THE
HIGH
CRUSADE

Naero's War
The Citation Series:

Book 2

THE
HIGH
CRUSADE

Mason Elliott

Naero's War
The Citation Series:

Book 2

High Mark Publishing

High Mark Publishing
www.highmarkpublishing.com

Seattle & Portland, Los Angeles, Chicago, London

THE
HIGH
CRUSADE

Naero's War
The Citation Series:
Book 2
by
Mason Elliott
Createspace Edition

Published by High Mark Publishing
ISBN 978-1-930451-21-6

Watch for other titles by this author in the future.

Cover Art by
Mike Leonard
madmanmike.deviantart.com

Edition Notes
If you do not see this edition note here in this spot on the copyright page and on the very last page of your eBook or print version of this title, then you are not getting the final, polished version of this novel that the publisher, editors, and author intended for you to receive. Please contact either the publisher or the author via their emails or websites if you do not see the following update code:

High Mark Publishing Update Code F0215A

Become a fan of my books.
Please join my Readers List:
http://bit.ly/1L2QpUL

Thanks, from Mason Elliott

1

After Nilar-2, Mystic adept Naero Amashin Maeris was officially attached to the Marines of Bravo Command, and rushed to join her new official unit on Ovedar-3. No longer just an advisor, but as an MCL, or Mystic Combat Liaison, she would serve her first mission with Marine Company 36, 250 elite Bravo Marines in total.

Marine Company 36 consisted of five reinforced platoons of fifty Marines each. One Command or HQ platoon, one mek/heavy mekanized weapons platoon, and three rifle platoons. Their commander was Major Ivana Luna, and the XO was Captain Viho Cheyenne. The Combat Field Commander was Captain Samson Konrad, with Combat Field First Leftenant Yaeden Adams. First Sergeant Samuel Gordon and Gunnery Sergeant Peyton Valmont and all of their aides filled out the Command staff. Each of the five platoons had their own leaders, squads, and fireteams.

She had never met or served with any of these people directly, nor they her.

Naero had obtained permission from General Walker himself to join her new unit in disguise at first, as just another new recruit/replacement named Miranda Allen. She wanted to get to know her new mates on a personal level before they just saw her as a Mystic ringer who was simply tacked onto the company like a secret weapon of some kind.

And she wanted them to get to know her, as well. If they were going to be fighting together during the course of a long war, she wanted all of them to be on the same wavelength.

Miranda-Naero jumped down to the surface of Ovedar-3 with all of her Marine gear. The planet was an earthlike with extended polar regions, not glaciers. The habitable zones were contained in a band that covered about two-thirds of the planet's surface, centered around the equator up through much of the tropics.

Ovedar-3 had been a peaceful, Joshua Tech border world with the Alliance before the war. The Ejjai Invasion had penetrated this far and had been attacking and killing on the planet's surface for only thirteen hours.

Thirteen hours too long for any world.

The blood red invader fleets quickly overwhelmed the sparse system defenders, on a world that had not known any hostilities in more than a century. Now, Ejjai clone shocktroops swarmed around and encircled the ten largest population centers on a sleepy world of three billion sentients, mostly human landers. Now those landers scrambled in terrified panic to defend themselves with any meager means of defense that came to hand, against a hyper-violent, implacable foe who simply wanted to process them all into frozen, carrion meat blocks.

Miranda-Naero reported for duty, a replacement for a Marine who had been seriously wounded in the action on nearby Kulator-6. Naero had briefly read about the intense action there.

She wanted to meet her new mates and settle in with them, see how they operated, win them over a little before she went all MCL on them. Her actual rank would put her equal to or just under the commanding major, and that could be a barrier as well.

She wanted to be one of them. One of their team.

Elite warriors were a rare, complex breed, and as close-knit as any family that depended on each other for their very lives.

To be accepted as a part of such a family, she would have to earn it—as a Marine, a Spacer, and as a person. Just jamming her in with them did not gain her anything. And even worse, from what she had heard from some of the other Mystics, MCLs were often shifted around by Command on whim and impersonal appointment. Many Spacer Marines viewed the Mystics as something spooky, or even inhuman.

"Pfc Allen," the platoon leader on duty called out to her on sight. The second leftenant ushered her into a nearby nanohut and went behind a desk to confirm the new replacement's arrival and duty orders.

"Just a moment, Allen."

They were inside, out of view, so Naero snapped to and saluted, ready for anything. "Yes, sir!"

The officer looked up with a smile and returned the salute crisply. "At ease, Allen. Welcome to forward base Baker-3. I'm 2nd Platoon Leader, Second Leftenant Ana Wilde. Get you and your gear squared away with your new squad next door, Squad 2, under Staff Sergeant Owen Valmont. You'll be in Fireteam 2 with Sergeant Milton Ramsey. You know what you're in for with us, right?"

"What's that, sir?"

"This is a large scale invasion war, and it's going to be fast and hot– a deadly marathon. We could drop down every day and slug it out in a new place, even a new world. Each day you're going to fight until you collapse. Bravo's going to be the tip of a very bloody spear, and it does not end until the invaders are all crushed. You got that, Marine?"

She nodded. "Copy, that, sir. That's what I'm here for."

The leftenant grinned. "Good. Again, welcome and dismissed. Get over there and join your squad."

Naero saluted again. "Yes, sir. Thank you, sir."

A few steps across the way and she entered an even larger, barracks-style nanohut for 2nd Platoon and its four squads. It almost exactly resembled their quarters aboard their awaiting Marine dropship.

With the soundproofing, you couldn't hear anything from the outside. The mixture of noise and quiet that she walked into like a sudden wall within was to be expected.

There were about forty-nine other Marines besides herself, all sleeping, joking around, reading, arguing, gambling craps with dice off to one side, or checking their gear. A few were sparring in pairs or practicing blade techniques in other open spaces.

The barracks was dark inside, except for the well-lit parts over by the bunks and the latrine.

Miranda-Naero spotted a bored-looking corporal on watch duty, sitting at a tiny desk, sipping a citrus lix pak and yawning as he watched a WebBall sports match on a pad.

He didn't look at her. "Name?" he muttered.

With a sudden tumult from further within the nanohut, Naero hadn't heard what he said. "What?" she tried to shout over the din.

The corporal shouted, "What's your name, rook?"

3

She walked up closer to the desk. "Pfc Miranda Allen, attached to 2nd Platoon, Squad 2, Fireteam 2."

The corporal froze his pad and put it down, crumpling up the lix pak and tossing it over into the recycler. He was a mid-sized man, in excellent shape as all the Bravo Marines were. Maybe in his mid-twenties, but his eyes already looked sunken a little. A plain face, with plain brown eyes. This guy did not smile much she guessed, for whatever reasons.

He muttered a question under his breath as to whether they were sending them midgets now. Naero was very short.

But she still took offense.

"Who sent you here, Allen?"

"I just saw Second Leftenant Wilde–"

Scott started a bit and raised one eyebrow. "You saw the Anaconda…and she was in a good mood?"

"I…guess so. Why do they call her–"

"Leftenant Anaconda Wilde. They call her that because she throttles the life out of dumbass rooks when they inevitably screw up in the field. Then she swallows them whole, digests them, and shits out their bones. Got that, rook? You don't fuck with the Anaconda"

"I didn't. Loud and clear, Corporal…?"

"Scott. Corporal Baylor Scott. Call me Baylor, Scott, or Corporal." He waved a finger for emphasis. "None of that Scottie crap, or you'll wake up wet in your bunk with your cute little nipples sliced clean off, sweetness. Copy that, rook?"

"I copy, Corporal."

"Okay. I'm sorry. Not trying to be a prick. I'm just sensitive about my name, is all." He looked over at the mob and yelled out, "Hey, Sarge…Sergeant Val!" A tall, lanky sergeant with red hair looked over. Scott muttered under his breath again. "Yeah, you, ya moronic ape. Look this way." He spoke out loud again. "Stagger over here, Sarge. Come hold the hand of our new little rook, Allen. She needs some milk and cookies. Tuck her in tonight and sing her a lullaby before she gets her dumb ass shot off tomorrow."

The sergeant bounded over with long strides of his gangly legs. He was like a huge gamboling puppy, with oversized hands and feet.

But he seemed cheerful and good-natured enough, compared to Corporal Scott. But Non-coms could be mercurial in nature. Sweet and supportive one second, bitter and harsh the next. Valmont even shook her hand.

"Welcome aboard," Valmont told her. He had hazel eyes and short red hair. He was early to mid-twenties at best. He probably couldn't even grow a full beard still. "Is Scott giving you his brand of shit?"

Miranda-Naero grinned. "Why no, Sarge. Except for threatening to de-nipple me in my sleep, he's been a perfect gentleman."

Valmont chuckled. "Makes the gals swoon, he does. Scott's a regular Max Lii. It's a wonder he's still single. Come with me and store your gear, find your bunk, and meet the rest of these goons, Allen."

"Oh, goodie!" she squealed.

Scott only glared at them both for a second, and then flipped his pad back up.

Of course all forty-seven of the others either ignored her or tried to overwhelm her at first.

"Yeah, yeah, show some imagination," she told them. "All of the short jokes are too easy. I've heard 'em all before, many times over. So think up some new material!"

Miranda-Naero did her best to hold her own and keep up as she stashed her gear in her equipment locker, her personal effects and extra clothes in her trunk. Valmont helped her re-code her seclocks with her thumbprint.

Finally she came to her bunk up top and could relax a bit. The others tried to settle down and go back to what they were doing.

Sergeant Valmont did his best to make the initial formal introductions. "All right you goons, shut your holes and listen up. This is our new rook, Miranda Allen. Look out for her and show her what to do, if there's something she don't know."

The others howled at him. "Yeah, yeah, Sarge. Sure, sure."

Someone from one of the other squads shouted over as soon as it got quieter. "Tell the dumb bitch she's on her own, you jacking tossers!"

Some laughed, some shouted insults back at the heckler.

Valmont suddenly roared at them, "Shut the hell up, you stupid rock apes!" That put them down.

Sergeant Valmont picked up where he'd left off. "Allen, welcome to 2nd Platoon, led by Second Leftenant Ana Wilde. I'm the second in command of the Platoon, Staff Sergeant Owen Valmont, leader of Squad 2 and Fireteam 1, along with Debra Steiner, Waylon Aztec, and Wallace Archer."

A few said "Hey," or waved briefly, but they didn't look at her. The others kept gambling. Miranda-Naero waved weakly, but didn't say anything.

Valmont kept going. "You'll be in Squad 2, Fireteam 2, with your fireteam leader, Sergeant Milton Ramsey. Milt, say hello to Allen, your new rook."

Sergeant Ramsey was too busy rolling the bones, and winced as he went bust. "Shit it all–snakes!"

Miranda-Naero just grinned. Valmont kept going. "And here's the rest of Fireteam 2: Bessa Jackson and Acer Adams."

Jackson was up in the top bunk across from hers. She had dark eyes, a big smile, short, straight, glistening white hair, and skin like dark chocolate. She was long, powerful, and curvy. "Damn, itty-bitty. You'd best watch yourself among these horndogs. Us gungals gotta stick tight. You let me know. Any of these go-go-rillas even looks at you wrong, and I'll kick my size eights so far up their hatch that we'll have to have 'em made inta boots!"

Everyone liked that one, even Miranda-Naero. They all had a good laugh.

A handsome looking mook with short, dark, wavy hair leaned out from the bunk below and smiled, exposing his guns as he stretched what looked to be a pretty amazing physique. Intense gray eyes openly leered up at her. "They call me Acer, baby-girl. Acer Adams. Cause I ace everything. Every foe I've met has tried and died, and my women all stay satisfied. And I'll be under you tonight, honeycakes–dreaming of you moaning in my arms, and giving me your tight, sweet, sweet love."

Miranda-Naero rolled her eyes. "Haisha, Ace. You know, I hate neutering lover-boy clowns like you. All that blood, and the girlie-screams when I make that slice. Owie. Please, let's not go there."

The unit hooted and hollered at both of them.

Acer was unfazed. "Yeah…she wants me. Only a matter of time. They all come around."

"Yeah, sure," Bessa said, "and that's just the guys." More laughter.

"See? Everyone wants a piece of this," Acer said, quite pleased with himself.

He had to duck and dodge when the others started throwing stuff at him.

Sergeant Valmont laughed right along with the rowdy lot. "All right, you goons. Ace, keep that diseased tool of yours in its cage. Allen, you already met our other loverboy, Scott. He's the leader of Fireteam 3 with Chime Fox, Falco Borelli, and Trisha Marshall."

The three of them actually looked up and nodded. In unison, they all said, "Hey, Allen."

Miranda-Naero smiled back. "Hey guys."

Chime Fox was also shorter–but still fifteen millimeters taller than Miranda-Naero. Chime had brown eyes and short golden hair. She had a stack of paperbacks–real-life actual books-in a plascrate next to her.

"Great! A new gungirl. Do you like to read? I just love books; I've got some great ones. All kinds. We even have a Book Night, every Fourthday." Chime tossed her pretty head and rolled her eyes. "I'm kinda like the unit lending library. Just tell me what you like. Lots of great netbooks on the webnet, too–if you want them on your pad."

This one was a little too bubbly and kooky. But Miranda-Naero couldn't remember when she had last read an actual, physical book. For fun. Not since before the wars. Poetry, maybe. What a novelty. "Uh…thanks, Chime," she said. "I'll let you know."

Falco Borelli seemed to be big into the craps games. He watched the dice and the action like a turkey vulture swooping in on a carcass. "Do you shoot, Allen?"

Miranda Naero shrugged, and pulled out her own green Sharbanian dice. "I do. Sometimes, when I get sick of other stuff."

"Sharbies. Nice. Well, let me know if you wanna roll. The guys and I will be happy to strip you of your creds, whenever you feel like losing them to us."

Trisha Marshall walked over to her and spoke quietly, handing her a piece of Devanian silk chocolate wrapped in foil. "This one's on me, Allen."

Miranda-Naero smiled. "First one's always free, right?" She unwrapped it and savored the rich taste. Really exceptional chocolate. Marshall had a sweet, innocent face like someone's kid sister next door.

But she was a business person. Naero could tell.

Marshall came right out and said it straight. "I'm the platoon scrounge. Junk food, poteen, other booze or fun stuff. If you want it, I'll find out how and where to get it."

They both said the words in unison: "For the right price, of course."

"Thanks for the treat, Marshall. Could you, say, get me a borbble of Jett?"

Marshall blinked for a second and then knitted her brow and curled her lip. "The soft drink? That's what you want?"

"Sure do. Our dispensaries can't get it from the Corps, due to the war, from what I hear."

"Some of my local sources should have some, I guess. Give me a day or two."

"Sure. Thanks. I'd really appreciate it. And what about some Spum, while you're at it?"

7

Marshall smiled wide like a blurtwall ad. "The only blue meat?"

"That's the one," Miranda-Naero said..

I got two pods left. Some of the other guys like it, too. I'll get more."

"Dang, I'll take 'em both, Marshall. You're my new best friend. How much?"

"For you, a rook and all…thirty creds.

Miranda-Naero felt her eyes widen. "Thirty? For only two pods? Why, you opportunistic rat bastard."

Marshall chuckled. "What happened to me being your new best friend?"

"Haisha, I can get a whole shelf of Spum on Nilar-2 for that much, you bloody crook!"

"Ah-ha, but that's the ancient law of supply and demand, and this isn't Nilar-2, and here the going rate is two pods for thirty or one for twenty. Or just go without." Marshall shrugged, completely indifferent.

"Okay, okay, hang on. I'll take 'em." She made the transfer from her wristcom. "And they better not be out of date."

Marshall shook her head and made a face. "Spum? Out of date? Impossible. That could never happen. Spum keeps forever, as long as the package isn't violated."

"Well, get away from me before I change my mind and do a little violating of your package, you flipping scrounge!"

Sergeant Valmont made it back around to her. "All right, Allen. Seems like you're fitting in with the other kids, so far. At least they haven't killed, cooked, and eaten you off the bone like the slashers yet. So that's a good sign. When you get around to it, introduce yourself to the other three squads. Try to get to know everyone. I know it's tough at first. Let me, Ramsey, or Scott know if you need anything or are having any trouble."

"Thanks, Sarge. I will."

"Get some good rest, Allen. We'll see some action tomorrow. I'm sure of it."

"That's what I'm here for, Sarge. Ooh-rah!"

"Be careful what you wish for, rook."

*

They loaded up for battle early the next day. The Anaconda called out to her as they boarded their dropships. "Pfc Allen. You're with me this ride."

Miranda-Naero snapped to, ready for anything. "Yes, sir." She didn't salute outside, out in the open.

2nd Platoon Leader Anaconda Wilde grinned, and came toward Miranda-Naero in all her combat armor and gear. She did move like snake, with the easy grace and sure agility of both a commander and a warrior. She stood 1.83 meters, even without her stealth armor battle suit. Each of their suits had a built-in, assault gravwing and a squad-level shield pod.

Wilde had her battle suit set up in black wraith mode, an E-5D assault blaster carbine slung and secured on her left. An E-P17 microgrenade machine pistol was strapped to her right hip. Float-seeker smartmines, more microgrenades, fusion claymore slappers, and shield negation bombs filled out her load.

The Anaconda was true to her totem, a deadly armory and arsenal just on her own.

Her hi-tek armored helmet and its sensor and visual arrays was secured behind her back, and her long auburn hair, pulled up tight in Spacer battle-fashion for helmets, gave her the look of a warrior goddess with large, amber-gold, Clan Wilde eyes.

The eyes of the lioness.

The platoon leader looked her and her gear over. "I appreciate your eagerness, Allen. No one better. But you're still a rook, still green. And I haven't seen you fight yet. No offense, Marine."

"None taken, sir."

"Good. Stay with me and my Fireteam 1: Moses Fay, Trevor Lakota, and Michael Borelli are as good as they get. We're your guides on this little outing. Follow our lead, shoot straight, fight well, and you'll be all right. Did you get the sitrep down cold? Do you understand our mission role on the combat grid?"

Miranda-Naero nodded. "Affirmative, sir. Like ice in my head. Let's put some slashers down."

"I like your calm intensity, Allen. Outstanding. I like to see that in my people. Keep your fire hot in your suit for now. We need to do a lot of snooping up front, first, and get in close. Initially, we'll conduct vital forward ops and targeting confirmation and coordination. We'll paint them all up and lock them down."

The platoon leader smiled. "When things do go hot and the fire comes down, we'll have a front-row seat at the fireworks, with key targets of our own to burn and light up. So stand ready."

Leftenant Wilde moved on, checking with the rest of her 2nd Platoon, Squad 1 Marines.

Then she called out across the dropship bay, "Sergeant Vaughn, any further word on when our new MCL will be joining us? Has there been some kind of delay? Why do I not see her with us on this op? Do we even know our MCL's name or any deets on her or his abilities, yet? Tell me something I want to hear, Vaughn!"

Vaughn saluted; Wilde shot it right back. "Negative, sir. I've been up the chain a few times with HQ; as yet, they have no further info for us on that issue. Our MCL status is still pending, and could be sent to join up with us at any time."

"Keep me informed and updated, Sergeant. Listen up, 2nd Platoon. Suit and weapons check, complete in two. Slap and tap and look your jump buddy over with genuine love. We're going into the heat, and we go in heavy and silent, but ready to burn. Each of you hotcheck your Intel fixers and direct your feed links into the combat grid. Command and HQ wants us to slide in quiet and paint and confirm all enemy elements in our combat sector for overlapping, indirect light up firing profiles for our unit CPA.

"Do you hear me, Marines?"

"Yes, sir!" they shouted eagerly, performing their prep tasks.

"As I have stated, stealth is essential to the tactical success of our coordinated mission. And as you well know, we will not engage the enemy in any way, for any reason, until our unit Coordinated Plan of Attack is in full effect and green to go. Then and only then will you engage, put fire on our new invader friends, and turned their furry asses to burning shit beneath our boots. I say again, until our CPA gives the order to attack, we will maintain and perform our roles as forward observers, and I mean like ghosts, people! Is that clear?"

"Yes, sir!"

"Just like fucking ghosts, Bravo! Prepare for battle, Marines. Take the fight to the bloody bitches in the black, and drop it on them hard and hot. Ooh-rah!"

"Ooh-rah!" 200 Spacer Marines echoed.

Wilde and Fay finished their battle checks.

Miranda-Naero did her checks with Trevor Lakota, who had his rig war-painted Native Clan style, including holographic feathers.

"Nice war paint spolymer," she told him.

Lakota grinned. "Very interesting, Allen. You've rigged your suit in a custom shadow ghost mode I haven't seen before. Most of us just use black wraith because it's so simple and reliable for up-close combat. You really prefer your rig this way?"

He called her Allen, not rook or newb. She appreciated that. "It has the same non-detection profiles as black wraith, but it's better against the Ejjai sense of smell, and conserves juice eleven percent better, and cuts down on shielding scan echoes."

Miranda-Naero drew two wicked-looking combat blades and spun them. "Plus, as long as I don't use any energy weapons, I can still slice and dice with my blades with a very low chance of detection."

Lakota raised an eyebrow, his suit bristling with various blades, much like her own. "You're good with blades. I can tell. I see you have a Clan Apache fighting knife among yours. I won't ask how you got that."

She smiled. "It was a gift."

He nodded to her. "Then we must fight one day, when there is time. The old way. No practice blades. My iron against yours."

Miranda-Naero met his gaze and sheathed her blades. "I'd like that."

He really smiled this time, raising his eyebrows. "I will, too. That's a very specialized customization for a rook, Allen. Fight well beside us today."

"Thanks. Fortune favors the bold." He sounded a little suspicious of her, but she had a ready answer. "My brothers and most of my family served with the Niners during the Annexation War. They all suggested I rig my suit this way. It got me through my night-fighting school training to qualify me for Bravo, so I guess I'll stick with it."

Lakota nodded. "You're green to go, Allen. Stick close with us. You'll do all right. Whatever else you are, you're no rook. How about me? Am I good?"

Naero finished her prepcheck on his suit. "Everything checks out. Thanks, Lakota."

He nodded at the others. "Go meet the rest of Squad 1 while there's still time. Sergeant Vaughn, Allen needs an intro here. She's swapped out with Borelli in Squad 2 for this jump."

Vaughn was tallish and all muscle with a doughy face and roundish features, sandy hair and brown eyes.

"Let's make this quick, Allen. Get ready to lock and load. I'm Sergeant Selby Vaughn, leader of Fireteam 2. Meet Suki Lii, Josh Elkins, and Whip Konrad. Corporal Parsival Patton leads Fireteam 3, with Luca Abraham, Razor Wilde, and Keesha Aztec."

Miranda Naero nodded to them all. "Hey, guys."

"Good luck, rook," Suki said.

"Yeah," Razor added. "Don't get your dumb ass killed."

Miranda-Naero grinned. "Copy that. Death is to be avoided. And, thanks for the vote of confidence."

She glanced over at Konrad, who was sweating and looked wired.

"Hey, Marine…Konrad," she said. "What's with you? You sick or something?"

He ignored her and muttered to himself, "I'm gonna get it this time. This time they're going to get me, I'm sure of it. I'm already a dead man...dead man."

Suki grabbed Naero's arm. "Don't worry about Whip, gungirl. That's how he does it. Every time we jump, he rambles on about how he's going to die, he's already dead, and all that whiny shit. Haisha. Bastard fights like the rest of us and never gets a damn scratch. I say it ain't fair."

"2nd Platoon," the Anaconda said. "Lock in and prepare for gravwing insertion. Green in ten minutes. Mark."

All four squads of 2nd Platoon fell in line all around the drop bay hatches, in ready order.

Each of them conducted their final checks.

Second Leftenant Wilde shouted out once more, "Prepare to shoot in on target. Insertion in five. Activate stealth mode. Fixers up in same. Everyone online. We drop and slip in to cover the objective in spiral-6 sweep and scan approach. Paint, ID, and double confirm and lock all targets in our combat area."

They dropped in on the lead elements of ten invader divisions, tightening their bloody noose on the northern arc of the gigacity of Elaris, capital of Ovedar-3. Home to nearly a billion people, spread over a hundred square kilometers.

The Marines penetrated the enemy jamming and scanning fields without a glitch. The enemy jamming field kept the Spacer Naval fleets in orbit blind, unable to properly scan and target the invader forces on the ground.

Once the forward observing units scanned and painted each enemy target with nano-trackers, all targets and objectives could be computed and prioritized in an optimal CPA. Commanders and battle comps would dispense orders and modify the CPA as the battle developed.

An excellent combat plan of attack normally guaranteed a near complete pacification of enemy forces. Often up to ninety-eight percent. Most enemy forces were taken out completely within minutes of the initial engagements. The overwhelming, interlocking firing profiles were that devastating, efficient, and effective. No foe could stand up to such levels of intense, coordinated indirect and direct fire for very long.

Especially when those waves of destroying fire were unleashed suddenly and without warning. The initial engagement was often the only engagement, and became the deciding factor in most battles. In many instances, the local landers could move in and take over the cleanup in the aftermath, once the main groups of invaders were crushed and obliterated.

Couple these amazing tactics with Bravo's elite night fighting abilities, and the combination made for a furious, one-two punch that the invaders could not survive.

The Ejjai did what they did, with ruthless efficiency. They were already pounding and shelling the gigacity of Elaris with heavy waves of massed rockets and artillery. These violent attacks were meant to soften the civilians up, in prep for violent swift assaults by waves of tanks and gunships, and hordes of ruthless, armored infantry.

The invaders were not soldiers. They were murderers, sadists, and butchers, cloned to crush weaker, lander populations and feed them into the horrible factory meatships. Meatships that would feed the next generations of clone hordes, spreading their horror and terror from world to vulnerable world.

It had been proven time and time again that the invaders could not stand before an equal-sized and properly equipped and trained force of real warriors and soldiers. But the Ejjai were never looking for a fair fight. All they wanted was to slaughter and torment helpless civilians.

And infect the entire galaxy with their evil, if no one stopped them.

It was time to stop them once more.

And Bravo was the hammer.

The despised enemy meatships were usually the first targets marked for certain destruction. Then any enemy command and control, dropships still full of troops, and equipment carriers. After that, deployed artillery, tank formations, and gunship waves–and finally–all enemy firing positions and individual troops.

Each Ejjai invader was painted by the complex targeting system. Their weapons and gear were scanned and analyzed. All of this data was fed into the Spacer Marine battlecomp array for evaluation and tactical analysis.

When the advanced targeting profiles for all of the Marine units involved went out, the various assaults and attacks were planned in unison and almost flawlessly executed. It was an amazing system, and normally, when it worked, it worked extremely well.

But in every battle, on every new system where they combatted the invader, the enemy would do everything in their power to disrupt and beat the system. The invaders upgraded weapons and tactics in a never-ending attempt to outwit their fierce opponents.

And the Spacers and their Marines did all that they could to maintain their edge of superiority.

The difficult part for forward observing teams on such missions was waiting and completing all of the scanning and targeting in order to set up a crushing, wipeout attack.

It took grim discipline for the Marines to hold back, watching and doing their duty, preparing while the hated enemy continued shelling and attacking such helpless cities and their populations. The slashers, as they called the invaders, slaughtered innocent civilians each second. The Ejjai gloried in their bloody work, and murdered all that lived with a rapacious glee that was staggering.

But simply rushing in and attacking without sufficient planning and coordination was never as efficient, and took much longer in the end, providing the invaders with much more time to keep killing.

The Marines and their commanders quickly understood that their hi-tek, disciplined approach actually saved many more lives on both sides in the long run. They could cut the foe down faster, and move on to the next objective just that much quicker. Even the Ejjai killing machine was nothing compared what the Marines could accomplish, once they were properly led, directed, and unleashed in all-out, split-second timing.

Anyone who witnessed these lightning attacks would never forget such an experience.

Finally, all of the Bravo forward ops finished their tasks and required scans. The orders of what to attack, where, and when filtered down to the forward Marine units, and Bravo Command positioned their forces to unleash their direct assaults in waves of sheer fury.

Adrenalin kicked in even more as the war on that system was about to soar hotter, to an almost infinite degree. Miranda-Naero got set with her fireteam.

2nd Platoon positioned itself perfectly to sweep in fast on an enemy mechanized infantry unit, a full company, a hundred strong, with armored support vehicles and mounted heavy weapons and unit shielding teams.

Miranda-Naero carried the latest, E-19A5 version of the standard Marine pulse rifle with updated, advanced targeting optics. It could also be used to launch either microgrenades or float-seeker smartmines that would lock on and autoseek available targets. The direct fire of each Marine like herself was coordinated by the CPA for maximum effectiveness.

The tek in her advanced helmet array fed her and Command constant data flows on the best evolving patterns of attack to use in order to engage the priority targets nearest to her, and quickly brought up secondary and tertiary targets in a rapid progression.

It even tracked her remaining weapon systems and reminded her when to reload or switch ordnance types for more effectiveness, and could even have her fixer help her with such functions. All of this was coordinated not only within her entire platoon, but also their company and the other units all around them on the evolving combat grid.

Yet automation on the battlefield could take a Marine only so far, and sometimes the data flows came in too fast or grew confusing. Miranda-Naero knew from experience that in some cases, after the initial assault, it was often better to switch over to semi-reflex, instinctive shooting. In that mode, all of the AI suggestions could be muted, taken as valuable suggestions, and processed by the individual shooter, letting her decide what to fire up.

She selected three-shot burst on her selector switch over full auto fire. Miranda-Naero trusted her marksmanship.

The call went up over their links.

Commence attack in five seconds, mark. Green and hot in five-minus.

Engage and fire at will. Follow the flow of battle as directed.

Their helmet shields instinctively tinted darker to shield their eyes.

So much happened all at once.

Miranda-Naero cut loose with a spread of ordnance and put down all six of her initially assigned targets in less than a split second.

Waves of concentrated fire lit up the enemy positions in blinding blasts and flares of white-hot oblivion. More than half of the invaders were cut down in those first few instants.

Bravo moved in swiftly, shields in front, even as the heat and light flared.

Miranda Naero already snapped calm, precise fire at her next round of secondary targets. She drilled each one in rapid succession in a priority sweep, squeezing off precise bursts, quick and calm.

With nearly every trigger pull, an enemy dropped, lost a head, or was torn apart. And the formerly triumphant invaders withered and died in droves, wherever they stood or attempted to fight.

Tertiary targets. She pumped microgrenades and seeker mines into enemy vehicles, shield pods, fuel supplies, and ammo and ordnance pods and carriers.

For a short time, they crouched behind their own shields to let everything in front and around them finish blowing up and cooking off. No sense rushing into all of that.

More targets. This time the CPA directed them to pop up into the sky and interlock their fire with units rushing in below and around them.

They took sporadic but growing return fire from all of the built-up areas around them in the gigacity itself. The enemy wasn't done just yet.

They fought the invaders not just in the air, but in a three hundred and 360-degree battlefield all around them. Once they penetrated far enough in, enemy fire could come at them from everywhere, even hidden and concealed underground, just buried and waiting.

But the Marines piled it on, and attacked the invaders wherever they showed themselves.

Another set of targets, this time more spread out and not as concentrated. An autogun emplacement here, a pocket of infantry or a sniper there. Miranda-Naero nailed eight targets in rapid succession, proving once more, according to standard Marine doctrine, that a superbly trained sharpshooter was still one of the most deadly weapons, even on a hi-tek battle field.

And it wasn't just her. Each elite Marine was an incredible shooter with highly advanced weapons and optics. They punched enemy tickets to hell in rapid order, the CPA keeping them all shooting at different targets, and not wasting time firing up the same ones. The combined fire was so precise that many aimed for enemy helmet after helmet, tearing them off in kill after kill.

Like all of the other units, 2nd Platoon continued to advance at assault speed, sweeping the invaders away and leaving nothing but death in their wake, as ordered. At one point they were six hundred meters up or more, fighting among the gigacity pyramids and high-rises.

The Anaconda suddenly led them back down in good order to press the assault on a hardened enemy position, where the slashers were attempting to blow up and collapse an enormous skyscraper down across the forward line of battle.

Everything seemed to be going well. So why was Miranda-Naero's sense of warning going nuts?

She checked in with Om, the Kexxian AI defensive protocol secretly existing inside her mind. Om, I know you're monitoring everything all around on the nets and the fixer arrays. Is the enemy getting ready to surprise us with one of their tricks?

N, I'm striving to make sense of their actions and movements, but I think so. Okay, got it. Very slight traces of high EM signatures, scattered throughout this half of the entire gigacity grid.

Miranda-Naero kept maneuvering with her squad and firing on her available targets. Are all of those signatures underground, Om?

Yes, and many more than I first detected. There are hundreds and thousands of them in specific patterns, many coupled with an explosive device with the yield of a handheld fusion bomb. But what are the others? Why haven't they set these devices off, and what would they accomplish? Our forces aren't even near most of them, yet.

Teknomancy. Miranda-Naero used teknomancy to try to assess the situation. She quickly studied the scans of the tek on hand and the level of electromagnetic signature echoes and all of the other strange reads.

What purpose would the enemy have for setting up countless EM burst generators and these other things?

Then the answer hit her and Om nearly at the same time in their shared mind. And neither of them liked the conclusions.

N, those aren't just–

I know, Om. Some of them are devices specifically designed to cause massive EM burn waves–across the full spectrum of our tek frequencies and energy patterns. Those pulse blast EM effects will knock out all coms and active tek within the range of their blast net. All our tek in this region will be taken down and rendered useless at the same time.

And as you suspected, N, the other objects buried in the ground are powered-down, shielded enemy troops, waiting to pop up after the tek-crippling EM waves pass over us. Then they'll simply fire up their tek, which will still function, and charge in to mow us all down.

The enemy did a good job setting this trap, Om. They'll wait until we sweep in closer, thinking we've all but won. Then they'll knock out our coms and our tek.

Our people are in trouble, N. I calculate a full enemy battalion alone nearby, hiding just within the radius of half a klick. They have huge numbers waiting to hurl at us, once our tek goes out.

Hurry, Om. Translate that assessment through the fixer nets and shoot the intel to HQ and Command. Spread the word. I have to get the Leftenant to notice before it's too late.

"Leftenant Wilde," she called out over their secure link. "We have a situation."

The Anaconda spun in mid-air, pumping fire from her carbine and her microgrenade pistol into an hidden enemy hardpoint in the skyscraper, where the slashers had an artillery piece and several autoguns set up.

2nd Platoon attacked the position directly, coming under heavy return fire, degrading their defensive screens.

"Not now, Allen. Stay in front of me and keep firing down the building. Nice shooting percentage, by the way."

"Thank you, sir. But you need to look at the scans we have flowing to HQ from the fixer nets. Strange patterns, echoes, and energy signatures all around us and even to our rear. I'm guessing its some kind of concealed minefield."

"Minefield? Show it to me Allen."

Naero pweaked it a bit to make the findings slightly more obvious.

Wilde stopped firing and even pulled back in mid-air, drawing off the platoon with her. "Holy shit, Allen! That's no goddam minefield. 2nd Platoon, halt and stay with me, inverted Victor double defensive lines. All shield pods up and online in sphere defense."

They fell back slightly and took cover behind the next large building over that way, where the fighting had already passed them by.

The leftenant scrambled to call in the vital significance of that data directly to HQ and on to Intel and Command. "HQ, HQ, get me Major Luna and shunt this all the way up the chain. Patch us directly in to General Walker himself. This is an Alpha-Charlie-Negative One Alert. Situation Red. I repeat. Situation Red.

"The threat is preparing to set off a tek-crippling EM blast net. That way, we couldn't detect it, the way we could if they had used a large EM bomb. They will most likely cripple all of the tek of our forward units in this area. They also have large numbers of combat reinforcements buried, shut down, and concealed underground that will not be affected by the blast net. They are waiting only for us to move further and deeper into their trap–just as we are doing now by pressing our attack. Then their fully functioning troops will emerge and wipe us out."

Wilde suddenly sounded frustrated. "What do you mean, where's my proof? Damn it! It's all right in these scan reads, if you've got brains enough to know what you're looking at, and you can see the tactical patterns and analyze the energy signatures. Who the hell is this? Goddam it. Get me Major Luna or one of her officers. I don't care which one. Here's the data push once again. Show it to someone who's got a clue! Analyze the situation and advise. Over. Yes, I will hold the link, goddam it!"

Some degree of static blipped over the link and a well-known voice cut in. "Ana, this is Major Luna. Hold your position, Leftenant. Hold and stand by while we confirm your findings. Alerting all Company 36 units. Assemble on new priority orders and prepare for a heavy enemy counterattack, possibly from all sides and directions."

Shortly after that, Bravo broke off their initial assault, withdrew to a defensive line, and pumped up their shields.

Om almost screamed at Naero, *No, no! Make them power down all shields, N. Tell them to do so, before it's too late. Maxing all shields is exactly what the enemy wants us to do!*

"Leftenant!" Miranda-Naero called out. "We're playing right into their hands. They're going to negate all tek with a massive pulse surge. Even maxed out, our shields can't stop it! Insist that Major Luna have Bravo power down and button up–just like we would against atomics. That will protect us, and we can still power back up and fight! That's what the enemy is planning."

Wilde got on the horn, and the relay went from her to Luna, and then straight to General Walker. But orders were already filtering down from Intel and Command. Other heads had figured out the danger as well.

Most of Bravo had barely shut down and covered up, when the wide-reaching EM pulse flashed through nearly everything in the gigacity's western half.

All exposed tek was burned out: friend, foe, or civilian. Everything cooked and went down.

The game was up, and the hidden enemy forces then powered up and emerged from their hiding places underground.

They fully expected to crush and obliterate everything living around them.

Bravo command powered up and met them head on, picking up the new assault on the evolving combat grid.

Intense firefights erupted close in, in a ring of fire and death all around Elaris. The Marines slugged it out face to face as only they could, nailing targets at will, taking fire from all sides and giving back better.

At one point Naero was about the press the assault forward.

She felt a strong hand on her shoulder holding her back.

Trevor Lakota pulled her into an alley. An alley filled with dead Ejjai, butchered like cattle.

Lakota wiped his long battle blades on the hide of a dead Ejjai Alpha.

Naero hadn't detected anything or heard a sound. The slashers had been hiding there, holding back, ready to ambush anyone who came near.

Lakota had slipped in behind them fast and scythed them all down.

"What do we do now?" she asked him.

Lakota smiled. "Wait a moment. Little brother Fox is tricky. He knows his business. He and fourth squad have some tricks of their own to play. Then we can join in."

The other squads held their positions, making the advancing enemy pay.

Then three score enemy strikers raced in fast and low to ground on gravwings.

Float-seeker smartmines popped, taking the foremost Ejjai and halting their advance.

Jonny Fox and the rest of Squad 4 cut across the jumbled up enemy like flashing razors, gunning them down.

More foes tried to rush in.

Squad 4 suddenly shot straight up.

A mek platoon uncloaked and shredded the enemy reinforcements with interlocked autogun and rocket fire.

By this time the enemy and their reinforcements were fully exposed. Marine and naval close air support dropped down and became a crucial factor.

Then several naval warships also swooped in to assist, modified for ground attack and further close support over the heaviest engaged portions of the rapidly expanding battlefield. They pounded the invaders wherever they showed themselves in excessively large numbers, chewing them to pieces.

After that, Bravo command pushed in at numerous key points and carved the remains of the enemy trap into manageable chunks that it could envelope and eliminate in efficient, short order.

Company 36 and 2nd Platoon assisted in pinning down Ejjai strikers in high-rises, pyramids, and skyscrapers all around them. While they held the attention of the enemy up front, more Bravo units slipped in stealth mode to finish them off. This system worked time and time again.

Sometimes they switched off.

Sometimes others kept the enemy busy, and 36 went in to take out the Ejjai up close. At one point, the slashers tried to use hostages and human shields.

Marine Company 36 went in like ghosts and took the enemy down, up close and personal with blades in order to limit casualties to the civies.

Much like herself, she saw Trevor Lakota fight fiercely at several points, with a gory blade in each hand. He zipped through a dozen Ejjai like a surgeon, slicing windpipes and spines, nearly severing heads, piercing hearts and lungs. The invaders barely knew they were dead before they hit the ground. Even the civilian hostages were stunned at what occurred.

Miranda-Naero grinned as she moved forward, cutting down Ejjai on her own.

Her knife sparring matches with Lakota were going to be a hoot.

Miranda-Naero didn't hold back for once, and passed through the astonished enemy in a whirlwind of flashing, spinning kicks and deadly steel. She left almost thirty invaders in bleeding pieces in her wake. All told, 36 cut down several hundred foes in a matter of seconds, and did so in almost eerie silence, except for the grunts and yelps of the dying Ejjai.

Hundreds of severed Ejjai claws clutched weapons, grenades, and explosive devices that they never had a chance to activate.

The Anaconda grabbed her and yanked her back for a second. "Allen! Where in the hell did you learn to fight like that? I've only ever seen one other Spacer ever fight that way–The Invincible Cyclone!"

Miranda-Naero grinned and shrugged. "I grew up watching the fight circuits," she said.

No time. Word came down. They needed to execute another gravwing assault on an enemy hardpoint nearby. They left the startled civies confused, but alive, to fend for themselves. The combat grid would not wait.

Five hours later, the primary fighting was over, with the invaders eliminated as a major threat. The landers and the remaining Corps forces could handle the mop-up.

The Spacer Navy and Bravo Command had liberated four gigacities from the brutal attacks of the invaders, thanks to heavy naval fire support. Then they all packed up to go free the other six.

When Ovedar-3 was finally pacified the next day, Leftenant Wilde still seemed a bit suspicious, but she commended Pfc Allen for her detection and observation skills in the aftermath, during their stand down.

"Good work spotting that 'minefield,' Allen. Exposing that raw data to Command and Intel early on gave them the time to figure out what it was. Bravo avoided what could have been a major disaster for us, because of you. I think we'll call you 'Bright-eyes,' from now on. Anything else ever looks funny to you, you just sing out and let us know."

The Anaconda even saluted her. Miranda-Naero returned it, with great respect. "Thank you, sir. I will, sir."

"Damn right. These slashers are tricky bitches. What do we need with MCLs who don't show up on time when we have rooks like you! Well, you've seen you're share of action these past two days. Excellent work, Marine. You've done well, and you're not a rook anymore. Congrats!"

"Thank you again, sir." They exchanged the warrior's handshake, all the way up to the elbow. And before that night was over, she had shared it with every Marine in 36, her new company.

She had fought and endured beside them in the furnace of combat and put down their enemies. She was one of them now.

2

With the mop-up proceeding on Ovedar-3, Bravo packed up and hopped over to their next mission, an all-out assault on Ptolemy-5. The system there was yet another earthlike with slightly higher gravity. Everyone had to take ACDs to compensate, and adjust the gravitics on their suits accordingly.

Since it was the next invasion world over for Bravo, the jump in system took less than two days.

But it still gave Miranda-Naero a chance to get to know the Marines in her platoon and rifle company better.

She ate with them, gambled with them–mostly shooting craps– goofed around them, and grabbed some badly needed sleep.

She liked some of her new mates better than others, and some felt the same way more or less about her. Miranda-Naero strove to keep her personality neutral–not too extreme in any way. Not too hard or soft, not too quiet or loud.

There was always someone there to test the new guy.

A big stocky Marine named Luke Barrett from Squad 3 shoved her out of his way and into a wall kind of hard. She could take it, but it was still a provocation.

"Outta my way, Suga' doll. Little kids who block my path can get stomped on. 'Memba that."

Miranda-Naero turned and wheeled into Barrett with two blinding spin kicks. She broke his nose, blackened both his eyes, and put him down on the deck. She nearly knocked him out cold.

Then she glared down at him. "I would advise you to take more care about who you shove around and stomp on, you stupid rock ape. Some of us kids know how to stomp back."

Laughter and hoots erupted.

She shot a look at Barrett's mates coming to collect him, Patton and Ramsey. "You two gonna say or do something?" she asked.

They both glared at her with weird, dopey looks of sudden desire.

Uh-oh. Now she'd done it. She didn't expect them to get turned on by that. But most of these guys–and gals–were major ass-kickers in their own right. And they respected and even savored that in others.

"You'll know if we do, Allen. Better watch yourself."

"Ooh, like I haven't heard that before," she snapped.

"Dang," Patton droned, as if entranced. "I think I'm in love. Haisha, Allen. You are so bee-yoo-tee-full. Will you marry me and have my bay-bees?"

"Hell no," Miranda-Naero said with a grimace. "Your right hand might get jealous and try to strangle me in your sleep."

More laughter followed. His mates helped walk Barrett to the infirmary.

This was Thirdday, what the landers used to call Tuesday, after some ancient god or goddess or some such. Every day of the standard week, the Marines did something special at night, if they weren't on duty.

Every Thirdday was food night, and Company 36 made special dishes or shared special treats with their mates. It got pretty wild, along with the regular crap of gambling, bitching, posturing and trash talk, sparring, and couples pairing off and sneaking away for monkey love.

The next day, Fourthday, the old Wednesday from the past, was strangely enough: reading and Book Day, Chime Fox's fave day.

First, 36 began to settle down and study their sitreps for Ptolemy-5. There'd be an initial briefing before they geared up and dropped.

Later that day, the gravity went off for a bit during their reading time. Naero thought it was very humorous, and took vids of her and nearly a hundred of her new chums with some of Chime Fox's paperbacks, floating about and bouncing around, reading and turning pages. She seemed to have a little bit of everything.

"Wanna meet my second cousin Jonny in Squad 4?" Chime asked. "I'm the older cousin, by several months. I'm sure he'd like to meet a hot little dish like you, Allen."

Miranda-Naero sighed and frowned. She remembered seeing Jonny in action during the battle. "I'm willing to meet anyone, but I don't need you pimping me out to your Clan there, Chime."

Chime laughed. "Don't be that way. Jonny's a sweet guy–unlike most of these goons, and he's a great Marine. You'll like him. Come on."

Miranda-Naero shrugged, and Chime led her over to Squad 4.

Someone whistled when they floated over into view. That was Terrence Decker, ripped, 1.91 meters or bigger, and short blue hair on top like a coarse brush, blue eyes and bold-ass naked, reading a murder mystery. "Oh, man. Lookee here, Jon-Jon. Your hot cousin's here to screw my brains out...again."

A guy who looked a little like pretty Chime frowned and droned, "That shouldn't take long, Decker. Imagine her surprise." Jon Fox was average size, medium brown hair, well-built and in perfect shape, with soft green eyes. He was reading a historical romance by the cover, possibly even a regency.

Decker either didn't get the jibe or ignored it. "Ooh, lookee-lookee. My lucky day. She brought a cute friend. It's the hot little rook. Looks like a threesome ta me!"

Chime burst out laughing. "In your dreams, you troglodyte. Put some man-clothes on and go hump a dead mammoth or something. But you stay away from me and my new gungirl galpal, Decker, or we will both kick your balls to mush. You haven't seen her fight. I have. We got a regular Cyclone among us."

"Ooh, I like it rough."

"Hey! Decker," Jonny Fox suddenly warned, with an edge to his voice. "Chime's my Clan and my blood, so just frost your dumb ass."

Decker grinned. "Sure thing, Jonny. Later, honeydolls."

Jonny smiled at Miranda-Naero. "Don't mind him; he can't help it."

"Mental defective?" Naero asked.

Jonny chuckled. "No...he's just a dick. Gets stupid when purty girls are around and too much blood rushes to that tight little head of his."

Chime and Miranda Naero tried not to giggle at that one.

Miranda-Naero glanced at his book "Regency, huh?"

"What can I say. Those fancy clothes are a turn on, and I'm a sucker for happy endings. What do you have? Hard boiled detective, huh?"

"Yeah…the butler did it."

He halted. "Isn't that more of a whodunit or a cozy? And what the hell was a butler, anyway?"

"All right," Miranda-Naero said. "Then it's the smoking hot dame with legs that won't quit. Oh, and a butler was a kind of house servant."

"There, that's more like it. And thanks for the info."

Chime just stood by, watching and listening to them go back and forth. She put her hands on her hips. "Well Haisha. Should I leave you two kids alone with your books?"

All three of them laughed. "Hey," Jonny said. "Let's float over to my cold stash and have something tasty."

"Sure thing," Miranda-Naero said.

When they got to a coded storage hatch, Jonny punched it open with his thumb. "I got three bottles of ice cold Spacer poteen," he bragged.

Naero nearly fainted.

He also had about six four paks of Jett behind that.

"Make mine Jett, please," she nearly stammered. "In fact, I'll pay you top market price for one of those four paks, and be your goddam friend for life."

Jonny Fox took out one of the cold four paks and tossed it to her straightaway. "No, charge, Allen. Consider it a gift…friend for life."

By then Miranda-Naero had snapped one open and guzzled it down.

Chime laughed. "Haisha, I think she likes that stuff."

"I do, too," Jonny said, and grabbed a pak for himself. Chime still took a bottle of poteen for herself, holding it protectively.

"Dang, that was good!" Miranda-Naero exclaimed, chucking the empty borbble into the recycler. "I sure as hell needed that. Guys, I'd get transfusions of this stuff if I could. I love it that much."

Jonny closed and secured his stash, and smiled. "Well, if anyone blasts my cold stash open, I'll know who the hell it was, Allen. I hear they call you Brighteyes now."

"Oh, they're just being generous."

They wandered into the ship's gallery to play some vidgames. Other Marines joined them there, and they had a great time goofing off.

Jonny Fox pulled her aside at one point. "Hey, Allen. Do me a favor and help me look after my cousin Chime. I worry about her."

"Why is that? She seems as competent as any other Marine, just like the rest of us."

"Yeah, I know she can handle herself. But it's a long story. We're the last two surviving kids our great-granny has. Everyone else died off during the wars. And sometimes, I just have dreams about something bad happening to her. Not me. I'm a survivor. But I keep worrying something bad is going to happen to Chime. She was always greatgran's fave."

"Friend for life, you have my word. I'll look out for my gungirl Chime. Good enough?"

"Thanks, Allen. Very glacier of you." They clicked Jett borbbles together.

They sat up bullshitting and drinking Jett while Chime sucked down Poteen and fell asleep between them with her head on first Naero's and then Jonny's shoulder, smacking her lips in her sleep. Chime looked very pretty like that.

A Marine named Peter Cooper came by to return a book to Chime. Naero took it and assured Pete that she'd tell Chime how much he enjoyed the hell out of that historical thriller she gave him.

Miranda-Naero went to sleep in her bunk that night, after putting Chime to sleep and dodging Acer's stupid advances again.

She was going to have to kick that dumbass Romeo silly at some point.

She sent a quick report to Klyne, coded through normal channels, noting that she had not revealed her special status with Company 36 as yet.

Somehow, she had a feeling that it was going to come out at some point on Ptolemy-5. On this system, it was a full-on, planet-wide war that they were jumping into.

And as usual, the local landers were slowly losing. The Ejjai invaders had only been onworld for ten days. The entire local population of two billion Joshua Tech humans had done their best to fully mobilize to resist them, and continued to take heavy losses. Only their superior numbers were holding the enemy off, but they were clearly no match for the invaders on their own.

Intense fighting raged around and throughout all five of the major gigacities. *Hot* did not begin to describe what Bravo Command and Company 36 would be storming into. They had been lucky on Ovedar-3. Bravo had caught the invaders before they could do their worst.

But the meatships and the cloneships were busy, and on the move.

On Ptolemy-5, the enemy meatships still operated full bore, day and night. Without assistance, the planet would be stripped clean within a month.

This was already a straight-up fight.

They were simply joining the dance fashionably late.

General Walker started off by dropping down five Divisions of Bravo Command Marines, including Company 36. One division each would take on and engage the five enemy battle groups of ten thousand Ejjai each.

As Walker put it, delicately, they were going in to take those Ejjai clone bitches by the throat and knife open their guts through the spine. And once each enemy battle group was fully engaged, more Bravo Marines would be poised to drop in at the best points to wipe them out even faster.

Naturally, reports of atrocities by the invaders were already routine and to be expected. The usual hi-tek war was waged trying to keep the invader broadcasts of those horrors to a minimum. The invaders went out of their way to be brutal, ruthless, and cruel. They rejoiced in such activity–even wallowed in it. And in keeping with their hyper-violent nature, they fought without quarter or mercy to butcher anything that lived.

Bravo killed–hot or cold–quickly, and efficiently, only too happy to oblige the foe and surpass them in ferocity, if nothing else.

The Marines went in at night, just the way they liked, did their homework, and got into position.

They hammered the enemy hard, catching them in the middle, between the defenders. Yet the Ejjai were many, well-armed, and almost always fought to the death, laughing their eerie, chortling laughter.

The war quickly fragmented like glass into scores of pocket battles, various unit campaigns of fronts, rears, and flanks. This pitted specific units against one another in a rather normal, conventional war.

There were advantages and disadvantages to this. There was no way to separate the attackers away from the defenders, and the invaders were also attacking the civilian population and refugees at the same time. This made naval and Marine air and ground support far less useful and effective.

This meant that most of the war had to consist of close-up fighting. Unit shield flared and disrupted against unit shield, with weapons barking and punching back and forth. Microbombs, negation grenades and various ordnance burst among both side.

2nd Platoon took on two hundred Ejjai at four to one odds. Undaunted, Leftenant Wilde led them into coordinated battle. They set their unit combat shields layered and full front, and charged them into the foe.

The Anaconda sank her teeth deep into the invader throat, while her coils encircled and wrapped around them to throttle the life out of them.

Not only that, but Marine reinforcements and support units dropped in out of nowhere to exploit enemy weaknesses wherever they appeared.

Air and ground support couldn't dust the entire area for fear of taking out friendlies. But they could use negations blasts to take down enemy shields over the invader positions, with little harm to friend or foe–except for exposing the slashers to direct fire without their shielding.

Once their shields collapsed across the line, even the lander forces could exploit such advantages.

2nd Platoon marched in behind a drop of meks and gunned the Ejjai down point blank, filling the enemy's armored faces and chests with blaster fire and glowing holes.

Bravo broke them down. Then the local defenders demanded the right to take their vengeance upon all of the foes who remained. The Marines gave them that right, and went along only to back them up and help protect them from any enemy traps and nasty surprises.

In almost every engagement, even when outnumbered, the elite Spacer Marines eventually outwitted, outfought, and overcame the Ejjai invaders and soundly defeated them, always with pitched fighting.

Yet as always, new problems and complexities presented themselves. Every battle and combat situation was different.

At the next gigacity, the Ejjai were nearly in complete control, dug in and entrenched in all of the built-up areas. On top of that, they used captured civilians as not just hostages, but active human shields.

Bravo again waited until nightfall, making their plans for another stealth assault. The city could be taken, yet there was no way to prevent hundreds of thousands–perhaps millions–of civilian deaths at the hands of their captors.

Naero and Om had some ideas of their own, but to make them known, Shetanna could no longer remain silent.

Miranda-Naero went to her commander for the last time in her disguise. "Leftenant Wilde, contact HQ and Major Luna immediately."

The Anaconda looked at her funny. "What is it this time, Brighteyes? Another hidden enemy minefield?"

Naero hit her nano presets and morphed her stealth armor into her Intel variant, complete with her dark cloakcoat and Mystic battle mask. She undid her gleaming, long black hair and shook it free. Next she ignited her twin, blazing red Chaos katanas in both hands.

Then she made her blades and all of herself go transparent, until she was nearly invisible. "I'm sorry to have deceived you," she said. "Miranda Allen is but an alias."

Trevor Lakota stood by smiling slightly, not looking very surprised at all.

"I see," Wilde said. "Then I'm guessing that you are, in fact, our delayed Mystic Combat Liaison? How shall we know you, sir?"

"I am Mystic Adept Naero Amashin Maeris, of Clan Maeris. And I hold the matching rank of Strike Fleet Captain. My battlefield codename is Shetanna."

Wilde saluted. "That rank is the Marine equivalent of a major, sir. I'll bring you to the attention of HQ at once, and escort you there personally, if you so wish it."

"Please, out in the field and unless our superiors are around, let's be on a name basis, first or last, you pick. That's the way I run. Call me Naero, N, or Maeris."

"I'm Ana," Wilde said. "I like that as well. Thanks, N. General Walker has spoken very highly of you and your service both during and after the Annexation War. And who has not heard of your illustrious parents? I thought you had that fighting style down a little too well."

Naero nodded. "My thanks once again, Ana. You honor me and my Clan."

"So, N. I assume that with this flamboyant entrance of yours, you have some Mystic tricks in mind to unleash on our new friends, in conjunction with our developing night operations?"

"Indeed. Something quite radical, I would say."

The Anaconda showed her teeth. "Bravo specializes in stealth attacks, the radical, and the unexpected."

"First, I think we should send in everyone—even our reserves and any numbers that we can muster. And we do it quiet. They won't expect us to overwhelm them one-on-one with knives, battle blades, and swords. We gut them all silently in the black with blades."

Ana raised both eyebrows. "Interesting. Daring. No military force has attempted such a thing on this scale in centuries, perhaps millennia. At the least, in a thousand years."

"And Bravo is the only force that can pull it off," Naero said.

"You are correct, N. It just might work, and they would never expect us to do such a thing. We can coordinate the attack with the assistance of all the other MCLs present in this battle zone."

Naero was called in to meet with Major Luna, who was still technically her commander. Everyone on the command staff for 36 introduced themselves to her, and she to them. Naero and Ana outlined the plan together.

Then they contacted General Walker and Intel directly to gain approval.

That night, a powerful thunderstorm unleashed its fury on invader and defender alike. The weather played into Bravo's hands even further. Under the cover of that storm, waves of Marines moved through the shadows in a deadly sweep.

By dawn the next day, tens of thousands of Ejjai invaders lay dead, all with stunned and surprised looks frozen on their dead faces. Millions of equally stunned defenders and civilians finally began to realize that they were not only free, but delivered from the foe.

It was as if avenging spirits had walked about and among the invaders that night and stolen their lives away in silent waves of sweeping, whispering death.

Throughout the gigacity of Kolovan, and three others, the defenders found countless enemies cut down where they had stood and fought. Eyes staring wide in shock and fear. Throats slashed, necks and spines severed, eyes stabbed out, lungs and hearts punctured, heads nearly decapitated and skulls crushed. Guts sliced open and ripped out.

Bravo exhausted themselves, but they took out entire armies of invaders, struck down silently in the black.

And the legend of the deadly ghosts of Bravo Command only continued to spread and grow. Across all sectors, the invaders were freaking out, big time.

Naero walked among Company 36 and introduced herself once more, apologizing for slightly deceiving them the way she did. She had her reasons.

Jonny Fox laughed. "So, Brighteyes. Does this mean we're not really friends for life?" he asked.

Naero smiled. "It doesn't change that much. Hand me a cold Jett, ffl, and let's talk about it."

They did so. That night after the battle was another Fifthday, the ancient Thursday named after some other god. Fifthday nights were Chat Nights, and the Marines broke off into groups and pairs to talk, gripe, or get to know each other better.

Naero sucked down some more of her stash of Jett, sharing one of hers with Jonny this time. "So, you gonna tell me this long story of yours?"

Jonny Fox laughed, still so young that he looked like a boy more than a man. "Oh, I guess it isn't that long. Like I said, Chime and I are the only surviving members in our family besides our great-granny Farita. Everyone else died in the various wars. Great-granny Fari loves books, and always read to us when she was raising us. She made us read to her when we got old enough. If you haven't noticed, Chime's a little bit of a kook about books and reading and all that."

Naero chuckled. "Really? I had no idea. So, what do you want, Jonny?"

"Me? Not that much. As soon as this war's over, I'm done with the Marines. I'll muster out like a lot of Marines do, and get a little ship, somewhere nice and peaceful on some milk run for great-gran and me, and Chime, too, if she wants to tag along. A simple life in the stars for a Spacer. Maybe track myself down a cute wife and have some kids for great-gran to fuss over."

Naero nodded, drained her borbble and reached for another. "That all sounds like a pretty good life, Jonny."

He belched real loud. "I thought so."

They stopped talking for a while and listened to the other Marines around them.

Staff Sergeant Gerrold Donovan had three kids with his wife Kelly: Donald, age six, Mearal, age four, and Tarana, at one and a half. He showed pics and vids of his kids around for all to see. Corporal Poker Elkins and his wife Arrella had two children: Wilton, age five, and Karina, age three. Victoria Apache had a two-year-old daughter with her husband, Jim Williams. Everyone in the Marines was proud of their kids, if they had them, and liked to show them off to everyone.

Everyone had something, or someone to live for.

Trisha Marshall, their scrounge, had a Marine starfighter pilot named Jake Turner that she was crazy about. Vincent Fay had fallen nose over tail in lust with a medtek on a hospital ship, Shelly Baker, who apparently felt the same way about that gorgeous hunk of Marine.

Everyone was either in the Marines for life or, after this tour or war, they were going to take it easy and live whatever they called "the good life" somewhere else somehow.

Either way, everyone had big plans.

3

Zvigeny-7 was a special case. The local population of former Ramoran and Besh mining slaves had armed their world to the teeth since the Annexation War.

By the time the Ejjai invaders fought their way through the Alliance fleets, and the system mines and gunships, most of the Ejjai shock troops had been swarmed on and slaughtered.

So, why were the Marines of Bravo Command even there?

For one thing, the defenders were exhausted, and many of their best units and fighters had suffered heavy casualties during the initial phases of the invasion.

Next, one entire Ejjai battle group of ten thousand slashers were smart enough to escape with their remaining ships–including clone and meatships–to a continent on the earthlike planet that had not been settled. As a jungle world with dangerous creatures and unstable selontium deposits that disrupted and blocked coms and scanning, it was the perfect place to hide and lay low. Even fixers could not scan the continent and the thick jungles, although they could maintain some fleeting coms at close range.

Even worse, the Ejjai sent out distress calls to all available invaders on the nearby systems. Other invader battle groups kept trying to reach Zvigeny-7 and join the fight. Everyone was getting worn down in a ceaseless hot zone.

If the Ejjai maintained their foothold on that key system, the world-hopping campaign of the Spacer Alliance could not go forward and would stall-out. The enemy could flood more forces forward and seize even more worlds.

Unless these Ejjai were eliminated, they would only continue to cause major problems. The depleted system defenders weren't in any shape to pursue the holdouts. And there was always the threat of the enemy meatships and cloneships creating more enemy troops on their own.

Naero finished studying the sitrep on her holopad screen and turned to Staff Sergeant Owen Valmont, leader of Squad 2. "Okay, so it's a mop-up, but a tricky one."

Valmont seemed to be in agreement. "With a few complications, you are correct, N. We'll insert in stealth mode, scout the target areas, and then bring the heat down where it's needed."

As the company MCL for Company 36, Naero went in on point, ahead of Squad 2 in advance recon mode.

Staff Sergeant Valmont, Deb Steiner, Waylon Aztec, and Wallace Archer in Fireteam 1. Sergeant Milton Ramsey in charge of Bessa Jackson, Acer Adams, and Sender Konrad in Fireteam 2. Corporal Baylor Scott led Fireteam 3, with Chime Fox, Falco Borelli, and Trisha Marshall.

Five minutes after they dropped into the dense jungle, a hunting pack of twenty or more midsized carnasaurs started tracking and sizing the Marines up for a snack.

Naero sighed and zipped back to Squad 2.

"We don't have time for this crap. Fighting these dinos will attract too much attention. Everyone with me in stealth mode. Hop-jump three klicks southeast of here. Form up on my mark, vector close. Mark!"

That slight hop got them out of scent range from the pesky hunting pack.

An hour later, Naero guessed that they had to be getting close to their quarry.

The Ejjai were both messy and efficient. That section of jungle had been stripped of all life, huge or small. Anything that was meat. The invader meatships could process huge dinosaur carcasses as well as civilian humans.

No scans worked, but from visuals alone, the old blood trails and kill spots were slightly less than a standard week old–about six days. That meant at least one or more meatships, and most likely a cloneship, as well, was feeding off the local fauna.

Given time, the invaders would expand their own numbers, producing more and more of their violent kind, training and arming them to fight and kill relentlessly.

It only took about a standard month of thirty days to create a fresh crop of Ejjai clone troops. They'd be meatship-fed and shunt-memory trained, complete with manufactured gear and weapons, ready to go forth and fight and feed on their own.

This was the plague of the Ejjai invaders that the enemies of all humanity had unleashed on the Alpha Quadrant.

Om cut in. *Scanning and communications are greatly reduced, N. Fixer waves have spread out over this section of jungle and pursued the visual signs of enemy unit passage. Three Ejjai hunter-killer teams, thirty-five kilometers, heading in a northwest direction on these headings. Combat armor and energy weapons. They are also posting small pockets of troops around them in a defensive perimeter pattern. These small groups of Ejjai have cloaking tek after their own fashion.*

Most likely scout/sniper teams on the outer perimeter of their base, Om. Good work; you and the fixers have located the outskirts of their base.

Naero notified her recon team. "If we pop them too soon, they won't report in, and the enemy base or bases will know something's wrong and have advance warning. The bulk of them might be able to slip away before we can wipe them all-out."

"Copy that," Sergeant Valmont said. "So, we paint them on the combat grid map and bypass them. They'll get theirs later from the other units, when the main show starts up."

"Leave no stone unpulverized," Corporal Scott added. "Fox, Borelli–paint the enemy scouts and snipers with your fixers and relay their positions up the fixer chain that we established on the way in."

"Affirmative," they both said.

"Squad 2, move out," Naero said over their close link. "We mark all of the enemy positions, numbers, and makeup on the way in. Watch for any additional secposts. Locate the primary targets, and paint them on the short combat grid."

Up close, on the ground, the Ejjai were easy to track. So what if scanners didn't work?

The slashers left a trail of death in their wake. They killed and ate anything that moved. Leftovers went into the spinning, processing blades of the meatships. No waste.

The enemy kept their scouts and listening posts in concentric rings, two klicks apart. With the enemy on the move, the rings would fall back at times, following the path of death that the main camp carved through the jungle every day or two.

In the event that one perimeter ring was attacked or did not report in on time, the entire battle group could alert the rest and close in for defense, or scatter in several directions to vanish and escape, and link up somewhere else at pre-arranged rally points.

Bravo had seen this pattern of operation before, yet without coms and scans, the situation was that much more complicated.

"Got a buried gravtank," Pfc Steiner noted.

"Ejjai gunship completely concealed up in a huge vine and tree complex," Pfc Aztec noted. "The slashers exposed their position by dumping their waste down the trees, thinking no one would notice."

Pfc Konrad cut in. "Don't let the slashers empty a latrine catch on you, kids. You'll never get that stench out of your filters."

"Quiet, you goons," Valmont ordered.

Pfc Archer called out, "Two slasher listening post at these points, halfway up the leeward hillside among the rocks."

"Another three enemy sniper team, hidden in this group of trees, mark these points," Jackson added.

"Heads up," Naero warned. "Our first forward infantry defensive line…complete with hardpoints and autogun emplacements. Enemy troops dug in. They must be protecting something further in."

"Copy that," Sergeant Ramsey stated. "What are those positions, N? Say again?"

"Here's the feed again, Milt. Don't blink next time. Off our two o'clock position, east by southeast. We've got vehicle movement and engine noise, half a klick in."

"Got it. Copy that," Valmont said. "Let's swing in and check it out. Stay on approach, just under the tree canopy, ten meters off the deck, rearward triangle assault pattern. Fifteen meters between fireteams. Team 2 take point behind our MCL. One left and three right. Everyone glacier in, quiet and cool."

Naero led them in, three hours before sunset, as they painted everything they could on the way through.

Bravo Command closed in and encircled that area, taking up assault positions, processing all data feeds on the expanding play map.

The rest of Bravo stood poised to bring overwhelming firepower to bear on the invaders, once their exact positions and locations were known.

Naero and her team counted and marked three separate meatships, two cloneships, and four automated factory supply ships–all running full tilt.

Enemy transports brought in dead dinosaurs and jungle animals to be fed into the meatship blades.

Squad 2 and Naero continued to paint gravtank units and gunships, troop emplacements, two battleships, three cruisers, and five destroyers–all concealed in the dense jungle vales, along with assorted transports and lesser support vessels.

Even Naero grew alarmed. "This battle group is much larger than we originally thought," she said.

"Copy that Brighteyes," Valmont said. "We'll call in more units from command, and alert the Navy. They'll make ready to intercept any ships that try to leave the atmosphere."

In the end, the secret enemy base covered an area in a radius of only ten klicks. To Naero, it looked like a straightforward drop and pop. Bravo most likely calculated it that way, too.

"Uh-oh," Pfc Chime Fox said.

Staff Sergeant Valmont barked at her, "Dammit, Fox. You know how I hate to hear 'Uh-oh!' Report something if you have it to report. Now. I want deets and specifics."

"How's this, Staff Sergeant: I've got a feeding pen of three or four thousand friendlies. That's right, mates. Friendlies, all sexes, all ages. And it looks like some of them are rigged with explosives."

"Dammit to hell," Naero said. "Haisha! Just when we thought this was going to get easy…a damn feeding pen full of prisoners." Nothing was ever simple.

"The slashers like fresh meat," Pfc Borelli flatly noted. "Why are we surprised?"

"Now Bravo can't just sweep in and wipe out every slasher in sight." Chime said. "Haisha! Now we have to perform a rescue op at the same time."

"Okay, so we do it the hard way," Valmont said. "We secure that pen and get those civies out of harm's way. We do the job with finesse instead of sledgehammer."

"Aww…" Naero muttered in disappointment. "I like the sledgehammer."

Chime actually giggled.

"Can it, you two," Valmont told them.

"Very well. We'll survey the extraction site and prep the coming assault. Inform HQ about our complication," Naero said. "I want to try to locate the enemy command and control. We might be able to take them out right before the attack begins, with remotely detonated microcharges. Fireteam 3, with me. The rest of you work out what's best to accomplish here with Staff Sergeant Valmont."

Naero led Fireteam 3 around to the various starships, watching and observing for the right signs.

Finally, they spotted one. Ejjai troops came to the feeding pen and culled out several local pregnant women, and women with babies and small infants. About a dozen in all.

That had all of the earmarks of a snack for the invader high command, or whoever the officers were in charge of the battle group.

Grimly enough, the Ejjai leadership hoarded the best meat for themselves, and feasted regularly, as the disgusting, greedy gluttons that they were.

"I'm going in," Naero told her fireteam. "You four stay put out here and do what you can. If I'm not back in half a standard hour, and I send no word, I order you to return to the rest of Squad 2 and assist with the primary assault."

"Be careful, sir," Corporal Scott told her, a little sheepishly.

"Aww…why, Scott, you bad boy. You do care about me. The last thing you said to me was something about chopping off my–"

"I-I'm…really sorry about that, sir. I was kinda having a bad day, you know? I'm hoping you'll kind of forget about all of that."

"Sure, consider it done, Scott. And besides, the medics tell me it only takes a day or two in the regen tanks to grow your nips back. And they say even say they come back all pink and pretty and even perkier than before, so good news!"

Naero left him staring with his mouth hanging open.

Yep, always leave them either laughing or wanting more.

The rest of Squad 2 also wished her good hunting and told her to be careful.

"I'll be fine," she told them. "If you hear a commotion, that will just be me giving our visitors holy hell. But I want to stress that we should all do our best to remain undetected until just before the assault begins. You guys have your orders."

"Yes, sir," they all said, mostly in unison. There were always a few stragglers late to the party.

Naero zipped away on her gravwing, working her way above the heads of the terrified captives and the jeering, chortling guards escorting them to their grim doom.

Those captives had to know very well what was going to happen to them, where they were being taken, and why.

Naero despised this part, and the Ejjai even more for forcing the issue.

She was under direct orders to do nothing. And she had to watch the looks on those people's faces, sometimes as the enemy tortured and killed them. That wasn't right and it wasn't fair, but sometimes that was war.

The Ejjai troops herded the dozen or so captives into the nearest cloneship, shaped like a big red, round dome. Within, Ejjai techs, mostly the smaller, scrawny males, labored hard at developing, shunt training, and freezing ten thousand Ejjai shock troops in only thirty days.

Left on their own, the clones would only live for about ten years–and could still reproduce the natural way, as well.

The enemy cloneships were obviously far more efficient for military purposes. The Ejjai clones never seemed to question their situation or existence. They gleefully relished any opportunity to exploit, torture, kill, and devour all life that got in their way.

The leadership for this battle group consisted of one Ejjai admiral, two combat generals, and their closest direct command officers–all female. That was customary, being that hyaenanoids were strictly and brutally matriarchal.

On the big cloning vessel, the invader leaders had set themselves up a little playroom, like all good warlords, complete with implements of torture, butchering, and cooking and eating supplies. The Ejjai leadership took for themselves the best of everything, including the most prized meat.

The Ejjai leadership and about a hundred of their closest officers shut themselves up in their playroom, ready to have a little fun.

Naero even overheard them give explicit orders not to be disturbed for the next few hours. Only if there was a major attack on the base.

That made things interesting.

Naero checked her wristcomp. Still, that gave her almost two hours before Bravo moved in to take out the enemy base.

Ejjai could do a whole lot of nasty in two hour's time. The additional dozen fresh captives joined about threescore others, huddled together in holding pens and cages.

Naero estimated. She could channel only so much more Cosmic energy this day, and most of it was still in Chaos forms. Her Mystic powers were not infinite, so she had to use them sparingly to the best effect.

Om, I think we have to take out the leadership on our own. Bravo can take these other clowns down without me. But we need to call in a new plan for Squad 2.

Let me guess, N. You want them to leave you to it here, and go assist with saving the rest of those captives in that pen when the attack goes down? Correct?

That's where they'll be needed the most, in order to cut down on the casualties. We know there will be a few, no matter what we do. They can help reduce that number even further. I'm calling it in.

"Squad 2, Squad 2. This is N. Go help save the people trapped in that pen. I'm good to go here. I'll take out the leadership and rescue the prisoners here. Catch up with me after mission completion."

"Are you sure you don't need any help or back up from us, N?" Scott asked. We could leave you a fireteam, if nothing else."

"No, thanks, but I don't think so. There's only a hundred of them."

"Only a hundred, eh?"

"Funny, Scott. Just do me a favor and don't let our people waste this cloneship until I've signaled that myself and the other prisoners are all-out. Luck to you all. Fight well, 36."

"Affirmative, sir. You do the same. Squad 2, over and out."

Om, I need you and our fixers to cut and bypass any alarms and keep us sealed up in this little Ejjai playroom for the next hour or so. These bitches want to be alone with their meat? Let's keep it that way. Oh, and jam all of the coms and links, while we're at it. Two can play at that game.

Fixers on it, N. Nothing will get in or out until you give the word.

Thanks, Om. Watch our six.

As always.

The Ejjai leadership were pickier about their meat that the rest of their kind. They began washing the captives and carefully stripping them of their clothing, careful not to bruise or damage their prizes.

But very soon…things would take a turn for the worse for the captives, and get extremely messy soon enough.

Naero focused her abilities and prepared herself.

She set up a company-level shield pod near the holding pen where the invaders were herding in all of the clean meat. The victims shivered, wet and cold and afraid.

As soon as the last selected captives were tossed in, Naero had a fixer flip the switch on the shield pod.

Now the captives were all as safe as she could make them for the next several minutes.

Shetanna could go to work.

At first she remained cloaked and shot many of the Ejjai on the perimeter with stun needles from her needle rifle. She could have chosen explosive needles, but she had time to kill…literally.

The Ejjai flipped out, firing weapons in all directions, killing and wounding each other.

Then her mines and microbombs went off.

When she had whittled them down to about thirty or so, she made herself visible to them and their leadership, twin red katanas blazing and crackling in her hands.

The invaders snarled and roared, going on the attack.

A few tried to call for help. Naero cut them down first.

Some others tried to attack and kill the shielded captives.

Shetanna struck them down next.

Next she flashed among the remaining Ejjai with Mystic-trained speed and strength. Pieces of Ejjai flew in several directions, their screams echoing in the air and filling the isolated chamber.

The leaders held out among a final pocket of a handful of troops, weapons blazing.

Shetanna set her personal shield full front and strode toward the band deliberately, ignoring their fire. She stalked them slowly, eyes set.

She walked in among them and killed them all, one by one.

She saved the leaders for last.

By then they were reduced to cowardly gibbering and balling up in terror in their own wastes, as Shettanna slowly carved off their heads with her glowing blades.

All the terror the Ejjai instilled in their poor, helpless victims. And yet, when put to it themselves, they were all nothing but gutless cowards at heart.

Naero took the time to free and see to the Ramoran and Besh captives, allowing them to reclaim their clothes and gather up weapons, if they so wished.

While they put themselves together and made ready to depart, Naero made sure of any foes who were only stunned.

Some of the captives began shooting any Ejjai who twitched and still moved. Some just liked shooting up their captors.

Other than being traumatized by their entire ordeal, most of the captives seemed all right. Two of them were actually experienced transport pilots.

That would come in handy.

As Naero guessed, the leadership had an escape transport at hand. That included room for at least a hundred persons. She put the captives in and sealed it up, giving them orders to fly out after the Marine attack started up.

Naero made sure to paint the transport as a captured vehicle with friendlies on board, not to be shot down or destroyed. She sent a relay alert to her mates and HQ, to make certain that nobody fired upon the prisoners as they fled.

After the attack began, and the transport left the ship, Shetanna turned back and went after the Ejjai troops still on board the cloneship, and the troops protecting it outside.

Once again, with her unit shielding shimmering around her, Shetanna quietly walked out to face them.

At first they just stared at her in shock and disbelief.

Shetanna yawned and calmly, casually stretched, as they rose groggily to their feet.

One of the alphas snarled at Naero and pointed, looking around. "See if it's a holo. The spacks get us to shoot at holos, a lot. What is this, spack? Some kind of trick?"

An Ejjai actually tried to come close and poke her.

Shetanna shoved a blazing blade through the invader's eyes. "No, tricks, filth. It's the real me. Get your strength back. Stop shitting and pissing yourselves. Take your time. Lift your weapons. Let me know when you are ready."

Shetanna smiled and narrowed her eyes. "Let me know when you all are ready to die."

The enemy blinked at her as if she or they were all insane.

Weapons came up.

"You aren't getting out of here alive, spack."

Naero flexed her neck casually. "Yeah, yeah," she muttered, stray blasts deflecting off her shields.

The Ejjai simply did not know what to make of this, apparently forgetting about the battle rapidly sweeping toward them all.

But they still tried to encircle her.

"Why aren't you scared, spack? You should be trying to escape."

Shetanna laughed and grinned at them, pulling up her Mystic battle mask. "I could say the same thing to you, bitches."

"Are you crazy? Can't you see how many of us there are? All of the firepower we have?"

"Yeah," Naero said calmly. "I guess I only wanted a light work out today. Thanks anyway for trying." She sighed and lifted her swords. "I guess your dumb asses will just have to do!"

Sonic attacks and telekinetic mind blasts drove the foremost attackers crunching into supports and the hull when they rushed in on her.

Enemy weapons barked and cut loose.

Naero unleashed an expanding wave of Chaos energy attacks and techniques that cut the attackers in half within seconds.

A spray of Chaos energy spikes and rods shot out from several directions and drilled many others full of lethal, burning holes.

Then they exploded, shredding the invaders where they stood.

Shetanna ripped into the last foes like a flaming wheel of blazing swords and flashing, crushing kicks.

When Naero rejoined her unit, everyone was in a somber mood.

They had endured one casualty. A gigantic carnasaur slipped in during the battle and snapped its huge jaws on Sender Konrad of Squad 2, Fireteam 2. It chewed him and his armor up and swallowed him whole, before his mates could track the damn thing down and kill it. They had to blow the carcass open with charges to retrieve Sender's remains, which they put into a standard casualty bag.

Marines took care of their own dead whenever and wherever possible.

With the mission complete, 36 returned to their dropship and went back into orbit that night, attached to the strike cruiser, *The Black Bulldog*.

Staff Sergeant Owen Valmont led Squad 2 and the rest of 36 as they solemnly carried and escorted Sender Konrad to the ship's mortuary, where the honored dead were prepared for burial on the third day, after their wake. At times, if there were many casualties, the wakes would be held, but the dead would be kept frozen, and launched into the nearest star when the mission was over.

The Marines marched slow. Valmont's voice rang out. "Let the call go out into the Beyond. For a Spacer Marine goes forth upon the next journey. Let him be welcomed and embraced, by all of his blood, and his mighty brothers and sisters who have gone before him. Let them welcome him in honor."

Sender's mates had already said their goodbyes to him along the way and during the ride up.

They handed the remains over to the funeral teks, and went back to their quarters. Marines were almost always quiet during the first few hours of losing one of their own. Then slowly, they returned to their regular routines.

Seventhday had what many called Sparring Night. Others also called it Dance Night, but Naero had never been much of a dancer. Although from what she heard, 36 had some of the best dancers in Bravo Command. Everything with the hyper-athletic Marine Companies was a hot and heavy competition.

Naero spent much of the evening knife fighting with Trevor Lakota in a practice room.

They had a fantastic time.

Just as she expected, Lakota was superb with blades. Without her Mystic strength and speed, he would have beaten her half of their matches. The man was that good.

Even with her prowess, he drew her blood seven times.

"You should have been a Mystic," Naero told him.

He smiled. "That is not my way, as it is yours, Naero of the Brighteyes. I am but a simple warrior at heart. While you, you were borne of the blood of your mighty parents to become the great Spirit Warrior that you are now, and that you shall yet become in the future. Any who have eyes can see this in you."

Naero sighed. "I carry a Cosmic monster within me that I cannot control," she confessed.

Lakota nodded. "You may call it that, but it is you. You are the darkness and the light, both good and evil, and they constantly war within your soul. The Great Mystery itself has touched you, and invoked its powers of Life and Death within you. I fear, that your destiny shall be both great and terrible–a very frightening thing indeed. I would not wish such a life. Yet it makes me glad, that I am but a simple warrior."

Naero asked him about the Marine they had lost, and then about several other people in the company. Lakota always gave her his honest opinion.

At one point Naero grinned and was curious. "You like the Foxes, the cousins Chime and Jonny. I can tell you do, but you seldom talk to them or hang around them as friends."

Lakota grinned. "Big sister and little brother Fox? Yes, I have great love for them, and they need it, because of the great sadness of their family. They often make me laugh, but I can only take so much of them. Yet they are good Marines and warriors in their own right, and have my respect. I am a quiet man by my nature; I usually keep to myself."

"You know they're cousins, not sister and brother, right?"

"That does not matter. They were raised together like brother and sister by the last of their elders, but the little brother always tries to look out for the older sister. He protects her like a brother should and has a good heart."

"I would agree with you, though, Lakota. Chime can be a little much at times."

Lakota sighed, "It's because she's crazy. If she survives this war, and finds the right person to love her well, Chime will be all right I think."

They talked for another hour, drinking lix paks. Lakota informed her about several others in the company that she would enjoy matching iron with, half of them from the other native Clans.

Naero gave him one of her special Clan Maeris battle blades, and showed him all of its powered features.

Lakota's eyes twinkled and he smiled. He unfolded an ornate leather wrapping with intricate beading and gave her a warrior's knife from his people. He said the hilt was buffalo horn and that the blade was sacred to his Clan.

Naero gasped slightly, actually sensing a touch of Cosmic power within that blade.

Naero made certain to thank and honor her new friend with great respect. Honor was something that was paramount to all Spacers; something that they all shared and could understand.

4

Metra-4's lush, green, primordial forests and grassy plains covered most of the three main continents, sprinkled with a few mountains and foothills here and there. There were very few deserts, and extremely small polar ice caps.

The Metrans had a system population of only 1.8 billion souls–almost all of them Besh, with their gray-green skin, green-black hair, and small ears. Mining and lumber were, of course, the two biggest exports.

Here the Ejjai invaders had primarily split their forces and were locked in two separate, all-out struggles with the locals, naturally around the two largest gigacities, Bronten and Turam, each on a different continent.

Ejjai military doctrine consisted of having their battle groups surround the two gigacities within rings of artillery, gunships, and gravtanks. They proceeded to shell the the defenders relentlessly and without mercy, while gunships and warships modified for ground assault raked the defenders and the civilian population indiscriminately.

Once the defenders were sufficiently beaten down, the invaders began to collect the locals for the meatships, efficiently wiping out area after area.

This strategy was very effective against mostly static, planetary defenses with weak militaries.

The Marines of Bravo Command slipped onto the surface of Metra-4 without being detected, and organized two massive surprise assaults directly against the two main bodies of the invading forces.

When night came, and darkness shrouded Bronten and Turam, the Marines unleashed their carefully orchestrated assault plans.

Naero had been forward, scouting as usual with Company 36, and Squad 3 of her assigned recon platoon. Squad and Fireteam 1 leader Python Wilde, younger brother of the Anaconda, led the rest of her fireteam into harm's way, consisting of Rebecca Cooper, Neesha Flynn, and Felix Blooding–no near relation, apparently, to an assistant cook Naero had known during the Annexation War, famous for a certain gravy he made.

Fireteam 2 was led by Corporal Chang Han, Vincent Fay, Nicholas Kowalski, and Ted Kim. Squad 3 was rounded out by Corporal Lance Allen, Bryan Mitsubishi, Gabriel Patton, and Luke Barrett in Fireteam 3.

Shetanna and her dozen Marines watched and painted Ejjai gravtanks and vehicles, belching forth out of a big enemy transport, assembling into their attack formations.

They put all of those vehicles into play on the main combat grid, where they would be tabulated and assigned targeting profiles and priorities. Yet as they watched, another similar transport came down and began to disgorge its forces, making for a very tempting profile for an advance attack.

Every enemy target couldn't always be engaged at once, especially as enemy forces increased in size and became very numerous. Thus they had to be prioritized and attacked in the best order possible for maximum success.

Naturally, higher value targets had a higher priority in the flow of attack and were engaged and eliminated first. This was done according to the integrated firing profiles of the Spacer Marine Battle Command System, its series of linked, powerful AIs, and the leadership, right on up to General Walker himself.

"Sergeant Wilde, that's a lot of enemy armor coming online," Naero noted over their secured helmet link. "That's going to be a major problem for everyone when they start to maneuver and fire."

"Yes, sir. I agree, sir."

"Wilde, let's drop the *sir* stuff when we're on our own. There's no brass here."

"Copy that."

"How can we possibly resist such rich targets of opportunity? What say we seize the initiative here, swoop in and use up all of our explosives and ordnance. I mean drop it all where it counts–grenades, charges, microbombs, and float-seeker smartmines–everything we've got–in order to take out those two transports and perhaps some of those other ships, while they're still unloading those tanks."

Python nodded. "I like that idea a lot, N. But after we do all that, we're still in the middle of a combat zone, completely depleted, with nothing but our primary weapons. And then the fighting really kicks in."

"I've thought of that. Let's see what our fixers can do about resupplying us along the way from whatever they can recycle. Let's keep them busy working for us."

Python studied the gravtanks and grimaced. "You know, it's too bad we couldn't get a unit of our own meks or gravtanks over here. They'd have a field day. That's what we could really use."

Naero thought about it. "Everyone here knows how to operate a tank, don't they?" she asked.

All of Squad 3 clicked in. "Affirmative."

Naero looked back the way that they had come in.

The battlefield was awash with a litter of ruined, damaged, and abandoned enemy gravtanks from prior battles with the local forces.

"I think we might just go for a little ride. Let me and the fixers do a bit of teknomancing and upgrading, while you and Squad 3 go set those transports to go up in flames."

"We're on it, N. Pick us out some good ones. Four or five. We can put two or three people in each one."

Naero handed all of her remaining explosives over to the sergeant to put to good use.

She and Om sent some fixers to scrounge and recycle the battlefield for more ordnance and explosives they could dole out and utilize.

But the bulk of their small fixer cloud they sent to work on a handful of mostly abandoned and lightly damaged enemy gravtanks that could be teknomanced, modified, and somewhat improved upon. Perfect for a little jaunt in the country to see the sights.

By the time Squad 3 joined back up with her, Naero had teknomanced four enemy gravtanks back to life, and even better than their counterparts– with a few upgrades and modifications of her own.

"Here we go, Wilde. You wished for armor? Haisha! I give you armor. Our chariots await. When things go hot in just a few minutes, and those transports cook off, that's when we make our move. I say we jump in these

48

hopped-up babies and take them for a joy ride. Our fixers have painted them so that our people won't fire upon us, and we can have all the fun we can manage."

Python turned to Squad 3. "Split up, three to a ride, just like the lady said. We slip in from behind if we can and knock out their rearward lines while they're still forming up. We hit hard and fast, do as much damage as we can, and keep going. If your tank gets shot up or destroyed, cloak and fly out on your gravwings to support the assault."

"I've increased the firepower and the rate of fire on these guns," Naero told them. "Keep all weapons blazing. In the middle of a couple of enemy tank battalions, we're bound to hit something. Ram and slam. I've also boosted the armor and the shields, and the speed and power plants. These tin cans can take it, and we don't have to give them back. Keep your fixers active around you to repair any minor damage on the fly. Fight well, and enjoy the ride!"

She and Om kept the controls basically the same. By now they were all familiar with the invader Marauder IV class, standard main battle gravtank. They had fought against and taken out many of them and their variants.

Naero merely improved upon their known weaknesses.

Normally, operating such gravtanks took a crew of four to five slashers. Naero simplified and used fixers to automate the systems so that two or three persons could operate the gravtank and its systems effectively. At the very least, there had to be a commander/spotter and driver/gunner.

"Everyone settled in and clear on the mission?" Python asked. "We go in fast, strike from their rear, and roll them up. Pop as many targets as we can, and then bail out when we must."

"Arrowhead-3, loose armored formation," Naero said. "Three gravtanks forward, one guarding the rear–I'll stay cloaked until you need me. I'm your wild blade. I'll do whatever I can to keep the enemy from swarming on you and dragging you down. Don't get stuck. Move fast, and keep dodging, maneuvering, and firing. Fight well, my brave tankers."

"We're about to go hot very shortly," Python advised. "In no time, there will be fire coming at us from all sides, even if we do everything right. We are descending straight into a hornet's nest and blowing up the hive. The slashers are going to be pissed as hell. Your tank gets hit too bad, everyone bails on gravwings, cloak, and regroup to continue the assault with the remaining elements. Keep as much heat on the foe as you can for as long as possible."

"Exactly," Naero added. "We do as much damage as we can, and then if they trap us, we scatter and slip away, regroup as assigned, and find another place, another way to keep fighting."

Python checked his combat feeds. "Mark. Hot in 1.45 minutes when the main attack kicks in with our explosives. Everyone frost down, check your systems, and get ready to ride."

Hundreds of invader gravtanks had unloaded by the time the transports blew up and became an inferno. Fuel, ammunition, and power cores cooked off as the flames soared.

Squad 3 became a gravtank unit, and vectored in toward the enemy rear under the cover of all of the chaos and confusion.

Then they swung their guns around and blazed a path of destruction in wild, crazy, slashing arcs. They cut a zigzag trail of burning and exploding gravtanks and vehicles, where they were still hemmed in and packed too closely together to be able to move and fire effectively.

The commander of each tank stood up in the turret, behind a unit shield pod, integrating the targeting systems in his or her helmet, patching into the battle command system and the fire control systems of each tank by itself as a separate mobile gun platform.

The commander could also engage targets of opportunity and paint them into the profile with his secondary weapon, a viper gun–an even more devastating version of the basic autogun. The high rate of fire from these energized gauss cannons was blistering, and could degrade and destroy practically anything but another tank itself. Concentrated fire from a viper gun could even eventually take out a tank on its own. And it was positively lethal again all other soft targets with less armor or shields than a tank.

That included other enemy tank crews and personnel out in the open.

And everything popped by the viper guns was automatically painted and lit up on the targeting arrays.

These feeds poured in to the main combat system, where indirect and adjacent direct fire and units could be applied against priority targets.

The gunner operated the main gravtank energy cannons, confirming targeting patterns and redirecting rapid fire as needed. They struggled to stay several targets ahead of the actual guns, which fired very quickly and efficiently after Naero's modifications.

They fired so quickly that some of their firing profiles couldn't help but overlap. They also cancelled and redirected fire away from targets already destroyed, to new targets of opportunity.

The gunner helped monitor the onboard systems and kept them operating at peak effectiveness. That also includes shields, damage control, and fire suppression. The driver helped keep them moving, in a pattern that was not predictable, but allowed for good firing profiles to be executed.

The four modified gravtanks roared over the enemy's rear and–in the words of Naero's father–tore them a new ass.

They very quickly fought within what seemed to them to be spinning wheels and spheres of exploding fire all around them, lit from within.

The steady bump and pulse of the tank cannons punching, rocking, and hammering at the hapless enemy tanks quickly disrupted the invader formations in several directions.

The sweeping spray of the secondary viper guns and the launching of smoke, mines, and missiles only added to the destructive confusion.

Because most of the enemy tanks didn't have their shields up yet, Naero's little joy ride with Squad 3 raked and blasted the foe by the dozens with each second.

Burning hulks and wrecks were soon everywhere in their passing.

Naero also guarded them from above, enclosed within a red star of Chaos energy, whenever enemy gunships of starfighters tried to wing in. Like a guardian spirit, she bobbed above them, flitting from tank to tank, deflecting or absorbing incoming energy blasts and hits.

She returned fire on her own, concentrating on knocking out any enemy gunships or starfighters in their vicinity who tried to get a lock on them.

The Navy and the Marine starfighters were a big help with that. With the sky clear and dominated, Naero focused on helping her tankers pop and kill as many tanks as they could. Om and the fixers assisted them with fine-tuning and computing their own targeting profiles in a target rich environment.

Many invaders adjusted and began to respond to the surprise assault within less than a minute. But by then, Shetanna and the Marines had shot up significant portions of both massive tank formations.

What a ride.

The world all around them continued to light up and explode.

As they suspected, the remaining enemy gravtanks reacted eventually, activating their shields and maneuvering to envelope the raiders in a dome of deadly, interlocking fire.

Shetanna and her tanks took multiple hits as scores of gravtank cannons came online and started to beat the hell out of them.

Naero could no longer attack.

All of her efforts soon concentrated on deflecting and absorbing waves of incoming attacks. And even she could not intercept them all.

The high speed and rate of fire, and their beefed-up shields and armor, would endure only so many hits.

Each second that their four gravtanks kept firing, they destroyed more and more enemy armor.

The invaders concentrated nearly all of their intense fire on the rearguard renegade tank in order to take it out and break the defensive formation. While at the same time, Naero focused all of her efforts on protecting it.

The rear tank lasted for several seconds longer before it started getting blasted to pieces.

"Tank 4, Tank 4. Get out of there. Bail out now!"

Allen, Mitsubishi, Patton, and Barrett barely ejected with their gravwings, joining up with Naero, and fired their weapons under the cover of her shields.

Tanks 1 and 2 continued on forward, pressing and leading the ongoing attacks. Tank 3 whipped around and assumed the rearguard position, protecting their backsides.

They managed to fight for a few minutes longer before they were fairly trapped.

The three remaining crews bailed and ejected almost at once–right before their battered, speeding tanks with their power cores set on overload, plowed into another wave of enemy armor, disrupted, and detonated under a storm of concentrated enemy fire.

Everyone heard Corporal Chang Han's scream cut off over the link, as one of those waves of fire enveloped him. A split second meant death. That's all it took.

Han did not slip within Naero's unit shield barrier fast enough. A half an instant too slow, and he and his combat armor were vaporized.

There wouldn't even be any pieces of him to go back and collect.

"Hornet scatter and cloak fade," Sergeant Python said, just before Naero was going to say the same. "Regroup at R-point Delta-5."

Naero was about to be overwhelmed by those same intense waves of fire, locking onto her no matter how she evaded.

The enemy was so intent on destroying her, that they didn't notice that they were blasting each other, and ignored all of the other Marines who had manage to disappear.

Naero and Om called down an electron wave pulse burst, and several decoy and holo drones, and they cloaked as soon as the rest of Squad 3 was safely away, scattering in all directions away from that growing, misdirected firestorm.

In the confusion, the enemy continued blasting not much else but each other for a few seconds longer, taking damage.

Meanwhile, at rendezvous point Delta-5 nearby, Shetanna and Squad 3 regrouped.

"I know we lost Han," Wilde noted. "But that wasn't anyone's fault. It was just dumb luck. We did good. Han did good. We knocked out and damaged nearly one quarter of the enemy's armor. Not bad for a dozen–plus one–goons on a joy ride!"

Vince Fay nodded. "Han went happy. I saw him smiling. He was having a great time. He knew we were doing well."

Han's best buddy Kowalski still looked in shock at the loss of his best friend. That was always hard on anyone.

All of their fireworks also quickly got Command's attention.

Not seconds later, a Marine mek unit snaked in to engage the remaining enemy armor formations while the foe was still disorganized and reeling.

Marine air strikes also pounded the confused, enemy armor formations.

Two naval destroyers swept over the rest to finish the task and keep moving.

Naero had their fixers stay busy.

"Everyone," Naero told them. "It's time for presents. New orders filtering down. Prepare to move and fire. Re-sup with our fixers. They have demo-charges, grenades, microbombs, and float mines. A full spread of toys for all of us. Load up and let's mission on, for Han. Tighten it up, Squad 3. Let's fight, Marines!"

"Our MCL's on the nose," Sergeant Python Wilde shouted.

"For Han!" all three remaining members of his fireteam yelled.

"Ooh-rah!" the rest roared.

Naero screamed right along with them, and loaded up double for their next fun ride.

Once the battle was over, and the mission was won, Naero and 36 went back to where they lost Han and tried to find some remains.

Nothing. No good.

When they went back up into orbit, they took an old, spare suit of Combat Armor that Han had once worn, and kept for spare parts, like most of the Marines did. They put some of Han's personal effects inside the empty suit. Stuff that reminded his mates of him. Then they added gifts of food, drink, and trinkets. Then they put the suit into a casualty bag, along with busted up enemy weapons as trophies, and took it all to the funeral teks as they always did.

Sergeant Python Wilde led the procession, spoke the needed words, and handed the substitute for their lost friend over to be placed in a Marine casket. They went back, and Han's mates helped Kowalski gathered up the personal effects and gear to be sent home to the family and Clan Chang. Marines took care of their own.

5

Bravo replacements for Company 36 reached them on Tecumseh-2 their next drop point. That world was a vast desert planet with huge, cacti forests and dry-bed rivers with quick dust sink holes that could swallow up tanks and small vehicles.

These wind-whipped, dry-bed rivers snaked through the continents, canyons, and towers of rock and crystal formations.

2nd Platoon had three reps, or what the Marines usually called rooks, come in from Command on the next supply run.

This trio of newly minted Bravo Marine recruits consisted of: Tucker James, Kemela Anthony, and Kokey Miles. Second Leftenant Anaconda Wilde got them in and sitched with their squads.

The day was Firstday, and that night was going to be another Vid Night. Everyone got together and watched their favorite vids.

As the company MCL, Naero came around that evening to meet the new blood. Elite units could be very tough on rooks, and in some cases, they needed to be. In others, not so much.

Naero wanted to examine them and meet them for herself.

"I'm Naero–"

"We all know who you are, sir," Tucker said.

"Your parents, too, sir," Kemela added.

All three rooks stared at her as if she were some kind of spirit being or something.

"I'm the company MCL for 36. Welcome." She offered them all her hand. They each took it, up to the elbow.

"All of us hoped to get a chance to serve with you, sir," Kokey told her.

"Well, be careful what you wish for, Marines. You'll get a perfect introduction to what we do very shortly. Tonight, we'll be hunting, in the black, just the way Bravo likes it. I want you to be extra careful, and listen to the people in your fireteams. The Ejjai are also hunters, and they can be tricky at any given time."

James spoke up again. This one had lots of attitude. She could see it. "Permission to speak freely, sir?"

"Granted. And that goes for all of you. Fire away, James."

"Sir. With respect, we've been here less than half a day and we're already extremely tired of all of this rook, newb, and green crap that we keep getting heaped upon us."

Naero smiled. "I understand."

"No, you don't, sir," Kemela added. "What with being an officer, a Mystic, and an MCL and all."

Kokey sided with her new mates. "We've all been fully trained, sir. All of us are ready to bust someone up the next time they dump on us."

"Listen up, Marines. Regardless of what you think I know or don't know, I'd stow that frustration of yours somewhere deep and dark, and save your busting for the enemy. You want it straight? You know damn well this is just what happens when you're new. After your first action, it will ease off. You wanna change things? Then think about how you're going to treat the next batch of rooks who come in after you.

"We all go through crap like that and the general stupidity of the mob. And yes, for your info, I've been there. I've served with the Niners and with Bravo–and not just as an MCL, but as a regular jarhead, fire-eating devil dog. A Marine, just like you. And yes, I was a rook also. So suck it up and go relax and enjoy some vids. Talk to your new mates. Freeze those hot heads of yours. You can't be worried about things you can't change and that don't matter. Focus on the mission and the enemies we face tonight. That is what real Marines do. I'll be around, if you need me."

"Sir," Kokey asked. "What are the slashers really like to war against?"

"None of you have fought Ejjai anywhere, yet?"

"We only know what we've read and what we've heard and seen on the webnets," James added.

Naero took a moment and sat down with the three. "The Ejjai are animalistic killers more than soldiers. They're pack-minded. They are no match for us Spacers one on one. They will never fight you fair or one at a time, either. They will come at you a hundred at once and pile on more. They see everything that lives as their prey, and will kill and try to eat it. They are stupid in some ways and very cunning in many others. They've just been barely uplifted from the point of being animals, but are clever enough to remain who and what they are–a major threat to civilian populations."

Kemela said, "We've been trained by the best, to be the best. Why should we be afraid of them?"

"Kemela, I never said anything about fearing them. Just be smart. Respect every foe for what they are and for what they are capable of doing. All of you. No amount of training can completely prepare you for what the real experience of this war is like. The people you are replacing were all good Marines–better than you three–only because they were more experienced. But war is always unlucky. If you buy it by bad luck, that's one thing. You just don't want to buy it because you did something stupid that made you dead.

"Haisha, by the law of averages, with all of the shooting going on– even if we are cloaked and invisible–some of us are going to get hit, wounded, and even killed. That's war."

All three rooks rolled their eyes. "We know the odds, and we don't care about that," James said. "We're Marines, sir. And we're ready to scrap, rooks or not. We just want some respect."

Naero grinned a second time. "Never said that you weren't, Marines. Luck to you tonight. You want respect? You'll have plenty of chances to earn it."

She passed Whip Konrad, pale and hugging his knees, rocking back and forth and stammering. "Arty, arty, artillery…th-th-that's how they're going to get me. I'm dead. I'm dead. I'm dead. Arty. Dead man…"

Then a delay came down, and the mission was postponed until the next night.

Secondday was Gear Night. Everyone went over gear, and talked gear while waiting for the call. They inspected their rigs and compared notes and mods, met with teks, and fine-tuned their systems. All three of the new replacements listened in and learned plenty that they had not heard before.

After that, they went over the sitrep again.

Unlike many other Alliance worlds, on Tecumseh-2, the population of fifty or so million were scattered across the habitable zones in relatively small towns and modest cities. Because of the scarcity of fresh water, both surface and ground water, the sentients there had outlawed any city larger than a hundred thousand souls in any one given region.

This was a world of the Silesians, near-humans, often called frogs or even toads, because of their wrinkled throat bags which they could swell up and use to add to several specialized vocal effects for their species.

Silesians still courted each other by chasing each other and singing various mating or love songs to one another. Among them, throatbags remained a sign of status and virility.

As a race, Silesians also had a rep for discriminating against other sentient races, and being very abrasive and difficult to deal with. They delighted even in insulting each other at great length, let alone other sentients.

But after suffering hard from the Ejjai invasion on several of their ancient homeworlds, even the normally abusive Silesians had met their match and become desperate, and begged and pleaded for any assistance and deliverance from any quarter, against such a determined and vicious enemy who did not care anything about them, and saw them only as yet another source of meat.

Then they got the word. The mission was on.

That night, Kokey Miles had a major stealth suit malfunction an hour after sunset. A fairly rare incident with their stealth tek, but it did occasionally happen. Things broke down.

Leftenant Wilder sent her back to one of the Company 36 dropships to effect repairs, before her suit lit them all up for the enemy to locate.

But when she arrived at the camouflaged dropship, she noticed a stray unit of several dozen Ejjai skirmishers just happening by that way on their gravwings. Now they were getting into position and preparing to attack the transport and its crew of eight.

Non-working cloaker be damned, Kokey took cover and attempted to get closer, warn the transport, and reach Company Command and HQ.

As it happened, coms in that localized area near the drop zone were being widely jammed by the enemy. She couldn't even warn the Marines on that transport without being spotted and attacked herself.

One against a hundred or so Ejjai were not very good odds, but Kokey immediately prepared to execute a high velocity, ring-sweep strafing attack via gravwing, in order to alert everyone that something was up.

First she had her fixer reconfigure most of her gear into an E-88 particle beam mini-gun.

Then she increased her velocity and swooped in without hesitating, not only gunning down the enemy skirmishers in droves, but lighting them up and painting them as available targets on the combat grid.

She kept up her sweeping arcs of intense fire, her shields full front, and began to take small arms fire in return.

Kokey killed and wounded several Ejjai, but more importantly, she exposed almost a full company of them on the combat grid in a big way, and took down many of their shields.

Pop-up turrets on the transport responded with supporting fire behind unit shielding. Several Marines guarding the dropship down below and from within were alerted to the enemy presence and moved to engage them as well.

Finally, the dropship itself lifted off and decided to change locations, since that one was now exposed and hot.

Things got dicey when another nearby enemy unit swooped in to assist the first, which by then was being cut to pieces from three different attack vectors.

The heavy Marine transport drew most of the fire, absorbing and blocking it with its shields. They could take it. And that allowed the defenders, like Kokey, to keep cutting the invaders down.

Then a pod of Ejjai gravtanks and two gunships also swept in, and a running fight ensued. The dropship took a major hit from one of the gunships.

In the hail of fire that was exchanged, Kokey's shields and gravwing went down under intense fire, but her armor saved her.

She dropped down hard onto the roof of a high building, more or less stranded there.

To make things worse, another large contingent of Ejjai marched in from below on the streets of the small town, attracted by the fighting. By now, they were all 0.7 klicks from the original DZ.

The dropship blasted off, leaving the enemy behind.

But that also left Kokey behind.

Kokey found herself surrounded on top of that building. She fired her mini-gun, holding them off as best she could from above. She had her fixer convert more of her tek into an autogun, and kept up a steady rate of fire while she also hurled and directed smart grenades, microbombs, and float-seeker smartmines at targets.

Still the Ejjai kept coming.

Once she was out of explosives and ammo for her primary weapon, Kokey drew her backup blaster pistols and dueled with the enemy as they advanced.

At the last instant, a rear guard Marine element appeared directly behind the Ejjai and cut them down out of the sky and below down on the street.

Shetanna popped in back-to-back with Kokey, making the Marine jump. The MCL threw up a unit level shield pod around them both, right as about two dozen foes swarmed over the top of that roof.

Together, they took the rest of the attackers down, although Kokey only managed to shoot three more.

Shetanna buzzed around and hewed through the others with her glowing red sword blades in less than a flashing second.

"Hey, Miles," Naero told her, clapping her on the back. "We'd better get that lousy suit of yours fixed. What's wrong? I had eyes on you as I was circling in, staying out of your firing profiles. You were doing great. Although you did start to look a bit serious and concerned there toward the end."

Kokey breathed a very visible sigh of relief. "Thanks for the assist, sir. For a few secs, I thought they had me."

"Hey, like I said, you did great, Miles. Very adaptive. I came along and decided to lend a hand. I knew you had the situation under control. You didn't mind a little help mopping up, right?"

"If you say so, sir. Not at all."

"Hey, and good news. You're not a rook anymore. Again, welcome aboard, Marine."

Miles rolled her eyes, still catching her breath. "Ooh-rah, sir."

Shetanna grinned back at her and clapped her on the shoulders once more. "That's the spirit, Marine."

Kemela Anthony tripped a shielding negation mine later that night, right before an attack started, exposing half of one entire platoon.

The Marines quickly overwhelmed the enemy position in any case. Anthony fought well.

Shetanna came by and told her not to worry too much. Such mines were everywhere and tricky for anyone to avoid. Everyone triggered one at some point during their various actions. It was a gaffe everyone made, eventually, even Shetanna herself.

Tucker James got jumped by several Ejjai who snuck in, concealing themselves under heaps of dead Ejjai prepared for fusion burn disposal.

He had his shields up. The slashers knocked him around at first with various grenades, and finally took down his shields. Then seven of them swarmed on him as he took them on and fired. The enemy went at him close up with various blades and energy blades.

Bad move on their part.

Most Spacers were experts with blades, and elite Marines received special blade-fighting training.

James drew two Spacer Marine battle blades, one of them energized, and proceeded to carve up six of the slashers as if they were big hams.

The seventh Ejjai was about to stab him from behind when a blazing red katana sliced away the alpha's blade hand first, and then her head.

James whirled an instant too late and instinctively impaled the headless torso with both of his blades. Then he kicked it away.

"Too late, James," Shetanna told him. "Line them up or arc them. If you let them surround you, and you're not fast enough, one of those bitches is going to gut you wide open. And, from now on, let's all scan those gut piles for any life signs before you go to burn them, as well."

James shook his head. "Sounds good, sir. So, I guess everyone's going to have a laugh tonight at the rook's expense, eh?"

"Well, only if you're stupid enough to tell them. I'm not going to say a damn thing. I'll just remind everyone to look out. The Ejjai infiltration teams have just started trying to use this trick. Everyone needs to be wary of it."

"I wasn't sent here to burn any of them. I was just sent to dump off a deposit."

"Doesn't matter, Marine. Either way, from now on, we guard these dumps with fixers, if nothing else, and we send a full fireteam along with the burn teams to dispose of the trash–not just one or two. I'll notify HQ and Command, and these disposal sites will be kept under better security from now on to defeat infiltrators. See, James? You almost dying here might just save many other lives, by alerting us to a new problem to deal with."

"Just doing my job, sir. And…thanks for having my back." Tucker offered her his hand. Naero took it, up to the elbow.

"You're welcome. Let's get back to work, Marine."

When they returned to 36 at the dropship after the fighting was over, they learned that they had already lost someone else that night.

Perice Logan, crushed to death during an op when a building suddenly toppled over on her squad. She went down warning others and shoving them out of the way ahead of her. She never made it.

A demo team had to recover her crushed body from the rubble. 36 and the new Marines brought Logan in and showed them what was done.

On top of all that, it was Food Night, and now with their newest loss, they needed one more rep.

61

6

Haitha-1 was a jungle/swamp world of the Silesians as well, who, on that planet, chose to build their homes in gigantic, stone oak trees that naturally petrified from within as they slowly died, due to the minerals and crystal residue in the swampy, underground water.

There were many of these small tree cities, with a system population of only 1.3 billion.

As they did on many such worlds, the Ejjai invaders broke off into smaller, hunter-killer units and teams. This made them harder to track down and eliminate, with them being so scattered across the planet's surface. And they could engage many more targets at once, better matching the equally scattered population.

In one region in particular, a small enemy sniper team was causing havoc, panic, and death over a wide area, wherever the enemy chose to strike at random. And they kept moving and popping up in the vicinity, only to cause more.

Shetanna and 36 assumed that this was the work of an elite Ejjai sniper unit. They had encountered standard op enemy sniper units similar to this one on several different occasions on other worlds they had served on.

The sniper team would show up, find the highest vantage point in a local area, and then kill as many civilians or military personnel as they could. Then, by the time any troops or competent authorities did show up to combat them, the enemy sniper unit had already packed up, melted away, and was long gone.

These were radical new tactics for the Ejjai, meant to cause Chaos and terror, and not simply bloat their meatships.

They clearly chose a new area, at random, and repeated the bloody process.

From the signs of things–initially, at least–the enemy snipers and their small team also apparently had advance scanning and jamming tek that defeated all normal attempts to pinpoint their locations and firing positions.

That became a problem for the Marines and their teks as well.

These ruthless enemy snipers struck at several random points planetwide, and had already killed thousands within a few days, terrorizing an entire region with small groups of such forces. They obviously had at least one starship, most likely a small insertion ship, with highly advanced stealth tek.

Then something even worse happened the very next day.

A hundred sniper teams just like the first one struck the same region all at once. Civilians, lander military, and even Spacer Marines fell victim to the enemy sniper onslaught.

Bravo Command and 36 organized into rapid-response, anti-sniper teams.

Shetanna formed up with Squad 4, an attached tek unit, and three superb counter-sniper teams, composed of Marine snipers and their spotters.

Sergeant Maria Bucci led Squad 4 with Terrence Dekker, Sarah Maeris, and Pete Cooper in Fireteam 1. Corporal Veronica Nelson led Fireteam 2, with Ken Ryan, Tavis Marshall, and Zina Gordon. Fireteam 3 was comprised of Corporal Braeden Kowalski, Karla Cherokee, Jonny Fox, and Dillon Kothari.

They were thirty klicks away when the call came in about an enemy sniper starting to kill among the locals.

Shetanna and her team swept in fast.

For good measure, Shetanna transported in ahead of them cloaked, and spread out a rapidly expanding cloudnet of specially modified detection fixers.

Let's locate this sniper and take her down, Om. She's not going to show up on any normal scans.

Got it, N. I have local reports of six casualties. Four civilians, one local police, and one medical response person. Nope…make that seven KIA. The sniper just fired again and took down another first responder.

Any kind of trace-back trajectory, Om?

They were meters away from where the action was going down, and still no one, including Naero herself, had heard any conventional shots.

Nothing yet. Fixers almost in place. Net up and running.

Any anomalies or background scatter feedback or blips?

None. Nada. Nacha.

Naero sighed. Then I think I know what this is, Om. We faced something like this back in the Annexation War, remember?

Phaze rifles?

Exactly, Om. It was originally Triaxian Hevangian tek, but I'm guessing our new enemies have improved upon it and taken it to the next level. Adjust the fixernet; watch for subtle energy fluctuations in the near psyonic ranges, similar to the spectrum flux frequencies and vibronic patterns of Astral energies. Have the fixernet track, triangulate, and follow any spikes or even blips.

Adjusting and tracking along those bands that you have specified and anything close. Uh-oh. You're not going to like this.

What, Om?

Four more KIA–a mother and three kids. They were caught in the open, running down a street looking for cover.

Om, if we don't find this sharpshooting invader bitch and neutralize her and her team, there's going to be a lot more death. Find her so that we can ghost her hairy ass and put an end to this slaughter.

N, we have reports of over a hundred such enemy units, doing the same thing on this continent alone.

We crack one of these teams, scan their gear, and send it to Intel, and then we'll figure out how to nail all of these bitches.

There's a flood of data. I think they're trying to confuse our efforts by overwhelming the nets with bursts of useless chatter junk info. I'll shunt it to the tek unit to sort it out.

The tek team called her back seconds later over their link, breaking up a bit from the enemy jamming.

"Talk to me, guys."

"We've computed various anomalies from the fixernet, and gotten rid of the intentional data garbage dumps obscuring the real info."

"Do you have a lock?" she nearly demanded.

"Not yet, but we're close. We can tell you where the sniper last fired from."

"Boys, what good does that do us?"

"Sir, they move thirty meters left and then back thirty meters right, popping targets of opportunity from that position in any direction, at random."

"Then what? That can't be all of it," Naero said.

"Hmm, the full analysis says that they move again within five to ten minutes at most, and they set up again within one minute and start shooting again."

"That's tight, guys. Thanks a lot," Naero told them. "These sniper teams are elite and extremely well-trained. They excel at this."

"Sir, we still can't locate the next exact location of the shooter, but we can pinpoint several possibilities. May we suggest having auto or miniguns ready to shred all of those areas at the same time? We might get lucky with a scattershot approach?"

"Negative. One sign of something like that and they'll just fade away and set up shop somewhere else, where we aren't."

"What if we mass stun the blanket area and sort it all-out from there, sir?"

"No good either, guys. Stunfields won't affect phazed troops. We know at least that much. Explosions or indirect fire won't, either. Their rounds only un-phaze an instant before they hit their targets. We can only detect them for sure when they pause to recharge."

"Sir, didn't phaze armor originally kill the users in some horrible fashion?"

"It did. Phaze-sickness. But we think the enemy has improved upon that tek by now, although it sucks up lots of juice to function. They will still be forced to recharge at some point, or swap out energy paks or some such."

"Sir, we've got just such an apparent recharge spike."

"Get it up on the Combat Grid locator."

"Wait a sec—no good, sir. We've got five more bursts of charging echoes just like it, all within thirty klicks. Probably just echoes."

Shetanna kept up the feeds live to Squad-4 and the others, now positioned around her, ready to go in. Then she spotted the pattern and what it meant.

N, those aren't echoes or feedback scatter and chatter.

I know, Om.

"People, listen up," Naero said. "Each one of those pockets of blips is coming from a six-person sniper team operating in this area, each of them independent. One or two spotters, two shooters, and the other pair are mostly guards or lookouts. That's how they're making this work."

One of the attached snipers called in. "That's how they make all of this work so well. The shooters kill as much as they want. Then they vanish with their team before the area gets too hot, and they go do the same thing somewhere else. I bet they already have the next location selected before they even move."

Word reached them. An enemy sniper had just killed Spacer Marine Macon Abraham with a clean head shot.

"Now the slashers are killing us. Suggestions?" Sergeant Bucci asked. "How do we break them down and take them out?"

"Let me try something," Corporal Nelson suggested. "Maybe our MCL can help. I happen to be a telepath myself, a very strong one."

"Nelson," Naero said, "I'm a Mystic. I've already tried to detect their minds. But you can't detect a mind that is *phazed* or even cloaked, for that matter."

"Hear me out, sir. You can do so…if you're phazed right along with them, at the same time."

"You can phaze, Nelson? I didn't know that. Not many Spacers can. I sure can't."

"Yeah, I can phaze. I just can't move very much while I'm doing it–and it's exhausting. My whole family can do it, more or less. We used to play hide and scan, and we figured out the whole phaze and telepathy thing."

Naero zipped over to Nelson's position and they found some cover nearby. Naero focused and opened her third eye. Then she placed her hands on Nelson's shoulders, studying her through a mindlink and with biomancy, all at once.

"Go ahead, Nelson. Go ahead and phaze. I want to study everything you do at every level. I'll mindlink with you and study your flows when you phaze. I'm a quick study. Once I see a talent performed, once or twice, I can usually learn to imitate it. Now, find the enemy for us. Show me where they are."

"If you don't mind, sir, I'll have to lie down. If I phaze successfully standing up, I'll slip right out of my armor and flop down on the ground naked. The neutral flows of the ground strata will act as a stabilizer. I won't fall into the ground while I'm phazed."

"All right. Go ahead. I'll stay right with you to maintain our mindlink."

"Oh, we have to turn our stealth suits off, as well. That will also interfere with the process."

They lay there under cover, and Nelson went still, into a psyonic focus trance. Naero matched her, keeping one arm across Nelson's shoulder and another hand on the Marine's other shoulder.

Then Nelson phazed.

For an instant, Naero winced as if she were on fire. Phazing was painful at first. Their link almost shattered defensively as Nelson compensated. Naero kept pace with her and phazed right along with her, the very next instant.

Nelson was already scanning and searching the nearby areas with her racing, telepathic mind. Once more, Naero caught up with her counterpart.

Nelson most likely did not know this, but being phazed was a lot like being in the actual astral plane. But instead, this felt more like a small pocket dimension that was temporary, and on a slightly different frequency or flux energy band of Cosmic existence. Only a Mystic would be able to figure out all of that.

There they were: the six members of the enemy sniper team were within range. Nelson and Naero could see and spot them, but without being telepathic, the Ejjai could not see them in turn.

The enemy team had moved once more, and quickly set up to start shooting again.

"We've got them, Om. No one else is dying here. Can the fixers paint them some way to light them up on the combat grid?"

We can't paint them while they're phazed, but we can paint the air around them and their positions so that they show up. They won't see it. But what good will that do? Our weapons and any of our fire will simply pass right through them.

You forget, Om. My weapons and I are also phazed.

Naero spoke to Nelson. "I'm going to take them out."

"Sir, wait. Moving while you're phazed is incredibly taxing. You'll quickly exhaust yourself and become vulnerable!"

"I've got an idea, Nelson. Back in a sec. Trust me."

Shetanna transported right in on the enemy sniper team with her blazing red katanas appearing with her, already rammed right through their bodies. There was no time to react. Their eyes blinked in surprise and froze in death.

Then Naero noticed that she was both phazed, and naked.

She had her swords, which were a part of her, but she had teleported her phazed body right out of her stealth armor.

Not that anyone besides Nelson might notice.

If that was the trade-off for taking out the enemy sniper team, so be it. Naked never hurt anyone.

She quickly flashed back to Nelson and teknomanced into her gear.

"Did you get them, sir? How do you feel?"

Naero caught herself, and un-phazed along with Nelson.

When Naero tried to sit up, she felt lucky that she was already lying on the ground. She barely had the strength to move.

"You were right, Nelson. I'm almost completely drained. But yes–I got them. We got them, thanks to you."

We did get them, right, Om?

Gathering the bodies and all of their gear as we speak, N. The teks are swarming over them and sending the scans and feeds back to HQ and Intel for full analysis. They're having a field day. Fireteam 4 is securing the area and going over everything with the teks. Intel's already got a rapid response ship on the way.

Om, I'm spent. While I'm lying here resting, let's at least teknomance the enemy gear and try to find a weakness we can exploit right now. There are too many invader sniper teams like this one at work, all around us on this continent, as we speak.

Your attacks damaged some of the suits and their functions, and they disrupted and appeared as soon as they un-phazed and dropped. We have their advanced phazed weapons, also. Let's take a look and see what we have, N.

Right with you, Om.

They poured and sifted through the data flows and the tek scans even as they were being made.

Oh, let our friends know that the rapid response fixers and I have already deactivated the deadfall fusion charges in each suit that would have melted them and the guns into useless slag.

Thanks, Om. You're a wonder.

Such flattery.

Hey, take a look at this, Om.

I see. We can use that. If we can interface it with the spyfixers, we can use those tek patterns to detect both the suits and the guns while they are in use.

Not only that, Om: we could also modify an electromagnetic pulse wave from orbit to do so over a wide area, paint and light them up on the combat grid, and maybe even focus it enough to disrupt them.

Let's send it up the chain through the Intel fixers. What are we waiting for? They can experiment with it from here.

One of the teks absently suggested something like that on the fly.

It was fairly easy to lead them along the same path of discovery, and pweak some of the data to get them on board.

The flows were already hitting HQ and Intel.

"Intel, this is MCL Maeris with Company 36. We need a full spread of EM pulse bursts over this targeted area. Alert Bravo Command that our pests should be popping up on the combat grid very shortly. Attention all Bravo anti-sniper teams–be advised–prepare to modify your gear and get ready to hunt down the hunters."

Naero sighed, still on her back, her Cosmic energies rapidly returning as she and Om focused all of their efforts on regenerating. She inhaled a foodbar and some lix to help matters along.

There are still some things that only flesh and blood can do–not machines, Om.

Machines still helped a great deal, N.

I know that; don't get touchy, Om.

Nelson was still exhausted from her efforts as well.

Once Naero was feeling better, she used biomancy to bolster Nelson back up. "Thanks, Veronica. We couldn't have solved the problem, or done any of this without you and your ideas, and your help. And you've shared and given me something extremely valuable–part of your own gift and talent, which I learned from you. Now, with your permission, let me give you something back in return."

"What are you going to do, sir?" Nelson drew back slightly and looked a bit worried.

"Relax. Most don't know this, but one of my Mystic abilities is that I can quicken or increase psyonic abilities in others. Would you like your talents to be stronger? I can make both your telepathy and your phazing much stronger, now that I've linked with you and I fully understand them. How about it?"

"Sure. What Spacer could say no to that? Then I can help my squad and the unit even more."

Naero linked with her again. "Very well. Just hold still."

It took Naero only a few minutes.

"There…now your telepathy will be much stronger and tax you less. The same with your phazing. I see how it works now. Both of us will now be able to both phaze, and move, and even shoot and attack. I want you on counter-sniper team ops from now on. Get out there with me and help us take the enemy down when they try this crap!"

Nelson rose to her feet. "Copy that, sir. I feel like a zillion creds. Let's hunt those bitches down."

They split off and rejoined 36, who were in the process of taking out first one, and then another enemy sniper team trying to escape the area.

Within the span of two hours, most of the enemy sniper teams had been located and gunned down.

And the cloaked insertion ship or ships most likely fled.
Unfortunately, none of them were ever located or shot down.

Then the defenders realized something chilling from the Intel scans of the sniper teams.

The primary enemy sniper was always an Ejjai male. A clone of the same exact male, shunted with the same elite training and ability. The other five members of the enemy sniper teams were always the same five females.

Like the shock troops, the enemy was mass-producing these sniper teams and turning them loose in droves.

By the next day, Bravo Command finally had the planet under control, and the invaders on the run.

Veronica Nelson was quickly promoted from corporal to sergeant and then to second leftenant, helping train the new anti-sniper program working with the Mystics, to locate, eliminate, and defeat enemy phaze snipers.

By the end of that week, they were able to stand down and rest after days of constant hunting and fighting. This was Sixthday, the old Friday, and that meant Binge Night.

Chime Fox and a few others read a bunch of new books that just came in. Marines gorged themselves on junk food and delicacies like gluttons. Some still got drunk or gambled the whole time. Others slept as much as they could. Couples took their leaves together and vanished for a day or two of romance. Entire groups jacked into vidgames and played them competitively 24/7. It was a time for relatively harmless excess. A time for everyone to loosen up, and do whatever they wanted.

Within certain Spacer limits, it was all fun.

7

Suvanna-6 was a winter world with most of the continents in the northern and southern hemispheres locked in glacial ice ages. Only a small temperate band existed around the equator that was even remotely inhabitable.

Yet because of active vulcanism and rich mining deposits, half of Suvanna-6's population of two billion were Miner Consortium miners, living in dome cities around their mining interests–a mix of several sentient races.

The original native population were Zotchans–near humans who were physically mute, without vocal cords. As a species, they had telekinetic, shining hair tendrils, similar to those of jellyfish in many ways.

The Ejjai invaders hated Zotchans, because without vocal chords, they couldn't be made to scream. Torturing them wasn't any fun for the invaders…almost.

At first, everything went well. Up close, the Marines had very little trouble taking out the Ejjai invaders.

Then Company 36 went missing in their dropship.

All of them.

Minutes later, Naero received a mysterious, telepathic signal from an unknown entity. It was not an Ejjai mind–but something unique, and very different.

Yet it was still working for the enemy.

Curiouser still, this being had Mystic-like powers. No. Correction. Cosmic psyonic powers. It could cloak itself from detection, even from her and Om both. And from what she could sense, it was extremely dangerous.

All of these things had Naero incredibly intrigued.

This entity challenged Naero to a formal duel. Just the two of them. Naero wasn't particularly interested into being lured into such an obvious trap. Their enemies had tried such tactics before–many times.

Then the entity revealed that she had Company 36. All of them, in their dropship, frozen in stasis. If Naero did not agree to the duel, the entity would be forced to hand her Marine brothers and sisters over to the Ejjai.

Naero followed the instructions to the letter. She piloted a starfighter to the south pole to meet the challenge. She asked the entity to release her friends. Naero had held up her end of the bargain.

The entity replied that she would do so, only if Naero won the duel and defeated her.

Of course, this duel was going to be to the death.

Om, I'm certain that this is all still a trap, planned just to take me down. We have to be ready for anything. 36 is merely the bait. I hate to think this, but they're probably already dead. Yet something does feel very different about this one. This entity appears to operate with some autonomy. She isn't the usual mindless, grunt slave of our unseen foes.

She doesn't know about me, N. I'll be ready to back you up, no matter what. And my fixers will be searching for 36 the entire time, and trying to find a way to secure and free them. I'm your wild blade.

Thanks, Om. I'm really going to need you on this one, I think.

As soon as Naero transported near the given coordinates, she felt as if she were being hunted.

She quickly located and eliminated the units of Ejjai in polar armor.

A fierce Antarctic storm whipped up, obscuring all visibility and taxing shields, armor, and even psyonics.

Naero had just started to wonder what was next when a familiar telepathic signal went out to her, trying to contact her.

If she linked with and answered it, the entity could pinpoint her location and possibly attack her.

Om, help me. I can't get a fix on it.

Sorry, N. I can't either. This opponent is both powerful and tricky. Be careful. There's still so much we don't know about this one.

They waited for the telepathic message to be repeated, or for another to go out.

Nothing.

If this strange new entity was, in fact, holding 36 hostage in stasis, that was a lot of mental and lifeforce energy to mask.

N, this entity is extremely powerful. She's even shielding them from us. That's a very bad sign.

I'm worried about that as well, Om. This entity rivals the High Mystics in raw, psyonic power. Although to my senses, she appears to be primarily a telepath. I've yet to sense any kind of direct Cosmic powers and abilities beyond telepathy. And the energy levels are so strange. Not raw Chaos, but Chaos mixed with several other types of energies that I cannot sort out.

Naero had yet to complete her Mystic training. There were still gaps in her knowledge that one could pilot a battleship through, and that could always be dangerous.

Something else, N.

What's that, Om?

We already know that this isn't an Ejjai mind signature. Whatever it is–it's a sentient from a race we've never encountered before.

I agree, Om. And the funny thing is, I keep sensing this deep regret. I might even call it resistance. We've never encountered any servant of the enemy that emanated regret. They're always fanatical. We're walking into the unknown. Our foes went to a great deal of trouble to bring this new threat against us. They must be pretty sure that it is stronger than us. They expect us to fall before its might. We can't afford to underestimate this one.

Finally, they drew close enough that Om detected the cloaked, heavy stasis fields through the enemy shielding.

They'd found 36 at last.

Naero transported in, struggling to mask her presence psyonically. Om and the fixers checked. 36 was alive and well, but helpless, at least for now. Luckily, the Marines and their entire dropship were entombed in a massive stasis field in an underground ice cave.

They did not appear to be under a direct guard, but there were security sensors on the ship, and massive explosive charges set to destroy the craft.

Om, you and the fixers neutralize those fusion charges and devices without alerting our hosts.

On it, N. You'll need to buy them some time. A distraction or diversion wouldn't hurt. This is a big job.

The right remote signal, or the wrong attempt to free the Marines, and this entire ice cave would go up in flames.

I've got the perfect distraction, Om.

What's that?

I'm going to knock on the front door. And spring their little trap. Keep those fixers working down here. Get our people out if you can, when the time comes. Don't let them use 36 against me.

Will do, N. I'll signal you when the task is done, as soon as I hear from our fixers.

Great, Om. Let's start this party. We want the enemy completely focused on me.

Surprisingly, the entity sent out another summons a few seconds later.

"Shetanna, the time has come for us to meet, and test our skills against on another. The moment of our duel is at hand. Answer me, or I regret to say that the lives of your companions are all forfeit."

Naero transported directly out of the underground ice cave, and half a klick in front of the large dome of the pop-up complex's main entrance. The storm outside had only increased in violence.

"Shetanna. I know that you are out there near the dome. I can sense your presence now. You are close. You're flitting about in that storm, trying to find a way in. I feel you resisting me. You're keeping me from locating your exact position. Very clever. Your friends are still here with me. The only way to free them, the only way to save them, is to face me in single combat.

"Where I will take your life, or you will take mine."

Naero continued stalling for time, for as long as she could. Either way, this couldn't get over with too quickly. She needed to draw it out to give Om and the fixers a chance to free 36.

"I know you can hear me on this channel, Shetanna. There's no other way to do this. Defeat me and take my life, and they go free. Or, I defeat you and they die. Or, you attempt to free them, and they die, and we still fight each other anyway."

Om, I'm kind of running out of time here. Have we stalled enough?

I think so. Go ahead, N. Start the show.

"Shetanna, I challenge you to face me!"

Naero zipped in right up to the front of the dome itself.

"Shetanna has come," Naero announced.

A nanoportal irised within the dome's entrance surface. She stepped in, and it closed behind her. She was alone within the shielded dome, a hundred meters in diameter.

A perfect, level platform for a duel awaited her inside. Within was sparsely decorated and supplied, only with a few furnishings and pods of equipment and gear here and there.

Her mysterious opponent rose up from a concealed nanolift and hatch, near the center of the dome's floor.

Of course she was taller than Naero.

Wasn't everyone?

"I am Riel."

"I am Shetanna."

They circled each other slowly like predators.

Species unknown. Riel looked female, by all appearances. Near-human, or at the very least humanoid. Riel was, in fact, a hand taller than Naero, although that wasn't difficult to manage. Sleek. Athletic, with superb muscle tone. Riel looked strong, agile, and fast.

Riel was a warrior, warrior-born, or from a warrior people, and she looked proud of that.

She had an odd skin coloration pattern, blazing white up to her neck, supple and shiny.

Yet only through the middle third of her body. The outer thirds of her form were sleek, shiny, and black, including her dexterous hands and feet. She wore thin boots and gloves of what appeared to be a black nano material, similar to Naero's own flight togs.

Riel's head was round on top, her face humanoid and shiny, jet black. She had large, attractive sapphire blue eyes, the hue of gleaming, light blue steel.

Small nose, expressive mouth with bluish lips and white, omnivore teeth, within the human range. If Riel had ears, they were small and recessed into the sides of her dark head, or perhaps concealed under her coat, or fur, or whatever it was that covered her body. It was some kind of protective layer.

Naero had spotted the thin nanogloves and boots right off. Now she noticed that Riel wore a tight pair of shorts, and some kind of sleeveless bodice top over a high, mid-sized bosom, under her coat.

The nanomaterial of her clothing barely covered her hips and shoulders, exposing most of her front torso, perhaps her back, and her arms and legs.

Riel touched some kind of preset on her waist on the shorts, and her garments, boots, and gloves included, began shifting and shimmering–

flashing with strange, almost hypnotic patterns of black and white, which became very distracting.

The thin, black leather belt at her hips was set with bright metal squares or some kind of control buttons. At a closer look, there were strips of material up the sides. The outfit was not so much a garment as it was a harness from the hips to the shoulders. Both hips held what appeared to be finely shaped sword hilts of intricate design, without blades or scabbards needed.

Are those energy weapons, Om?

There was something incredibly odd about those hilts and their energy signatures.

Naero, there are indeed strange Cosmic energy signatures around those sword hilts. And they are made of a rare substance–Ur-metal. The power levels of those weapons are being well-concealed, as long as they are not activated.

"I sense very well that we are warriors of honor," Riel said. "Know that I bear you no ill will, Shetanna. I offer you my hand, before our contest begins. Champion to Champion."

Naero took the hand, firm and strong; strength enough to match her own.

They pulled back.

With her biomancy, Naero had some fleeting insights into Riel's species.

"You have a layer of insulating skin…and something like…fur? It covers your entire body, including your hands and feet. Intriguing."

Riel smiled slightly. "Even my eyes are protected, by an insulating layer of clear film. Almost my own natural EV suit. All I really require is a sealed helmet and a source of breathable air."

"A shame I didn't get to finish my perception analysis of your genotype and species."

"So, you are a biomancer as well? You are indeed quite formidable, Shetanna. Very much so. Now I am curious. Can you phaze, or transport, or both?"

Naero grinned. "Does it matter right now? When the time comes, you shall know these things."

Riel smirked. "I suppose that is fair.

Something else. Riel wore a wide, golden nanotek collar, padded on the inside. A very hi-tek collar from what Naero and Om could detect. Almost constricting.

Om, suggestions? Is that some kind of throat protection, or is it really a control collar? Our enemies are forcing her to do all of this?

Both, as it would appear. The tek is highly advanced–on par even with the KDM. Without being able to study it, I cannot fully identify or determine its makeup or function. Yet it is also neutron detonation device, similar to the suicide device you wear upon your wrist.

So, Om, do we think someone among our unseen enemies is controlling Riel against her will? Are they making her fight for them? If she disobeys or tries to escape, I'm guessing they can blow her up?

With a yield that will take out half a kilometer in all directions.

Then they must want to be very sure that she is dead, if she steps out of line.

Control collar or no, she is obviously a hired blademaster, sent here from far away to slay the great Shetanna.

Shetanna spoke aloud. "Tell me, Riel. Where do you and your people hale from?"

"From the Gamma Quad–"

The golden collar around her neck suddenly flared and flashed.

Riel's eyes bulged and she winced, grinding her teeth suddenly together in pain. She hissed and clenched her teeth again and looked down for a moment.

"It…it doesn't matter where my people are from, Shetanna."

"I…suppose not. My people were descended from mammalian rodents and primates, and came to the stars after purposely, genetically altering their sub-species in order to thrive in space. Now they are a people of warriors and poets. Are you descended from polar sea mammals who gained sentience, Riel?"

Riel smiled, and felt her collar for a moment. "A close guess, Shetanna. Not mammals–avians."

"Birds? You're descended from birds?"

Riel nodded. "Yes. Flightless, polar sea birds, actually, who mostly took to land, at some point, becoming fishers and hunters, and then warriors, singers, and dreamers. First we sailed the seas in ships, and now the stars. Very similar to you and your kin."

"So, you are not covered in dense fur?"

"No. Dense feathers."

"Despite that, it seems that we have much in common, Riel. In another situation…we and our peoples could be friends. Perhaps even allies."

Riel shook her head sadly.

She winced again as her golden collar jolted her once more. "Yet not today, I fear. Today we must do battle, Shetanna. That is why we are

77

here together, and neither of us can avoid that now. One or both of us shall know death this day."

"It does not have to be this way, Riel. By all that I see, you seem very honorable. You are clearly being forced into this. To serve those who are controlling you. Why must we fight? I would much rather us be friends, and comrades."

Riel sighed heavily and rested both hands on the elaborate sword hilts at her sides. "I'm afraid that is impossible, Shetanna. I have no choice in this matter. My will is not my own. We have been brought together to duel. How then, shall we begin?"

Naero nodded. Om and the fixers still required more time.

"Very well, Riel. Let us square off in the center, salute one another–and test our prowess."

"Very acceptable. Proceed."

This was a formal contest.

To the death.

Naero summoned her bloodred Chaos katanas, sizzling and crackling. She saluted her opponent with great formality and respect and puled up her Mystic battle mask.

"By my family name, I am Mystic Adept Naero Amashin Maeris of Clan Maeris of the Forty-Nine Free Spacer Clans. Yet in combat and war, I am also known as Shetanna, the Dark Angel of Death. I have never known defeat in single combat with blades. Let us match swords."

Riel drew forth her two blades in one fluid motion, igniting them in her hands. The two long swords were a marvel.

One blade seemed to be fashioned out of black lightning. The other sword blade blazed blinding white.

Naero instantly recognized those Cosmic energies.

The Darkforce and the Lifespark.

Riel saluted her in return, striking a fighting pose. "I am Riel, daughter of Shuno and Glaithel, swordmaster of the star children–the Pelani. Wielder of the swords of Death and Life–Nohk and Laha. I salute you, Shetanna. Prepare to do battle!"

They clashed in a blur, all four swords crackling and crashing together. Sparks and Cosmic lightning erupted.

Naero wheeled, struck, cut, thrust, and kicked.

Riel flipped, twisted, and lashed out with several intricate combinations and techniques of her own.

They tested each other, time and time again.

Riel probed for a weakness, and found little that she could exploit.

She's extremely good, Om. I just might be in trouble, here.

Naero waited patiently for Riel to make a mistake.

There were none. Riel was flawless.

Both of them sprang further away, parting briefly.

They saluted each other once again.

"I commend your skill," Naero said. "You have had exceptional training."

Riel nodded. "I have never faced such a champion as yourself. Truly impressive. You are indeed a worthy opponent!"

Riel sounded excited, eager.

Naero felt the same way.

"Again, Riel?"

She nodded. "Again, Shetanna."

They clashed once more, lashing and striking and swinging and thrusting in a blinding fury. Their clashing weapons showered sparks and flared.

After similar results, they circled each other.

"Do not hold back," Riel told her. "I can take it."

"Don't worry. I'm not."

They clashed for another long exchange, and then broke one more.

"Might I suggest a way to accelerate this challenge?" Riel said.

"How?" Naero asked.

"Would you at all object to fighting in zero-G?"

Naero grinned like her characteristic self, raising one eyebrow. "I was born in null gravity."

Riel showed her teeth eagerly, a characteristic expression apparently for her. "As was I. Very well then."

The gravity in the dome ceased.

Naero activated her gravwing.

Riel switched on gravitic filaments laced throughout her battle harness, accented and guided by telekinetics, flight, and repulsion deflection.

The two combatants slipped through null gravity like sharks through water, slicing and jabbing at each other. Their weapons crashed. More sparks and lightning ripped through the air in several directions.

They parted.

Naero came to a grim conclusion.

Om put it into words. *N, you are almost evenly matched, but her reach is slightly greater than yours, and she is a bit more maneuverable.*

He was right. Riel had the barest advantage, but it would eventually win out. She flipped, twisted, and rounded as if part of her body were made of nanoflex rubber. She was…amazing.

N…that will eventually give her the decisive edge.

I know, Om.

No one said a word yet.

She knows it too, Om.

Then why is she hesitating? What are you going to do?

I—I don't think she really wants this. I'm going to try to end this, fast. Before she's forced to wear me down.

Naero launched herself at Riel in a blistering, all-out assault.

Riel wisely retreated, feinting, dodging, and withdrawing–her defenses perfectly timed and executed.

Then they switched suddenly, and Riel pressed Naero relentlessly in every direction. Naero tried to get away and break. Riel cut her off with a stunning reversal.

A thrust, and then a twist cut passed through Naero's flowing hair and arced toward her neck.

Completely unblockable.

Naero transported…in the last split instant before Riel severed her head from her shoulders.

Excellent, N.

No. Not excellent, Om. She's better than me in zero-G. I can't keep transporting. She'll just wear me down.

Naero, get in close with her. She doesn't know about me. I can take her out.

No, Om. Promise me you won't.

What? You can't be serious, N. You'd rather have me stand back and watch her kill you? Kill us?"

Yes. That's what I'm saying. It would be dishonorable to defeat her that way. I don't want you to help me. I forbid you to interfere! Wait…I just thought of something. Riel might have been trying to tell me something. Send me a message. Let me try something."

Riel circled in for another attack.

Naero focused all of her efforts on attacking Riel's forearms, wrists, hands, and fingers.

Riel read the attack and responded with the appropriate defensive techniques, and then she always went back to reaching for and striking at Naero's neck.

This left Riel's own neck and head open to attack.

Riel hesitated a fraction too long.

Naero got in a lightning-fast snapkick that rocked Riel's head back.

Riel whirled and head-spiked Naero full in the face. For a split second Naero saw stars.

They cut, sliced, and broke away. They charged back in at the same time, just as fast.

Naero distracted Riel again with kicks, taking a light cut on her left thigh. Her Spacer smartblood quickly sealed up the wound.

She blasted Nohk out of Riel's left hand with a sonic attack, and pierced her opponent's right hand with a few Chaos spikes, causing her to let go of Laha.

A Chaos blast right between them flung Riel away, slightly scorched, blistered, and staggered.

Riel's swords extinguished shortly after being released.

Naero scooped them up and attached them to the nanomaterial on her thighs. She flew over and brought the gravity back up slowly, and she and Riel floated slowly back down to the dome floor.

Riel stood up defiantly from crouching on her hands and knees. She clenched her fists, spread her stance, and lifted her head high. She swallowed slightly. 'It is done. I am prepared."

Naero spoke. "Hold. I've figured out a few things. Except for your swords, you don't actually have any of my Cosmic abilities…do you, Riel? Although I sense great power within you…yes. You have not learned either to awaken or use them–have you?"

Riel lowered her gaze slightly. "That does not matter now. You have won. My life is forfeit."

"It matters to me." Naero tossed Riel's sword hilts at her feet.

"It was wrong for me to use Cosmic attacks against you when you cannot yet respond in kind. This is a sword duel. From now on, we will just rely upon our blades, and our skill."

N…we won. Are you sure of this?

I'm sure, Om.

Riel grinned and blinked, looking more than a bit surprised. "You…you greatly honor me, Shetanna." She bent down to pick up her sword hilts.

As soon as Riel had them in her hands, Naero sliced both of her katanas at the back of the Pelani's exposed neck.

She cut off Riel's control collar.

Om transported the device out beyond the dome in that same exact instant.

The resulting detonation from the enemy control collar took out the area close by, rocking and damaging the structure.

Naero took down her defensive shield from around herself and Riel, after the blast wave and the thermal effects swept by.

Riel gasped suddenly, and felt around the burned and blistered ring encircling her neck where the control collar had repeatedly tormented her. She sobbed, and a look of disbelief washed over her face.

Then she knelt down and burst into tears.

"You got my clue. That I wanted you to find a way to remove my collar. I knew you would figure it out."

Naero nodded. "I did. You attacked my neck repeatedly and exposed yours. I used my abilities to transport your collar away from us just as I sliced it off of you. And by the way, you're welcome. You know, I trained for years to learn how to do something just like that."

"Shetanna, I–"

Naero put her hands on her hips.

"Haisha, Riel! Dammit all. Don't you dare tell me that you still wanna fight me to the death?"

"No…I–"

Naero breathed a sigh of relief. "Whew! Good. And please, call me Naero, or N."

"You can't possibly know what this means to me, N. There is so much to say, and no time to say it all. I am free now. The Pelani are not, and now they are in even greater danger. Forgive me, but I must depart immediately. My homeworlds are in peril. I…I must free my people in the Gamma Quadrant."

Naero thought her eyes were going to pop out. "So, you really are from the Gamma Quadrant?"

That put the Pelani on the far side of the galaxy.

"I must reach the enemy ships, Naero. They specifically captured me and brought me here…to eliminate you. But I must make it back, or they'll depart, and I'll be stranded with you here in the Alpha Quadrant. I must get back, but we're about to be attacked by an invader battle group, sent along to make sure we're both dead, if something like this should happen."

Om?

Riel is correct. A full Ejjai battle group is closing in on this position, at this very moment.

Om, I just assumed. I never asked. Did you get–"

Way ahead of you, N. Company 36 is not only free, they are fully awake and ready to fight. They've even set up a little surprise for that incoming battle group, with all of those captured fusion bombs.

You mean–

Exactly. They're going to put all of those explosives to good, practical use.

A massive chain link of explosions rocked the ice shelf, annihilating most of the Ejjai battle group, even as it closed in.

Naero and Riel jumped on the black, enemy stealth ship–a unique design that Naero had never seen before.

"Riel, what kind of vessel is that?"

"My ship, which they captured and took from me. A Pelani spy ship. Very advanced."

"Do you need any help subduing the Ejjai guards and crew?"

Riel snorted in disgust. "Not now that my will is my own. There are only a dozen or so of the scum left, and my collar is gone. They will pose no problem."

Bravo Marines came out of the ship suddenly.

Sergeant Python Wilde spoke up. "The Ejjai on board have already been neutralized, N. Per your request, we're leaving your new friend with a suit of the new and improved enemy phaze armor that we captured recently, as well as a small team of various fixers to assist her. This is a formidable vessel."

"Good work, Sergeant. Get our people clear. Our new friend has somewhere important that she needs to be."

"Yes, sir. Squad 3 and 3rd Platoon, with me. This way. Back to the dropship."

Riel, champion of the Pelani shook her head. "I came here a slave, sent to slay you and all of your comrades. And yet you assist and help me so freely?" She quickly undid her belt with all of the buttons on it and handed it over to Naero. "That is my computer belt. It contains most of the technical knowledge of my ship and my people. I gladly share it with you and yours. Consider us allies now."

Naero merely touched the Pelani computer belt and now it was her turn to gasp, as she and Om automatically teknomanced with its complex structure.

Naero. Haisha! Their tek is overtly Kexxian in nature.

She looked up at Riel. "You're people knew the Kexx?"

Riel smiled. "And the Drians as well, from ages past when our rise to sentience began. They were our guardians, as they were yours. They protected many of the younger sentient races and species. It seems that we are all their children, and now we war against the same fearful powers which threatened all things back then."

Naero threw her arms about her great an noble new friend.

Riel embraced Naero in return. "Thank you, Naero. My people and I thank you in high honor. I must go now, to do all that I can to free them from the oppression of our terrible foes. Good luck with your war here, N. I perceive now that we but fight the same evils in different places, you and I. If you or your people ever reach the Gamma Quadrant, we could use such allies as you. The battle which has been joined there is even greater than you could imagine."

"Wait just a few minutes, Riel. I know you must go, yet I have more gifts to bestow upon you."

Naero formed a mindlink, and then used biomancy to unlock Riel's own third eye and awaken her own latent Cosmic Powers.

It took a few minutes.

Riel gasped, staggered back, and stared wide-eyed for a moment. She blinked and had trouble catching her breath. She nearly transformed into an energy being right before Naero's eyes. The vertical right side of Riel's face turned white, while the left half remained black.

"What have you done?" Riel exclaimed, staring at her glowing hands in awe. "All that I can see now–the enlightenment. It is astonishing."

"I gave you nothing that you did not already possess. I have only awakened that which was already deep within you, Riel. Now you can begin to use those gifts, to help you and your people."

Naero had sensed the Cosmic potential lurking deep within the Pelani champion. Those powers were mighty indeed.

"Is this real?" the Pelani asked in disbelief. "All that I am feeling, experiencing, and awakening within me. How can I ever thank you, my sister?"

"Go. Save your people. As I intend to save mine. And if we should meet again, let us indeed do so as sisters–and the mightiest of allies."

Riel bowed and saluted Naero and her people. "All honor to you, brave Spacers. Thank you, once again."

"Safe journey, mighty swordmaster Riel, champion of the Pelani. Fight well against our foes."

"I shall. May we stand together once more, someday, my sister Naero of Clan Maeris. Though an entire galaxy of foes rises up between us."

A minute later, the sleek Pelani spyship lifted off, heading up into the Suvanna-6 atmosphere. It cloaked and vanished, as the southern lights blazed high in the sky.

8

Silvion-9 was yet another hot stop on an invaded, Zotchan homeworld. Bravo command and 36 were there to break yet another enemy back, and free another invaded world.

There were still many worlds to free that desperately called for help.

And that was just on the Alliance side of the border. Many either forgot or chose to forget that enemy invaders also raged virtually unopposed on the Gigacorps side of the border.

Many Spacers and Alliance people ignored that fact. But Naero knew for certain that such attitudes were both unwise and unjust. Many claimed that the Corps worlds deserved their punishment at the hands of the Ejjai, because it was their governments who at first helped or allowed the Ejjai Invasion to be unleashed in the first place. Even the Corps hadn't known that the invaders and their masters would betray them so thoroughly, and attack Corps worlds with just as much impunity and horror as they attacked Alliance worlds.

It became clear very quickly that the real enemies fully intended to vanquish all of humanity in the Alpha Quadrant, no matter who resisted and who did not. That no longer mattered. To the enemy, all humanity–Spacers, landers, and whomever else–were their foes.

And the road to enemy victory and eventual triumph over the humans was a sheer numbers game. The Ejjai had to conquer and defeat so many hundreds of worlds before they would become numerically and strategically unstoppable.

And that number was only in the hundreds.

After that, little else would matter.

If the enemy did not win those worlds on the Alliance side, they could still achieve victory by tallying enough defeated worlds on the disadvantaged Corps side.

Technically, the Corps by far had more worlds to defend. And that meant the invader tide could shift and spread over them. Continuing to refuse to help the Corps worlds, while the invader might still be contained and defeated, could yet turn out to be a huge and deadly mistake.

Each day that the invasion raged on, the enemy still grew stronger. And very little retribution would actually reach the governing heads of the Corps. It wasn't many of their families who were at direct risk of the invader meatships. At least not yet.

It remained that the innocent civilians and helpless Corps slaves on multiple worlds, those with no choice in the matter, who would in fact pay the highest prices for the stupidity of their careless Corps leaders.

They always did.

Even with that stark realization, there was little that Naero herself could do beyond what she was already doing each day. She and Bravo 36 system-hopped as quickly as they were able. And most people knew that they were rapidly exhausting themselves.

But what choice did they have?

This was also a campaign of endurance. Everyone knew that extended fatigue would cost more Marine lives.

Like all of the other rapid response units, Naero and Bravo were being stretched and spread thin. They grabbed rest and food wherever they could.

But once more, what choice did the Spacer Alliance have?

Every hour that they chose not to fight, the relentless Ejjai hordes slaughtered millions of innocents. Bravo knew the odds, knew the risks, and chose to fight on. As one of the premier rapid deployment forces in all the known galaxy, and from the top on down, they chose to fight. And they took the fight to the enemy time and time again and put the invaders dead upon their backs.

Silvion-9 had been a key agro world in its region with wide swaths of prairie, grasslands, savannahs, and steppes in different climes. The weather had been modified to support large scale crop and livestock production. It had originally been transformed into a rich livestock world by the Corps, before becoming part of the Alliance during the Annexation War. Now it was known as a key producer of both crops and livestock.

Continuing in those roles, it had a population of only six hundred million, but it also possessed a huge wealth in almost every form and kind of cattle and livestock ever known to be profitable.

The Ejjai invaders sent twice as many meatships there, in an attempt to process all of that livestock for their war needs. They simply included humans, near-humans, and other sentients in with the rest.

Therefore, the major drawback for the defenders was that wherever they went, wherever they fought, they could not escape huge herds of panic-stricken livestock, and the massive quantities of uncollected manure and waste products that such large masses of creatures could produce on a daily basis. It quickly became a health hazard.

Fertilizer was also a major export of Silvion-9's economy, after livestock and crops.

Shetanna and Bravo nicknamed Silvion-9 "Shitworld." They laughed at first, but the jokes only lasted for about an hour for new arrivals.

After that, fighting, getting wounded, and dying in shit all around stopped being so hilariously funny.

Spacer noses and senses were keen, and the Marines suffered from the exposure. Most troops saw it as a toxic environment and elected to remain buttoned up in their combat armor suits, as if they were actually fighting a biohazard war on that planet.

With the increased chances of disease and infection running rampant, that was partly true.

Not only that, but there had been several dangerous and even lethal methane explosions–just another hazardous bi-product that added another threat to combat on such a world.

Clouds of methane could build up or sweep over contested areas by nothing else but prevailing winds, then explode and ignite fires. Fixers began monitoring the methane clouds and their buildup and movement. If the level reached the danger point, the fixers would trigger alarms and emit warnings. Flame stations and burn-off towers were set up in an attempt to burn off these flammable gases before they reached explosive and life-threatening concentrations.

Naero came across a Marine one day, gagging and choking, his filters rapidly clogging and cutting off his treated air supply. Another serious risk.

She quickly teknomanced the suit system and cleared it.

Corporal Scott looked up at her and smiled, true thanks in his eyes.

Naero smiled and he offered her his firm hand. Naero took it, up to the elbow.

"Thanks, N," he nodded. "I was in a bad way there for a few seconds."

"Sure thing, Scott. Glad to help."

The corporal was less sour to her and others after that episode. Some better part in him seemed to kick in.

One day, Naero was still sleeping after a long night op. The next thing she knew, someone kicked her boots slightly where she had crashed.

That was warrior code for "Get your ass up, Marine. You've had enough shut-eye, Sleeping fucking beauty. Time for another op."

That went for MCLs, too. It wasn't always a wise thing to wake elite troops on the edge in a battle zone.

Had someone shaken or touched her anywhere else–say her head, shoulders, arms, or hands curled around a battle blade–Naero might have come up fast, ready to fight and even kill.

To frontline elite combat troops, a wake-up touch anywhere else but the boots or feet and ankles could mean that they were under attack. Jump up and be ready to fight.

As it was, Naero sat up, and had the nanocannisters in her sealed helmet gently mist and flush out her eyes. But even with her stealth suit sealed, she could still smell Shitworld, and groaned at its filtered reek.

She only imagined how bad it would be if she opened wide and sucked in a deep breath.

There was one tactical advantage: the reek also played holy hell and havoc with the keen Ejjai sense of smell. The invader would be hampered and messed up even worse by the smell.

Despite the fact that the Ejjai lived in crap and filth. They even ate crap, in a pinch. Rotting carrion was a delicacy to them–their favorite food–but they could still stomach offal and dung as part of their diet. Eating it didn't bother them. Smelling it all did. Go figure.

Naero had slept so hard, she still couldn't believe that it was night again.

The sitrep for that enchanted evening called for Bravo 36 to coordinate with a planned, mass assault on two complete invader battle groups. In doing so, they would attack and take out more than twenty enemy meatships, that had worked night and day to process both animals and people, all lumped in together.

Leftenant Anaconda Wilde went over their precautions and protocols for the op. "This is going to be another close-up fight, Marines. The Navy can't hit these sites from orbit because there are too many civies and local ground units still caught up in all the fun. Yeah, I know. Expect a real mess.

"Make sure of your targets. Don't pop any locals in the black, and more importantly–don't let them pop you. The rest of the sitrep's pretty clear and self-explanatory, for those of you goons who can read. Mark and coordinate the objective protocols and timing calcs in your battlecomps. Load up, check your gear, and take your positions on the line, Bravo. People, don't forget to flush your filters out to avoid clogs at the worst time. Do it now."

Command directed them flawlessly and wove them into position with the other units in the combined ops that night.

Enemy positions, targets, and objectives lit up on their displays and scrolled with each turn of their heads, in order of priority. Their primary targets were selected and locked.

Leftenant Wilde cut in again. "Go hot, 36. I say again: go hot, my dark children. Mark. Fifteen seconds. Begin the assault and fire on Command signal. Follow your directive targeting feeds and scans thereafter as the op flexes and shifts. Good hunting, 36!"

Overlapping waves of direct fire erupted out of nowhere.

Half of the enemy targets across the line for many kilometers in either direction, along several tiers, withered and collapsed, obliterated by the stunning Spacer Marine combined arms assault.

Naero was already several minutes ahead of her profiling schedule, using her Mystic-trained speed to enhance and quicken her attacks. She finished taking the head off the last Ejjai gravtank commander on her array profile–all of her primary targets down as she flashed among them, swords blazing.

The ghost warriors of 36 came right in behind her like an invisible tide of death. They neutralized an entire forward enemy armored regiment in seconds.

Then Naero's sense of warning went wild, even as she and 36 shot up into the air, cloaked and on gravwings. The enemy gravtanks cooked off below them without warning.

Their new targets came up all around them.

The armored regiment had only served as the bait to lure them in.

Om called out to her, adjusting the fixer arrays to give her and the Marines advance warning. *Naero, look out. Several hundred enemy stealth troops, converging all along this portion of our front lines. It's a counterattack with heavy weapons and explosives. Converting scans to these patterns and frequencies. They're almost on top of us.*

Om, light this up for 36 and Command. "36! Hit the enemy counter-assault forming above us. Flip up and proceed to these positions above and around them and commence attack!"

36 broke, reformed, and struck the enemy as the Ejjai dropped grenades and bombs on where the Marines had just been.

Bravo endured heavy direct fire and regrouped their assault patterns in response, targeting arrays shrieking and scrambling to adjust.

But the Marines shot out of harm's way just in time, and spread out the counterattack in order to thin it out and overextend it. Then Bravo pounced again on the new arrivals.

36 unleashed everything they had on the enemy attackers, despite being outnumbered at that juncture seven-to-one or more.

At least their efforts stalled and confused the exposed enemy numbers and positions, painting and lighting them up on the combat grid.

Then 36 swept away on another vector, on direct orders from Command, with the enemy in hot pursuit.

Swaths of Marine starfighters swung down so fast that they passed by in a blink. Yet they took out most of the enemy stealth troops with coordinated air bursts.

Something they could not have done with Bravo in the way.

Direct fire hunted down and eliminated the rest of the enemy for the time being, and the front line of battle crept forward.

"Good work, sir," Anaconda said to Naero. "Those late arrivals from the slashers could have really crashed our party and messed us up."

"Thanks, Ana. Hey, I thought I told you to drop that 'sir' stuff when the brass aren't around."

Ana laughed as they were directed forward to their next target. "Sorry, N. Old habits. Left, on our left, 36! 3rd Platoon, watch our right. 4th Platoon, protect our six."

"Enemy units advancing to plug up some of the holes we've made. Targets coming online. That's a lot of them. Stock up and fire!"

Four to five hours later, all twenty invader meatships were accounted for and on fire. Local troops marched in to clean up.

Back at their base on their armored and shielded dropship, Naero sat relaxing with her mates in the protected rear, taking another breather and preparing to grab some more rest.

They had done good–real good–as the Anaconda informed them. Only four wounded and no KIA–thus far, at least.

By that time, half of their number were already asleep, wherever they happened to crash. Many slept in their gear. Why bother taking it off?

Naero felt a bit drowsy herself.

She leaned back, mumbling, going on about Jett and how good it tasted.

Whip Konrad of Squad 1 laughed at her. "Why do like that stuff so much, N?" He only did his crazy thing right before a drop. Other than that, he seemed normal.

"Well, Jett is just so tasty," Naero said. "Sorta wish I could have some today of all days."

"What's so special about today?" Suki Lii asked.

Naero sighed. "Guys, today's my birthday. You'd think a gal could get a sip of her fave lix on her birthday. It's not like it's booze. I meant to look into it, but there just hasn't been much time. I'm out. Jonny's out. Even Marshall is out, and that slank charges four or five times the going rate!"

Sergeant Vaughn sneered. "What? On Shitworld? What the hell are you thinking, girl? Not much chance of that, Brighteyes. Plenty of dead livestock around, though. How about a nice putrid steak? You like blue meat?"

"Only Spum. The only edible blue meat."

"We could try to find a carcass that wasn't completely rancid yet," Trevor Lakota said.

"No, thanks, guys. I appreciate the thought, but with this stench, I probably couldn't choke it down. Hey, there's Abraham and Aztec, back from HQ. Over here, guys!"

Naero started to doze off even more.

Someone placed something cold up near her head. She could see it frosting her face shield and registering on her reads.

Even through her helmet, she made out the familiar and beloved shape of an icy fourpak of Jett, right next to her helmet.

Naero sat up and put a hand on it. So nice and cold, even through her gloves.

Then she noticed that 2nd Platoon was up and standing all around her.

She unsealed her mask.

Surprisingly, the air inside the jump ship wasn't that bad at all. Then she cracked open a borbble, and smelled something even more heavenly.

Steaks did in fact get handed back from the mess hall.

A fat, juicy steak came Naero's way, a bit salty, but juicy and good as she tore into its steamy texture with her hands and teeth.

"We sent a special request all the way up the chain to General Walker himself," Anaconda said. "When it came in, Luca Abraham and

Kesha Aztec had to go to HQ and fetch it all back when the time was right. Our mess hall started cooking the steaks immediately. And we got this place filtered out and scented, so that we could relax a bit and chow in it. In your honor, N."

Naero's cheeks were so bloated on both sides that she could hardly talk. "I'm speechless, guys. I might even cry a bit."

"And hey, N," Acer Adams said. "Good news. In honor of your birthday, my calendar's free, and I can pleasure you all night tonight. I've got thirty millimeters of hot, hard joy with your name on it, and you can ride me and scream all night."

"Haisha, Acer," Naero said. "What the hell, man? Did both of your goddam hands go numb at the same time? Again?"

Everyone in 36 roared with laugher.

"Seriously, my friend," she went on. "You ought to get that situation checked out on the double. Might be a nasty, repetitive stress injury or crippling nerve damage, in your case."

She yanked a borbble free and then was stricken. It felt too light.

One of her precious borbbles of Jett…was already empty.

"Aztec, Abraham…what the hell is this? What's the deal?"

Naero pointed to one of the borbbles in panic–completely empty with the cap still sealed.

She held it up and turned it around.

A neat and clean blaster hole had been shot right through it.

Aztec shrugged. "Sorry, N. It must have taken a hit through my pak, when we were on our way back during the end of the assault. I thought something was wet and sticky down my rig."

Abraham laughed. "Buck up, Brighteyes. At least three of 'em made it through the lines."

Naero looked at the empty and sniffed. "Now I know I'm going to cry."

That night Naero sat up with Chime Fox and a few others–Bessa Jackson, Pete Cooper, and Deb Steiner–listening to Chime's story about her and Jonny's family. How everyone but their great granny Fari had been killed off by the wars.

"That's where Jonny and I got our love of books," Chime said. "You know, we were left alone a lot. As the oldest, I more or less raised Jonny and myself through books, and the people we met inside them. We'd play this game where we could close our eyes and pretend to go right into the different worlds of all of those stories. It was fun while we could make it last, but we always came back to being just two orphan Spacer runts, bopping around in a beat-up old merchant ship run by a half-crazed old lady."

Chime sighed.

"Sounds terrible…and fun," Naero said.

Chime laughed sadly. "It was all that. Yet we missed everyone. We were still old enough to miss all of those people in our family who had loved us."

Naero sighed. "Some don't even get that much, Chime."

Chime was getting sleepy. Her friends all looked at their resident booknut and smiled at her. "I know," she said. "I'm grateful, and so is Jonny."

Naero took a slug of poteen, with her Jett all gone. "So, I know Jonny wants a little merchant ship after the war, for himself and your greatgran. What do you want, Chime?"

Chime fluttered her pretty brown eyes and smacked her pink lips. She gestured weakly with her hands. "What I'd really like is to fill a merchant ship full of books and go peddle them all over the Alpha Quadrant and beyond, wherever it takes me. Maybe I could even shanghai some authors and whisk them away on some book tours. That would be so awesome."

"That sounds pretty nice," Bessa said.

"I agree," Pete added. He was always tapping away on his pad in the background doing something, maybe playing a vidgame.

Naero nodded. "Give it a shot, Chime. But what about romance?"

Chime rolled her eyes. She was very cute, even if she was a bit of a kook.

"I don't know, N. I surely do want some handsome guy to love my socks off, but I'm a lot to put up with, you know? And he'd have to deal with all of my books, and my mania. How am I going to find a guy like that?"

Naero shrugged. "All you can do is try, I guess."

Chime shrugged and started to drift off. "I guess so."

In another minute, Chime Fox was breathing peacefully.

She didn't look so crazy now. In fact, for a young devil dog Marine, she looked sweet and innocent for once. Like a pretty little orphan girl one might find asleep in an alley, in a sad story or some fairy tale.

After everyone else filtered off, Naero carried her friend back to the bunks and tucked Chime in. She caught Trevor Lakota glancing up at her where he still sat up awake, carefully sharpening the keen edges on his knives. He smiled and nodded to Naero.

9

Guta-8 was fully engaged by the invaders when Bravo deployed. Once more, the population of eighteen billion was locked in combat with the ruthless Ejjai, in a life-and-death struggle across the surface of the entire world.

Guta-8 was mostly a Pietto world of tiny mining people. Piettos were a sentient, humanoid, spacefaring race who were only thirty to sixty millimeters tall. They were small, but incredibly fierce for their size, especially when their homeworld was threatened.

They swarmed on the invaders, fighting them to a standstill. And that was saying something. It said a great deal about the courage and tenacity of the diminutive Piettos.

They were the masters of small microweapons, needlers, and microbombs. Their weapons were small, scaled to their size, but they still packed a sizeable, lethal punch.

For every Ejjai who landed on Guta-8, a thousand Piettos came against them to defend their world.

The enemy was forced to retreat under such an onslaught, and finally sent large tank formations, meks, and mass stunner ships to knock out large sections of the frontlines and the gigacities. They dropped the locals in droves and multitudes.

Even such valor as that of the little people could not hold out forever against superior tech and ruthlessness.

The Ejjai gathered them up in baskets and collection haulers while they were still alive and helpless, and dumped them into the meatships. The invaders heated pits of fat and oil with flame guns and incendiary grenades, and callously feasted on deep fried locals.

It was a grim thing indeed for the drop troops come down and see so many of those small skeletons, strewn haphazardly behind the enemy in their wake. Just like chicken bones.

The only way to stop the Ejjai was to exterminate them to the last. General Walker and Bravo Command developed a new strategy to crush the invaders as fast as possible.

A lightning-wave assault should weaken and confuse the invaders and get their attention. Then an even larger assault upon their rear areas should rake them viciously, and reduce their numbers and technology. That would leave the remaining slashers open and exposed to the vengeance of the local forces to flood over the enemy before they could even catch their breath. The Piettos yearned to be able to finish the job, liberate their world, and have their vengeance.

Every MCL present went in hot with their units, under orders to use all of their powers and abilities–to exhaust themselves, if need be–in order for the twin attacks to succeed. It was a one-two punch designed to knock out the enemy hard and fast, with the least loss of life for the defenders.

Naero fought at point with 36.

Every Marine pulled out all of the stops, loaded up heavy, and went in hard, hot, and fast. They carried double loads and even dispersal drop pods that could be jettisoned when empty.

Marine stealth craft filled the air and began the show, taking out key invader positions.

Next, Marine starfighters and fighter bombers blotted out the sky and dominated the air. Then lines of cloaked Bravo Marines on gravwings, heavy with smartbombs and drop pods of seeker ordnance, went in next.

The combat grid lit up with countless prioritized targets of opportunity, organized on their profiles. Those targets were wiped off the combat grid just as cleanly as they were wiped off the field and the face of Guta-8.

In seconds, the gigacity capital of Allonorah was lit up like daylight itself, ablaze with war and the fiery fury of the Spacer Marines.

Naero screamed at top speed, leading 36 into the teeth of the fray.

Her sense of warning suddenly spiked.

Up ahead, several Marine starfighters dropped from the sky. She raised a priority alarm. Something was happening.

Om, what is it? What's the enemy doing?

An ion pulse EM wave. The biggest I've ever seen. They must have triggered it under the capital!

Naero shouted over her links across all channels, "Incoming EM pulse. Uncloak and max your shields to these flux patterns as the pulse wave hits. They'll go down, but your suits and weapons won't be burned out and lose power. Do it now! Mark, in three seconds!"

The EM knockout wave hit, exactly three seconds later.

36 and many other units maxed their shields and avoided the EM pulse burnout. They lost their shields, but the fixers that survived could eventually bring more shield pods back up or online.

They still had a job to do. Shields or no shields.

The Marines pursued their objectives, dispersing their smartbombs on their objectives at hand.

Behind them, Ejjai positions and targeting blips vanished off the combat grid in large sections, and the gigacity lit up once more.

Few invaders could survive a firestorm such as that.

On to their next objectives, as their shields slowly came back online.

Multiple enemy autogun emplacements cut lose from the city high points and buildings at several level.

First Leftenant Yaeden Adams led them against those sheets of death and caught a burst dead on. The autoguns blasted her and her armor to pieces.

Just like that, she was gone.

Shetanna dodged in, cutting down several of the guns and their crews, scything them in half as she went.

Fixers went in, and at Om's direction, reduced many of the heavy gun emplacements to useless scrap.

Time. Time was essential. The wrath of the Marine assault did not let up. Ejjai lay eradicated behind them in concentric rings, exposing the enemy defensive patterns.

The enemy responded by marshaling all of their forces, unleashing every bit of firepower they had, and rushing their reserves to the front as it continued to collapse in toward them.

The Marines were rolling up their lines faster than the enemy could bring up fresh forces to support them.

By the time the main assault completed neutralizing their objectives, they had pounded more than half of the gigacity, and all of their ordnance was depleted.

Bravo drew their primary weapons, swept in lower, and drove the assault forward at close range. Another bright line of firefights punched into the enemy-held parts of the capital, continuing to press and reduced vast numbers of the invaders each second.

In a one-on-one, up-front fight, the slashers were simply no match for the Spacer Marines. And the enemy lived in abject fear of the Marine MCLs and shit themselves when the Spacer Mystics appeared, because that meant death in all manner of creative ways.

Naero spotted fresh lines of Ejjai, scrambling to set up more autoguns in an attempt to hold back the tide.

Shetanna whirled and wheeled into them, extending her katanas, sweeping and banking through them, hewing them in half as she passed among them. She unleashed clouds of pea-sized unstable Chaos energy. Microexplosions blasted Ejjai reinforcements in a wide swath.

Bravo charged in, guns blazing, overlapping their firing profiles and catching the enemy before they could reset their lines and their weapons.

The enemy defenses suddenly buckled and collapsed almost entirely in that area.

36 and other available units of Marines poured through that breach to exploit it, bringing devastation and death with them on a wide scale for the invader.

In a last-ditch effort to survive, a fleet of enemy destroyers rose up over the gigacity from the enemy's rear areas furthest behind them, configured in ground assault mode. They began strafing everything in sight, whether friend and foe.

A direct link cut in from HQ, from Major Luna herself. "Naero, General Walker is ordering you and every MCL present to hit those destroyers with everything you've got. They will decimate our people on the ground, and you Mystics are the only ones who can take out entire warships like that in short order. Destroy as many as you can!"

"We'll do our best, sir. But that's fifty warships and only about a score of us. Get the Navy in on this. Break half of our forward wave off and have them board those warships and disable them. If our people are going to go down, at least let them go down against those ships that are going to kill them anyway."

"Copy that. We're on it, Maeris. Now just follow orders, before those strafing ships wipe out everyone. Do what you can to slow them down!"

"On my way to engage as ordered, sir. Over and out."

Silence.

Then a moment later, General Walker himself cut in over all the available links. "All forward elements–divert from original plan and board the enemy ground attack ships and divert them away from the city at all costs. Put fire on them. Take them down, Bravo!"

Hundreds of Marines soared up, swarming at each destroyer as the strafing ships came on.

Naero was already getting tired, reaching the limits of her Cosmic and Mystic energies and abilities.

Om, help me any way you can; we have to push it.

Conserve your energies and use them sparingly, N. Think and fight smart. Make it count. I'll give you everything we can muster up.

Thanks, Om.

She remembered something insane Danner had done when they fought.

Naero swept over the lead destroyer and attacked the aft section of the ship with a shearing plane of Chaos energy.

She neatly sliced off the warship's engines.

The lead destroyer crashed straight down and exploded over the enemy held sections of the city.

Next, she scythed her way into the destroyer on the immediate right, and severed the power core.

That ship nosed down and cooked off.

She raced over to the next on the left, transported right into the bridge itself, and cut down the command staff. Marines rushed in to take control of the vessel, and continue the fight with the enemy on board.

Naero knew how to command a ship. She quickly took charge of the vessel and overrode the security with teknomancing.

She lifted the ship a bit higher, and swept back over the left flank formation, pounding the line of destroyers with her batteries as she passed over them.

Marines cheered.

MCLs on the right flank helped capture a ship and did the same on the right.

Major Luna cut in once more. "MCLs, there are still too many enemy warships. Focus on capturing the bridge of each vessel. Then turn control of the ships over to the Marines, and move on quickly to the next."

Despite their best efforts, several destroyers scattered out of the original formation and began their ground attacks. They annihilated everything beneath them.

"Dammit, Bravo," Luna commanded. "Take down those ships!"

Naero dragged herself toward one, already close to blacking out.

One destroyer suddenly exploded. Naero got caught by part of the blast and hurtled through the air.

She heard Om speaking. *Gravwing damaged. Can't reactivate. Fixer net racing up to catch us. Must keep us from impacting.*

Whether she liked it or not, she was at her limits and beyond. This battle was effectively over for Shetanna. She had done all that she could do, and there just wasn't anymore juice.

She was more or less a spectator as 36 and the other Marine units rallied around.

Her own Marines caught her and carried her, handing her off, shielding and protecting her with their very lives.

No foe got anywhere near her without getting gutted and shredded to death.

Naero never lost consciousness. She smiled and allowed her people to protect and care for her. She listened to the flow of battle over her links.

Bravo and the MCLs took down the rest of those destroyers, as command launched their next attack from the enemy's rear.

The local forces of the Piettos got their wish for vengeance, later that night. By morning, the battle for the capital gigacity and the planet was all but over.

In the aftermath of the battle, battered and exhausted but triumphant, 36 went back to their dropship for a breather.

It was another Fifthday, and that meant Chat Night again.

Gabe Patton bragged about how much fun he and his gal Devin Scott, a Marine from another Bravo Company, had on their last few days together. Penelope Valmont showed some vids of herself and her husband, Calvin Cooper, and their two-year-old son Louis on her last visit with them. When Penny cried, several people cried with her.

Sergeant Omar Steiner had managed to be present for the birth of his first child with his wife Vessara Evans. They named the squashed, beautiful little girl Madelyn. Omar planned on calling her Maddy, and she was already daddy's little girl. He watched those vids over and over, celebrating with his mates.

Chime gave Naero a heads up that her younger cousin, Jonny Fox, was feeling blue. Naero went to cheer her friend up with some Jett and some delicious, marshmallow cookies she had been saving.

She found Jonny against a wall by himself, pretending to read a book so that no one would bother him.

Until Naero noticed that he wasn't turning any pages.

"Heads up," she said, and tossed a borbble of Jett his way. He caught it with one hand. They had both managed to restock.

He smiled up at Naero, but it was a forced smile.

They sat and finished their drinks. Naero handed him another.

"So, what's got Jonny Fox so blue?" Naero asked.

He let out a long breath. "I've just realized today that I'm in the wrong line of work, N."

She stared at him. "How can that be, Jonny? You're one of the best Marines I know."

"Yeah, but that's just the thing, N. I've suddenly realized that I don't like to kill things that much. Seeing all of these little people dead–these Piettos. I don't know why. It just got to me this time."

"Jonny, dead civies are always tough. For all of us. But we didn't do that. The enemy did."

"I know, I know. But I'm just tired of it, that's all. Tired of seeing all of this death. Tired of killing things. I'm sick of it. Sick of all of it. Sometimes I just want to stop." He paused and almost sobbed, "I don't want to have to kill anything more."

Naero put a hand on his arm.

Tears started running down Jonny's face, and Naero wept with him.

He suddenly gasped out loud. "Then I look at all of those dead civies lying around, and something just snaps and I go all cold inside." He paused and then went on. "I just want to kill Ejjai until there aren't anymore of them to kill. And sometimes, I'm afraid, N…I'm so afraid of…of…"

"What are you afraid of, Jonny?"

He looked her right in the eyes and swallowed hard. "That I won't come back. That I'll just go all cold and hard inside and never be able to get back to being just me again. That's why I'm sick of killing things. I don't want to kill anymore. I don't like it."

Naero touched his face. "Oh, Jonny."

He shook his head and threw up his hands. "But I'm a Marine, dammit. And I'm good at killing–a trained expert. None better. And the sooner we stop the Ejjai, the sooner I can stop dreaming about all of those dead civies staring up at me. The ones we couldn't save. And there's just more and more of them, on every new world we hit."

Naero rested both hands on her friend–her brother. "Just stay with me, Jonny. We'll make it stop. We're going to put an end to this nightmare."

He nodded again. "All right. I will. I'll do it. But after this, I'm done, I tell you. I'm done killing. I don't want to kill anything, ever again."

"Sure, Jonny. All of us will be free again. You can go some place where you won't have to do anything you don't want to, with your greatgran and Chime. You'll have your little merchant ship you always talk about and you can all be happy."

Naero and Jonny Fox chatted together all the rest of that night.

10

Palmyra-3 was different.

First off, it wasn't an earthlike world. Next, it was the system that contained an advanced Joshua Tech research facility with only about forty-four thousand sentients working there.

And finally, Shetanna and Bravo got there first–before the invaders could strike.

This was indeed something new and strange.

They raced in with only two fleets deployed, uncertain as to when the invaders would drop in to pay them a visit. They couldn't just extract the staff. That would leave behind far too much sensitive data and equipment, some of which had to be removed as well.

The defenders were in the process of accomplishing those vital tasks when six invader fleets hit Palymyra-7 only hours later. While the naval forces duked it out up in the black, Bravo held their positions against everything the invader battle groups could hurl at them them on the ground, pummeling the defenders without let-up.

Naero observed the unfolding war on the combat grid display screens at HQ, with XO Viho Cheyenne. So far, there wasn't much in general for an MCL to do, held in reserve to defend the evac if need be.

"Static defenses are nothing but delaying tactics; standard Spacer Marine strategic and tactical doctrine, Viho."

The XO smiled. "This one only has to hold for another hour or two, N."

Naero sighed. "And by then, our other fleets will pull up and wipe the black with these guys."

"Exactly. By the book. Watch it all unfold on the grid screens."

Something still bothered Naero.

Then her sense of warning went nuts.

Om broke in. *N, Chaos sword attack. Phaze, cut, and thrust right behind the XO. Do it now!*

She did so without hesitation or question. Instinctively, she phazed and activated her Chaos katanas. She slipped around Viho to protect his back, executing a Spacer sword strike combination.

Something she sliced through disrupted and exploded.

"Intruders!" Naero shouted as the alarm went out.

Bloody pieces of an Ejjai assassin in ruined phaze armor sparked and clattered onto the floor behind Cheyenne.

Naero hit her presets and morphed into full Shetanna-mode, shielding herself and the XO.

Viho busied himself checking HQ and the facility, taking security steps.

Shetanna cloaked as Marines spread out in security patterns and called up reinforcements. She phazed herself and opened her third eye.

Let's go hunting, Om. How many infiltrators do we sense? I'm locking onto their minds. Help me track and expose them. Have our fixers mark them, even if they are still phazed.

Naero gasped slightly.

One hundred and twenty Ejjai, N.

That many? Haisha! What are the hell are they doing, Om?

Most are busy setting multiple fusion and neutron charges throughout this complex–including the escape ships currently docked in the starport. They aren't bent on attacking yet. It appears that their primary mission is sabotage. They'll continue setting charges.

Have our fixers neutralize–

Trying. Already ahead of you, N. Fixers in progress as we speak. There are a few enemy techs attempting to hack our systems, seize equipment. Some few are wandering about, like this one was that you took out. They are snooping to see who and what they can come across. Even with the alarm, with their phaze suits, they still think they're safe.

Silent orders went out. Intel brought out anti-phaze guns and started popping isolated Ejjai in order to test them.

The new vesper guns function, but take time to recharge. And the anti-phaze shimmer particles dispersed in the air will work, but they will also take time. They show where the phazed troops aren't by outlining their negative astral frequency echoes with an aura. Five more intruders down, thus far.

It's a start, Om. Let's go take down a few ourselves. I can spot them by their minds when I'm phazed as well. She closed in on the infiltrators closest to her.

Shetanna didn't fool around. She pierced an assassin's head with spikes of Chaos energy and then exploded them.

After she cleared her section, she double-checked with Viho again. "XO, XO, launch all ships from this starport, ready or not. Fixers are neutralizing demo charges and mines all over the complex, but the intruders have been busy for a while; they have this entire complex rigged to blow. Get those transports out of here. The rest of us can fly out under our own power if need be. This place could still go up any second."

"Affirmative, sir. Clearing starport. Emergency evac."

They had stripped about eighty percent of what Intel wanted. That would need to be good enough. They could blow the rest.

Naero checked the combat grid again.

Just as she thought. Not good. The invaders stepped up their game, throwing in another enemy heavy battle group for good measure.

The Ejjai were all in. All of their efforts and main attacks focused on taking the defensive shields of the complex down and overrunning it.

"Shield control. Maximize your security and prepare for an all-out attack. Take all Intel precautions again phazed infiltrators. Maintain all defensive screens at maximum deflection, no matter what."

Then Naero noticed it as soon as Om did.

N, shield control is the only sector that the enemy phaze troops haven't penetrated. They didn't even try to go there.

That's crazy, Om. Why wouldn't they go there first? That's what we would do. We'd better check it out.

That worries me, N. Perhaps they know something that we do not.

Shetanna phazed again and scanned the area around shield command with telepathy, her third eye wide open.

It doesn't seem logical, N. We are greatly distracted and fully engaged on all fronts. This would be the best moment to hit shield control.

Copy that. You're right, Om. Okay–got them. A full platoon of phaze troops, heavily armed and rigged for suicide bombs, approaching our positions on these vectors. I'm going straight at them. Send our fixers in to neutralize those bombs. Alert the XO!

Sending reinforcements.

Transporting now. No time, Om.

Shetanna attacked the sortie directly while starships continued to panic-launch from the starport.

One of the ships suffered an explosion and barely limped into orbit.

Shetanna used swords and Cosmic attacks to take the infiltrators down quickly. But even with her powers, she could only engage several targets each second, and the sortie scattered in a dispersal attack pattern.

She had taken out more that half of them when several large fusion and neutron blasts rocked the shielding generators.

Defensive shields around the complex collapsed, and heavy enemy indirect and direct fire immediately slammed into it.

Shetanna hunted down the remaining phaze troops, while she still could.

Marine dropships came down under fire, attacking the enemy battle groups swarming forward from the rear areas. They attempted to take some of the heat off of the beleaguered facility, but the bulk of the enemy forces stayed on task.

Naero knew they were in a bad way, despite all of her efforts to prevent exactly what was happening.

Marine armor and meks stood their ground, fighting back against the onslaught and pouring fire into the advancing enemy lines. The two sides duked it out up close.

With the starships up and out, at least the Marine transports could come down in near-crash drops and try to extract Bravo.

These dropship pilots were the best in the business. The best combat insertion and extraction pilots in the galaxy. Only they were brave enough or crazy enough to endure that level of fire to come in, gather up who and what they could that remained, and then launch back out the way they came to escape.

The last transport came racing down into the fire to do the same thing.

This was it. The last ride out. Anyone left behind after that would be force to fight their way past the enemy in order to escape.

Two other dropships had taken heavy fire and peeled off.

The last shielded dropship literally crashed through the advancing hordes. Above, Navy and Marine starfighter pilots slipped down to lend their support, trying to hold the enemy off.

Finally, in a boldass maneuver, the battleships *The Okinawa*, *The Guam*, and *The Midway* dropped straight in on near-crash dive vectors. The three gargantuan warships interposed themselves and their heavy shields in a triangle around the facility, and crushed many of the attackers flat.

Then they aimed their massive batteries at the enemy lines and pounded them to dust at point blank range, kicking up huge craters in the surrounding area. But they endured heavy concentrated enemy fire.

That gutsy move gave the last bunch of Marines and civies a chance to regroup, and take out their remaining attackers or get on the last dropship.

Naero kept stalking the last of the enemy phaze troops to make sure they didn't do any further harm or slip onto the dropship. All the while, the main battle still raged.

The final orders to all personnel came down. Withdraw or be left behind with the dead and the dying.

The three battleships had done all that they could, and were taking too much damage even now. They had to launch back up into orbit and effect repairs in the fixer clouds.

Time to go.

Naero rejoined 36 and dragged a final group of teks onboard *The Okinawa*, the closest ride at hand.

The rear defense Marines fell back in good order, and also loaded up, still under fire.

Squad 4 from 36 was one of the last units to come in, racing toward the lift ramps, flying on gravwings, bounding and firing as they retreated, still covering each other.

From out of nowhere, several modified enemy gravtanks phazed into the complex and began firing on the battleships.

One of the tanks cut off Fireteam 3 of Squad 4 and rammed into them, as the battleships pulled away.

They have tanks that can phaze as well?

Naero shot out of the relative safety of the loading bay and back out into the mix. She couldn't leave her Marines behind. She deflected fire off her shields, raced at one of the gravtanks, swords blazing.

In a feat of sheer Cosmic might and fury, Shetanna hewed the gravtank in half, flung the exploding pieces to either side, came to the side of her dazed and stricken mates.

Kowalski, Cherokee, Fox, and Kothari were down, wounded or stunned.

Naero picked them up and tossed them bodily into the open cargo hatch, battered armor and all. Jonny Fox was the last. She slung him over her shoulder and shot toward the closing hatch.

Hands stretched out to her. Marines from other hatches returned withering fire at the foes on the ground and dropped explosives.

When the hatch closed before she reached it, Naero transported herself and Fox inside, spilling onto the floor, exhausted.

Bravo and the Alliance had held on to the facility, and gotten most of the people, and much of the base's secrets out safely, under great duress.

Naero learned later, after she recovered, that the Spacer fleets had quickly arrived after the evacuation, and blasted the remaining enemy forces on the ground directly to hell.

Chime came to Naero and thanked her personally for saving her cousin Jonny.

That night happened to be Seventhday, and that meant Sparring Night. Marines squared off in matches, both with practice blades and hand-to-hand.

Naero begged off the latter. With her Mystic training, most of the several Marines she trained with were clearly not a match for her one-on-one, and by now her mates understood that. She still enjoyed blade contests–if she held back. There were always a few exceptions. She had had several very interesting matches with Trevor Lakota and a few others.

Then something really freaked her out. After the sparring matches all ended, the Marines began clearing the floor and turned off the gravity.

Strobes, lasers, and holographic light shows started up.

What the hell was all of this?

"What's going on?" Naero nervously asked Trisha Marshall, who by that time was drunk and hanging all over Acer. He never seemed to mind stuff like that.

"Seventhday just isn't for sparring, N. Oh, no. It's also Dance Night!"

Naero's jaw almost shot through the floor to the next level. She was deathly afraid of something exactly like this, and had avoided it all thus far. "Dance Night?"

She had to get away.

Several of her mates suddenly blocked her every path of escape.

107

"Yeah, come on, N. Wait until you see these skills at work," Bessa boasted.

Chime slapped her hands to the beat and began swinging her narrow hips. "Haven't you heard? 36 Marines are some of the best dancers out there!"

"But all you people know are Marines, you nutjobs," Naero protested. "And besides–I don't dance!"

Marshall laughed. "Then how can we be wrong, Brighteyes? Come on, Acer. Let's stomp on the ceiling! Cut loose, N. Dance with us. Let's throck out and have a gigablast!"

"Oh, fuck!" Naero groaned, pulled and pushed into the mix by her laughing friends, entirely against her will.

Naero Amashin Maeris was a lot of things…but a dancer just wasn't one of them.

Haisha! But after a while, damn it if Trish and the other gungirls weren't dead on. It was kind of exciting and fun just to let go and be wild.

As the music and the lights continued to spike and flare, 36 continued to erupt into complex dance moves. The Marines were shaking it down everywhere, in groups, in couples, showing off on their own. These amazing athletes wowed her with their moves, and they were everywhere, on the ceiling, the walls. Some of them were spinning and floating up in midair.

Naero had seen discos, jackpits, and spinspheres on gigacity playworlds that weren't this hot with action.

She tried to jump in and have fun as best she could, but she clearly wasn't anywhere good enough or drunk enough to try to compete.

That in itself was humbling.

When the Marines put the moves down, they nearly tore the goddam place apart. Major Luna herself finally had to intervene, and threatened them all with stungas, just to restore order.

11

Kariinga-12 wasn't a planet, but a water moon world with ninety-eight percent hydrographics. Almost no land to speak of.

Yet leave it to the industrious little Piettos to construct a network of underwater cities and rich mining facilities for its population of 1.7 billion. Underwater mining and robotic fishing ventures were well established and booming there–until the invaders showed up.

Below the roiling, stormy surface of that moon, a terrible, ruthless war was being waged.

The invaders converted a great deal of their war tech to underwater warfare. They systematically raided and destroyed undersea cities and robot fishing fleets to bloat their meatships of all sizes. What was more, the fighting taking place underwater made the enemy much more difficult to track down.

Bravo arrived on scene, prepared for underwater combat.

Submersible ops were a lot like zero-G ops in many ways, complicated by additional environment issues involving pressure, undersea concussion effects, and various weapon and movement modifications and considerations.

Some energy weapons still functioned quite well under water, with some slight adjustments. Fixers also worked very well.

Shetanna couldn't use her Chaos swords; that was a pain. But many of her other Chaos powers and Mystic abilities still functioned perfectly fine.

Exploding needle guns fit the bill nicely, in most instances, for primary Marine weapons. Rockets, microbombs, and float-seeker smartmines became incredibly useful.

Cloaking actually worked even better under water. Bravo was able to sneak up on the enemy units and take them out as they were blasting away at another civilian sea city shielded dome.

Shetanna and the Marines learned that gravwings could be modified to work very well in the deep.

The battles on Kariinga-12 became a running contest of undersea hide and strike.

This was how it usually went.

One side would expose a unit, sometimes even on the surface, baiting the trap. This was called drawing fire.

Then the other side would take the bait and attack. Combatants would pile on as the skirmish or all-out war escalated from there.

There was one problem for both sides. Starships and submersible craft could mask themselves and hide very easily in the oceans. Marines and Intel had trouble locating and destroying the enemy fleets underwater.

Naero and Om were still in the process of knocking their teknomancing heads together in an attempt to lick that obstacle. While Bravo could take out attacking units when they struck, the enemy fleets remained relatively safe—free to produce more clone troops.

And that was exactly what they were doing. Giving the rapacious Ejjai access to rich, plentiful, underwater food stocks was not a good idea. Abundant mineral resources also gave them resources for the enemy production factory ships to produce more war materials.

In short order, the Ejjai would soon be churning out clone fleets and forces faster than the defenders could destroy them. And they could launch them to help overwhelm Kariinga-12, and then to help harass and subjugate other neighboring systems, perhaps for years to come.

Then, on the hunt one day, Naero spotted two dozen enemy squid ship raiders—scuttling along, looking for trouble.

Squid ships were the equivalent of underwater tanks or assault ships and troop carriers of various types and sizes. The smallest and most basic held a crew of four, and eight troops.

"Let the small fries pass through," Shetanna ordered her cloaked Marines over their secured link. "We want the bigger fish today, guys. These are just scouts. Paint them on the combat grid and let our people pop them later."

Corporal Murphy Daniels, Fireteam 2 leader from Squad 4, added. "Hey Brighteyes, I'm sensing some psyonic static with my telepathy again." Most Spacers had a psyonic talent by the time they were twenty. Murphy's was telepathy.

Naero focused her own Mystic abilities and opened her third eye. Many telepaths and MCLs had encountered this phenomenon before, but no one could make any sense of it.

Any ideas, Om?

N, you know as much as I do on this. All analysis reveals some kind of psyonic shadow or feedback echo. It appears out of nowhere, and then just fades or vanishes. There's no source or anything to trace it back to.

And yet the phenomenon was being repeated on a regular basis, and noticed by anyone sensitive to telepathy. It had to mean something, and she worried that it was some kind of new threat.

Om, plot all known occurrences on the combat grid history.

Naero, that's already been done. No direct connection has been found between any enemy attack patterns or projected troop movements.

Humor me here, Om. Project and scan for any directional flow patterns of this phenomena. Compare them to that of the enemy attack patterns and the flow of battle that has occurred in the last half hour. Hey, look at this. A full analysis has just been released by Intel. Include all of that data.

Wait. Tabulating new data. I think there is something here, N. Counter-intuitive algorithmic patterning suggests that the occurrences of the phenomena has them flowing away from all major attacks, directly before those engagements by the enemy. They move away from the attack patterns, against the logic. Everyone assumed that to be significant, that they would need to flow toward the attack locations.

Good work, Om. Now, what does it mean? Can we use any of this to predict their next waves of attacks, or predict attack patterns and targeting?

No, N–not yet, unfortunately. The parameters and indicators don't work that way exactly. But we can use the data we have, combined with this new analysis, to guess where they won't attack next. And from there, we can begin to make better guesses as to where they might attack. We need more info, and we still can't be sure when they would launch such attacks and from what directions.

Well, a better idea of where they might attack is better than what we had, Om. Instead of just responding to their attacks, and allowing them to pick the time and place, we can be more ready. Next time, when they do strike, we just might be waiting for them. Transmit our initial findings to HQ and Intel and ask them to apply and test them—on my order codes.

Will do, N. Transmitting now.

Hours later, they predicted a high probability of three new major enemy attacks on three unrelated, removed locations.

The telepathic ghost echoes were also reported in those vicinities, within the acceptable parameters of the prediction models they were testing.

Om, if only we could locate all of those submerged fleets. There has to be a connection between these phenomena and the enemy.

After a few minutes, Om came back to her. *N, I think there might be a way to located those enemy fleets.*

How, Om?

Well, as usual, the attempt to do so would prove risky—to both of us. It might very well sap all of our strength within about an hour or so. There's even a chance that it could kill us.

Screw that. What's the chance of death, Om?

About twelve percent.

Hmm…but we could locate the enemy ships, even if they're cloaked or concealed under the ocean depths?

I'm eighty-seven percent certain of that, N.

I think we have to risk it, Om. I'm not worried about us. We're tough.

Well, as usual, I'm the sane one. I am worried about us.

Since when did you get to be the sane one?

Like, forever?

Nero chuckled. Om, if we can pinpoint those enemy fleets, our people could destroy them and end the conflict on this system in no time. That means we can be done here and move on to the next world that needs us, saving more lives faster. We can't get bogged down here on one planet.

Moon.

Haisha, whatever. The point is, we can't get stuck here, trying to out-weasel the enemy. Let's jump on this and make it happen.

They informed Intel and brought Squad 4 with them. They took over a scanning ship orbiting the water moon.

Working with the fixer clouds attached to Naero, they modified the sensor and scanning arrays.

Naero and Om teknomanced with the modified craft and tek, becoming one with it all.

Naero became the conduit–the heart and brain of an enormous psyonic scanner, passing over the watery moon, searching for any active or passive mind signatures.

It would take them one standard hour to complete a full sweep of both hemispheres.

And it was not fun. All the while, Naero felt as if her Cosmic energies were being sucked out of her by hordes of vampires. And the feedback waves of cosmic and psyonic pain and pressure ripped through her with fresh agony at random.

No one guessed that the interface would be that painful or dangerous, except for Om. They were proceeding into uncharted territory with untested new tek.

Damnation, Om. You didn't say that becoming part of this sensor array was going to hurt this bad.

Sorry, N. I'm feeling it, too. Right with you. I did say that there was a slight chance of death. The various energy flows passing through a biomechanical form, even one as powerful as ours, does make some physical discomfort extremely probable. There, does that make you feel any better, now that I've quantified it?

Hell no, Om. Some physical discomfort? Some? Haisha! I feel like someone's ripping my teeth through my body and out my feet!

Naero clenched her teeth, breathing hard.

Naero, reach out with your expanded senses. You are one of the most powerful telepathic scanners ever devised. Ignore the fact that you could burn out any second. Concentrate. Focus. What do you see below us in the oceans?

She controlled her breathing and calmed herself, ignoring the pain as best she could, closing her eyes, but opening her third eye and her mind, boosted by the amplified intensity of the array she was jacked in to, adding to and magnifying her awareness.

At first, all of the sensations and data were simply too overwhelming. Then she and Om worked together to order and make sense of them all.

Naero saw the entire moon on the telepathic wavelength–in the realm of pure psyonic energy.

Even as the effort slowly drained her and tore at her mind and body.

I see them, Om. I see everyone. I see all and everything. Are you getting this? Are you recording the data?

Brilliant, N. Recorders on. Loading data to the combat grids as we speak. You've done it, N. The sheer scope of it is staggering.

You've scanned an entire system psyonically.

Om, I'm fading. I can feel it. I'll need to unplug soon. The hour's almost up. I can't take much more. I'll try to hold on a bit longer. Make sure that you pinpoint the locations of the enemy fleets and relay them to our orbital navy and coordinate targeting profiles with battery fire command. That is imperative.

Transmitting enemy locations as they come to us. Hold on, N. Processing raw data and psyonic telemetry as fast as I am able. Only a few minutes longer to complete the full scan. Hang on.

Om. I don't think I can. I'm losing it. The array, the energies. They're tearing me apart!

She steeled herself and called upon her finite reserves.

Just a few minutes more could save the lives of billions.

Naero saw the enemy fleets as clumps of cloaked minds in their ships and units. She could easily differentiate them from the other mental signatures of sea life, Spacer Marines, and the locals.

She could spot and locate every enemy vessel, craft, and individual trooper. That was how powerful the new array was.

The heavens lit up with fire.

Massive combined orbital batteries locked on and opened up on the water moon. Naero watched as those enemy mental signatures winked out and were snuffed out.

There were many more foes in system than they had assumed.

The sweep continued, and more invaders were eliminated each second. Fire from the sky continued to rain down.

The enemy probably didn't even know what hit them or how the Alliance had located them.

Naero's torment intensified, and her energies ebbed.

A massive feedback wave disrupted the sensitive scanning array. It began to melt down and tear itself apart, with Naero still jacked in to it. She was still part of the array as it destroyed itself.

She screamed, too damaged and fried to disengage from her teknomancy links to the vessel and all of its tek.

Veronica led the attempt by Squad 4 to cut and blast her free from those links and all of the hardware.

The scanning ship was about to go critical.

The order was given to abandon ship.

Squad 4 ignored those orders and at last tore and blasted Naero free. Then they stuffed her into a rescue ball and sealed their armors.

Four Marines blasted their way out of the hull with shaped boarding charges.

They fled into the black on their gravwings, heading away from the burning ship as it first imploded, and then exploded.

All hands managed to get away to a safe distance, and awaited retrieval from the rescue teams and vehicles swarming their way.

Veronica mindlinked with Naero shortly thereafter, when they had their MCL on a medbed. They shared some of the last remnants of the psyonic pain that was still pulsing through Naero's mind.

Veronica did her best to syphon away that pain and take it upon herself. Together, they kept Naero's mind from collapsing and being destroyed.

Did...did we get them all?" Naero asked her.

Veronica checked. "You sure did. Great job, N!"

The orbital batteries did their work, completing the task.

Even as Naero and Om recovered, Bravo's water weasels began mopping up whatever was left of the enemy.

The very next day was Thirdday and Food Night once again.

To celebrate their victory on the waterworld, Naero purchased a bunch of top-notch food supplies and took over the mess hall.

She made enough fresh, seafood and crab bisque to feed all of Company 36, and then some.

Her mates gobbled it up and came back for seconds.

Acer Adams broke down and proposed. And it wasn't a joke. He seemed pretty serious about it.

The guy completely lost it and went for broke, gesturing wilding with his hands. And he wasn't even drunk, that much.

He even had tears in his eyes. "Naero, I really love you, babe. I just can't take it any more. I dream about you all the time. You kick ass like a warrior goddess. I can't take my eyes off the way you are shaped, and that cute little butt of yours just knocks me out. It's usually your face I see in my sex dreams–more of than not. I...I have never felt this way about anyone.

"And on top of all of that...you can fucking cook like this?"

Everyone within earshot simply stared in stunned silence.

Naero rose, stood before Acer, and then leaned down to whisper into his ear.

"Acer, you enormous ass howitzer. You stop humiliating the fuck out of both us right now, or so help me, I will rip your genitals off with my bare hands, cram them down your throat, and choke the living shit out of you with them until you turn every color in the rainbow and die. Nod your head if we have an understanding."

Acer didn't say another word. He nodded slowly, swallowed hard once, and then quickly made his way back toward the mess hall, presumably for more bisque.

12

On Pixie-6, Bravo Command got their wish. Bravo loved to fight in the black. The black was their home, their element. They were raised in it, nursed on it, and fought in darkness like no force in the galaxy. And they defended their domain with a devotion and a ferocity that had made them legendary.

No one. No elite fighting force in galactic history owned the night and fought under its dark mantle with more finesse and tenacity than the Marines of Bravo command. Bar none, they were the finest night fighting force that had ever been known to exist.

And they took any challenge to their dominion very seriously.

Nowhere was that fact made more evident that during the fierce battles that raged across the planet called Pixie-6.

That planet had a very radical trajectory to its axis that made the declination to the sun very odd at times during its year. As a result, almost half of the world plunged into a winter of almost sheer darkness for months at a time.

Without moons and a cloudy atmosphere, it was a world that suffered the Ejjai invasion in a complete blackout of cold terror.

And the situation would not change, alter, or let up for many days to come.

The locals were, again, mostly the Piettos of those sectors, barely thirty to sixty millimeters high. Fierce in their own ways, but still terribly outmatched and outgunned by the militaristic hordes of the Ejjai invader. One quarter of the local population of twelve billion had already been slaughtered during the invasion, before Bravo Command arrived on scene and hit the enemy with all of the blazing fury that the Spacer Marines had come to be known for.

Yet the invader had had time to entrench themselves right in the middle of numerous, key population centers on the planet's surface. The enemy meatships were being stuffed to capacity each day. And the cloneships were already churning out fresh enemy units of cloned shocktroops, tens of thousands at a time.

With each day that passed, the war of numbers still appeared to be tipping in favor of the invaders.

Projections showed Pixie-6 as possibly becoming the first invaded world where the enemy could not be directly defeated by force of arms. At current rates, they would eventually tip the scales, and overwhelm all of the defenders.

Then there would be no choice but to eradicate all remaining life on the planet in order to take out the enemy. Of course, by that time, the local population would be dead, so razing the world by atomics and mass bombing to exterminate the invaders would be the only choice, before they could continue to spread their disease further to other systems nearby.

That was a very grim plan of last resort, and always ended in the planet being uninhabitable.

Bravo took on the challenge for what it was, and brought in all of their reserves and allies.

The invaders had already been pushed out of the area where the sun still shone.

Bravo and 36 raced into the black, knowing full well what was waiting for them. They rode headlong into battle with honor, and with unparalleled ferocity, to face down the invader at their strongest, in a stand-up, all-out war in the black.

Bravo went in to blast the enemy to perdition. And they did so at one hundred to one odds, a hundred thousand Bravo Command Marines against ten million Ejjai.

The Spacer Navy sped one hundred fleets–five thousand warships, to back them up on this one key engagement.

It was very possible for the tide to turn in the enemy's favor.

The invader might use its numbers to hold out against the best that the Spacers had to offer.

Shetanna helped lead the coordinated assaults against the meatships and cloneships. They had to be put out of business fast, or the Alliance would never overtake the enemy's expanding numbers. Destroying those factory ships became an absolute priority.

Invader clone production had to be stopped for any of their goals and plans to succeed.

Every MCL available worked closely with their attached units to see those ops through.

Shetanna and 36 haunted the invaders like destroying ghosts and phantoms until the enemy lived in terror of them. They hunted the meatships and cloneships down with a vengeance with cloaked ordnance, mines, and fusion neutron charges that were nearly impossible to detect until they detonated.

And then it was too late. That was the idea.

Cloaked fixers could ferry in tons of ordnance to the advancing Marine raiders, who also went in loaded down with gear and weapons to accomplish their tasks.

It took ten hours to prepare one of the largest initial assaults on meatships and cloneships, key communications centers, and command and control. All of these were targeted across a wide expanse of the dark battlefield by most of the Marine units who were not already engaged.

At the twelfth hour of the watch, over one third of the enemy's existing cloneships and meatships exploded and were reduced to dust and burning wreckage.

That was the signal for the main assault to begin.

Up in the low clouds, the naval fleets targeted and kept up a steady bombardment of the invader within an expanding ring of fire and death.

Nothing that was of the invader escaped that ring alive.

Bravo appeared in great numbers wherever the enemy least expected them–even at the enemy's very center–at the heart of its power and vast numbers.

They took the foe by the throat and shot them full of big glowing holes until the startled invaders stopped twitching.

The enemy had fully expected massive attacks around their dug-in perimeter, but not deep within what they had thought to be their most secure core.

Bravo proved to the invaders that the Marines could attack at will, wherever and whenever they chose, with impunity. Marine raiding parties, led by their amazing MCLs, continued to methodically attack and destroy the meatships and cloneships on the hour, striking wherever those vile craft could be located. And the hunt continued.

In the open battlefields, Marines continued to march forward in rapidly advancing formations of heavily armed troops in powered armor, meks, gravtanks, and Marine ground support gunships, starfighters, and fighter bombers.

Even large units could suddenly smash through the enemy, appearing as if by sorcery, unleashing precise interlocking and overlapping waves of combined arms, direct and indirect fire upon the stunned enemy positions.

Most Ejjai were dead before they even had a chance to react, so sudden did the Marines unleash sheer hell upon the foe.

Right after many attacks began, the cowardly Ejjai were often cut down as they fled, abandoning their positions, even when fighting back might have still given them a chance at victory.

The invader never wanted a fair fight. They wanted to butcher helpless civilians. They didn't have the stomach for a stand-up fight in many instances.

That was their worst flaw of all, as the Marines saw it.

The invaders had no honor whatsoever. They were completely devoid of it. The concept did not even seem to exist among them.

They might fight out of spite or hatred, but that was it. They fought only to destroy. They couldn't fight for each other. They didn't give a damn about the clone invader next to them.

They flung their own wounded into the spinning processing blades of the meatships and laughed at them while they did so.

Naero had seen Ejjai wound the troops next to them to slow them down, so that they could get away for a few seconds longer. There was base, self-preservation instinct, and nothing more.

How could any force, however numerous, hope to achieve victory, when they meant nothing, to themselves or even to each other? When they fought and killed and died for no worthwhile reason?

The invaders were a plague unleashed on humanity. Huge swaths of them were being systematically eradicated on numerous worlds at every passing minute. And the Alliance, led by the Spacer Marines, was the cure. The Marines often saw themselves as if they were antibodies defending humanity as a whole, eradicating the invaders as if they were germs or viruses of a deadly illness or infection.

In the battles in the black, when the foe did return fire, they more or less pinpointed their positions on the combat grid and helped Bravo plan their next coordinated attack. The enemy fired in panic, knowing that they were about to die. They poured direct and indirect fire in all directions, hoping beyond hope to eventually hit something. At times they got lucky and did.

Often they hit their own troops, damaging each other in their terror. Some enemy units could wipe each other out, each thinking that they were firing at the Marines.

In some battles, very quickly, the disorder and chaos among the undisciplined invaders was nearly complete. The Marines timed their assault wavers and coordinated them precisely. They organized the combat grid and modified it on the fly, directing and guiding its unrelenting flow.

New units swept in, conducted the ops, and then swept forward or back out to regroup and hit another vital target nearby. Some units needed to rest and resupply themselves before their next turn on the line.

The Bravo Marines sustained these withering attacks on the invader in ways that were precise and relentless.

Shetanna and 36 pulled back to their rally points and turned aside briefly to watch several more enemy meatships and cloneships detonate behind them. They had been moving constantly, setting charges, and attacking for many hours straight in the combat zone.

The order came down finally. All of the them could withdraw to make room for fresh teams to go forward, and take a well-deserved breather.

Naero marveled that they did not see any of the locals in the rearward areas. Intel and the Alliance had done their work very well this time, and these sectors were clear and secure.

In many areas, the brave Piettos had offered to fight if they could only be armed.

If there were any locals in the area left to fight. Many times there weren't. General Walker considered the Piettos to be a very valiant people, despite their small size. He always considered and granted their brave requests when and where possible.

Naero soon learned that this time, the Alliance had decided that it would be best for the locals to simply take shelter in rearward areas, so as to stay out of the way.

That allowed the determined Marines to go in, confident that there were no locals in the way. They could take the fight directly to the enemy and do what the Marines did best.

As General Walker put it, in his more or less exact words, Bravo Command was there "to blast the living shit out of the Ejjai invaders, and rip the screaming heads off of these assholes who so richly deserved and required to have such done to them, with all speed and dispatch."

Shetanna and 36 continued to make their way back, leaving nothing but burning death and terror in her wake.

At one point, they spotted three companies of Marines on a crested hill and vale, engaging at least two thousand Ejjai troops and armor sweeping up the slope.

As one, the heads of almost every Marine snapped to Shetanna, and awaited her orders.

She knew what they wanted.

Orders be damned. They were here. They wanted to go help those other Marines who were already fully engaged and fighting so courageously.

They could see the weaknesses that they could exploit in the enemy formations from where they stood.

Shetanna sent several holos of herself on fixers into the enemy formations to confuse them and draw their fire.

Shetanna ordered an attack of opportunity and sent their supporting action up the chain to show up on the grid.

By then, 36 was helping those Marines turn the tables on their attackers.

The Dark Angel of Death tore through the enemy center, bloodred swords arcing and slicing in flashes and gouts of scarlet fire and lightning. She unleashed a full spread of Cosmic attacks, gutting the leaders of the attack and hollowing out their heavy weapons formations.

After she passed through, more reinforcements arrived, and the specters of Bravo trained hundreds of E-88 mini-guns on the enemy and ripped them to bloody shreds.

After the smoke cleared, there was nothing left of the enemy counterattack but burning chunks and lots of Ejjai corpses.

Bravo cloaked and proceed on to their next objective.

36 kept on heading back to rest.

Naero passed by a sizzling, burning frozen meatblock, blasted all the way here from the explosion of one of the meatships they had taken down earlier. She and her Marines stared at it in fascination and horror, even though they had seen them countless times.

Anyone could still make out the twisted, chopped-up pieces of little local Pietto bodies, packed together and making up that sick cube. Like little dolls and skeletons, pressed and frozen together in fear.

This was the enemy. And what the Marines felt for the invaders was beyond even what could be called hate.

There was no word for it.

This was what the enemy was, what they did, and what they wanted to do to humanity, and with all life that they encountered.

This was why the invaders had to die, as quickly and as soon as such could be achieved. Nothing would be able to return to any sense of normalcy until that reality was made true.

There could be no Ejjai. The entire race had to be eradicated as if it had never existed.

The shock and disgust at just watching that one meatblock sizzle and burn brought it all home to them. Why they were fighting, and what it was they were fighting for.

The end of shit like this.

What they were fighting against.

Shetanna snarled and lifted one hand, reducing the vile cube to ash with Cosmic fire.

Yet the stench of it was still in the air like a cloud, like the stink of death and misery of all the hundreds of invaded worlds. And that putrid cloud clung to them and stained them all.

On Pixie-6, it took the Marines eight long days of nonstop fighting to completely exterminate and slaughter the massive hordes of the Ejjai that were hurled against them.

Shettana personally selected eight invader generals and admirals who had been captured, gagged them, and bound them in chains and shackles. Once General Walker approved her request, these enemy officers were sent on a small ship to the next world Bravo was heading for.

They carried a message to all of the invaders. To let them know what had happened in the black on Pixie-6.

To let the enemy know what to expect, very shortly.

Bravo Command, Shetanna, and the Alliance were coming for them, head on and ready to take them down.

And there was no power in the universe that could prevent that, or save the invader's worthless existence, from the wrath and the sure vengeance of the Spacer Marines.

13

The Gort-6 system had a population of barely fifteen million. But it was a botworld, where all sorts of bots were developed and tried out before being shipped out for sale to various markets.

Unfortunately, that also included drone attack/defense systems and other warbots.

Even though the invaders attacked Gort-6 with only four fleets, they had been onworld for almost two months–during which time they had killed off more than a third of the local, mostly Naivatch, population, hunted the others wherever they hid, and also seized control of most of the 2.3 billion bots on the planet.

Only twenty percent of those bots were originally built for war, but the others could also be programmed to fight and kill, or at the very least get in the way as they attempted to cause harm. The sheer number of them made for a bizarre and extremely dangerous and unpredictable situation.

The Ejjai invader could sit back and laugh, waiting behind a sea of bots shielding them, and snipe at the Marines at will. While the Marines were forced to fight and slog their way through billions of pissed-off bots, reprogrammed to combat anything living that came near that wasn't Ejjai.

If the Marines couldn't get at the invaders, they couldn't take them out. What was worse, the enemy made certain that all of the bots they unleashed on the planet were randomly AI-adapted to various kill and attack modes.

The bots all operated independently. Therefore, there was no off switch, abort, or kill switch on the bot hordes. No central command or any way to shut the bots down in large numbers. Unlike in countless stupid vids, all fail-safes and safety protocols were off. There was no convenient self-destruct or deactivation code for the robot armies.

Available EMP attacks would take out the military equipment of the defenders as well as the bots. The Alliance was stuck. These bots would continue to attack and try to kill the defenders, even after all of the invaders were destroyed.

Granted, only the actual military drones and warbots constituted a real tactical threat. At first the Marines and the Navy focused on dealing with them as priority targets. But it quickly became apparent that the vast numbers of the other normal bots were a huge obstacle as well.

Shetanna and her strike teams from 36 focused on locating batches of the actual invaders directing and controlling the bot hordes. They either took out the invaders, or painted them on the main combat grid for other primary forces to take down.

At first the Marines found it rather comical to enter a gigacity area and have service bots, waiter and waitress bots, cookbots, janitorial and sanitation bots, and store clerkbots come at them with low level firearms or even knives and clubs.

The Alliance sent in clouds of fixers to deactivate or dismantle the bots into inert components and scrap.

In one illicit area, hundreds of sexbots flooded out of buildings to charge the defender lines with automatic weapons and grenades. They had to be dealt with swiftly and cut down.

Then there were suicide bots that simply tried to get close enough to the defenders and detonate the explosives rigged up inside of them.

After the first casualties, all of the jokes and the laughter ceased, as soon as the Marines and the civies suffered wounded and KIAs.

More waves of modified fixers were brought down from the Navy and sacrificed in order to take out hundreds of thousands of bot bombers, some of which had gravitics and could fly. The silent ones were the most deadly.

Leave it to Om to finally come up with a viable solution. Due to flaws in the invader programming, the bots did not attack Ejjai...or other bots. Therefore, a specially modified fixer went with each Marine and projected a masking, camouflage signal that made the Marines appear to be either Ejjai or other bots.

Such protection improved the situation dramatically.

The invader countered by remotely detonating suicide bots and many explosive charges set all over the city.

In the end, the sheer number of bots continued to be a hindrance and complicated the combat situation.

Yet they were a definite distraction, an obstacle. The battle for Gort-6 could not be won until the enemy invaders were hunted down and killed.

Naero and the hunter-killer teams proceeded to do just that, and kept it up as the actual number of invaders onworld deteriorated.

They managed to break into one of the bot construction factories where the female Ejjai shocktroops and their smaller, male tech counterparts were scurrying around, reprogramming and planting explosives inside a few thousand more suicide bots.

Grenades, explosive needles, demolition charges, and rockets brought the entire operation crashing down on the enemy's heads. The resulting multiple explosions sealed the deal.

Reports from long-range recon scouts stated that a large group of invaders was passing through some service and sewage tunnels, trying to reach a hidden pocket of enemy ships. The Ejjai were preparing to flee.

The Navy already positioned itself up in the black to intercept and take out any of the cowards who attempted to get away.

Meanwhile, Shetanna went down to drive a good portion of the slashers into a waiting deathtrap that 36 had prepared for them.

A small, cloaked squad maintained several unit shield barriers in front of either her or a projected holo of Shetanna.

All Naero had to do was appear menacing and advance on the foe. The slashers were already terrified out of their minds wherever the Dark Angel of Death appeared. They shot and fought with each other in their panic to escape from Shetanna's wrath.

All the Marines needed to do was keep their trap set, and just wait for the terrified Ejjai to more or less leap right into it.

Gort-6 was fully pacified, one day later.

Mission accomplished, the Marines loaded back up into their dropships and returned to their fleet carriers and other transports to depart that system for their next objective.

Then Naero received an alert from Om.

N, several strange disturbances in the fixer clouds. None of these scans or readings make any sense.

What do we have, Om? Some other kind of enemy stealth or phaze attack?

Not sure yet. Trying to track and filter multiple pings.

Naero closed her eyes and teknomanced with Om, adding her abilities and senses with his, reaching out through the various fixer nebulae in all of their configurations.

Om, let's try a vesper flea attack, and then an infestation strategy.

Got it. Tag, envelope, and then reveal.

Okay. We've got something forming. Looks like...hundreds of small ships. Haisha! What configuration are these? No jump drives. They're not starships.

Unknown design and origin. But they must be enemy craft.

What are they doing? Where are they heading? Is there some kind of pattern? Spy craft? Are they scanning our fleets? Maybe they're sabotage vessels?

They're rather large for that, but they could be remote drones of some kind. Why not just send in cloaked missiles or bombships? No atomics on board, other than cloaked power cores. Silent alerts going to Fleet Command and Intel.

Naero's heart froze the instant she perceived what they were.

They're phazed boarding craft, Om. Like nothing we've ever seen before. And the enemy's swarming on General Walker's Flagship, *The Iwo Jima.*

They're attempting to kill Walker and take out our command and control.

And right before the crucial Spacer Grand Conclave was set to begin. Was that just a coincidence as well?

"Major Luna," Naero cut in over the links. "Priority One Negative Alert Red, I say again, Alert Red. Company 36 MCL Maeris reporting. Hundreds of inbound, phazed enemy boarding craft are slipping in and coating *The Iwo Jima.* They will most likely attack any second. I know that you and first and second platoons are already on board. Secure General Walker and all command officers. Prepare to repel boarders. Make ready for heavy assaults by phazed enemy troop waves. Institute Intel Vesper protocols."

Intense enemy jamming disrupted all coms suddenly, as even the fleet ships were cut off from each other. As a further distraction, a dozen new enemy strike fleets and fighter waves jumped in to keep the Navy busy.

Explosions and fires suddenly rocked *The Iwo Jima*, taking out her power core, propulsion, and jump drives. She floated helpless in the big black.

All while hundreds of assault craft appeared along the flagship's length, injecting their lethal cargo of attackers and assassins at the same time.

Their officer's were already fighting and in harm's way with the first two platoons of 36. Naero called up First Sergeant Samuel Gordon and Gunnery Sergeant Peyton Valmont. Then they woke up Second Leftenant Holly Mitsubishi and she joined their link instantly, checking the sitrep.

"Top, Gunny, Holly–you're scanning the sitch. I have our dropship en route to dock and board the Flagship *The Iwo Jima* in seconds, near the bridge and command quarterdecks. Platoons three, four, and five are geared up and ready to fight, on my orders. More help is right behind us, seconds away."

"Good work, N," Gordon said, "by their own initial reports, the flagship is engulfed in heavy fighting on almost every level. They need us in there fast."

Naero nodded. "Copy that, Top. I'll take 3rd Platoon, you take 4th in, and Gunny, you take 5th. I want our most experienced people at the head of this. Holly, I know you're normally a combat field officer, but we desperately you to stay behind and run–"

"Already on it, N. I'm up and hot on the combat grid. 36 won't go in blind. Linking with stealth fixers on scene. Coordinate your three assault entry points on these three key locations and fight your way to the officer's quarters, the bridge, and General Walker's state room and command quarters. Lock and load Marines. Green to hit the mix in thirty-seconds. Mark."

Naero, there's something odd being reported about some of the enemy Ejjai boarding troops. Many of them are larger, and more powerful than any other Ejjai troops we have met before.

More Ejjai mutants, Om? Naero switched into full-on Shetanna mode, racing to join 3rd Platoon at the insertion tubes.

It appears so. Early stealth fixer genetic scans show them to be some kind of Ejjai sterodans, hyped up on strength and speed mods.

Great, Om. We've fought sterodans before. Let's kill these jacked up slashers all the same. They bleed. They die.

At the last instant, Shetanna split up their available meks evenly throughout all three platoons. Their extra might would help counter the new Ejjai freaks.

They went in blasting and fighting on gravwings in zero-G.

3rd Platoon entered near the officer and command staff quarter decks. On board Marines already had their hands full attempting to repel hundreds of invading troops.

One of the Ejjai sterodan mutants, a misshapen beast over two meters tall grabbed her and attempt to smash her against the hull of the battleship.

Shetanna stunned the creature with a mind blast and drove it back. She severed one huge, hulking arm with her right katana and then opened her third eye.

Three scarlet Chaos beams drilled out of her eyes and bored out the mutant horror's face and skull, leaving only a glowing shell of sizzling meat and bone.

She cut off the left arm and finally broke free of the huge corpse.

If there were many more of these creatures on board, they were going to cause a lot of havoc. She saw at least four more from where she floated.

These mutants could take an immense amount of damage before they went down. And they were stronger than even the meks.

The Marines swarmed on them, cutting them to pieces with autoguns, miniguns, and multiple explosives.

They were still heavily engaged when platoons four and five reported that they were meeting heavy resistance trying to reach their objectives and were falling back with other Marine units to regroup.

More enemies seemed to pour in from the boarding craft outside.

Yet more Marine units arrived each second, swarming on the flagship inside and out. The battleship rocked, twisted, and shook, shuddering with the effects of heavy fighting all throughout its length.

Shetanna needed to break the stalemate here fast so that they could move on.

She pierced one of the freaks with Chaos spikes and detonated them, blasting it to pieces, and even sending Marines in shielded combat armor flying. But they'd survive being kicked around.

Another with several ravening mutant heads was ripping through a Marine's combat armor, trying to devour her. The gungirl did her best to hold it off. She stabbed at the monster's horrid faces with an energy blade and unloaded her pulse carbine into its torso.

The abomination ignored blaster fire being pumped into its massive body, and continued to lash out, knocking other Marines away while it still tried to gnaw on the one.

Jonny Fox charged up and shot the freak with his microgrenade machine pistol but was also sent flying.

Shetanna dove in and then swept up, impaling both of her Chaos blades into the mutant's thick, hunched back. Then she ignited twin blasts of scarlet lightning up through the creature, shredding it's upper body into ash and charred fragments.

The hulking legs flopped lifeless to either side, and the battered Marine and her damaged armor fell away, into the arms of her comrades.

It was Chime. 36 pulled her back.

Another Ejjai mutant launched itself off the hull and came at Shetanna, hurling grenades. Shetanna intercepted the grenades in Chaos shield spheres that absorbed the blasts and shattered like glass, but contained the force of the explosions.

Shetanna screamed. Her sonic attack rammed the mutant back into the hull with heavy crunching sounds. Then a series of arcing Chaos blades shot out in waves from her swords, and sliced the thing into gushing slabs of meat and disrupting armor and ordnance. Even the hull of the battleship itself was damaged, deep gouges raked into its impossibly hard surface.

By then, most of the enemy were dead, including all of the big mutants. Shetanna called out to Sergeant Python Wilde. He just finished stomping his armored boot down on an Alpha Ejjai and blasting its head off.

"Python. 3rd Platoon. Let's move forward and press into the mix. Other Marine fireteams are coming up behind us to help secure these areas. Our Platoons Four and Five are bogged down and need our assistance. Let's give it to them!"

"You heard our MCL. Fight forward Marines, and drive on hot and hard. Our buddies need us. So, let's go!"

They arrived at the area around the bridge, mired in another heavy firefight. Both sides were actually packed in too tight. The enemy had made the mistake of stuffing the corridors too full.

Now they were crammed too tight with dead, wounded, and troops still struggling for anyone to get through.

"I'm going in along the ceiling," Shetanna told her Marines. "On my signal, blow open the outer hull walls throughout the length of this entire corridor. Coordinate that with the troops outside. Tell them to use cutting charges."

"Sir...N," Python objected. "You'll be caught in multiple blasts. You could be wounded, killed, and sucked out into space!"

"Python, just do it. Follow my orders. I'll be all right. This isn't suicide. Trust me. I know what I'm doing."

She shield herself as best she could, and shot in upside down along the ceiling. Sizzling red Chaos katanas sliced through and pierced skulls, and jabbed down into open mouths and throats. Ejjai blood geysered.

Om helped by dropping and dispensing microbombs and float-seeker mines onto the packed enemies. Any trapped Marines in the log jam would still survive out in space.

Shetanna gave the signal.

Marines inside and out ripped open that section of the battleship hull like a tin can, using a rocking series of shaped charges.

Almost instantly, the congested knot of enemies–most dead or dying from Shetanna's sweep–were quickly sucked out into the black. Marines waited to retrieve any of their own. Any Ejjai were sent spinning on their way, and shot up for good measure.

Fixers raced in to put up containment fields and automatically started repairing the damage.

The blockage jam was now free.

Shetanna dropped down and raced forward, cutting down more foes on her way toward the bridge and the heavy fighting there.

Another of the hulking mutants tried to grab her.

Shetanna jerked its entire right arm free from its shoulder socket and kicked the monstrosity in the head several times in the flashing space of a second, crushing its face. Then she ripped up through the groin with her right katana and sliced the freak into two halves from hip to shoulder.

The Dark Angel of Death swept through the boiling maelstrom of its blood in zero-G. She concentrated with her third eye, targeting multiple attackers.

Streaking threads of Chaos force pierced a score of Ejjai, transfixing them in sudden agony with their mouths open and gasping.

Those glowing red lines expanded into impaling rods and then detonated, shredding the enemy forward position. Marines charged in behind Shetanna's relentless advance, gunning the remaining enemy down at close range.

Finally they reached the bridge proper. The crew and their Marines held their position behind the last blast wall barrier. Enemy phaze troops penetrated that barrier. Other foes set charges, fired weapons, or mutants used energy weapons to slice at the blast screens in order to cut them down.

The bridge crew and defenders fought against almost a hundred foes.

Reinforcements of heavy Marines and meks surrounded the attackers in a circle of blazing death and came at them head on. Heavy weapons barked and scorched back and forth, shields disrupted, and the majority of the fighting was within two meters or less.

Shetanna cloaked herself and then concentrated. First she put up a ring of dense Chaos energy around the bridge defensive perimeter. With all of her Mystic might, she clenched her fists and tightened the ring inward, sweeping dozens of Ejjai off their feet and crushing them into the bridge blast screen. Those heavy blast screens buckled and cracked, but so did the foes smashed into them.

She reversed the ring, transforming it into a scything blade of scarlet energy slicing outward. She had to disperse it just as the right instant to avoid hurting any Marines. But the spinning blade of raw force cut down another third of the Ejjai from behind.

Shetanna left the last third of the enemy to the advancing Marines.

She transported into the bridge itself and phazed.

Phazed enemy troops positioned themselves all about the crew and defenders, preparing to kill all of the Spacers within. While they remained phazed, they were invisible and invulnerable to the defender's weapons.

Yet that did not protect them from Shetanna.

An orb of glowing chaos energy expanded rapidly in the grinning maws of seventeen Ejjai. The orbs quickly shattered their skulls from within, bursting outwards.

Then she caused the spheres to implode. Seventeen corpses in phaze armor topple over onto their backs.

The blast barrier went down, and Shetanna rejoined First Sergeant Sam Gordon and 4th Platoon. He held a mini-gun in his right arm, but his armored left arm looked crushed and slack.

"One of those mutants shattered my left arm," he noted. "Come on. Gunny Valmont just told me they're outnumbered and fighting beside General Walker and some of his staff in the General's state rooms!"

They shot forward, the rest of Platoons three and four behind them. "I'm with you, Top. But while we race over there let me biomance that arm of yours."

Sam nodded. "I'd be obliged. I've never had any Mystic healing before."

Shetanna grinned. "Well enjoy it. And by the way, it's probably going to hurt like bloody hell."

"Go for it, N. I'm a grunter, not a screamer."

She biomanced the crushed bones and torn ligaments and tissues back to usefulness.

Sam did quite a bit of grunting, wincing, and sweating as she did so, but he was right. He sure wasn't a screamer.

He worked his repaired left arm, still wincing a bit. "Haisha! Almost as good as new. Now lets gut these bitches!"

Dead and wounded Spacers and Ejjai lay strewn all about the corridors and large chambers around the general's quarters.

Any Ejjai who still twitched got shot in the face and head.

Naero and the Marines could both hear and scan signs of heavy fighting still taking place deep within. One large conference room, like a small arena, was piled up with mostly enemy dead and wounded. The walls and the hull were pockmarked with heavy blasts and multiple explosions.

As they finally reached General Walker's private quarters, all hell broke loose.

The hull buckled and then burst with multiple explosions from within. As the chamber exploded at several points along its length. Some foes were sucked out into space before the containment fields snapped up.

From the scans, over a hundred enemy attackers–almost a third of them the huge mutants, were doing their best to take down the General and his defenders, including Gunny Valmont and 5th Platoon.

Gunny had a large, two-handed energy sword in his hands, like the ones Naero's father had once dueled with. He was doing his best to defend the general's back, cutting down any foes who tried to attack the general from behind.

But General Walker, never one to hold back in any fight, was a terror to keep up with.

In fact, Naero was suddenly staggered at the sight of Walker completely enraged and let loose on the foe like one possessed. In his custom battle armor, he wore two enormous energy gauntlets on his big hands, powered by a small fusion power core on his back.

Those powered gauntlets glowed orange and yellow, and backed by Big Jim Walker's massive thews, they could rip through almost anything.

To prove that very fact, Walker waded into dozens of the packed mutants, matching them strength for strength and more. His large, energized fingers melted into their shrieking, screaming faces as he crushed their skulls and ripped their heads from their necks.

He tore a duranadium support beam free of the battleship and swung it in wide circles, clearing some room to fight and crushed the slashers with it. He flung crushed and shattered bodies away all around him.

The other mutants still rushed in to close with him, attempting to drag him down.

Walker came straight at them. He fought and battled them in close, hand-to-hand. Any who saw it would remember that fight for the rest of their lives.

Those glowing, energized gauntlets froze into and tore through armor and flesh. Walker tore the mutants to pieces like some kind of machine. He ripped into torsos, crushed and tore out hearts and lungs, snapped spines.

He tore their guts out. Within seconds he had slaughtered nearly a score of them.

In the face of such ferocity, even the big mutants broke and fled in terror from Walker, some of them coming right at Shetanna.

Anything to get away from those ripping, tearing energy gauntlets.

Shettana used Cosmic attacks and her blades to cut down half a dozen who foolishly thought that they had any chance to escape through her.

General Walker trampled and slew all the others, rapidly stalking and dragging them down.

Then Walker shut down his gauntlets, went back among his fallen defenders, and tenderly picked up the body of what looked to be a young female Marine. From the looks of the body, she had been repeatedly stabbed from behind, and her right arm and leg had been torn off, most likely by one of the mutants.

Then Naero saw the young Marine's face and understood the general's great wroth.

It was Walker's daughter, Captain Taillara, who had served with great distinction as one of his closest aides. She was clearly a casualty from the intense and chaotic fighting that had erupted during the attack.

Her mighty father had avenged his beloved child as best he could, exacting a terrible vengeance upon the assassins.

Still, in the midst of all of that carnage, the great man held Taillara's broken body close to himself, and broke down and wept.

Every Spacer present knelt down and mourned with their great leader.

Six stunned Ejjai sterodan mutants suddenly rose up out of a mass of tangled bodies where they had been clubbed down, shaking their huge heads, snarling and laughing.

Scores of Marines lifted their humming, glowing weapons, hot to cut them down.

"Hold your fire!" Walker roared.

"Don't worry," Shetanna told him. "I'll take them."

Before she could summon her katanas, Walker shoved his daughter's lifeless body into Naero's arms.

"See to my girl, Naero. I'll deal with these monsters. They're mine."

Walker ignited his energy gauntlets.

It was always surprising how fast a man of his great size could move.

The Ejjai freaks stopped laughing when they saw death charging straight at them with those gigantic glowing fists.

They attempted to run.

They did not make it very far.

14

When read on a data pad, the the ill-fated mission on Bodis-2 should have been a cake walk. The sitrep was almost a joke. Yet there was plenty of bizarre trouble from the get-go.

Some missions and ops were just snakebit. There was no denying it. No way around that fact.

First of all, Bodis-2 had a population of only less than two hundred thousand divided up equally between five dome cities, all on the same west coast of the same continent.

The mostly Joshua Tech and Mining Consortium people there were seeking rare minerals, crystals, and other materials that were only found on that system in sufficient quantities.

Yet the history of the short-lived colony was one of nearly constant accidents and mishaps that seemed to occur there with an alarming, out of the ordinary frequency.

Naero herself sensed something odd about the planet and its strange energy fields even on approach. Bodis-2 gave off incredibly goofy Cosmic vibes.

Could un-luck and misfortune be quantified, or concentrated in one place? Was such a thing even possible?

The enemy had had trouble trying to attack it, as well. Half of their invasion fleet got caught in a bizarre magnetic storm that swept by, and crash landed on the surface, with great loss of life.

Half of Bravo's work was already done for them, even before they arrived in system.

Estimates ranged between five thousand or fewer actual invader troops hiding somewhere on the surface, and they had no way to summon others, now that the Alliance and Spacer navies had arrived.

Shetanna and the Marines simply needed to locate the Ejjai and help eliminate them.

But the defenders soon found themselves plagued by numerous problems as well.

Even during the drop zone landing, there was trouble. All of this, despite the fact that their deployment went completely unopposed by the enemy.

Bravo still lost more dropship transports and suffered more injuries than in many other ops where they had gone in hot—under enemy fire with guns blazing.

First, the primary command transport with Major Luna and half of her command staff didn't even make it out of the launch bay hangar during the drop. One of their engines burst into flame without warning, and the fire threatened the power core before finally being extinguished.

Major Luna and her staff suffered one person killed—Corporal Darren Taylor in the initial explosion and fire within the hangar. Many others suffered smoke inhalation damage and several minor injuries. XO Viho Cheyenne and third-in-command Captain Samson Konrad departed in a second dropship, as was SOP, to take over the op down below onworld.

But the strange magnetic storm effects plaguing the planet suddenly returned without warning, and left half of the ships of the 127th and 863rd naval fleets disrupted, most of their warships floating helpless around Bodis-2.

Cheyenne and Konrad and their teams were soon floating helpless up in the big black also, waiting for rescue and retrieval.

The only junior grade command officer who made the actual drop turned out to be Second Leftenant Holly Mitsubishi, no direct relation to Naero's Mystic comrade, Hashiko. Holly assumed command, although technically, Naero outranked her.

Bodis-2 was a stupid little temperate rock, with some mildly active vulcanism. There were weird particulates in the mildly toxic atmosphere that made it unbreathable. Strange energy readings and odd levels that defied analysis or description were also present.

Correction. One could breathe the atmosphere and survive it, once exposed, but doing so made people loopy. Exposure caused people to flip out, hallucinate, and dive off cliffs or fall into the equally tainted rivers.

Everything on Bodis-2 seemed tainted with these drug-like, narcotic effects. The animal life seemed more or less immune to such effects, but they could at times behave in weird ways as well.

All forces remained under strict orders to stay buttoned up, as if they were fighting in a toxic and caustic atmosphere. All safety precautions and protocols had to be observed.

But their problems and mishaps only seemed to mount from that point on. 2nd Platoon leader Anaconda Wilde slipped and fell backwards off of a loading platform and fractured her neck slightly. Enough for her to get put on a medbed and await evac, along with a growing list of several others with equally unfortunate and bizarre injuries.

Whip Konrad, for once, said he had a good feeling about this op. He wasn't going to die.

Then a mining ore hauler ploughed into him. He could have been killed, but his crushed armor saved him and sent him to the medical ship for the first time in his actual Marine career.

Moses Fay's heads-up display went nuts and started playing movie vids only in fast forward mode. He couldn't unseal, and had to be led back to the dropship by teks as if he were blind.

The teks had their hands full with all sorts of malfunctions and problems. Along with the dropships acting up, almost every E-19 pulse rifle–only the standard primary weapon of the Spacer Marines–powered down and would only come back up in training mode.

Yeah, that was going to be a big help in combat.

Several Marines, such as Trevor Lakota and Michael Borelli, grew a bit concerned when their G-1, HE microgrenades started blinking as if activated.

The Marines scrambled to toss the grenades a safe distance away, but nothing happened. The platoons tested some of their grenades, but only half of those went off as they should.

Corporal Choti Donovan was on point with a patrol when suddenly her entire suit of stealth armor disrupted and zapped her into unconsciousness.

At first they thought she had struck or triggered some kind of enemy stun mine.

But a quick diagnostic said that her suit had shorted out when she took a leak. Despite the fact that the nanomaterials of those suits were specifically designed and engineered to process human waste internally. They functioned so efficiently that they were rarely even questioned. The fact that one had malfunctioned was in itself amazing.

Reports reached them from a few other Marines who got zapped when they tried to pee.

Kerrel Apache's gravwing had her bouncing up and down until she deactivated it. Mystaria Romanov complained that her comlink merely echoed and repeated everything she tried to say. She couldn't receive or hear anything.

Clive Luna—no direct relation to the major—said that his suit was filled with the overpowering scents of fresh flowers, nearly choking him. Everyone else told him to shut the hell up and go on smelling his damn flowers and quit complaining. There were far worse odors to be trapped inside one's suit with.

Corporal Kerrington's leg armor froze up and would not move. He floated back to the drop point to wait in line to see the teks.

Branton Taylor fell into a steep ravine and fractured his right foot.

Maurice James kept blinking into stealth mode and vanishing for no reason. Julian Kothari's suit, on the other hand, kept changing from one bright, flashy color to the next.

As these various concerns, incidents, and mishaps continued unabated, Naero called a halt to their advance.

"Everyone stand down, maintain security as best we can, and perform a level-1 diagnostic check on all of their gear—both armor and weapons. If you can't check your stuff, have someone else run one for you. We can't fight like this."

It was maddening. And they couldn't bring fixers down to the planet's surface for fear of them going haywire as well.

Running the diagnostics took well over an hour, and left their effective fighting force at about fifty percent efficiency.

Half of them couldn't fight. Fewer than three thousand troops were battle ready.

When there was time, Naero tried to help the remaining officers assess their status and form a plan of action.

They still had a primary mission: locate and eliminate the enemy forces on Bodis-2.

Om, can you give us any help? Om? Are you there?

No answers. Haisha. Even Om was down.

What the hell was it with this freaky place?

138

The remains of the strike force bounced around on the surface for several hours, more of them dropping like proverbial flies all the while.

And they had yet to spot the enemy or fire a single shot in anger.

Word finally reach them. "Call off the attack and search," Leftenant Mitsubishi ordered. "The enemy has been found and has already been neutralized."

Naero couldn't believe it. Who or what had done so? She needed to find out.

She got the coordinates to help check it out.

Five thousand foes lay scattered and dead across the sands, many of them at the bottoms of steep cliffs and ravines.

Mitsubishi looked as if she couldn't believe the reports. "For some reason, they all opened their battle suits up and went bonkers after breathing in the local narcotics in the air," Mitsubishi said. "Then most of them attempted to fly without their gravwings."

Naero almost got down on her knees. "Sir, I beg of you. Get all of us the hell out of here as soon as possible," Naero said. "This planet is the most snakebit place I have ever seen. The sooner everyone is off this whacked-out rock, the better."

Bravo departed Bodis-2 and fled that location with all haste and dispatch.

No one ever wanted to see or hear from that crazy world again.

Fourthday was another Chat Night, and all of the oddities of Bodis-2 were a big point of various discussions, at first.

Then the usual stuff and the mundane took over. Jason Ahmed's and his wife Karyn's daughter Dara had her second birthday.

Everyone shared vids of their kids and families and lovers. Any Marine who didn't like stuff like that could go somewhere else.

Jessy Ramsey was married to a tek named Thaedel Wang, and they had twin boys, age three, Thomas and Frederick. Miriam Decker was married to Melody Kim, and they had a one-year-old daughter named Yvonne. Mystaria Romanov and her medtek husband Mark Daniels just had the birth of their daughter Alexandra by a surrogate mother. Some female Marines on duty chose that option during their tours.

Actually, Naero didn't mind watching vids of happy people one bit.

It actually worked to help hold off the nightmares of countless dead civies, staring up from various battlefields.

Later that evening, Naero gravitated toward her gentle friends, Chime and Jonny Fox, and their quiet, easy-going ways. They weren't usually all hyper, or full of crap, or on the make like some of the jarheads were.

Chime sat there between them, smiling and laughing softly to herself as she read one of her books. Until she dozed off and fell asleep peacefully on Naero's or Jonny's shoulder with her thumb still marking her page.

Naero thought that her odd friend Chime was a pretty young Spacer, but she was definitely the most beautiful when she was asleep that way. There was a quality to her finely fashioned face that made her look fresh and at ease, and not either wily or distracted as she often appeared when she was awake. But she also looked childlike and vulnerable.

No wonder Jonny, her cousin, always felt protective toward her, and asked others in her squad to look out for Chime. But Naero came to learn that all of the Marines had each other's backs. Each was willing to lay down their life for their sisters and brothers.

And that fact ennobled the lot of them, whether they were fools, or dreamers, annoying twits, horndogs, or rat bastards on their own. In combat, there was never any question of that great and mighty fact. Everyone could count on it, and that was an extremely good and powerful thing.

Jonny sipped Jett with Naero and droned on a bit longer. He liked to talk about his future plans for himself, Chime, and their greatgran, after the High Crusade was won and over.

"Do you know what I'm gonna name my ship, N?"

Naero flashed him a smile. "Tell me Jonny."

"Gonna name her *The Green Fox*. And I'm gonna christen her with a big bottle of Jett. My first ship, like all Spacers want."

"You gonna join one of the booms, Jonny Fox? Gonna go off and explore?"

"Nope. Don't want any of that. Plenty of others to do all of that, and more power to them. I just want to set myself up with a nice, safe, comfortable milk run. I don't care where it is, just as long as it's peaceful and quiet. I've had enough excitement being a Marine to last me…forever. Maybe even find me a sweet little wife…and just maybe, some kids someday for greatgran to fuss over before she makes the next journey."

"Even for you, Jonny Fox? A wife, and even kids, someday?"

Jonny sighed and smiled. "Stranger things have happened. Even so."

15

General Walker's Marines from Bravo Command maneuvered into position under the cover of darkness using their stealth gear.

Naero agreed to slip in ahead and bait the trap, in her battlefield role as Shetanna–*The Dark Angel of Death.*

Get ready, Om. The show's about to start.

I will need some time to prepare, concentrate, and focus enough of our energies in reserve, before you deplete them all again.

Just get ready and keep us ready. I'm going to set our game plan in motion.

I will do all that I can to assist. Call upon me when you require me. Good hunting, Naero.

Thanks, Om.

The invaders would do anything to have a chance to destroy or capture her.

She was, in fact, the actual, literal bait, and the trap was being set for an entire invasion force of Ejjai elite that ravaged the Corps border world of Tholos-4.

No local planetary army, military, or militia had been able to stand before the horrific onslaught of the alien invaders.

The Ejjai hammered the local landers into submission with advanced artillery, orbital bombardment from Ejjai fleets, and close assault gunships and gravtanks.

Then the terrifying collection process began, and all the living, wounded, and dead were hurled into the shrieking, whining processing blades of the robotic meatships.

The horrible sounds of the meatships warred with the screams of their countless victims.

Given time, Ejjai mass cloning factories and robotic ship- and weapon-building factories would also be established onworld.

The murdering bastards had already wiped three major cities and their mixed populations off the surface of the hapless planet, before Naero and the Marines could even deploy onworld.

The enemy left those lost cities little more than red, blackened, burning scars and stains that could be viewed from orbit.

Nothing left alive.

Ejjai hyaenanoids loved carrion.

Every man, woman, and child of any kind, species, or age that the enemy captured was routinely tortured, killed, and processed into rotting ration blocks in the horrific, robotic meatships of the invading aliens. That included any sentients, pets, livestock–anything and everything that was meat.

The meatblock rations were frozen only to keep them from breaking down and decaying completely.

Hatred was too gentle a word for what most humans felt for the Ejjai invaders and their extreme methods. Spacers, landers, and each of the other known races that encountered the Ejjai quickly learned to feel the same way.

This vile, uplifted, intrusive, and opportunistic species needed to be completely exterminated wherever it was encountered.

The invaders proved that they were incapable of coexisting with any other living things.

The Ejjai could only dominate, torture, and destroy all life that they encountered, anything they could sink their teeth and claws into. Uplifting them, and giving them advanced weapons and starships had only turned them into a galactic abomination, an interstellar menace, a virulent plague.

An utter nightmare.

One that needed to end for the poor people of Tholos-4.

Naero and her Marine allies were there to see to that.

It was amusing that the Ejjai always saw themselves as invincible, the supreme warriors.

Shetanna and Bravo Command quickly intended to disavow the foe of such jaded notions, time and time again.

The Marines of Bravo Command were the textbook picture of professional warriors. A legend among all the known systems.

Naero loved serving with the elite of the elite. Together they made a fantastic team.

Even the Ejjai had learned grudgingly to fear them from their initial engagements, and the proof was there.

Every invader force that came up against Bravo Command had been completely wiped out—in record time. And then Bravo quietly packed up and headed on to the next world, ready to do it all over again.

The enemy struggled to halt the Spacer advance and throw it back.

They tried everything they could think of.

Increased enemy numbers.

Different tactics.

New weapons—traps and tricks of many different kinds.

The Ejjai generals turned themselves inside out trying to find a solution—a way to achieve victory against the Spacer advance.

Bravo Command slipped in and ruined the invader's sick, twisted party every single time.

And Shetanna, The Dark Angel of Death, continued to use all of her amazing, Mystic powers and abilities to help the Marines keep up the pressure and drive the enemy to terror, madness, and distraction.

General Walker worked closely with Spacer Intel, always making sure his leathernecks had the latest hi-tek toys, weapons, and armor that came online.

As a result, they landed an entire Marine division on Tholos-4 and slipped into position, without the enemy even knowing they were there yet.

By the time the Spacer Fleets swept in to destroy the enemy naval forces, Bravo Command would already be implementing their plan to put the foe down hard and fast on the ground.

Three Marine infantry regiments, one artillery regiment, plus specialized units of meks, armor, and air-to-ground support.

The ghosts of Bravo Command spread the impending Shadow of Vengeance and Death over their foes like an unseen net, without any knowledge or awareness among the invaders themselves.

Bravo and Shetanna prepared for another stunning series of lightning attacks.

All became poised and ready, while the heedless enemy celebrated their vile victories and atrocities.

Naero struggled to remain silent as she slipped in among the foe. Death and damnation to any invader who thought they could invade the human sectors with impunity, death, and cosmicide.

On every world, the invader needed to be taught that bloody lesson.

Naero strode right into the belly of the beast.

Alone.

Defiant.

By now she was supremely confident in her skills and abilities and all of her comrades depending on her and backing her up.

Her cloaked combat armor made her virtually invisible. The Ejjai could not even smell her.

She used her gravwing to slip into the most heavily guarded command and control bunker the enemy possessed. With her skill and her tek, she could crawl upside down on the ceilings like an unseen insect.

Her miniature vidcams and audio collectors fed data to Intel in real time, covering everything she saw.

Naero's small contingent of cloaked Intel fixers and microdrones stayed close, ready to disrupt key enemy systems and communications, planting microbombs and detonation devices as they went.

The Invader High Command celebrated their latest triumph with what one might expect from them–a huge, decadent, disgusting feast–held within a shielded bunker.

They set up their victory celebration within a huge underground arena, probably used by the Tholosians for some kind of urban or regional sporting events.

Ejjai got drunk on stinking, fermented grog made from human blood. They shipped it in from the meatships by the tankerful.

Under the bright lights of the hi-tek arena, tens of thousands of Ejjai feasted and celebrated their latest victories. The enemy generals praised their troops and used the huge arena vidscreens to plot out their next attacks on the three nearest Tholosian cities.

On the center of the playing field, Ejjai transports and appropriated trucks had also hauled in and dumped huge piles of human corpses from the local population for their undefeated troops to feed on.

Piles of fresh and not-so-fresh meat, diverted from the enemy meatships to help sate the troops in large numbers.

One of the piles was all dead children and infants.

Even worse, to Naero's horror, some of the bodies in the various meat piles were somehow still alive. They twitched or cried out in pain and

144

terror. Some weakly attempted to crawl away despite broken or missing limbs.

The Ejjai quickly seized them and began tormenting them even further, laughing hysterically at the sport. They stabbed, cut, and skinned them alive–or otherwise got creative.

As Ejjai were wont to do.

Ejjai were among the vilest, most disgusting creatures Naero had even encountered.

She resisted the very strong impulse to cut loose on them right then and there.

But she couldn't–not yet.

These monsters needed to die. Every single one of them.

And very soon, she would have a direct hand in launching the attack that would accomplish just that.

The timing had to be just right, so she steeled herself.

The generals. Reach the generals and stay ready.

Six Ejjai generals held court like warlords at huge tables overflowing with comconsoles, sensor stations, map screens, and piles of loot. And the bloody remains of horrific, eviscerated meals.

The bulk of all Ejjai clone troops remained predominantly female. Smaller male Ejjai concubines were kept around on leashes for fun, for the leaders. They even dressed them in human clothing and poorly fitting human lingerie.

As an oddity, one of the generals even had a human male dressed up as a concubine. But the poor guy apparently had to be kept in a heavily guarded pen off to one side–to keep all of the other Ejjai from devouring and murdering him, most likely in that order.

Naero circled around the generals and studied the arena, trying to devise the best way to take them all down.

She listened intently to the plans the enemy generals were making, feeding it all to Intel.

"So, are all of the atomics and genocide devices in place yet?"

Another general pulled up a mapscreen displaying all of their installation of such devices planetwide.

Naero instantly transmitted all of that data directly to Spacer Intel as well–priority alert.

Intel and Bravo Command were most likely already neutralizing the most vital elements of the enemy plot. These genocide devices could be scanned and located from orbit. But it was always good to be sure, and to know their exact locations.

The Ejjai generals scoffed. "We will be ready for anything the enemy can throw at us in less than a day," one of the other Ejjai generals boasted.

"They won't know what's going to hit them until it's too late."

"Good, very good. Speed things up if you can. Get it all up and ready."

"Don't worry, sir. We will be more than ready to deal with their so-called Bravo Command–and their spack witch."

All of the Ejjai generals had a good laugh and congratulated each other.

The lead general stepped up to a waiting podium and addressed the crowd.

"Great news, sisters! We have it on good authority that the spacks are sending their precious Bravo Command and their spack witch Shetanna against us."

Lots of cursing and booing about that roared up.

Their lead general continued. "This time, we are more than ready for them!"

Huge rounds of applause to that.

"Let me just say that we have some heavy duty surprises of our own ready and waiting and in store for our enemies. We can't wait for them to get here–and have them all for dinner!"

That brought an even bigger round of cheering, cursing, and applause.

"We will engage the spacks in a matter of days, and with our increased numbers and new weapons–I say we're going to kick their asses and stomp them bloody. We will gut them! I want all my girls out there to feast on spack Marine flesh until you puke!"

Further rounds of cheering and vile responses.

"We will ferment their blood in our huge vats and get drunk on it!"

More horrendous rounds of cheering and applause.

"And once we have captured their filthy spack witch, all of you will watch as I personally cut her up and rape her with red-hot knives, and torture her to death over the course of an entire week. She'll sing to all of us with her screams. Then I myself will feast upon her guts, and eat her heart while the light in her eyes fades. I'll crack her skull open and eat her brains!"

The Ejjai went crazy.

"Wait until we post *that* on the webnets for the spacks and the skinners to watch! I promise you victory. We cannot be defeated. And we will sweep the human skinners and all the other inferior races into our meatships and out of all existence. They are our prey! Yet another galaxy that shall fall to us and our mighty masters!"

More about their mysterious masters. Interesting.

Furious cheering continued in waves.

"So, my warriors. Feast on meat until you vomit, and then feast some more. Then prepare for battle as we crush our foes and ravage the rest of this world. We shall drown it all in blood and swim in it! Prepare for our ultimate victory! Our time has come. None can stand against us!"

They erupted in an orgy of celebration and vile gluttony.

Fights broke out among the meat piles, and the Ejjai fought with and murdered each other in their frenzy.

The lead general returned to the others, rubbing her claws together eagerly in the midst of the chaos.

"My sisters, I have a special treat that I've saved just for us, at this exact moment. Please, enjoy my precious gifts to you all." She motioned to a large knot of troops off to one side among some gravtanks.

A full squad of Ejjai in heavy battle armor led out six terrified human women, all of them naked and extremely pregnant.

None of them had a mark on them. Yet.

But from the looks on their pale faces, they all knew very well what the enemy generals intended to do with them. Each of them was heavy with child, in the later stages of pregnancy.

That they had remained unspoiled and unharmed up until now would quickly change for the worse–the worst fate imaginable.

Although they were unbound, there was no chance for any of these captives to break free or escape on their own against so many foes.

The generals each glared at them and gloated. The Ejjai generals slavered and drooled, snapping jaws and smacking lips.

Each general had a set of rusty, bloodstained butchering tools that they began to place out in front of them in heady, eager anticipation of their coming feast.

Then the squad of Ejjai troops guarding the six women suddenly staggered a few feet away as if drunk.

Some melted into slag where they stood.

Other Ejjai troops exploded.

The six human captives looked around in confusion.

The next instant, they all vanished.

The six Ejjai generals shot to their feet in stunned surprise.

They couldn't even speak, but a few flung cleavers and knives at the spot where the captives had stood.

Their weapons fell harmlessly to the ground.

All of this was captured and displayed on the big arena screens, and slowly attracted the attention of the astonished crowds.

Then Shetanna appeared as if by magic, right before the lead Ejjai general, resplendent in her full Angel of Death mode. She was all dressed in black, shining black hair flowing in the wind, violet eyes burning above her mask.

Twin bloodred katanas crackled and hissed in the damp air, at the ready in either hand.

Every eye fixed on her—while the mini-gravpods from her fixers whisked the six cloaked, female captives away to safety.

Naero only had to buy few more seconds for them to make it out. Fierce Marines waited nearby to take charge of them and keep them safe.

With the six captives out of the way, at last Shetanna could go to work.

"I have come for you, filthy Ejjai cowards. I am Shetanna!" she cried.

She rammed both of her swords through the lead general's eyes and out the back of the Ejjai's scorched skull.

Two of the generals tried to run.

The other three tried to attack her.

It did not matter.

Bolts of scarlet lighting tore forth from both her blades, ripping and blasting the other five into charred pieces of meat and bone.

Naero cloaked and shot away as the area around the tables was engulfed in torrents of enemy weapon fire the very next instant.

Then the gravtanks, gunships, transports, and other vehicles lined up nearby began to explode.

Naero projected multiple holos of herself all over the arena and in the in the air, drawing fire in all directions.

She used *the voice*, her words booming and echoing from several directions.

"EJJAI FILTH. PREPARE TO MEET DEATH. FOR SHETANNA IS THE DARK ANGEL OF DEATH, AND HAS NO FEAR OF MURDERING COWARDS."

The Ejjai fired in panic from so many angles that they cut down each other by the hundreds—just as Naero planned.

Fear began to infect them.

Gouts of red lightning lashed into the arena stands from several directions like gigantic whips of destruction. The devastation flung dead and dying Ejjai everywhere in a cyclone of slaughter, adding to the total chaos and confusion.

"NO MERCY, EJJAI SCUM. NO ESCAPE. FEAR IS MY MOTHER, DEATH MY SIRE, AND I THEIR DAUGHTER! YOU CANNOT HARM ME. THERE IS NO ESCAPE FOR YOU!"

Just as the enemy started to figure out they were shooting at holos and murdering each other wholesale, Naero merged with one of her mirror images in the midst of hundreds of Ejjai in the arena stands.

Multiple thin rods of red Chaos energy shot from her, fanning out in a diameter of thirty meters.

First she impaled hundreds of the shocked invaders.

When she spun, the red blades chopped them all into smaller gory chunks and pieces.

Torrents of unleashed Ejjai blood suddenly gathered and swept down the arena, carrying others away in a sudden red, rushing tide of gore.

Naero cloaked and flashed away again.

More enemy fire stormed and tore at her former position.

She took the place of another holo, and sent forth a sweeping hurricane of of Chaos bubbles and orbs of every shape and size into another section of the stands.

The explosions collapsed that entire section. Wreckage toppled inward.

Next she appeared on the field before the horrendous meat piles, in the midst of hundreds of more frantic enemies.

Half of them flung their weapons away and ran in terror before her as she raced toward them. So much for the valiant Ejjai.

"STAND AND FIGHT, SCUM!"

Naero surged and fought with the mob of foes, sweeping one way and then the other, cutting them down by dozens, by scores.

She moved among them so fast they could not focus their attacks.

Then she would abruptly change direction and sweep another way before they could hem her in.

She unleashed more scarlet lightning strikes.

She sent random Chaos blasts into packed pockets of foes.

At times she just whirled and passed through them with her swords fully extended, mowing them down in lines and bunches.

Once she had shattered them completely, she merely turned her back on them and began walking away quickly and with determination, toward the nearest exit.

Naero set her shield pod full-on.

Three enemy tanks roared at her, cannons blazing.

Naero dodged and deflected their blasts into the stands.

Two gravtanks she exploded with Chaos bombs.

She sliced the last in half with her swords and kept walking calmly, straight through the burning wreckage as the gravtank exploded directly behind her to either side.

She ignored all enemy fire directed at her, kept walking, and cut down anything stupid enough to attempt to stand before her.

She crackled with destroying red lightning as she passed into one of the exit tunnels, laying waste to anything before her.

The enemy regrouped and poured into the tunnel in hot pursuit.

Just as Naero hoped they would.

Another kill zone. How convenient of them to all bunch up for her.

She turned at bay, just before exiting, and focused all of her energies in an intense Chaos blast cone.

The massive detonation tore the tunnel apart and blasted shredded pieces of the packed invaders out the other end, right before a massive fireball that followed hard thereafter.

Naero cloaked, and called out over her secure link.

"You guys ready? I've got them primed, but I'm also almost out of juice."

"We're in place and ready to join the show, Shetanna. You okay? Do you need us to extract you?"

"Negative. I can finish my part. It just takes a lot of energy to sustain attacks at this level. You guys know that. Did Intel take care of those genocide devices?"

"Almost all accounted for."

"All right, I'm setting up for my final show. They'll take the bait, all right. You guys hit them hard when they do."

"Hard as we can, Shetanna. You know us."

"I sure do, and I can't wait to watch it all go down–right from the front row. Copy that. Make the legends proud, Bravo."

She took up her position in the center of the fallen city nearby, just outside of the shattered arena.

She formed a Chaos construct around her that duplicated her and her every move.

Her construct became a scarlet, gigantic version of herself, semi-transparent and fifteen meters tall, red and glowing with huge blazing swords.

She stomped on a meatship and slashed at it until it exploded.

Then she attacked the cloneship factory next to it.

"FACE ME, COWARDS. SHETANNA SHOWS YOU HER MIGHT. SHOW ME YOURS. FACE ME AND PERISH!"

Yet in actuality, her energies waned with each passing second.

It wasn't like being back on Janosha where there was limitless Cosmic energy to tap into. Away from the Mystic Homeworlds, Naero's energy levels and her abilities were not infinite or limitless. She made a good show of it, but even she could not sustain these levels of attack for very long.

The entire enemy invasion roared to life and locked on, bunching and sweeping her way, to engage her from all directions.

The Ejjai went insane with fury.

Up in the skies above and beyond Tholos-4, the Spacer navy sent the invader fleets spinning down in flames.

Thousands of Spacer Marines suddenly materialized out of the black at key points and positions.

Phantoms who owned the night.

The black was their domain, their element, and they surrendered it to no one.

Bravo Command unleashed a torrent of concentrated, interlocking fire against the bunched-up invaders. Veils of destroying fire, artillery, and ordnance rained down—a deluge of precisely timed destruction that no living thing could possibly survive.

Within a matter of minutes, a quarter of a million Ejjai invaders flashed and flared into a sweeping typhoon of white-hot death that overtook them.

Shetanna had done her job all too well.

Completely drained of all her Mystic energies for the moment, she could barely stand.

Even as she staggered away, a full platoon of gigantic Ejjai Sterodans in phaze armor appeared all around her.

They piled on and overwhelmed her with their greater mass and several shock charges that hit and rippled through both them and her. The shock charges rattled Naero's teeth in her skull.

The Ejjai and their mysterious masters still wanted her and the KDM alive and intact, apparently.

Naero grinned.

Yet another trap, and she had stumbled right into it.

This time, the enemy thought they had her at last.

Yet Naero knew something they did not, and called out into her own mind.

Om—you're up. They've got me.

Take these bastards down hard and fast!

16

Naero's insertion probe was knocked down out of the sky over Shuji-9, the first Gigacorp world that Bravo Command struck right after the events at the Spacer Grand Conclave.

The enemy, however, didn't give a crap either way. Somehow they detected her cloaked probe and filled the sky with so much fire and airbursts of ordnance that they had to hit something.

She and Om barely teknomanced enough to keep themselves from dying, but not from crashing.

Naero burst out of her insertion probe with her small cloud of fixers, just before the small craft crashed into a battalion of Ejjai gravtanks, with its power core and jump drive set to detonate.

The resulting small gigablast was nearly atomic in yield, and gave her cover to vanish and get away to assess her situation. Naturally, she and her fixers cloaked, and then shielded, under the additional protection of Naero's Cosmic abilities and Om's defenses.

But they were still more or less in the middle of a fully involved battlefield between the Ejjai invaders, and the locals, the avian/birdlike Quess.

The Quess were sentient, birdlike humanoids with various avian heads, styles, and colorations of feathers covering their bodies.

On some worlds, some of them had wings and could still even fly. On others, their wings or winged arms and hands were either vestigial to some degree, not even noticeable. All possessed the ability to reason and speak at very high levels of intellect.

They were a space-faring species in all of their many forms and variations, and held to be very ancient and wise. Yet such wisdom did not always avail them in combat. And the Quess suffered against the invasion as all the sentient races did.

Naero tried to reach some of the defenders to join up with them and attempt to explain that the Spacer Marines would shortly arrive to assist them. But the combat around her was too fierce.

Each time she attempted to move away, explosions from something batted her about. Being unseen did not save her from indirect fire. Her shields would serve to protect her, but only for so long. And the enemy bombardments seemed both heavy and endless.

The original plan had been for her to drop down and spearhead a big dropship assault by going ahead of Bravo and 36, and execute an attack on the invader's central command and control. She would help coordinate the drop, and then race ahead, slicing through key enemy positions in order to soften them up and spread confusion.

Something Shetanna seemed created to do.

But this DZ was clearly too hot to drop into. Bravo or anyone coming down into this level of fire would be shredded and take serious casualties before they even reached the ground. Naero got on her secure link and delayed the intended assault for the moment.

She had to find a new place on the white hot combat grid for Bravo to drop in and then start putting the hammer down on the foe. But it looked as if she was going to have to clear a DZ all by herself.

Perhaps if she could do enough damage or wipe out enough of the Ejjai in one place, the Marines could come down and strike while the invaders were still reeling and trying to regroup. Bravo didn't need a huge window to execute a drop and pop.

Shetanna would find a way to blow open such a window for them. She informed them to stand ready and monitor her progress.

Lucky her, she was right in the middle of the nightmare of an all-out invader attack on the native military defense forces. The Quess defiantly held their own, but they were slowly being chewed up and forced back by the intensity of the invader's combined arms attacks.

For the defenders, this grim fact was complicated by the attack taking place right within a heavily populated gigacity. Civilians and refugees attempted to flee in panic, clogging the streets and skyways, and trying to escape while the invaders poured withering fire at everyone in an attempt to cut them all down.

Wherever Shetanna scanned, there was grim, bloody fighting.

Om, link with our fixers. This place is a total disaster. Let's coordinate our attacks for maximum effectiveness on the local combat grid.

They picked their prime spot to clear for the new drop zone. Om and the fixers directed her to the site. Shetanna buzzed up her glowing red katanas and accelerated to attack speed.

She swept in and sliced her way through the enemy formations where they were heaviest, causing the most destruction.

She struck so fast that often she deflected defender fire just as much as invader fire off of her shields and swords, continuing to rip right through the hottest parts of several ongoing battles along the invader positions.

Shetanna lopped off enemy commander heads, sliced throats, and cut the barrels off gravtanks and autoguns.

A black and scarlet blur zipped through the mingled invaders and defenders alike, leaving behind destruction and death, but only for the Ejjai.

The local defenders had no idea what the hell this strange new weapon or phenomena was, but from their voices over their links, they quickly realized it was taking out the invaders. Orders went out not to fire upon this new force, whatever it was.

Soon the defenders rallied, regrouped, and charged in behind and around Shetanna's lightning assaults.

Om cut in. *I've reported in to Bravo over the enemy jamming that just started up. They are on their way down to secure these positions.*

Great, Om. We need them bad.

Shetanna spiraled up to take on a flight of enemy gunships roaring down out of the sky. She launched a full spread of float-seeker smartmines into the gunships, rocking and busting them up.

After a few minutes, she began to wonder. Where are our guys, Om? How come they're not–

Blasts and explosions walked in and stomped in all over the enemy positions as the cloaked Bravo Marine dropships came down hot, hard, and fast.

Shetanna continued to strafe the enemy assault lines at the perimeter of the DZ, deflecting fire from both sides. She helped smash the enemy's forward thrust at the dropships.

Om fed Naero the combat grid data as it evolved. *Our rapid deployment units have come out swinging and are already nailing the invader hard. Two other Bravo companies have gone ahead with your original mission to take out the enemy's command and control. They'll have to do without Shetanna's assistance.*

Good for them, Om. How are they doing?

Moderately well. They sent in two hundred heavily armed stealth strikers to perform the role that you usually serve.

Nice to know that it takes that many Marines to do what we do, Om.

They just want to be sure.

From that point on, Shetanna needed to conserve her Cosmic energies if she was going to fight all day and night beside 36.

She dropped the last of her microbombs and fusion grenades on an enemy arty position that continued to rain hell down upon the local population and its defenders and civies.

She left it behind her in flames.

Om, I'm out again. Get our fixers to regenerate a full spread of ordnance for me. I need to resupply.

N, hold still for a second and re-arm. The fixers can hardly keep up with you. Two full sets, ready and waiting to lock on and fill you up. Just give them a chance.

Naero chuckled. Hit me on the fly and let's lock and load, Om. We're burning daylight and I'm not letting up on these bitches.

Her fixers swarmed over her like bees on a queen bee, filling her pouches, pods, dispensers, and micro ordnance racks with all of the good stuff.

All while Naero maintained her racing attack arcs, her blazing red blades scything and hewing.

Om, maintain an automatic resupply of my weapons and explosives, bombs, and mines. Have the fixers fill me back up as soon as I use something, as able. If I brush them aside, just have them check back later and keep working on it. I don't want to run dry.

Will give it a shot, N. You zip around pretty fast.

Everywhere Naero saw the local Quess defenders getting licked, she swooped down and lent them a very heavy hand.

The locals stared at her as she flashed among the lines, ripping down the Ejjai. They looked upon her in wonder and awe at her fighting prowess. She made such an impact and caused such havoc among the enemy, that Bravo Command HQ allowed her the freedom to act as a wild blade of Chaos upon the battlefield and go at the enemy wherever she thought best.

In fact, both they and the locals cheered her on, directing her toward the heaviest pockets of intense fighting to either quell or soften up.

They sent 36 to support her, but she kept moving out in front of them so rapidly and erratically that they couldn't keep up with her.

They merely swooped in behind, adding their fury and firepower to the mix, pummeling the enemy further in her wake.

But at one point, Shetanna's Marines got cut off as enemy reserves poured in.

Corporal Parsival Patton was cut down from behind by several enemy grenades. And the bloody fighting continued the rest of that day and throughout the night.

The slashers tried to make off with Percy's body at one point.

Shetanna wasn't about to let that happen, and led a charge with elements of 36 that not only got Percy back with them, but shattered the enemy's entire left flank until the Ejjai broke in blind fear and ran.

When dawn rose up the next day, the invaders were on the ropes and on the run, routed and attacked viciously from nearly every direction.

The Dark Angel of Death had worked her black magic once again, and helped Bravo teach the Ejjai invaders the depths and the meaning of absolute terror.

The locals even started using holos and even human impersonators of Shetanna on the front lines. Wherever she or one of her fakes appeared, all over the gigacity, the invaders panicked in cowardice and battled each other in order to get away.

Shetanna and her sisters drove them like flocks of frightened birds, into trap after trap–destruction after destruction. The gutless enemy withered in the flames of battle and were consumed.

After a short rest, the real Shetanna calmly walked straight into the dissolving front lines, unknown to the enemy, protected by Om and several unit-sized cloaked shield pods placed over her in layers.

The invaders poured everything they had at the phantom. Withering fire that pulverized everything nearby, all to no effect.

Shetanna walked through those destroying waves of fire like an avenging spirit, an invulnerable juggernaut.

Let the foe do their worst.

Shetanna kept coming, drawing fire, getting the hysterical enemy to repeatedly expose themselves and all of their firing positions on the grid for Bravo to light up and take out.

The enemy continued to shriek and scream in panic, and withdraw against such apparent might. And thunderous cries went up from the defenders until they became a roar.

Shetanna.

Shetanna.

Shetanna!

On she came and the enemy threw down their useless weapons with shaking hands and open, shivering mouths and were routed. This was a foe beyond their comprehension—impervious, indestructible, and unstoppable.

Shetanna kept coming. Whenever one of her cloaked shieldpods went down, Om and the fixers brought up another in its place, maintaining the terrifying illusion.

Line after line, she walked straight into the teeth of their heaviest fire, her deep violet eyes shining, head held high.

Utterly fearless.

She used *the voice* and paced right at them. RUN, COWARDS. FLEE YOU FILTH. YOU WHO CAN ONLY BUTCHER THE HELPLESS. RETREAT AND DIE, FOR DEATH ITSELF FOLLOWS ME AND FALLS UPON YOU. SHETANNA, THE DARK ANGEL OF DEATH COMES FOR YOU ALL!

THIS IS THE BLOOD I COME FROM! AND IT IS THE FIRE OF BATTLE ITSELF. NO MATTER YOUR PUTRID NUMBERS, YOU SHALL NEVER STAND BEFORE OUR MIGHT!

Once the battles on Shuji-9 ended that night, 36 escorted and carried their Shetanna back to their dropship on a medbed like a champion upon her shield. Utterly spent once more, it would be nearly a full day before she could rise up again without weakness or pain.

They also saw to Percy, as they always cared for their own fallen.

The sooner Naero healed and regenerated her amazing abilities, the sooner Shetanna could fight once more. Bravo ghosted on toward their next objective, as they ever did.

Her mates came by as they always did, to check on her and give her shit.

She was up and around the following night, which was another Seventhday, and that meant both Sparring night and dance night, all over again.

Jonny Fox came to her as the sparring matches broke up and the dancing began. Naero still tried to slip away and hide somewhere, all to no avail.

This time, Jonny was not alone. He had an entire posse with him, including Trent Patton, Clive Luna, Razor Wilde, Acer Adams, Lance Allen, and Terrance Decker.

"What the hell is this?" Naero asked them. "You guys gonna take me on all at once? Let's rock!"

Jonny held up his hands. "Nothing like that, N. So, frost. We're just here to give you a little friendly education. That's all. Nothing bad. Trust me, even if you don't trust any of these other mooks, you know you can trust me."

"All right. I still don't get it. What's with the goon squad?"

They all laughed. Acer spun in place. "Cause we are the best at what we do," he said, running his hands down his sleek, athletic body."

Naero rolled her eyes. Kill me now, Om.

"Re-lax, gal," Decker told her. "We seen you bouncing around. We know for damn sure you ain't got no moves. So we gonna teach you some."

Her mouth almost dropped open. "Haisha! You…you mean you wanna teach me to–"

Patton called up some jump tunes. "That's right. 36 Can't have no asskicker MCL hottie like you who can't burn the lines. Unacceptable!"

"Haisha," Decker noted. "We've got a dance off with the other Companies in a month or so."

Acer jumped in. "It would be an embarrassment, girl. We gonna teach you to move with style and grace…and *Authorit-T!*"

Naero tried to back away. "You got it wrong, guys. I *don't* need dancing lessons."

Jonny blocked her path. "N. You really do. Accept it. You stink right now…but we can fix that. You are an amazing athlete. Watch what we do, and we can teach you."

Naero covered her mouth in humiliation. "I…I…can't believe this."

"Believe it sugardoll. We're gonna switch those lame-ass stomps from sour to sweet. Come on, now. Work with us."

Allen sang out. "No choice. You ain't got no choice, honeypod. Company 36 *always* brings the heat, and when we flare out, our delicious little Shetanna is going to burn them all down to the fucking ground in smoking ashes!"

Seeing that she had no choice, Naero and gave in. She laughed and danced, working with all six of the best dancers 36 had to offer.

"First you learn all of the basics and the current stomps over the next few weeks," Jonny told her. "Then we bring in our best gungirls to refine your steps, and all of your different acts and routines, and plans of attack.

Even costumes. Dancing is like combat, N. It's all attitude, and focus, and concentration. You size up your foes–execute–and proceed to take them down."

For hours Naero danced and flirted with the guys, laughing together and listening to them instruct her and give her attitude and crap. She had a great time learning from them all. They were actually great teachers.

Naero never had a clue that Spacer Marines were so into dancing. But they were all so hyper-competitive about everything else, she figured it only made sense.

By the time her first session was over, it wasn't just Acer. They were all madly in love with her and would do anything for her.

Naero hugged Jonny Fox and whispered into his ear. "Thanks Jonny. I never would have done anything this crazy-stupid on my own. Thank you, my brother."

"I know that," he flatly said with a wide smile.

17

Fathom-5 was a hot world, close to its star, used for smelting and forging. Lots of volcanic activity along its fault lines. A hostile and toxic atmosphere. As well as the mining and smelting operations onworld, there were numerous research labs, giving the world a population of about 2.5 million.

The Spacer Marines were not there to evac the population.

Bravo Command came to fight, to take the invader head on and beat them into the ground. Their goal was to exterminate the Ejjai and put the system back to work for the locals.

Because of the harsh environmental factors, all of the Marines and the MCLs were heavily shielded, with modified, hotworld battle armor. Or they could elect to use meks. Some Marines did so, knowing that in a pinch, they could evac the mek and still remain lightly armored and shielded.

The trade-off was that meks usually drew extra fire, from the enemy trying to take them out first.

While the Alliance and invader fleets fought up in the big black, Bravo and 36 came down in the role of being assigned to security details. Such ops usually meant protecting the remaining civies and neutralizing any enemy attackers who tried to come after them.

The invaders had similar protective tek, and were engaged in combat with around fifteen major gigacities and population centers. The slashers were backed up by the usual armor, arty, gunships, and factory meatships and the like.

Bravo had the available numbers and firepower, so they engaged all fifteen enemy positions at once.

With the Ejjai invaders being there mostly to process the local population into meatblocks, as usual, they weren't really very prepared to face significant military resistance of the elite variety.

The enemy had superior numbers on their side, and that was about it. Watching the Marines take the invaders apart was like watching an expert fighter chop and punch and kick her way through a gang of vicious thugs.

The thugs just kept coming, and the warrior kept taking them out.

This time, Bravo tried something new. The Marine units went in first and fully engaged the enemy. Then the MCLs were sent in last. They raced in cloaked and followed the directions of the field commanders as to where they should strike the enemy next. This way, the combat grid could process what had already been taken out in the initial assaults, and then send their favorite Mystic troublemakers in to exploit the biggest gaps and new weaknesses.

In one particular area, the invaders were using massed artillery batteries up close against the fighting, right inside the domes and smelting facilities. The sheer magnitude of firepower from these batteries was holding the Marines off, and wreaking destruction upon the locals.

Neither Bravo nor the Navy could go in and bomb them out, not without killing tens of thousands of civies in the process.

Then the enemy began rallying around that position, killing more locals as rapidly and efficiently as they could.

While those big guns kept blazing away in all directions at anything the Alliance tried to get going.

Shetanna ghosted her way in undetected, in an attempt to break the stalemate, crack the enemy positions open, and help decimate the foe.

Even as she attacked them, the enemy batteries kept up an intense barrage all about them.

A dozen Marine meks tried to drop in on the enemy. Ten of the twelve got slapped around hard and were driven back, forced to retreat behind the lines. Four Marines had to bail out and shield themselves as their damaged meks cooked off.

Messengers carried the wounded back to the dropships and field hospitals.

Captain Samson Konrad directed her through the enemy lines and positions over a secured link, in an effort to track down the battery fire control forces themselves. Yet, by then, there were thousands of Ejjai in that area, and more filling in as the slashers beefed up their positions.

Naero checked in on her link. "Sam, I could lop heads all day here and wear myself out quick, without making a dent by myself. I can't do this alone. We gotta try something else."

"You call it, N. Find a way to bust them up."

It was the massed big guns themselves that were the problem for the time being, not the troops operating and protecting them. The Ejjai could be dealt with later.

Time to take out those cannons directly.

The combat grid gave her priority targeting on 443 major batteries and gun emplacements.

Haisha, a regular walk in the goddam park for any creative MCL.

But she didn't have to take every single one of those big guns down all at once.

Shetanna went on a speed attack, and more or less ignored the invader troops, for the time being.

She extended the arcing, sizzling blades of her Chaos katanas before her, smiling her customary half-smile in battle, and buzzed among those big guns, not unlike an angry insect.

She also hurled scarlet lightning, explosive pods of unstable Cosmic energy, and ribbons of force that sliced and blasted their way through that forest of big, glowing barrels, several at a time. She lopped artillery barrels in half even as they attempted to keep firing.

Shetanna sent pods of explosive Chaos energy into the battery power cores and down the barrels and bores themselves.

The invaders filled the sky with every type of fire they could unleash, but usually, by the time they did so, Shetanna was already past those positions, and the secondary explosions were just starting to chain-react and take their toll.

Despite the fact that she remained cloaked as much as possible, the invaders simply wanted to fill the air with as much fire as possible, in the hopes of hitting her or anything else that might be up there.

The volume of fire and explosions behind her eventually caught up, and battered her around like a ball. Shetanna endured and kept at her objectives.

By the time she completed the arc of one pass, she had disabled or destroyed nearly one quarter of the massed artillery pieces, and that area was reduced to being a scorched wasteland. Explosions were still cooking off.

Om cut in at the same time that her sense of warning shot up off the charts.

N, get out of there!

Om...what–

No time. The enemy is filling the sky above them with airbursts.

At this range, the airbursts would inflict damage on the invaders as well, but they didn't give a damn about that. All they wanted was to take her out and halt her rampage.

The enemy used all of their remaining batteries, tanks, gunships, and ground forces to fill the sky overhead with showers of exploding ordnance, just as Om warned her.

She used her Cosmic energies to transport away from certain death at the last second, popping way over to the opposite end of the enemy's positions.

That was the key. Do what they least expected her to do.

They might expect for her to simply run for it. Shetanna stayed on the attack.

Speed, speed, speed. The enemy could only focus such concentrated airburst attacks in one small area. She simply had to keep moving and striking fast and hard in order to remain ahead of them.

Keep wearing them down.

But she was rapidly wearing herself down at the same time. Shetanna couldn't keep up such a pace forever.

The enemy did their best to lock in on her and intercept her with focused airbursts of firepower and explosives. If nothing else, they could track her by the damage she left behind.

Shetanna continued to just barely slip away, and then show up somewhere else and attack from there.

By the time she had reduced almost half of those massed big guns, she knew that she couldn't do much more.

Her warning sense shot up again. What now, Om?

Get the hell out of that entire area, N. The enemy have just uncloaked not one, but five atomic cosmicide devices. They are arming and preparing to detonate them!

163

Dammit, where are they, Om? Get our fixers on them. Paint them on the grid. Those atomics will take out the entire gigacity and half of Bravo and the Alliance forces with them!

That's probably their idea, N. Fixers en-route. I calculate that there's enough time to neutralize three of the five devices.

Naero got on the link with Captain Konrad. "Samson, come in, we've got a real problem here. I need help. Send in 36 with everything they've got. We must seize those devices before the enemy can detonate them!"

"I see them, N. 36 on the way. They should be right on top of you in seconds. We see the two remaining atomics that need to be taken out."

"Copy that. I'm going in."

Shetanna focused on cutting down the enemy teks and troops trying to activate the devices.

Two of the goddam things went live and armed. She was too late to avoid that part. Detonation was set for a few minutes away. The enemy was going to attempt to pull back.

Now invader troops swarmed on Shetanna, trying to take back the devices to activate the other three.

36 dropped in right on top of them at that moment.

Even in the midst of the intense firefight that erupted, picked teams of the Marines and teks ignored their own peril and attached gravlifts on the two live devices.

Fixers and I are jamming enemy attempts to set the devices off remotely, N.

Great work, Om. We still have to get these two out of here. We don't have time.

Naero encircled the floating devices in globes of Chaos energy and rocketed up into the sky, hauling them away from the battle zone.

Transport away from them, N.

Not yet, Om. I can't.

N, get us out of here!

Not…high enough…yet. Naero shrieked in agony. She was tearing herself apart to get the devices safely away.

Finally they reached fourteen kilometers up and still rising when the atomic cosmicide devices were seconds away from going off.

Om transported them back to the surface at the last instant.

Naero slammed into the ground, nearly unconscious, as the bright atomic airburst blinded the sky all above the gigacity, doing little damage.

It took Naero nearly two standard days to regenerate after that. Which brought them to another Secondday, and that meant Gear Night.

She and her mates spent the evening going over their rigs and various weapons, debating the latest mods and adaptations sent down by Spacer Intel's R&D weapons, armor, and shielding divisions.

There were new power cells that lasted hours longer. There was a hot new float-seeker smartmine with a radical new mini-AI command splinter.

Naero and Om were even amazed by them. "Haisha," Naero commented. "Talk about unleash and forget. These damn things could almost be turned loose to fight on their own."

Everyone present had the same epiphany all at once, and then spoke all together.

"Haisha, we can launch clouds of them from the ground attack ships."

"From drop pods on our suits!"

"From the fixer clouds!

"How hard would it be to cloak them?"

"Wait, what if the slashers figure out a way to turn them, and send them back at us? Remember what they did on that botworld."

Everyone got on the horn with Intel, shunting their various suggestions and ideas on how to best deploy the new smartmine devices.

After things calmed down and winded down later, Naero passed by Whip Konrad, wringing his red hands and going into his routine once more before the next mission.

"A dream. It was just a dream. But they say sometimes dreams come true. I dreamed the slashers knifed me in the back. That's how they're going to kill me. Knives in the back. I'll never see them coming."

"Konrad, you're an idiot. You gotta stop all of this shit."

Whip just shook his head and kept muttering to himself. "Knives in the dark. A knife in the back…"

Naero rolled her eyes and kept walking. If that goon wanted to waste his time being all crazy and sad sack like that. It was his own stupid choice.

A bunch of Marines didn't get enough of Chat Night on Fifthday, so they were bunched up in the vid room, sharing vids with each other, mostly of their kids or some trip they took on leave with a spouse or lover.

Luke Barrett just got himself hitched, to an extremely pretty girl named Thalia Kim, a fresh faced Navy ensign. Everyone was jealous and gave him crap about the honeymoon pics and vids–and how few there actually were.

Branton Taylor had sent himself as a holo to his wife Raiina Lii, and their little one-year-old boy Flynn. There was laughter and tears on both sides.

Maurice James broke down, mourning the fact that his three-year-old daughter Camilla, with his logistics wife Sarah Steiner, barely knew what he looked like. And his daughter had taken to calling one of her uncles 'daddy.' Everyone present tried to comfort Maury, and tell him it would be all right. In a handful of months, the war would end, and he would be back with them all.

Trevor Lakota laughed with his children as a holo, attempting to play and sing with them. Lakota did not normally laugh that much, and was very quiet and stoic. But laugh he did with his children. His wife Jenna was also of Clan Lakota, an engineer on a naval warship. Their children, Ronald, at two-and-a-half, and Elizabeth at age one were adorable, among the cutest infants Naero and many others had ever seen. It was clear how proud Trevor was of his family.

Then the vids ended, and he stopped smiling. His war face snapped back up. They were, in truth, still at war.

Trevor Lakota left his friends without a word to be alone with his private thoughts and feelings. All of the Marines had their own ways of dealing with their personal and private issues.

Naero left and heard deep sobbing coming from another area. d Fox, Bessa Jackson, and a bunch of the 36 gungirls were all huddled around Neesha Flynn. Flynn's Marine lover, Duncan Cherokee, had just been reported KIA. He died bravely during their latest action but his body had not been found and recovered until much later by the locals.

Duncan was dead an gone. Other Marines would give him a Spacer burial in the nearest star.

Neesha would never see him again, and she took the news very hard.

Each day during wartime brought so much joy and sorrow mixed together.

18

Delker-7 was the world where the shit finally hit the screws, in a temperate zone, during yet another joyous slugfest with superior invader numbers.

When the enemy attacked across multiple Marine positions, even threatening command and control, it was clear exactly what had occurred.

"All units. Our coms and command and control systems have all been hacked and compromised," HQ reported. "We don't know how they've done it, but the enemy has cracked our COMSYS and decoded all of our coms and can read our entire combat grid. For the near future we will be going blind and dark. So, all units be advised and act accordingly."

"Switch and dump all randomized, rotation shifting encryption algorithms and code batch sets," Naero suggested.

"That's a no go," HQ said. "We say again. They've somehow managed to crack our entire system, and all of its backups, ghosts, and shadows for the current SYSNET. They now own it, and we don't.

There's no other way to put it. We must go dark. All units on their own for a bit until we adjust, recover, and respond. Don't trust the coms and stay off them. All units will operate independently. Follow your commanders and your direct chains."

The combat grid that they had all come to rely on suddenly winked out and went completely dark. HQ and Command were intentionally jamming everything and shutting it all down until they had a solution.

Naero spoke with Om. How could such a thing happen, Om?

I can't say, N. I think we're looking at more evidence of highly advanced alien assistance here. Once again, the Ejjai clones are just lackeys, shock troops, cannon fodder–they do not even have the aptitude for this level of sophistication. Nor do they have anything close to the tek that would be needed to crack our system open like this–like so many eggs. And the enemy has managed to do so in less than a month. Scary, as you would say.

Yeah, it sure stinks, Om. This has alien overlords written all over it.

Bravo kept fighting and went where the fighting was hottest–directed by observation and instinct. They took down gravtanks and gunships. They fought the invaders day and night in the city streets and airways of the domes of another Corps gigacity where sometimes, the isolated locals still fired upon them just as readily as they did the Ejjai.

To the terrified minds of the landers, Spacers might be just as bad and bloodthirsty as the other invaders.

Yet without the Alliance's superior coms network and the all-knowing, all-seeing combat grid, the Ejjai were free to play a lot more tricks on them and jerk them around.

The Ejjai were masters at using humans as decoys, and had sadly even managed to brainwash and train thousands of Corps men, women, and children of all ages. These dupes, selected from several races, were broken and trained to do whatever the invaders told them to do, without question.

The fear of horrible death at the hands of the enemy or the blades of the meatships made many normal civilians pliable and willing to help the invaders–anything in order to stay alive, or keep their families or loved ones alive.

These dupes, brainwashed from the sentient races, helped lure the Marines and other Alliance and local defenders into many traps and ambushes.

Bravo called them puppets. Many of these puppets were terrific actors, and could be very convincing.

The situation grew so bad that whenever the locals pleaded for help, by default, Bravo had to start assuming that they were being played and drawn into another trap by more of such puppets.

Shetanna often played spoiler, and would sneak ahead, cloaked in her stealth armor, to check things out first.

She would spring, ruin, and otherwise expose such traps for her Marines to pounce on and wipe out.

The enemy puppets were trained to fear the Ejjai more than anything else, and do their bidding. They willingly lured other defenders into the enemy's firetraps and ambushes.

Once, Shetanna was moving up after another firefight, attached to Squad 2 under Staff Sergeant Owen Valmont.

Several pockets of heavy fighting were erupting within range. They merely had to pick one to join up with.

Out of the black, a new Bravo Marine joined them from another unit, a young woman with Cherokee tribal war paint and battle markings on her combat armor.

Tribal Clan markings or paint were optional in the Marines. Some Spacers used them. Some didn't. It was a personal choice.

Waylon Aztec in Fireteam 1 had his suit decked out like an ancient leopard warrior.

There were entire Bravo and other Marine units that were composed completely of all members from one tribal Clan. Or, such native Clan members could be scattered among the units as many were, all among of the other forces.

Generally, all Marines were free to customize the paint on their rigs, as long as the spolymers, decorations, and even holos did not affect function.

"I'm Corporal Meko Cherokee," the newcomer said. "My brothers and sisters and I are filtering into all of the units among the frontlines. We're here to assist taking our basic com and scanning system back from the slashers."

Sergeant Valmont nodded. "Welcome, Corporal. But just how in the hell is that going to work? The invaders have our system completely broken down into pieces. Completely cracked and wide open. If we try to use it, they know where we are, and they know everything we are trying to do."

Meko Cherokee smiled. She paused and spoke some kind of battle code language into her helmet link.

"That's already changing as we speak, Sarge. We're using something the enemy never expected, has any experience with, or knowledge of. We're using coded Cherokee battle language, on all new flux algorithms filtered through the fixernet. It's completely off the grid– never has been a part of Spacer Naval and Marine encryption systems.

"Trust us. The slashers are stumped. They have no frame of reference to even start with. They're tearing out their fur trying to figure out what's going on and what's being said. It's giving them fits."

"Outstanding," Naero said. "Thanks, Clan Cherokee. Your Clan has really came through for us on this one."

Corporal Cherokee saluted Naero in the confines of the hidden bunker, noting suddenly that she was an MCL. "Thank you, sir. What's your current sitrep? Once we get everyone linked back up with Command, we can coordinate and keep forging ahead."

"Valmont can tell you. He's running Squad 2. I'm just along for the fun. Sergeant?"

"Our original plan was to link up with the two forward platoons ahead of us on her two o'clock, on the right flank. From there we would assist assaulting the enemy's forward gun emplacements and clear a path for a mek unit penetration drive on to the troop ships still unloading more invader forces."

"All right. Let me link up and coordinate that with HQ. They'll advise us how to proceed."

Meko spoke rapidly into her modified helmet away. She exchanged info back and forth, answering questions for a few minutes.

An enemy artillery barrage walked in to the left and front of them on the enemy's own positions, less than one hundred meters away.

Meko smiled again. "The slashers think they're pounding us with that slop."

Cherokee listened a minute longer to the orders coming down. "Sergeant, proceed to these coordinates and prepare a six wave grenade and rocket attack on these enemy elements. All other Marine units not directly involved are pulling back to regroup, leaving decoy holos behind."

In the resulting confusion, Alliance arty fell right on top of 36. Felix Blooding in Squad 3 took a direct hit and was vaporized.

Meko got on the links and called off the barrage before they all died.

Suddenly the enemy positions up front vanished in a massive wall of fire that was blinding even in daylight.

"What the hell was that?" Shetanna demanded.

Om jumped in. *The enemy had rings of cloaked space mines concealed among their forward positions, waiting for us to overwhelm them and trigger those traps.*

Meko started explaining the same thing a few seconds later. "Luckily, we pulled most of our people back right before they detonated. Now push the attack forward. Those mines are all gone."

The enemy was willing to blow up their own units in order to cause more Marine casualties.

Bravo maneuvered under the cover of the dust clouds raised by those mines and large explosions and used advanced optics and scanners to pinpoint the enemy and put them down.

Meko and the Cherokee code talkers helped put the defenders and the Alliance back on top, and secure Delker-7 with much decreased confusion and loss of life for everyone.

Everyone but the bewildered invaders.

36 brought in what little they could find and retrieve of Felix Blooding. Mostly just melted fragments of his combat armor. But at least it was something–some part of him to put into his casualty bag along with an empty parts suit of his armor. They always tried to included pieces of broken weapons from the vanquished foes that had been put down, as trophies to the dead Marine's valor.

They marched Felix's remains in and said the right and proper words for him, as it should be. His mates mourned his loss. Yet another of their fellow ghosts would no longer fight directly beside them in the black.

Two days later at Blooding's wake, anyone who was from Clan Cherokee was also praised as a hero on what just happened to be Sixthday and Binge Night.

As a general rule, most of the native clans did not drink or get drunk out of personal choice and preference. But they feasted, and laughed, and danced and sang with the best of them, and celebrated another hard-won Bravo victory all the same. And their special role in that triumph.

Naero had great respect for the native, or tribal Clans, as they sometimes called themselves. And many of them respected her, her warrior parents, and her Clan. She loved sparring with them. She could never resist a sparring match with her native Clan friends, especially with their love of knife fighting, which matched her own to the point of both art and obsession.

She would sit among them at times, as they spoke about their ways and Clan customs which had evolved along with them as Spacers. Naero's family and her Clan had no links to the native Clans, and so the tribal Clan ways were exotic and fascinating to her mind. She had always been interested in other cultures and peoples. Just like her explorer parents.

Those who were worthy of respect should be given it. The native Clans who had survived for more than six centuries were a big part of the traditions and social variety that was scattered among the Forty-nine Free Spacer Clans as a whole. They had proven themselves time and time again as warriors, brothers and sisters of wisdom, and superb friends and allies.

The honor which they possessed was beyond question, and stood as a noble example to all the Clans, and to the enduring spirit all free peoples everywhere.

19

Tolon-10 was a winter world of cold, snow, and ice–even at the equator. The poles on that world were so cold as to be uninhabitable. The planet's population of only three hundred million miners and research developers were scattered across the equator and the tropics in shielded domes that were just ripe for invader picking, not unlike eggs in an open nest or low-hanging fruit.

By the time Bravo arrived onworld, late to the scene, half of the mostly Pietto population was already dead and processed–just frozen blocks of meat in storage on the enemy meatships.

The other half of the population remained under siege, holed up in a handful of mountain fortresses of stone, ice, and snow at the edges of the tropics.

Those mountains were littered with hundreds of thousands of frozen, dead civilians: Piettos, humans, and Ejjai.

Many of them were locked in eternal combat now. Others had simply been overcome by the harsh elements and their failed, emergency environment suits. A simple, crack, rent, or hole in such flimsy Corps suits could spell frozen death to the wearer in a matter of minutes under wartime flight and combat conditions.

Such emergency or rescue suits were never designed for long term use or combat.

With the fighting remaining fierce and constant, the invaders had not had time to collect all of those frozen bodies.

Bravo Command jumped down to punch through the enemy deathring blockade and relieve the defenders at last.

Down below, the bulk of the Marines were already slugging it out and degrading the enemy massed battle units.

Up above, the Ejjai kept up their assaults on the defenders, fighting and killing as quickly and as efficiently as could be done, no matter how the battle turned out below and on those mountains.

Shetanna and Company 36 were the lead elements of five hundred Spacer Marines–just one of several relief units being sent in to crack the siege and break through to the defenders.

They started by smashing into the attackers along a stretch of key supply lines leading up from base camp to base camp, all the way up to the front battle lines of the mountain siege.

Once they hit the enemy hard and caused confusion, they began their campaign to trounce the enemy combat lines, systematically destroying invader ships and vehicles.

Shetanna ripped into any sticking points that 36 got hung up on with the enemy, from the top down.

She had her work cut out for her. Scarlet blazing katanas hissed and crackled in the near-blinding snow. She took out officers, troops, gunship pilots, and tank commanders.

Several thousand Ejjai reinforcements swept up the mountainside, weapons flaring.

Bravo was already barely holding the mountain.

Shetanna called the next op. "Everyone up and out on my mark. Get ready to move. Mark! Tell the defenders to button up."

Tentacles of Chaos energy lashed out, crisscrossing the mountain and the advancing enemies in an energy net.

Then Naero hit the mountain rock and snow shelves with more than half of her ordnance.

And a tremendous blast of explosive Cosmic lightning.

The Ejjai shrieked as the massive resulting avalanche swept them off the face of the mountain and the planet.

The remainder of the enemy attempted to make a run for it.

Bravo and Shetanna were already waiting for them by then.

A little mop-up near the top. Then, it took hours to convince the locals that the fighting was actually over, and that they could come down.

After so much loss, their world was finally secure once more.

The next Fourthday and the accompanying Book Night had Naero feeling a bit edgy and uncomfortable. She had picked out a steamy romance, with Chime's help of course. But the steamy parts proved a little too suggestive and invigorating to Naero's mind.

There was always a deep part of her that was incredibly lonely, and felt the intense need for love and everything that came with that.

But she sighed. Would she ever find a man—a lover who was her equal? Who was all that she could wish for?

And like her parents, they could stand beside each other and face and fight whatever came at them. Together.

Would she ever know such a love?

Naero sighed very deeply. He certainly wasn't going to be found between the pages of some soft-core, nearporn bodice ripper, however cleverly penned by the author.

She couldn't read anymore without having to face down the strong urge to go take an embarrassingly long mist shower, as many of the Marines did. And she wasn't about to take a tumble with goons like Acer or Decker, who just lived to bang the lonely and the troubled into meaningless, empty release.

Goddam it. She wanted to be loved. Like what her parents had for each other. Naero wanted that at times more than she wanted to keep breathing. Nothing else was even going to come close for her. And she wasn't ready to settle for anything less.

Naero loved her Marines, but just not in that sensual way. She liked a lot of them very much and had great respect for them. But even men like Lakota and Jonny were more like her brothers—not potential lovers. There was no attraction there. No spark.

Naero wondered deep within herself when she would ever meet a man that she would feel that fire for.

She found Chime later with two bottles of cold Spacer Poteen sweating next to her, as the booknut just finished what she called a rousing medieval style fantasy novel, part of one of her favorite series. It had been written nearly six centuries before, by an ancient Earth author.

Naero returned her book to the plascrate and nodded at the Spacer poteen bottles. Another of their friends, Peter Cooper, came along, eager to get that exact book in the same series. Chime went on for a time about how much he was going to enjoy it, without giving any spoilers.

"What's the booze for, Chime?" Naero asked, when Pete was gone.

Chime grinned and licked her lips. "For you and me, babycakes. I decided on no sex for me tonight. So I was waiting for you to come around. Sit and get plastered with me. I'll guzzle mine. You guzzle yours. Deal?"

Suddenly, Naero felt an intense kinship with her looney friend.

They proceeded to do just what Chime had suggested.

"N, what's wrong with me?"

"You're mental, Chime."

"I know, I know. Batshit loopy. But I'm fun. I'm funny…fricking hysterical. Not a bad looker. I clean up well. And I'm pretty good in the sack…I think. Although I don't get much practice at that, with these dumb apes. Why can't I find some guy to worship me as the goddess I am? That's all I ask for. Is that too much?"

Naero giggled and finished her bottle first.

Chime bent her pretty brown eyes and glared at her. "You're not supposed to laugh, actually. This's the part where you're supposed to be supportive, dammit. Say something like: 'Sure thing, Chime. You deserve some good looking stud to worship you and love you until you both pass out. Sure thing.'"

"You'll find him, Chime. You'll find all of that and more."

"Great. I knew I would. So what the hell's taking that jerk so long?"

Chime polished her bottle off and then promptly fell asleep, looking radiant as usual and snoring in Naero's lap.

A while later, when she recovered enough to be able to walk herself, Naero put her friend to bed, and turned in herself.

Yet Naero could tell, as she looked around at 36. All of their world hopping was starting to get to them all, and break them all down.

20

Naero had never seen the Ejjai fight so fiercely.

Company 36 moved in on the Marchant-4 main starport, in the capital gigacity of Tharis. The Marines quickly captured four starliners, disrupting their power cores with new Intel disrupting charges specifically designed for zapping and temporarily disabling enemy ships and securing Alliance vessels that the foe attempted to utilize.

Around the gigacity capital itself, Bravo Command performed a perfect encirclement and containment strategy, moving and maneuvering leaping units in precise, lightning-fast ops. They popped and dropped slasher units left and right on the way in, carving the invader up and consuming the pieces.

Fixers took out most of the demo charges and booby traps on the starliners.

They also neutralized an additional nerve gas cosmicide device, with Om's assistance via Naero.

Shetanna trashed a squad of enemy gravtanks as they swiveled their turret guns to fire upon the vulnerable starliners.

What the hell was inside of those vessels that the enemy was protecting so fiercely?

She and the Bravo boarding teams raided the first liner they came to up close.

Shetanna transported into the bridge cockpits, cutting down the Ejjai crew. Even as the enemy tried to activate grenades and fusion charges. She sliced through their wrists firsts, if she had to. When that crew was dead, she popped over to the next two cockpits and did the same thing.

In the fourth, she was a second too slow.

She fled as the fourth starliner cockpit exploded and cooked off.

On all four rescued starliners, Marines popped out the inflating nanoslides and started tossing stunned kids out and down to the tarmac.

Om warned her. *N, that last starliner with the burning cockpit is going to go nova in less than three minutes.*

"Bravo!" Shetanna commanded. "Speed things up. Get your asses out of there. That last liner is going to blow."

Sergeant Maria Bucci answered back. "We can't, N. The whole ship is stuffed full of stunned kids–thousands of them. Foam sprayers are on the way to suppress the fires."

"There isn't enough time, Maria," Naero said. "I'm on my way; I'm returning to assist."

Shetanna needed to come up with some kind of solution.

She floated above the burning liner. The flames spread rapidly.

First she sheared off the entire front burning section with a Cosmic slicing wave.

That took a lot of Cosmic juice, but if that part blew up, it could still take out the rest of the starliner and maybe even damage the others.

Om, please, dig deep. Help me place layered Cosmic blast shields all around the part that's about to blow. We've got to contain the explosion.

N, it's too late. We can't.

I don't want to hear it, Om. Help me! Just do it. Knock us out if you have to. There are four liners filled with kids and our Marines who are counting on us.

The blast ignited less than ten seconds later.

When Naero came to, everything around her seemed to be on fire. Chime Fox from Fireteam 3 dragged Naero's scorched and battered suit of combat armor with her still in it, out of immediate harm's way.

"I got you, N," Chime told her.

"The liners?"

"Scorched, but secure. Between your shields and the foam trucks, we just barely kept it all from going critical and from engulfing everything in this sector in flames and explosions."

Naero gulped in air.

"The fires will be out a few minutes," Chime said. "What do we do then?"

Naero shook her still-fuzzy head, and blinked. "What are you talking about, Chime?"

"These stunned kids. What the hell do we do with all of these stunned kids, in the middle of a frickin' battlefield? There are thousands of them."

Naero tried to clear her head and ponder that problem for a moment. "Have the fixers refit the remaining three starliners, enough to get them up and running. Fly 'em out. Get those kids the hell away from here."

Chime protested. "But we just disabled them all to get the enemy from getting away with them!"

"The fixers can do it."

N, actually, only the first two of them are flyable. That leaves 4,631 kids age seven to eight months in imminent danger.

Naero checked the combat grid. Om was right. Incoming enemy attacks. Ground assault ships and gravtanks waves inbound.

The starliners were sitting ducks for the enemy to fire upon and destroy on sight. Naero had no doubts about that.

Om, how many Marines do we have on hand in this forward area?

Around six thousand, N.

She spoke out lout. "Get with HQ. We can do this fast. Line up the Marines. Get the two fixable ships the hell out of here. Then, on the damaged ships, each Marine grabs and carries one kid. Strap them on, use slings–haisha–use glue if we have to. But we're getting out, and we're taking those helpless kids with us, even if we have to fight our way out."

Chime called back. "Major Luna has confirmed the op and shift in objective. We grab the kids and race toward these coordinates to a safe zone."

"What's there, Chime?"

"A secure staging area for evac refugees. There are about twenty thousand civies there, waiting for a ride out of here. They've agreed to help care for the kids if we can get them there safely."

"Tell them to be waiting," Naero said. She pulled her pulse carbine off her back where it waited. She locked and loaded.

She might be out of Cosmic juice for the day, but she could still fight.

All the while, the Marines filed into and out of the ruined starliners to grab kids and secure them. The two rigged starliners that could fly were already limping away into the sky, in the opposite direction of the fighting.

The remaining Marine force deployed layers of float-seeker mines and prepared a rear guard action to delay the advancing invaders and buy the bulk of the Bravo forces time to get away with their new charges.

Marine and naval starfighters came down to harass the enemy's close assault ships rumbling in. The enemy was backed up by invader armor and reinforcements.

"Shields up! Let's move," Shetanna commanded.

The rear guard barely held.

Enemy skirmishers still managed to squirt through cracks and soon attacked both flanks.

Bravo fought their way out of the starport area, guns blazing.

Time and time again, Naero saw Spacer Marines cover their charges and take hits on their shields, on their armor, and even endure wounds, just to protect those kids.

The defenders used up their grenades and microbombs three times over, despite near constant replenishment by their fixers.

Just before they reached the designated safe area, the enemy tried to cut them off from the air with a gravwing assault.

Corporal Guy Kendall took a direct hit through his face shield and was killed instantly. Fireteam 2 towed his body and his charge in, with his mates still fighting.

Naero and most of 36 rose up, firing with precision, and shot the attackers out of the sky.

Bravo made it to the safe area and handed the stunned kids off to the waiting civies.

The Corps landers stared, hardly able to believe that the feared Spacer Marines–people they had been conditioned all of their lives to fear and hate–would sacrifice themselves and risk their lives just to rescue so many lander children, when they could have simply left them all to their fate.

Shetanna stood up, and spoke to the landers, telling them to be sure to remember that, and tell others of their people and all the worlds of the High Crusade what they had witnessed.

36 prepared and marched Guy Kendall's body into the halls of the honored dead. This was war, and Marines died. Everyone had to accept the fact that during any battle, at any time, it could just as easily be any of them. This led many to live life only for the moment.

They might very well die the next day.

On the following Seventhday, Naero had another dance night practice session, this time with the guys and the stomping gungirls of 36. With this being her fifth session, she was starting to get the hang of things. Dancing was a performance art, a competitive sport, just like anything else.

With much help, she was even coming up with moves of her own, but her dancing friends still had to tell her whether they worked or not. Some did. Some didn't.

After Vid Night the next day, Naero, Chime, and Jonny sat around with several other more philosophic Marines and yammered and argued about love, and what it meant to truly love another person.

Sara Maeris, a very distant cousin to Naero, if at all, spoke openly and freely about her depth of feeling her beloved, Aeden Taylor, a spacer tek in the Navy. She very clearly, simply, and eloquently stated what love was like for her.

Suki Lii spoke of the love she still felt for her deceased husband Garrett, and how much pain his loss caused her. But even more than a lover, Suki went on and on about the love of a parent, a mother. She expounded on the overwhelming depth of love that she felt for their two-year-old daughter, Brenda.

Keisha Aztec told them about the deep, appreciative love that she felt for her father, but not so much for her cold and distant mother. How she always regretted that. Now that she was married to her Marine husband Kevin, and she had a child of her own, a son named Omar who was a year-and-a-half, she was going to amend that in her life with her children. She wanted to be close to them.

Jonny Fox said that he didn't want to marry a Marine. One in the family was enough. "I just want her to be a cute little Spacer chick who's crazy about me. Maybe just a simple Spacer merchant girl, or a tek. Maybe even a medtek. Then she can heal me and make me all better when I do something stupid."

Naero laughed and couldn't resist. "She'd better get used to that with your dumb ass." Everyone laughed. Jonny's cousin Chime simply sat next to her cousin, hugging her knees and daydreaming off into space with a kooky smile on her face.

While the regular boneheads and horndogs just barged in and went on and on about straight up sex and the virtues of meaningless, monkey love.

21

Pulweii-11 was an archipelago water moon, with weird planetary electromagnetic effects that played havoc with tek, coms, and scanners. How convenient.

The place was practically an Ejjai invader's dream. Pockets of hundreds and thousand of helpless natives, human and Cumi, and Corps researchers scattered across a network of countless islands. Total population about one hundred million.

Ten invader battle groups scattered a hundred thousand Ejjai over the planetary surface, broken up into smaller, murderous bands of one to several hundred raiders and skirmishers.

The Marines and locals faced something else new—mini-meatships, which were much smaller, more numerous, and far easier to cloak. That made them much harder to track down and destroy than the full-sized vessels.

The mini-meatships were about the size of a regular, private merchant ship, cheap and relatively easy to mass-construct. One of these lesser processing plants could easily accompany each of the smaller invader raiding parties.

A new miniature menace.

For one of the first times during the High Crusade, Bravo units sent to Pulweii-11 found themselves outnumbering the invaders. That was a switch.

Yet because of the planetary EM effects, the advantage in numbers did not translate into the field. In fact, it did them little good in this situation. The Spacer Marines could not scan or locate the enemy in order to quickly wipe them out all at once or in a series of lightning fast ops.

They could resort to playing a cat-and-mouse waiting game. They could monitor the planet from orbit and responds to attacks with drop troops, but the enemy could often hit-and-run fast enough–melting away before the drop troops could fully engage them.

Another first. Bravo was stymied, stuck waiting for the invaders to attack and show themselves. The Ejjai could play lots of tricks on them and jerk them around.

Naero went to Om. Nothing's working, Om. We have to find a way to track down the invaders. We can't be everywhere at once in sufficient numbers to defeat attacks. Both sides are well aware of that.

I'm afraid it gets worse, N. Signs point to several cloneships and factory supply ships at work onworld. The enemy numbers are only going to increase, and they can feed off of the food stocks in the oceans for months and swell their numbers without ever attacking the humans on the islands, if they so choose.

We can't ferret out the slashers we have so far. More will only make things worse. We have to take out those cloneships and the equipment factories.

N, what about our fixers?

What about them, Om? We tried that. Fixer scans don't work on this moon any better than our regular scans.

No. What if we blanket the planet with fixers, creating an entire chainlink network of them? We can locate and track the enemy on real-time visuals alone, and then coordinate our efforts with the combat grid to take them down. They'll just be a grid extension in a mechanical, physical form.

Rely primarily on visual sightings? Sounds good, Om. How long would it take to cover the planet with linked fixers?

Fourteen days, three hours, twenty-seven–

No good, Om. Too long…unless that's our only option.

Then something else occurred to Naero. The moon's surface was effectively almost ninety percent hydrographics.

The exposed landmass of the various island systems were under eleven percent, in total.

Om, what if we blanketed just the island land masses in visually linked nets of observation and alarm fixers?

Less than two standard days.

Great. Get on it, Om. The invaders could be using submersibles in large numbers, or starships in those modes for short periods of time. Yet I'm still guessing that the bulk of their forces are hiding somewhere on land.

Naero brought up a holo map of the system from the sitrep and studied it again.

Once we can locate and track them visually and on a live basis, then we can begin to wipe them out, and pinpoint and predict where they are going to attack next. That will prove decisive.

Not only that. We can find out where their fleet ships are, including the cloneships, factory supply ships, and even the new smaller meatships.

Brilliant, Om. Prioritize the fixer network to cover the largest island networks first, and then work their way down the list. Bravo can start attacking the invaders as we locate them.

Yet that gave the enemy about a day and a half free rein to strike at will and kill and plunder, more or less unchecked.

Together, Naero and Om cooked up a response for that as well.

Naero went before HQ herself and explained the strategy to Major Luna and the Command Staff, using holo screens, simulations, and growing data feeds.

"Most of the random enemy attacks have still hit the larger islands and island network. The local population centers are the big draw, and there are still only so many of those. So by the numbers, there are only a finite number of places that they are most likely to hit. Those top locations are where we should concentrate our rapid response and drop forces."

Major Luna nodded in agreement. "Looks good, until the slashers figure out our game and try something else."

Naero was ready for such objections. "Yes, but this should help us for a day or two. That's all we need, because after that, our visual fixer net will blanket this system, locate the enemy bases, and hand them to us on a silver platter."

Luna grinned. "Outstanding. I like it. Let's get on this, people. Good work, Maeris. We'll purposely make it look as if we've spread our forces too thin across the planet, even using some holos and fake patrols over water."

Luna continued. "That's an invitation to be attacked. The invaders won't be able to resist what will appear to them to be a chance to hand us a major defeat."

Viho Cheyenne, the XO, chimed in before Naero could even jump back in. "They will attack for sure, eager to take us down along with the locals. Then we reveal our true strength, spring the trap, and split their chests and bellies open for the carrion eaters and the worms to feast upon!"

The HQ staff got quiet for a moment, staring at Viho.

"Haisha," Naero blurted out. "Damn straight. What the XO said!"

Captain Samson Konrad, third in command, was already gaming the combat hub and shooting out orders and logistics. "Got it. We bait the most likely traps, and then we keep rapid response forces cloaked at key points nearby, ready to respond to any attack. That provides better economy of force to threat ratios and probabilities. It will give us the best chance to respond to and defeat the invader over the next two days. We just have to hold out that long."

Naero brought them full circle. "Then the new fixernet will be up and online."

That first day, Bravo Command was able to intercept and destroy three main enemy attacks.

Five other enemy attacks still managed to hit and run and get away. But even they were cut short and interrupted by the new protocols and procedures put into place.

Four mini-meatships were destroyed. No clone or factory ships were located or taken out, as yet.

The next day went much better. Bravo foiled well over half of the stepped-up enemy attacks and crushed them outright. They took down several mini-meatships, one conventional meatship, and even destroyed three cloneships.

As predicted, as soon as the fixernet came online later that second day, it quickly became an even worse day for the invaders.

But even when exposed and trapped, the enemy never failed to fight to the death, and spend their lives trying to do as much damage to the civilian populations before they were cut down.

Bravo was more than willing to oblige with the cutting-them-down part.

By day three, the invaders were on the run, broken, and attempting to flee. Shetanna and the Marines were the masters of fear, and the invaders had finally had enough.

The Spacer Navy had a good deal of target practice as the remaining, panic-stricken Ejjai warships tried to scatter and escape.

Very few, if any, managed to do so.

When Bravo left that world behind, another Fifthday and Chat Night came up, the big topic of conversation was the end of the war, and how it might turn out.

At least now the end of the war could be imagined, and everyone began to speak about the aftermath of the High Crusade. What would happen to the Corps? How many of them would survive?

Who was really behind the Ejjai Invasion? When and where and how would these terrible new foes strike again? What were these new aliens like?

Speculation ran rampant.

But Naero, the officers present, and the non-coms reminded everyone to glacier down, and not get too ahead of themselves. The current war wasn't even over yet. By any estimates, there were still many worlds to rescue, and at least a few months of heavy fighting ahead of them. If their mysterious enemies didn't spring anything new on them in the meantime.

Mundane and personal matters always took over at some point each night.

Wallace Archer was very worried about the marital problems he was having with his wife, merchant Spacer Diana Taylor, and how it might affect their two-year-old daughter Vicky.

Falco Borelli and his wife, Stephana Wallace, were concerned with their one year old son, Trenton, since he fell and broke his arm. It was already healed, but the infant seemed to be holding back after his first painful injury, and didn't play with the abandon he had before. Many others advised them to give the little guy time. He would soon forget about the incident and go wild once again.

They came across Nick Kowalski, passed out in a corner and covered in his own sick, several empty Spacer Poteen bottles scattered and broken around him.

Chime knitted her brows in concern. "Nick was never a drinker before. Takes a lot to make a Spacer puke himself."

Jonny sighed. "C'mon, guys. Let's get him cleaned up and put him in his bunk. Nick's best friend was Chang-Han. Nick's been keeping to himself a lot since his buddy's death. We need to watch him and help him if we can. Try to bring him around."

Part of Naero suddenly worried if they were all like that in a war. At the very least a little damaged. War always changed people. Even after the war ended, no one could ever go back to who they were before. She knew that she couldn't. She'd always be different now. All of them would.

By the time they put Kowalski to bed, out of nowhere, some of the Marines began singing old Spacer songs. Songs that everyone knew. Songs their parents, grandparents, and greatgrans sang to them.

Other voices joined in. Naero joined in and sang right along with them. Soon everyone was belting out the old songs. When one song ended, they took up another.

This was their history. This was their mighty heritage and who they were–as a people. Spacers were singers, dreamers, explorers, warrior poets, and philosopher queens and kings.

Then at one point the Marines took up a new song that had been around for a few months on the webnets and dumptune stations.

Naero herself had heard the song a few times, although she did not know all of the words.

She learned them as her mates sang them to her. As she wept with joy, and sorrow, and open pride before her sisters and brothers. They honored her, her blood, and her Clan as everyone sang:

The Ballad of the Omaria.

22

Shetanna and Company 36 drew the lot to be the final mop-up team to prepare to depart from earthlike Vantar-5.

That system had had a very rough time. Their initial population of eight billion, mostly Moh-Karran, was now down to only two billion left, after months of heavy warfare.

The Spacer Navy and Bravo had carpet bombed nearly entire continents that had almost been completely controlled by the invaders. They were festering with factory cloneships, meatships, and equipment factoryships.

The enemy had even sent out several more invader battle groups to join the attack on other nearby systems. The remainder of the shattered lander population basically hid and pulled back in shock, over the course of a handful of days, while the Spacer forces took over.

On this mission, Naero passed by Whip Konrad and heard him muttering about head shots. That was how the enemy was going to get him. Just a clean shot to the head. Pow! Done.

Naero shook her head at that loon, but it did seem to work. He worried and fussed so much, but nothing hardily ever happened to him.

And once the fighting began, Whip fought as well as any other devil dog. He never hesitated or held back.

Like everyone said, that was just his crazy ass process.

Fresh to the fight, the Spacers eradicated and hunted down the entrenched invaders, who up until that time had considered themselves more or less victorious.

Then the Spacer forces moved on to the next world in the system hopping plan.

Company 36 was about to depart as well.

Then the strike cruiser, *The Tiberion*, that they were then attached to had a major jump drive failure. Not wanting to risk a misjump, *The Tiberion* set down in the gigacity of Vantar, at the main starport to affect repairs. Estimates ranged at one or two extra days.

When three new invader battle groups suddenly attacked at random, out of nowhere. That changed everything.

They shouldn't even be there still, and now they had to find a way to hold out until other Alliance forces could either reverse course and return, or fresh forces could arrive to help.

The first thing the enemy did was destroy *The Tiberion*, the only Spacer warship that they could find, while it was still docked for repairs.

Fewer than seven hundred Spacers and Spacer Marines were on the run, in their dropships and other assorted starfighters, transport craft, and vehicles. They faced more than thirty-thousand enemy troops landing onworld to come at them and begin the invasion all over again.

Company 36 had all the gear and supplies they could salvage from *The Tiberion*. They also had a small fixer cloud and did all that they could to expand it at short notice.

They mustered twenty thousand support troops from the battered landers, who were thus far poorly armed and led. But at least they were additional numbers.

Even as the defenders attempted to flee and hide, in order to regroup, they still came under attack. Many things started to go wrong. The Spacer Marines were too few and spread too thin to properly support the slower moving local forces. From the very outset, their hard-pressed defenses and all of the helpless civilian areas now re-exposed quickly began to collapse.

Help would still not reach them, at best, for almost a standard day.

And a standard day outnumbered by the Ejjai invaders could be a either a very long, or an abruptly short time during the war

Bravo Command ordered them to do their best, and if possible, to find an optimal place to make a defensive stand and hold their positions until relieved.

The first thing Naero and Om did was nail the invader fleets and landing craft in the distance with a surprise attack of makeshift atomics, while the overconfident slashers were still taking their lazy time unloading their gunships and gravtanks.

That reduced the odds somewhat.

Bravo and the defenders hid behind layers of unit shielding and slugged it out against sortie after sortie of enemy attacks upon their positions. The fixers were taxed in their monumental efforts to maintain and replace the shield devices repeatedly going down, and scrounge for weapons, ordnance, and explosives of any kind from the battlefield to hold the enemy off.

Naero had to hand it to the locals. They knew what was at stake, after all that they had gone through. A few more volunteers trickled in to pick up weapons from the fallen, but they only slipped in a few hundred at a time.

The defenders fought and sacrificed bravely as the situation remained grave.

Then something very strange happened.

A bright green glow appeared in the sky off in the distance, and according to the long-range scans of their fixers, something, or some powerful force over that way was drawing off the enemy in large numbers, and attacking and destroying them with impunity.

Then a similar red glow appeared in the sky on the right rear flank of the enemy, and the fixers reported the same thing. The invaders faced some other kind of unstoppable force or forces and were being devastated.

These new threats the enemy faced took some of the heat off of Bravo and the locals, giving them a much needed breather.

Shetanna led a stealth platoon out to scan the enemy lines. They took over a small force of enemy gravtanks and attacked the enemy lines in sweeps. Then they brought the captured, modified tanks back to their own lines, to dig some of them in and use that armor and additional firepower to hold the enemy off for three more crucial hours.

In the end, the enemy finally managed to knock out all of those captured gravtanks.

More fresh enemy gravtanks poured in. Bravo took them out with the last of their pulse cannons, float-seeker smartmines, and autoguns. Most of their Marine meks were already destroyed by that time.

Waves of Ejjai shock troops increased their attacks, sensing weakness. The weary defenders gunned them down with small arms and hurled them back again and again with grenades and microbombs.

Yet all the while, the constant fighting also slowly wore away at the defenders.

Naero and 36 led a final sortie under cover of their last shield pod, to gather weapons and gear from the heaps of enemy dead. The fixers also helped collect the gear and distribute it among the remaining defenders, less than a thousand in all.

These were all the weapons they had left to make their final stand.

They immediately came under heavy fire. Their last shield pod went down as they retreated back behind their reinforced defensive positions.

Spacer Marine snipers maintained a steady, withering, lethal fire against any troops who showed themselves, in or out of vehicles and armor.

The defenders retreated further within their tiers of defensive positions as the invaders pounded them with artillery and tank fire.

As soon as the artillery barrage let up, the invader wave attacks swept in once more.

Firefight after firefight erupted, waxing and waning, blazing back and forth.

Then the slashers unleashed another tank and artillery barrage, right in the middle of yet another infantry assault and firefight. They didn't care if they cut down their own troops, as long as they could blast the defenders to dust at the same time.

Naero could hold back no longer. If she did not act now, they would be swept away. She had been conserving the last of her Cosmic energies and abilities for the final need.

This was it.

At least they had the enemy whittled down to the point where she could make a difference.

In the confusion, she slipped out, cloaked, with a single cloaked fireteam.

They hit the enemy artillery batteries and tank emplacements with all of their remaining explosives and everything they could muster. They took out as much as they could as fast as they could in the enemy's rear where it was least expected. That would buy them some more time, until the enemy could bring up more big guns.

They ravaged the enemy's rear areas on the way back, doing what damage they could.

At last the enemy cut them off and completely surrounded them.

A squadron of enemy gunships dropped down at the worst possible time to pour concentrated fire directly into all of the defensive positions, while more Ejjai shock troops charged in up close.

Shetanna and her fireteam rose up on their gravwings and attacked the gunships directly. They quickly damaged each of the enemy ships, crashing seven of the craft down into the packed enemy troops and exploding them. Three of the last five gunships turned and limped away, heavily damaged.

The final two gunships the Marines took over, and pulled back behind the defensive positions and trained those guns on the fresh waves of invaders.

A massive, all-out assault of countless foes swarmed on the final defenders.

Shetanna charged out with her Marine backup, cutting the enemy down and blasting them back with Chaos power lightning blasts, detonations, direct fire, and grenades. She speared the Ejjai on rods of Chaos energy and cut them down with wheeling sweeps of Chaos force and gouts of flame and blast effects.

Baeven's voice, of all things, suddenly roared over Naero's secured link. "Hold on, Naero. You and your people hang on, any way you can! Gaviok and I have done every thing we can on your flanks. More Marines have dropped in and are advancing on your position. Just stay alive, damn it!"

So that was what those strange lights had been in the darkness the night before. Baeven, Gaviok, and his strange crew had come to assist, and had done their best to aid them.

"Hold on," Naero shouted to everyone. "Help is minutes away. Keep fighting Marines. Everyone fight to stay alive!"

She employed every trick that she could think of, burning through her arsenal. Every defender and Marine who could keep firing made every shot count. They kept shooting and backed her up.

Still the enemy pushed them back, by sheer numbers and ferocity, trying to drag them down.

They were fighting hand-to-hand with the foe when the first relief force struck, and dropped down among them to startle the soon-to-be-dead invaders.

Naero and her most of her people collapsed. They had plenty of wounded, but no KIA, amazingly enough.

Within the hour, the final enemy forces were crushed at last.

36 would *not* be the final mop-up unit next time.

Naero ducked away just long enough to send out a special thank you to her outcast uncle Baeven, Gaviok, and the rest.

How her uncle always seemed to know when she was in deep trouble still amazed her, but she was more than glad that he was out there, keeping tabs on and looking after her.

Back on the 36 dropship, Naero also made a point of checking on Whip Konrad.

Again. Not a damn scratch.

His insanity seemed to work, at least for him.

Anyone could call up the charts and see in general how the war was progressing through the invaded system and along the broad arc of fire in the hot zones. But most frontline troops still focused only on their chunk of that front. The Alliance continued to advance. It was more or less a meatgrinder of attrition now. As long as they could keep going, each day brought them closer to victory.

Thankfully, they had avoided a point of no return with the invader numbers. But for the first few weeks and months of the war, that had been a very real and serious concern.

Fourthday and another Book Night had the Marines reading their selections and floating around once more in zero-G.

Their buddy Pete was laid up with the wounded. Chime and some others took some books to them all and even offered to read to them in shifts, while they recovered.

Naero stayed behind this time and read some poetry and some comix, but she just didn't feel much like reading.

Her and Jonny Fox sat around sucking down Jett and gobbling up paks of Spum. Nearby, Ted Kim bragged about how smart his daughter Nikki was at two-and-a-half. His wife, musician Rena Young already had their infant little girl playing the thiolin.

Zina Gordon had just returned from a leave with her husband, Loader-Chief Lawrence Donovan and their one-year-old son Darren.

Naero turned to Jonny. "Do you want kids some day, Jonny? I might at some point, but I think I might need to find a guy first."

Jonny yawned. "That usually works out best. But if I get married, I want either two kids…or four. You see, I think it's better if you have them in even numbers."

Naero laughed and almost blew Jett out of her nose. "That's batshit crazy, you moronic goof. Even numbers? What the hell does that have to do with anything?"

They laughed together.

"Well, I'm old fashioned," Jonny said. "I want to take whatever we get by chance, and not know ahead of time. But I also want at least one girl, and one boy. One of each."

Naero flapped her lips and gave him a raspberry. "With your stupid luck, you'll probably get stuck with four boys, or four girls. Why risk that? Trust me. Let the docs help you out. It's easy these days."

"I'm serious, N. That's just not my way."

"Get a brain, Jonny. So, what do you want these two-to-four kids to do with their lives? Wash or load ships in some backwater starport?"

"Oh, I don't care very much what they choose to do–as long as they're Spacers and happy. I'm not going to push them into anything."

Naero stared at him. "Well then…what if they want to become Marines?"

Jonny Fox sighed. "I mean what I said, N. I'm not going to push or prevent them. When they come of age, they'll make their choice. I'll love and support my kids in whatever they choose to do."

"That seems pretty fair."

He smiled and belched real loud. "I think so."

A big commotion broke out suddenly nearby.

Tavis Marshall and Luke Barrett both happened to be drunk and mean-dog ornery at the same time. In seconds they were fighting and trying to kill each other–for real. Luckily it was just hand-to-hand.

Naero and Jonny raced in, helped break it up, and separated the two idiots before they did any real damage.

The officers on duty came in and dressed both of the goofballs down, telling them to save it for the slashers.

23

Bravo's fleet ships were overdue for repair and refit in the fixer clouds, so they were sent back behind the lines to Naraden-6, for a few days of well-earned rest and leave.

It was spring on that world. Spring on an earthlike planet in all its verdant glory and exploding new life. Radiant sunny days, cool breezes, and warm rain showers.

The Marines of Company 36 were at a very low point. Several of them had wrestled down Nick Kowalski in Squad 3, Fireteam 2, when they had caught him trying to stick a blaster pistol in his mouth and pull the trigger the night before.

Suicide in the Spacer Marines was still extremely rare, but in the course of a long and bloody campaign, it did occasionally occur in various ways.

Since the death of his best buddy, Chang-Han, Nick had gone slowly off the deep end with grief and survivor guilt. In the end, he just couldn't shake it, and had to be subdued before he ate a bolt.

Kowalski had seen enough and done more than his share. Time for him to get some help and get out. Time for him to get himself healthy and do something else.

The High Crusade continued to drag on, heavy fighting from world to world. It might still go on for another month or three.

But sadly, it now felt to many of the Marines as if it might never end. And that was the real fear.

Everyone was already weary, frustrated, and sick of the constant cycle of system-hopping, intense fighting, and relentless killing. They were sick of the atrocities. Just plain sick of everything. Naero felt it as much as anyone.

To make matters worse, they had just left Gurian-4.

On that isolated Corps world, many of the locals had not been properly informed about the Spacers coming to help them. With invader jamming, it just wasn't possible. Landers went in with the Marines to help educate and inform on the fly, but in the chaos of war, the landers couldn't be everywhere.

At first, the already panic-stricken locals thought that the Spacers were trying to take the world for themselves. To their minds, Spacers only fought with the Ejjai because they were in the way and competing with them directly.

Before all of these wrong conclusions could be cleared up, many of the local forces had fired upon Bravo Command from the start, treating them like another enemy invader. They ignored all coms to the contrary. Hatred did not go away easily. Corps conditioning could be very hard to break.

For generations, the population of Gurian-4 had been brainwashed to fear and hate spacks. The Corps spoon-fed them about what would happen if the vicious spacks ever invaded their world.

In many remote areas, even after the Ejjai were put down and defeated, there were still many among the local populations who still didn't believe that the Spacers would actually ever go away, without subjugating the system for themselves or, at the very least–looting it in some fashion before they did depart.

Rumors and lies quickly spread. Hatred caused atrocities that had clearly been committed by Ejjai to be blamed on the spack Marines.

The old hatreds did not die easily and tensions ran high. Even as Bravo Command marched and loaded up to depart, mobs of enraged locals had repeatedly insulted, hurled garbage, shit, and even spit on the very warriors who had just saved them and their world from the Ejjai. It was a grim tragedy.

All of the Marines had been pissed off and infuriated at being treated that way. Razor Wilde, younger cousin to Anaconda and Python, cursed and pounded the hull of their dropship. "The rotten bastards. We just saved them and all of their kids and old people from the meatships! And there they had to spit and shit on us, and say good riddance, bloody spacks. Get the hell off our stinking world!"

Tempers continued to ignite. Luca Abraham jumped in fuming. "Yeah, they had the guts to spit on us? To fling shit in our faces? They'd all be meatblocks if it wasn't for what we did for them. They wouldn't have any goddam world left if it wasn't for us!"

Naero and the other officers let the Marines vent and hurl stuff around for a while. It was pretty tough to choke down.

Major Luna agreed that 36 needed a break, and they were long overdue for one. When she explained the situation to General Walker, he also agreed with her.

Their ships changed course, heading for Naraden-6.

By the time they jumped there, at least the sullen Marines weren't ready to bite heads off and chew them up.

As they came down into the enormous starport, Naero ordered the blast panels on the transport opened up.

Brilliant sunlight poured through the large, plasteel viewports.

As they came down, 36 looked out, seeing peaceful meadows and grassland fields surrounding countless luxury hotels.

Naraden-6 had been a playworld, a vacation retreat world. But because of its proximity to many of the worlds that had been invaded by the Ejjai, it was quickly appropriated and transformed into a hospital world, a place for recovery, for refugees, and for shore leave for burned out troops.

Naero asked her Marines a question. "Do you goons know what Naraden-6 is famous for?"

Everyone just stared at her.

She answered her own question for them. "Many of the orphan and refugee children, rescued from many war zones, have been brought here to be kept safe until they can be sorted out and sent home once the war ends. Many of them will need new homes, but that can be sorted out later.

"For now, the weather here is stable and mild, and the local population is nurturing and supportive. Many healers, doctors, and caregivers have flocked here from many worlds to assist with that great task. If you are an orphan child from this war–after all of the hell that you've been through and survived–Naraden-6 might just be the closest thing to heaven that you could ever find. I think it's going to prove to be a pretty good place for troops to relax, also."

Josh Elkins threw his pack down hard. "So, what? What's your point, N?"

Platoons 1-4 stared at her.

She looked back at all of them. "My point is this. Do all of you trust me?"

They blinked and didn't know what to say to that.

"Do all of you trust me?" she asked once more.

Most of them finally nodded. A few of them looked pretty sad. Some of them muttered, "Uh-huh."

Naero called out to them louder. "Company 36. I am asking each and every one of you again. Do you trust me?"

First Leftenant Josie Stone spoke up. "N, we trust you with our lives, Naero. You know that."

Naero smiled sadly. "Then trust me now, and please, let me do something for all of my Marines. For my brothers and sisters. Please, follow my lead."

She shook off all of her armor and weapons, and let them fall to the floor.

Company 36 did the same.

Naero stripped right down to her Nytex flight togs, feeling suddenly free and relieved of all of her burdens for the first time in a very long while.

Her Bravo Marines went down to their togs.

"Form a gauntlet, on either side of me," she said.

In short order, two hundred Marines stood at ease, a hundred to either side of her.

Naero went among them on her right and left. To their surprise, she took their faces in her hands and she kissed each one of them, on the cheek, on the brow, sometimes on the nose. All of them remained quiet, silent, smiling back and forth at one another as Naero progressed among them, showing her deep affection for them all. No one was in a hurry for her to reach the end.

When she did so, Naero laughed.

Many of them were so damn tall, that she had to use her gravwing to reach their faces. "Haisha," she exclaimed suddenly. "Like I goof, I forgot something. Everyone put your gravwings on. Don't ask why. Just do it."

Others started to crack up and chuckle, but they were all still under her spell, and did exactly as she said.

Now, Om!

Om triggered the fixers behind each of the Marines.

Naero's presets transformed their nanotogs into soft, white, loose clothing, sized to each of them. Even their gravwings turned white. Hers were no exception.

"Bravo 36, you have been my angels of death in the darkness. Yet even more than that, you have also been angels of life. You have fought the High Crusade to save all of humanity–Spacer and lander–by your valor and your mighty sacrifice. On my own accord, I have sent word ahead of our arrival to the leaders of Naraden-6.

"All the people of this world, and the many refugees who have been brought here, have been informed about who we are and all that we have accomplished. You will forever shine as my heroes, Bravo 36. And you shall always be theirs as well. Now, follow me, 36. Follow me out of the darkness, and back into the light!"

Naero lifted off and the jump bays opened, washing out the darkness in rushing waves of light. When Naero flew free of the dropship, so did they, two hundred in all. They swept out into the blazing sunlight, beneath a flawless azure sky.

Naero closed her eyes for a rapturous moment and just felt the sunlight on her face and the wind in her long dark hair. She loved flying of any kind.

She led them down, and over the emerald expanses of grasslands and meadows like a flock of birds.

All upon a radiant day.

For as far as the eye could see below and to any horizon…tens of thousands of people, and hundreds of thousands of children, of all types, races, and ages, played, and supped, and rested at ease, happily watched, and cared for, and tended to by armies of guardians, teachers, medteks, and caregivers, many of them shipped in to assist with such a major task.

While they all floated a few score meters off the ground, Naero spoke to her Marines once again. This time, she used *the voice*, in order that they and all around them for many kilometers nearby could hear her words to them.

BRAVO COMMAND. MY ANGELS OF LIFE. GAZE UPON YOUR HANDIWORK BELOW AND BEYOND ALL THAT YOU CAN SURVEY. BY YOUR COURAGE, OVER ONE IN TEN WORLDS INVADED BY THE ENEMY OWE THEIR LIVES, AND THE LIVES OF THEIR CHILDREN, TO YOU AND THE MATCHLESS ARMS OF YOUR MANY MARINE SISTERS AND BROTHERS. YOU HAVE DEFEATED COUNTLESS RUTHLESS HORDES, IN EVERY ENVIRONMENT AND CLIMATE IMAGINABLE. YOU HAVE SAVED

TRILLIONS—LITERALLY COUNTLESS SENTIENTS—FROM A VILE AND CERTAIN DEATH.

Naero paused, took a deep breath, and smiled at them before continuing. ON THIS ONE RECOVERY WORLD ALONE, JUST A FRACTION OF THOSE LIVES THAT YOU HAVE SAVED: ONE BILLION CHILDREN STILL LIVE, AND BREATHE, AND SMILE, PLAY, AND LAUGH—BECAUSE OF YOUR BRAVERY. ONE BILLION. AND I SAY AGAIN, THAT IS ONLY A SMALL PERCENTAGE OF THE LIVES THAT YOU HAVE SAVED.

MARINES OF BRAVO COMMAND, YOU ARE MY HEROES. AND YOU ARE THEIR HEROES AS WELL. YOU GO FORTH AS WARRIORS, WITHOUT COSMIC POWERS OR MYSTIC ABILITIES. YOU ARE OUR CHAMPIONS, AND YOU SHALL NEVER BE FORGOTTEN.

A great cheer went up from the people below, and Naero let it continue on for a long while.

Then Naero touched her presets and transformed into Shetanna mode, briefly flaring her psyonic wings and her scarlet, glowing katanas. Then she made her swords vanish.

Weapons had no place here.

Everyone below recognized her in an instant and shot to their feet. They raced toward her and called out her name.

Soon they were chanting it.

Shetanna! Shetanna! Shetanna!

Shetanna hovered before her Marines above a low hill.

Countless people flocked toward that place.

Shetanna called out to them, using *the voice* once more.

HEAR MY WORDS, ALL. PLEASE, STOP AND LISTEN. NO ONE PERSON CAN FIGHT A WAR ON HER OWN. SHETANNA WOULD BE NOTHING WITHOUT HER SISTERS AND BROTHERS IN THE SPACER MARINES BACKING HER UP AT EACH POINT ALONG THE WAY. MY MARINE FAMILY HAS SAVED MY LIFE MORE TIMES THAN I CAN RECALL. IT IS NOT SHETANNA WHO IS WINNING THE WAR OF THE HIGH CRUSADE. THAT WOULD BE IMPOSSIBLE. EACH DAY, IT IS THE SPACER MARINES AND THEIR DAUNTLESS ALLIES WHO TAKE THE FIGHT TO THE INVADER, AND PUSH THEM BACK TOWARD DEFEAT, AND OUR FINAL VICTORY!

YET I AM SAD TO TELL YOU THAT WE JUST CAME FROM A WORLD THAT, UNFORTUNATELY, HAS BEEN TAUGHT TO HATE AND DESPISE ALL SPACERS. EVEN THOUGH OUR BRAVE MARINES FOUGHT AND DIED LIBERATING THAT WORLD FROM THE INVADERS, THE PEOPLE THERE MISTAKENLY ABUSED THEIR OWN SAVIORS AND CURSED THE MARINES AS THEY PACKED UP AND LEFT. THEY SPIT ON OUR MARINES AND FLUNG SHIT INTO THEIR FACES,

AND TOLD THEM TO AWAY SOMEWHERE AND DIE. AND THAT WAS VERY WRONG.

AND IT HAS COME CLOSE TO BREAKING THEIR SPIRITS AND THEIR HEARTS TO BE TREATED SO.

I WANT TO MAKE THIS VERY CLEAR, MY FRIENDS. I WOULD BE NOTHING WITHIN THEM. MARINES SUCH AS THESE ARE THE REAL CHAMPIONS AND HEROES OF THE HIGH CRUSADE, AND YOU NEVER HEAR THEIR NAMES. THEY ARE MY HEROES. AND THEY ARE YOURS. PLEASE, IF EVER YOU WERE GRATEFUL FOR YOUR FREEDOM AND YOUR LIVES, THANK THE MARINES OF BRAVO COMMAND AND THEIR MANY ALLIES FOR SAVING YOU AND YOUR WORLDS FROM THE ENEMY. PRAISE THEM WITH GREAT PRAISE, AND GIVE THEM YOUR THANKS. HELP HONOR, AND HEAL, AND SAVE THEM AS THEY HAVE SAVED YOU. LOVE THEM AS I LOVE THEM, FOR WE ALL ARE ONE. WE ARE ALL HUMAN. FAREWELL.

With that, Shetanna vanished.

At first the crowd was disappointed, but then new cheers quickly rose up from below.

Bravo! Bravo! Bravo!

Spacer Marines! Spacer Marines! Spacer Marines!

Company 36 formed a ring, and came down upon that hilltop amid cheering and singing. Then as a festive atmosphere spread, they went down and walked among the many children and people rushing up to them.

Naero's brothers and sisters moved among that gentle, smiling, laughing throng of thousands of voices on each side of them and encircling them, calling out their thanks and gratitude. Small children climbed up on them, into their arms, and onto their strong backs.

Marines went down laughing under waves of grinning, giggling kids.

Thereafter, as the celebration spread and continued, the Marines sat among them all and spoke freely, while people of all races and ages, came before them to offer gratitude and thanks.

Even the hurt and the lame struggled to come to them and speak their thanks. With tears in their eyes, some of the people they had saved attempted to kiss their hands and feet while sobbing and weeping, and the Marines stopped them, humbled and overwhelmed all the more.

Soon after that, the Marines were giving rides to the children up in the air with their gravwings. This was a huge hit. They zipped the laughing and shrieking kids around in the bright sky, going slow so as not to scare the little ones. Below, long lines of others anxiously awaited their turns, shivering and hopping with glee and delight.

Word spread quickly. Other Bravo Marines nearby from many other companies learned about the celebration, and configured themselves at first in white, and then thereafter in a rainbow array of colors, and came down all over the planet, spreading the growing celebration of life.

Then it was learned that there were many children still in many hotels converted by fixers into hospitals, all over the planet, who wept and cried in their recovery beds because they could not join in.

In response, the growing numbers of Marines checked with medical staffs, and arranged to swarm upon those hospitals like brightly colored birds. Any child fit enough to endure such fun, was visited and flown smiling out of their very windows. Even if four Marines had to fly them out upon their beds.

Across the world of Naraden-6, the skies and the heavens rang with the laughter of children. No child was neglected, not even in the regen rooms and burn wards.

And in special cases, some few little ones who at the last were deemed beyond all medical help, were allowed by choice to look upon or breathe their last up in the bright sky in the dazzling light, drifting off onto the next journey, smiling in the mighty arms of a Spacer Marine. Marines who had been among those who had saved them, and at least brought them away from war, to this peaceful and gentle place.

To do such a thing for a dying child was considered a great honor of the highest sort. At least these dying orphans of war did not pass on alone, unknown, forgotten, and unnoticed as mere casualties of the war.

When it came time to eat meals, clouds of fixers helped provide and distribute a merry feast for all. The Marines happily ate side by side with their many new friends, and even helped the caretakers feed the smallest, the injured, and the helpless.

There was great healing to be made and to be had on Naraden-6. Being with and helping with all of those many children healed the Marines in ways that could not be put into the words of any language. Yet there were now countless children on that world, planetwide, who would never forget them and their true power.

Word continued to spread fast.

Many more battle-weary Marines and naval personnel eagerly elected to come down and spend time among the orphans and refugees.

As was established now, the warriors left their armor and weapons behind, and usually just brought their gravwings. For the children, flying was always a big hit.

The authorities extended the Festival of Life over the next three or four days and beyond for other units in need of shore leave. Such a festival would also be scheduled on other hospital worlds.

For a brief time, many of the Marines returned to being like children themselves. All of them together, children who needed to heal.

Now it became a common sight at nap times to spot Marine volunteers and helpers snoozing serenely in the grass, in the shade, with rings of their little charges resting peacefully alongside with the other caretakers.

And if a Marine broke down for some reason and wept, his new little friends hugged her or him and even cried together, until they all finally stopped. And once they were cried out, they could all smile and play together once more.

An entire flock of tiny Pietto children came to Nicholas Kowalski in his recovery room to thank him. They laughed and sang for him until he wept and at last he could finally sleep.

Naero slipped away, and spent most of her time helping with the children who were still too injured or sick to go out.

Shetanna made many a special appearance in secret.

And if she also used biomancy to give some of those kids a little extra boost in healing, regeneration, or pain relief here and there–so be it. It was worth exhausting herself each day in order to achieve that much.

When it finally came time to depart, countless Marines from 36 and many other companies and units came to her explicitly, to personally thank her for what she had started.

Naero merely smiled and told them, "All I asked was for you to trust me."

24

Chodan-3 was just another world that Naero and Bravo hopped into. But it didn't matter. And despite Whip Konrad's OCD foreboding that this time, his legs were going to blown off and he'd pass out and bleed to death, Naero and the Marines went ahead as planned and did their duty as they always did.

At least by then, Intel had a new Comsys and Combat Grid up and running. Om had contributed a few rapidly morphing, Kexxian-style super-algorithms to that cause through Naero and the spyfixers.

Yet at some point throughout the course of such fierce fighting, something was was bound to happen to almost everyone. Clearly, it was all just the law of averages and dumb luck—unless one was on Bodis-2.

During further close-in action in built-up areas in another megacity on Chodan-3, Shetanna took her turn at being wounded and nearly killed.

A series of enemy artillery blasts rocked Company 36 as they assailed an enemy position on the combat grid. The attack injured friend and foe alike.

That was never much of a concern for the invaders. They were happy to cut down their own kind in order to take out some Marines.

Naero's shields vanished as the blasts kicked her about like giants using her for a kickball. She and Om attempted to hurl up Cosmic defenses against the destruction all around them, protecting them and the forward elements of 2nd Platoon Marines from Squads 2, 3, and 4.

Yet those fledgling defenses collapsed as well under the fury of that massive barrage.

The Ejjai invaders supplemented their normal artillery attacks with direct fire from the their orbital starship batteries, in an attempt to hold off the Spacer Marines from slicing through their positions.

Naero...Naero! Om called out to her.

She couldn't move. Her hearing was impaired from the proximity to the blast, and even with the depths of her own mind, it was difficult to listen, to focus on Om's words or anything else.

We have taken serious damage to our physical form. Instituting protocols to sustain life functions and place our physical form in healing stasis to avoid further injury and collapse of all bodily systems. Lots of concussive force damage. Routing all biomancy abilities and healing energies toward self-repair and regeneration. Staunching bleeding and maintaining life functions.

Naero couldn't even tilt her head and look down. Parts of her combat armor had been blasted away or melted off of her. She was effectively a scorched and bloody mess. Thankfully, all of her pieces seemed to be there still, but nothing would respond. She thought that she should have been in great pain.

But after being placed in stasis, she only felt numb. She didn't feel anything, and in a way that was even scarier–feeling disembodied. When her vision flickered and blurred, she had no way of knowing if she was merely losing consciousness–or dying.

We are not dead yet, N. I am doing all that I can to sustain us.

She thought she saw her good friend's face: Jonny Fox.

"Haisha, N!" He placed on hand on her face and checked her wounds. "This is bad. Don't worry, I'll do what I can. Medic. Medic!"

He's giving us healing...lifeforce energy. I was not aware that any of the Marines had a psyonic healing abilities.

Naero hadn't been aware of that either.

For a short while, she faded back in more and felt slightly better.

Where's Jonny? I don't see him. Om? I'm losing it again.

He passed out from aiding us, but he is merely unconscious. We're the one in serious trouble. I've called to the other Marines through the fixers. They're coming.

Then as she started slipping even further away, Naero heard other voices, more people she knew, like Trevor Lakota. Her awareness grew fragmented and confused.

Strong hands grabbed her and moved over her, deactivating and removing the pieces of her armor and weapons, checking her condition.

"Haisha! It's Naero and Fox, Sarge. Fox looks okay; he's just passed out. But Naero's down and she looks bad off. Like she took a direct hit!"

Naero knew that voice also and clung to that knowledge. That voice belonged to Suki Lii from 2nd Platoon, Squad 1, Fireteam 3.

Sergeant Selby Vaughn's voice came closer. "Damn it, she's bad off. Is she dying?"

Suki shouted, "I'm not sure, Sarge."

"She'll make it. Those slasher bitches can't take our Shetanna down that easy. Help me stabilize her, Suki."

"I'm with you, Sarge. Haisha, N's lost a lot of blood. Her suit's floating in it."

"Gravwings. Now. We have to get her to one of the aid stations or medical ships. I'm scanning the nearest one."

Whip Konrad called out, "Sarge, we have eight other wounded, most of them just as bad off. And the enemy's advancing on our positions."

"Form up and keep fighting, 36. Ana, we're moving the wounded to the rear. Back in a bit."

"Good work, Vaughn. Get our people to safety. We've got this here. Put in on them, Bravo!"

Fire from small arms and grenades crackled and exploded in front of them as the enemy came on.

"Her gravwing is junk," Suki complained.

"Get a gravlift on her from one of the fixers and keep her between us. Let's get her back with the rest. Stay low. Once we clear those building behind the forward line, we should be clear to fly directly toward the nearest aid station."

Sergeant Vaughn led them away from the battlefront as the conflict continued to rage behind them. She called out again, this time to Corporal Kooper Taylor. "Koop, log who's hurt, how bad, and let's start transmitting their vitals and their condition status to the aid station in advance. That way, the medteks can already have medbeds and medical fixers prepped for our people when we get there."

Kooper relayed the cs data, sometimes through fixers. "Cs feeds on the way, and we are inbound, Sarge. ETA, ninety-seven seconds. Summary is nine total wounded, seven of them critical, including our MCL. Multiple blast injuries and trauma, burns, shrapnel, and concussive damage. We have them stabilized as best we can for the moment. The aid station will decide if they make it."

"Shunt me the names of our people," Vaughn said. "I want to see who's hurt."

"Naero Maeris, Kesha Aztec, Moses Fay. Deb Steiner, Bessa Jackson, Acer Adams, Baylor Scott, Trisha Marshall, and Michael Borelli. All floaters in tow. None of them can help themselves."

"That's what we're here for. All right, people. We're far enough away from the front lines. Fly low and fast under the cover of the buildings and let's reach that aid station. Keep the wounded together in our shield pod perimeter. I want scans, eyes and ear, people. Maintain three 360 degree security all the way. No surprises."

Yet even as they sped on, a knot of thirty Ejjai skirmishers exploded out of a nearby building to attack the small band.

"Fly through that building for cover and keep going if we can. Protect the wounded!" Vaughn roared.

They vectored through the building noted, adjusting shields and providing cover fire all the way. Even as they passed within, a storm of enemy fire peppered their unit shield and the face of the building.

A Marine fighter dipped down and blasted the exposed pocket of skirmishers with air bursts of explosive, anti-personnel ordnance.

Nearby supporting units rushed in to take over, a sortie of two Marine fireteams sweeping in to finish the job. They shot any remaining Ejjai to pieces, and sent them spinning, burning, and exploding to the ground.

A few seconds later, Vaughn and the others finally reached the aid station. Medteks rose up to meet them in order to get the wounded onto the present, linked medbeds as quickly as possible.

The last thing Naero recalled before the medbed-induced coma took over was the medteks cutting off and removing the rest of her armor and weapons. Her nanosuit they dissolved in a hurry. She felt cold and vulnerable.

We're going to make it, N. We're here. Your medical people are very competent. They will save us.

A female Spacer medtek smiled down at her and touched her shoulder. "Don't worry, MCL Maeris. Your mates got you here. You're in our hands, now. We'll take over from here and get you fixed up. You just rest."

*

When Naero came to, she was covered in regen paks and bandages, still held immobile on her medbed.

A few medical fixers bobbed around, monitoring the facility and the area. Naero looked around, struggling just to lift her head.

All of our friends are here, N. Everyone who made it here is still alive. Although many, just like us, were pretty bad off.

I can't be on my back like this, Om.

Stop complaining. The more we rest, the faster we regenerate.

She told the doctors and medteks the same thing.

All of them laughed at her. "You damn fool. You and these others are lucky to be alive. Enjoy your stay with us for a few days. We'll get you back to the front lines soon enough. Crazy MCLs."

By the end of the next day, all nine of them from 36, in that shielded nanohut for recovery, were already going stir crazy.

They knew how these things went. In three to five day's time, the action on Chodan-3 would most likely be over. That would be about the time they could go back to the unit.

Although the sounds of battle continued to recede into the distance around them, it still sounded pretty furious, and probably was.

But there was no doubt that it was now further away, and they would probably sit out the rest of this action, whether they liked it or not.

The nine of them still couldn't move around much yet, but they could talk at each from where they rested, lying more or less fixed to their medbeds. Stasis fields kept them locked down. Those precautions were on purpose, to keep them from getting up and moving around, and possibly re-injuring themselves or someone else.

Elite troops were sometimes the worst at assessing their conditions. Hence the stasis fields.

"Hey, N," Trisha asked. "Where did you get hit?"

"All over, I think. Blast and shrapnel effects in numerous places. No broken bones, but lots of small blast fractures that are healing up inside. My armor and my shields saved my life, but they were practically shredded right off of me. Some of you are much the same, I assume?"

Moses, Deb, Bessa, and Baylor piped up in the affirmative, more or less the same as her–ragged and blown up.

Kesha Aztec called out. "I'm regrowing three fingers on my shooting hand, damn it. So I might be here a bit longer, guys. Anybody else missing any parts?"

Trisha cut them off. "I can barely see Mike over there. From this angle, it looks like the slashers took off that ugly growth sticking up on his neck. But our luck, it'll probably grow back. Because it's non-essential. Hairy warts like that are stubborn and hard to get rid of."

All of them laughed, including Mike. "Yeah, laugh it up, Trish. You only wish you had a mug as pretty as mine. And for everyone's info, I've still got my damn head. Think about it, geniuses. How else could I talk back at you goons?"

"Hey, Mike," Moses told him. "We all know your brains aren't in your skull anyway."

Deb laughed. "Mike, we all thought you were maybe a ventriloquist or something. Your lips always move, but the sound seems to keep coming from out of your ass." More raucous laughter.

"Yeah, yeah, you bunch of comedians. If you must know, I did get my legs all mangled up. But the medteks were able to save them. I gotta go through a partial regen to repair the nerves, ligaments, and joints. Then I'm going to kick all of your asses!"

"Oooh, big talk!" Kesha said.

"You couldn't do any of that before," Moses noted. "They giving you an extra leg or something?"

Bessa cut in and added, "So, I guess for now, you don't have a leg to stand on."

Everyone cracked up again.

"Boo! That was so bad, Jackson."

"Bessa, I swear, when I do get out of here…"

"Yeah, sure. What you gonna do? You gonna hobble at me or something? Well scuttle my way and bring it, crab-boy."

More bursts of laughter.

Trish sighed. "Well, guys. I might be here the longest, I'm thinking. They had to take my left arm at the elbow, and my left leg at the knee."

Kesha tried to sound hopeful. "I like the new regen process; they say it's only two weeks now, and a few days of hypertherapy to learn to re-use it."

"And it doesn't stink as bad. I'll drink to that," Trish said.

"She's right," Moses added. "Don't you worry. I got my right arm shot off two months ago. I was back on the line in less than three weeks. Three weeks!"

"Wait a minute," Naero said. "There's a system we haven't heard from yet. Is he out cold or something? Where's that loudmouth sonovabitch Adams? Somebody kick Acer or hit him with a rock and wake him up. What's his goddam story?"

They waited for a moment.

Acer Adams spoke out hesitantly. "Oh, I'm here, guys. I'm just resting and listening to all the jolly fun."

"Well, you're being awfully damn quiet about it," Mike said. "That's not like you at all. So spill. What the hell happened to you? You get a hangnail or something?"

"No, nothing like that. It's…it's a serious injury. I nearly died."

Kesha gasped. "Haisha! Oh my gosh. Holy krap–Acer got his balls shot off!"

"No, no, no…my boys are still here. Thank goodness."

Now Bessa gasped this time.

Acer cut her off. "No, don't worry, ladies, the heavy artillery is still there, too."

"Oh, come on, Acer. Just tell us," Naero insisted.

Adams took a breath. "I got my ass shot off."

After another pause, the other eight of them exploded with laughter.

"It's not funny, guys. Did you ever lose your ass?"

"In a dice game, once," Baylor noted.

They all roared even harder.

Finally it grew quiet again.

Acer spoke up. "I think I may have to kill all of you, once I get out of here."

They couldn't stop laughing after that.

"You're killing us right now," Trisha said. "By getting us to laugh ourselves to death."

"Get the medteks," Moses said. "I think I've torn my wounds open."

"No, wait. Wait. Quiet down, you morons. Be serious. Acer, look, tell us the truth. All of us got our asses shot off. It's just a figure of speech, right? Tell us true."

"Naero, I wish it was. My ass is completely gone."

They exploded with laughter again.

"Oh, and it was so purty, too!" Bessa said.

"Stop. Stop!" Trisha said. "My head's going to explode!"

"This isn't funny, guys. I have no ass!"

"Mercy! I can't breathe!" Kesha warned them.

"Well," Moses said, "I guess you'll be sitting around for a while in the regen tanks…re-developing you cheekiness."

"You won't be needing those assless chaps of yours anymore for Dance Night."

"Hey–how would we know?"

Another explosion of mirth.

Baylor couldn't stop laughing. "And picture this, guys. Somewhere out there–Acer's ass is just hanging out some place, just swinging or flapping in the wind. Or maybe it's just lying there, sizzling like two, juicy ham steaks on a griddle."

"No, no," Deb shouted. "Then a hungry slasher will stroll by, and say, 'Oh, my. Why what is this?' Then that snack-hungry bitch will slap those two pieces of fried assmeat together, and have herself a nice, dandy little hairy ham sandwich. Maybe with a little mayo, and a dash of mustard."

"I think I smell bacon," Moses said.

"I am going to hurt you," Acer fumed. "All of you."

Later that night, when they were just drifting off to sleep, all someone had to do was whisper, "Mmm…bacon!"

Then it all started up again. The bad jokes and the silliness just kept going.

"Hey, I went to pat Acer on the butt, and missed! It was like there was nothing there."

"Acer's going to be more careful at night, now."

"Why is that?"

"Because, it'll be darker. There won't be a full moon out for quite a while."

25

Wenga-1 was another winter world, but at least the atmosphere was breathable.

Currently, most of the planet was enveloped in various blizzard hurricanes, whirling and whipping across the endless plains and fields of snow and ice. Entire fleets were grounded in their starports for months.

Visibility was nil, nada, nacha. Scans were disrupted by the weather, the magnetic effects of the planet, and the metallics and particles in the swirling snow itself and the atmosphere.

This was winter in the northern hemisphere. Anyone would have to be insane to execute any kind of invasion under such conditions on a world such as this.

But the Ejjai invaders were never know for their sanity.

Besides, the population on Wenga-1 of 4.5 billion were all trapped in fixed locations, in nice, little, heavily shielded domes and pyramids.

How very convenient.

The Ejjai invaders spread their battle groups across the surface in groundtanks, armored personnel carriers modified and shielded for the harsh winter conditions. With the high winds, it was impractical to use anything that floated or flew. That left out gravtanks, gunships, and even starfighters.

But it brought back the use of something else.

A real blast from the past.

Megatanks.

Megatanks were gigantic tanks with guns as big as starship spinal guns, and secondary batteries larger than the regular artillery pieces that most armies deployed in battle.

They were vulnerable to air power and orbital naval fire, but in an environment such as this, they were nearly invulnerable except to direct assault.

With twenty battle groups in system, the invaders had ten megatanks onworld, and they were currently unstoppable.

The megatanks attacked in pairs to support each other. They pulled right up to dome and pyramid cites, wore their shields down, and blasted the locals into submission. Then the invaders inserted troops and a number of the mini-meatships to clean out the bodies and any survivors.

They moved methodically from one location to the next, wiping out everything in their path.

After all, they had all winter in order to do so.

Bravo devised their plan of attack and went at the enemy with modified ground tanks and meks.

The MCLs got in close enough to board the megatanks with insertion teams, and assaulted their crews and forces from within.

Shetanna and the Marines used a new form of combat armor that didn't so much rely on stealth, but focused on providing extra protection against the very real secondary threat: the intense cold and bitter high winds.

The battles for Wenga-1 turned brutal and up-close, at short range and poor visibility in the terrible weather, on a world where scanners were all but useless.

At times the visibility was so poor that the opposing units did not know where each other was until they actually started to slam and crash into each other, separating just enough to fire right on top of one another. Or they went after each other hand-to-hand or with blades.

Both enemy and friendly units even got crushed under the treads of the rumbling megatanks.

Corporal Reyes Keller from 1st Platoon, Squad 2, Fireteam 3 perished when he was struck by an enemy tank, became lost in the snow for a time, and then froze to death from his armor being cracked open like an egg, all in the course of a major battle.

Ops usually lasted from a few hours to one or two days. With determination and enough firepower, a megatank could eventually be worn down and blasted to scrap, from within and without.

But it was quickly discovered that MCLs and boarding teams could treat them like grounded starships, and destroy them much quicker from within. They killed off their crews and leaders, moved them away from the civilian cities, and blew up their power cores and ordnance, causing near atomic-level explosions.

The enemy countered by driving their last remaining megatanks right into the heart of the capital gigacity, the largest of them all.

Blowing up those four megatanks would do the enemy's job for them. The resulting blasts would lay waste to nearly the entire area.

That forced Bravo to attempt to use direct assaults, not to destroy, but the attempt to capture each of the megatanks, neutralize their crews, and remove them from the gigacity to a location where they could be safely destroyed.

Shetanna led the attack on one of the four megatanks, backed up by two thousand Marines, including Company 36.

They swarmed over the megatank like ants, fighting at first with all the Ejjai external troops and defenses. To anyone witnessing such an assault, it was indeed very much like insects clashing on a hill of metal with the addition of roaring guns and cannons.

Each of the enemy super vehicles kept blazing away at the stranded local population, tearing the gigacity open further, dealing death and destruction each second.

They had to be stopped.

Shettana didn't even need to blast or cut open a hatch. That would just alert the invaders to her insertion point. She used her Mystic abilities to transport straight inside and went to work where the enemy least expected her to strike.

By the time the slashers realized they did have a dangerous intruder, Shetanna had dozens or scores of other hatches and access panels open and marked for Bravo Marines to pour through and slug it out with the troops inside.

While the Marines did what they did best, Shetanna continued on, making her way either to the power plant or the bridge. In this case, they couldn't disable the megatanks until they got them back outside of the gigacity, so the best option was to take out the megatank leadership and ops.

The problem was reduced to fighting in very tight, close quarters with the enemy, but the Marines were already highly trained and used to doing that very thing on starships.

Shetanna could cut the Ejjai down quickly enough, but then their bodies would often block the way as well, among the confusing networks of tunnels and corridors.

Explosives and microbombs simply made too big of a mess, and brought about a greater risk of igniting fires that would grow out of control and lead to even larger explosions.

Om cooked something new up with the fixers and presented them to Naero. *Try these new microbombs, N. Immolation and incineration charges.*

She hit the Ejjai with them. The invaders burst into flames and shrieked, reduced to ash and charred bits of bone and melted equipment. Problem solved. No piles of dead bodies blocking tight passages.

That's the ticket, Om. Keep 'em coming!

All the while, Bravo Marines shot their way deeper and deeper into the core of the megatanks.

Om had the fixers send them all more of the new incineration microbombs and grenades.

Naero was closest to the bridge, while the Marines seized vital areas such as the engine rooms and power cores, keeping the enemy from disabling them or blowing up the megatank themselves.

"I'm going on to seize the bridge," she told 36. "If you can get control, move the megatanks out of the gigacity. Stop those guns from firing!"

Naero studied the layouts Om fed her and transported straight up, while the megatank she was in started clanking back the way it came. But half of its guns were still firing.

The enemy command crew attacked immediately when she appeared on the bridge like a ghost, and Shetanna was quickly the center of yet another intense firefight.

She raced upside down across the low ceiling, slicing and cutting the Ejjai heads and helmets open.

The bodies simply dropped to the ground. Plenty of elbow room on the bridge now.

After she cut the megatank captain in half, she jumped down into the fire control station. Using teknomancy, she quickly overrode the megatank sec codes.

In seconds, she poured heavy fire at the other three megatanks even while her tank retreated.

In short order, all three of the other megatanks stopped firing on the gigacity, and poured fire at the renegade megatank. Then more guns on the others went silent, and they began to withdraw. The last enemy tank that could still fire pursued the megatank that Nero was in and continued their duel. Soon both ginormous war machines were on fire, blazing and dueling away at one another.

"Keep it up until we're out of the gigacity," she commanded. "Bail out before they blow!"

Both dueling megatanks exploded just outside of the gigacity. Shetanna and the Marines on both vehicles just barely got out in time.

By then, all four megatanks were neutralized or destroyed, and the rest of the enemy invaders were hunted and cut down in a matter of two hours after that. Victory had at last been achieved.

36 celebrated on Sixthday Binge Night. Naero and Jonny scored some bottles of Spacer Poteen and went to get drunk with Chime and a few other of their mates.

But when they found Chime, she was all by herself in her bunk with what looked like a new book.

And a blaster pistol beside her within reach.

Even her cousin Jonny and Naero approached cautiously. Chime didn't always like to be interrupted when she was reading. She had been known to get a bit testy.

They watched and observed her for a bit, all the while inching closer.

As long as Chime's hand didn't drift to her pistol, they were fine.

Suddenly she slipped her golden book mark in, snapped the hardcover book shut, and tossed her head back with a deep and satisfied sigh.

Chime closed her pretty brown eyes, gritted her teeth, and stamped her drumming bare feet under her blanket in a little happy dance. She literally squealed with glee.

Jonny's mouth drooped open. "Wow. That must be some book!"

Then a serious look washed over Chime's enraptured face. "Haisha!" she yelled. "I've been reading all day. Get out of my way, guys. I hafta pee!"

Not wanting to get wet, they made way for her as she streaked for the head.

When she returned, they were still waiting for her.

Without even being asked, Chime began gushing about the book. "Guys, this was one of the best books I've read, in years. It's called *The Library of Alantia*, by Jack Ruel. There's this magical library, see? And it has the power to roam from city to city and world to world. Some of the books are magic as well, and allow the readers to actually enter those worlds. Those special books are actually magical gateways into still other worlds and dimensions."

Chime barely paused to suck in a breath.

"But the best part is the main character, named Chimaera. And it's scary, because this character is me. And I mean, she isn't just like me. She is me. Scatterbrains, and book crazy and all. She even looks like me. But Chimaera is in great danger. There's all of this sorcery and intrigue. Her parents died in a mysterious fire years ago that destroyed the book they were in and part of the library itself. And get this! Chimaera was raised by her batty grandfather, one of the chief librarians–and by and within the magical books themselves! And there are these evil mages and dark demigods trying to take control of this library, which is the last of its kind, thanks to the bad guys. Then there are the Vixani, the werefox people who are both allies and trickster guardians of the ancient librarians. Jimmy the foxboy is a shapeshifter friend that Chimaera grew up with, but they get into dire trouble up to their necks. And then, just when you think Chimaera is dead, this beautiful dark wizard boy named Aston saves her and they become allies and lovers and it is all so terrifying and wonderful, heartbreaking, and romantic! His own father is the leader of the dark mages, but his mother was one of the demigods who actually wrote the magic books for the libraries, and she passed that power on to her son–before her husband murdered her–but Aston doesn't know that yet. Whatever Aston writes in one of the Cosmic books actually happens in some dimension somewhere. The bad guys want to destroy the library, the magic books, and the remaining demigods who write them–

"Chime, Chime!" Naero kept shouting and waving her hands above her head to get her friend's attention. "That's great. We're all very happy for you. Where in the hell did you get this book?"

That stopped her in her tracks. Chime's mouth fell open and she looked completely stupefied. "Why...I...I don't know. I didn't buy it. I just found it on top of one of my crates today. I opened it up and started reading out of curiosity, and I just couldn't put it down."

They all chuckled.

Then Peter Cooper from Squad 4 walked up. "I gave you the book, Chime," he told her. "In thanks for all of the Reading Nights and great books that you've shared with all of us. With my great thanks."

Pete was one of the quiet and sturdy ones, a bit lanky, but still ruggedly handsome. He wore his dark hair rather long, and he had dreamy gray eyes that looked as if they could drill through titanadium.

Yet those eyes looked softer and even yearning whenever he looked at Chime. They hadn't noticed that much before, until now.

She glanced up at him and her lips parted slightly and caught her breath. "How did you know, Peter?"

He smiled at her. "Know what, Chime?"

"How did you know that I would love this book so much?"

Peter sighed, holding her gaze. "Because I'm the author, Chime. That's my pen name. I wrote that book for you. I know you from all of your books. I know what you like to read. You're exactly right; you are Chimaera. In every way."

Chime trembled and sucked in a deep breath. She came forward, placing her hand on Peter's chest, lifting her brown eyes to his.

Now it was his turn to gasp and close his gray eyes at her touch.

"You're Aston," Chime said. "In his language in the book it means the stone…the stone that never breaks. Just like Peter is for Petra, the rock. You wrote this book for me?"

Peter nodded. "And don't worry. Once you reach the end, it stops on sort of a dire cliffhanger, but I am working on a sequel!"

Chime clenched her fists. "Oooh, I can't stand this. I must read the rest now. Then you can show me the work in progress."

"I can't," he said with a laugh. "It isn't finished yet. You'll have to wait. Why don't we pick up where you left off. I could read some of it to you."

Chime was suddenly like a lantern or a beacon, lit from within. "I'd like that. We can read together. You do a chapter, and then I'll read the next. Oh, you must sign this copy for me."

"I already did. Didn't you see it?"

"Haisha, how could I have missed it? I just started reading. Who looks at the front matter anymore?"

They grabbed the book and strolled off together, babbling away.

Naero and Jonny Fox just stood there staring at them.

"What the hell just happened here?" Jonny said.

Naero giggled and tossed him a poteen bottle. "Your cousin's a lucky girl, Jonny. I think she just fell in love, and apparently with a secret admirer she's had for quite a while. How about that? Pete's crazy for your crazy cousin."

Jonny just stared after them, a worried look on his face. "Huh."

"Oh, come on," Naero told him. "Chime deserves someone exactly like Pete. We know him. He's a good guy, and a great Marine. A bit quiet, but the guy was practically made for her. Be happy for Chime."

Jonny Fox nodded. "I am, N." But he still looked slightly worried.

26

The invaders tried something different on Jamie-8. Unfortunately this was one of the first worlds where the invaders had struck, and they had been there a long while. Meatships and cloneships were running full tilt.

After losing half of its Capital Class System population of fifteen billion humans and near-humans, the entire planet was in disarray and abject confusion. Resistance was sporadic, and the invaders held sway over half of the planet.

While the Marines of Bravo Command attacked, the invaders suddenly cut their losses and attempted to flee, taking with them anything they could steal.

On Jamie-8, they had amassed fleet after fleet of all manner of stolen starships: merchant craft, liners, couriers, mine haulers, and yachts. Every type of vessel and starship imaginable.

These thousands upon thousands of starships, taken from their murdered owners, gave them many cobbled-together fleets.

Bloodships.

The invaders launched all of them at once, hiding behind the dense screen of smaller vessels.

At first the Spacer Navy closed in, trying to blockade the way. They started systematically blasting the ships trying to escape, cutting off others, and using Marines to board and pacify them when and where possible.

Then the Marines reported that the ships were packed not only with Ejjai and contraband—but with human captives and hostages, many of them pregnant women and children. Such prisoners were always the prized prey of the vile invaders.

"All ships, stop firing," Major Luna told the Navy. "Trap the ships or have fighters disable them. We must capture them and keep them from jumping. The Ejjai have filled all of their bloodships with hostages! I say again…"

The naval blockade closed in tight, closing off any attempt to escape. The Spacer warships still destroyed the invader warships— including the cloneships and meatships.

Marine boarding craft began systematically clearing the trapped ships. They stunned everyone on board or pumped the ships full of sleep gas.

Then the Ejjai started blowing vessels up on their own, rather than allow them to be captured.

Om, this is going to a bloodbath. Think. How can we head this off?

More rapid-acting stun gas, N. Have the fixers or Marines slip onboard and flood each of the bloodships with the new stun gas. If the boarding craft or naval ships can get in close enough, they can use mass stunners. That's the only way to neutralize the Ejjai and do this fast enough to save lives.

Naero proposed those exact courses of action straight up the chain, clearing them through Spacer Intel and Command. Om had already coordinated every fixer cloud and instructed the medical fixers to prepare large quantities of fast action stun gas.

The fixer clouds swarmed on the bloodships and filled each one that they could with the fast-acting gas. Even where the Ejjai wore EV suits or combat armor, special Intel cloaked insertion drones slipped onboard and immobilized any foes who could not otherwise be taken down by the gas. They used stun needles or actual shock charges or stun grenades, if nothing else.

Even so, with that many ships, it took a long time to dispose of that many Ejjai on all of the captured vessels. Marines and naval crews and landers chucked the invaders out of airlocks. Many of the Ejjai got sucked back down into the planet's gravity well and flared in bright sparks, burning up on reentry.

It would be a major undertaking to reclaim and deal with all of those remaining starships and captives onboard each of those vessels. But eventually, the bloodships were systematically landed in safe areas and emptied out.

There were still some pockets of heavy fighting onworld as well. Naero and Bravo Command focused on eliminating them.

The enemy did their best to conduct their military actions right in the middle of the most densely populated areas. It kept them from being bombed into oblivion outright, and allowed them to do the most damage possible before they were put down.

At times, Naero grew tired of the constant, brutal fighting.

But she was really good at what she did. As an MCL, she was one of the best, if not the best.

Killing and exterminating Ejjai, perhaps one of the vilest and most hyper-violent species ever encountered by humanity, was an art form to her now.

Each time Naero looked down at a dead civilian, sprawled upon a war torn street, she realized very clearly, exactly what her duty was: to utterly defeat and destroy the Ejjai.

The invasion had to be crushed, as quickly as possible, world by world. Every second that she kept fighting perhaps just brought the war that much closer to being over. And just maybe, fewer helpless people of all ages would be mutilated and killed.

For all defenders, dead civies and especially dead children were always the worst thing to run across. The invaders did not always have time to collect all of the dead for the meatships right away, especially in heavily populated areas. Yet that did not keep them from killing everyone in sight and then pushing on.

The invaders actually enjoyed rotting carrion.

They could always come back, given the chance.

Like everyone else among the defenders, Naero was sick to death of seeing dead kids. Their dead faces haunted her when she slept, and several times she woke up, already sobbing. Their slack, open, helpless little mouths, sometimes filled with water, dirt, mud, or blood. Their milky dead eyes. Their stiff, pathetic little bodies, limbs, and hands and feet. Sometimes they were in pieces.

Even worse, sometimes they were only near death.

Sometimes they could be saved.

Sometimes all efforts to do so failed.

Everything about the war became a living, walking, breathing nightmare.

If only Naero could go through the rest of her entire life without seeing one more dead child.

Part of her would be willing to give almost anything for that. But the sickening war still raged on each day, on too many remaining worlds ahead of the High Crusade to save humanity.

Realistically, her personal wants simply did not matter. The war was the reality. The war was what it was.

Damn the invader scum.

She fought them, and slew them in great numbers wherever she and her brave Marines were sent, on world after broken and shattered world.

They brought hope and victory, where before there was none.

Shetanna slew the invaders–calmly, efficiently, and coldly–as fast as she possibly could.

When the invaders lay vanquished and dead on one world, it was then time to pack up and exterminate them on the next. She knew that many of the Marines of Bravo command felt almost completely the same way.

She knew by now that her good friend Jonny Fox was also something of a slight psyonic healer. Since he had saved her, she saw him also do the same for others. His talent wasn't very strong, and he used it only in great need, to sustain life by giving his own life force directly to another. Doing so taxed him to a state of exhaustion and left him vulnerable or even helpless.

On three occasions that she knew of, her friend Jonny had saved the life of other wounded Marines in this fashion, keeping them alive at great risk and cost to himself until better help could be found.

One day, after a wild, pitched battle, Naero found Jonny passed out and near death himself, next to a dehydrated, dead lander boy of three. Jonny had clearly done everything he could to save the child, but in the end, it had all been for nothing. The little boy had been too far gone.

Naero used her own biomancy powers of healing to save Jonny's life, and carried him back to his squad. Neither of them ever spoke about the situation thereafter.

She had seen the tears streaked down Jonny's face that he had shed before he passed out, trying to save that poor lost little boy.

Everyone longed for the war to end. Haisha, let it end. And yet it dragged on.

Kill off the invaders to the last.

Rid all humanity of this scourge; end the atrocities.

End the vilest of wars that humanity and Spacers had ever endured.

And because the Bravo Marines so stoically shared her pain and torment each step of the way, Naero felt a deep abiding, familial love for her brothers and sisters. She fought jealously to protect them when she could, even to the point of exhaustion and taking harm herself.

Yet, in truth, they needed little protection. The elite Marines of Bravo Command were the premier warriors of their age, and warrior-for-warrior, they knew no equal.

With them, Shetanna grew to become even more than a legend among legends, revered even by the landers of the Corps worlds who had, before than time, hated and despised all Spacers and slurred them as murdering spacks. Now, Shetanna was nearly worshipped, much to the chagrin of the waning, out-of-favor Gigacorps who caused this entire mess.

In return, Naero's Marine brothers and sisters loved and defended her with a loyalty that far surpassed all devotion and ferocity.

They knew her weaknesses very well. Her Cosmic abilities taxed her, and many times she fought until the point of complete fatigue.

When she dropped, Bravo was waiting there to catch their dark angel in their arms and whisk her away to safety.

Woe to any foe who came against her to take her life.

The Marines fell upon any such threat that came against their fallen angel with an astonishing fury that was unmatched, and could hardly be believed, until it was actually witnessed up close and in person.

Shetanna's protectors fought like guardian angels, and shattered all comers. They crushed such attackers with absolute and astounding, stunning annihilation.

General Walker himself even joked that Shetanna should simply exhaust herself on a daily basis in order to channel the fierce loyalties and awesome ferocity that she awoke in Bravo Command. The end of the war would simply come that much faster.

Naero didn't have the heart to inform the general that that was how many days at the front actually went.

On Jamie-8, Shetanna and Bravo Command crushed the invaders without halt or mercy in nine of the ten largest gigacities on the planet.

Wherever they went, the lander leaders recognized them now, and cheered their names, flinging flowers at their feet, and heaped praise and adoration upon them.

Yet that wasn't what any of the victors really wanted.

They just wanted the fucking war to end.

27

Chickamauga-7 was a funny little world–an earthlike moon, actually, in an area of blank space, with only five hundred million people.

It wasn't even important enough to be part of any major trade route. Yet it was, just barely, a mining outpost, and a small naval base and research facility. Rumor had it, on good authority, that the system had been first colonized by accident, and then used as a hideout by smugglers and pirates for a time, before becoming slightly more respectable and useful.

Yet it had one thing that made it an a valuable oddity. The planet was the greatest known and almost sole source of the rare pseudo-element of Thelluria.

Thelluria was one of the rarest Cosmic substances in the galaxy–next to something called Ur-metal. Thelluria could be used by psyons and even non-psyons to either enhance or defend against psyonic abilities and powers.

Perhaps that was in part why the troubles began.

The enemy invasion forces were not especially numerous or any fiercer than any others that 36 and Bravo had faced.

Yet strange, inexplicable events began to occur during the course of several battles.

In one instance, a hundred local defenders and about the same number of Ejjai suddenly doubled over, dizzy and unable to go on fighting.

The only other weird thing was that an Ejjai corpse had been found missing its head. Not impossible, in a war zone, but it appeared that the enemy had gone out of the way to take the head themselves, and leave the body for some reason.

The very next day, several hundred troops at the front of a heated battle grew overcome with nausea and had to either retreat, or be carried off.

There was no scanned evidence of nerve gas or any biological agents present in the air. No one could figure out what was causing these strange, mass effects.

Then later that same day, in another gigacity nearby, thousands of defenders at the front were stricken and passed out, going into some kind of paralysis or induced coma.

This was not the work of mass stunners, which could be detected and countered quite readily. Nor, again, was it any biological or nerve gas agents.

More defenders poured in to defend the stricken.

They too fell victim to the same affliction.

For the time being, no more troops were sent into that area.

Yet strangely enough, neither did the invaders rush in to attack the helpless troops lying on the ground.

Why would they hold back? They never had before.

The enemy was obviously causing this, and knew something that the Alliance didn't. Suspicions grew among the MCLs and pointed to a possible link to psyonics. But the Ejjai had never shown any psyonic talents before, and had never been known to be psyonic in any way.

Psyonics usually required higher sentient brain functions to be present. The bestial, uplifted Ejjai were barely sentient.

Shetanna volunteered to sneak in cloaked and investigate with only a small, secret guard of one Marine Company–36.

An initial scan found hundreds of dead Ejjai shock troops in a single troop transport that had been shot down and crashed. The anomaly was that each of those troops wore helmet liners of precious, Thellurian alloy. The Ejjai were shielding their own troops against mass psyonic attacks.

Another unit came in from Intel to collect the bodies, and especially the never-before-seen helmet liners.

As soon as Shetanna and 36 continued on further into the area in question, Marines began to complain about feeling uncomfortable, suffering nausea and feeling dizzy.

A wave of special Intel fixers were sent in, and coated all of their armors in a Thellurian spolymer designed to resist and block out psyonic waves, powers, and abilities. Being a Mystic herself, Naero sensed bizarre pulses and bursts of strange, intense Cosmic and psyonic energy. Yet it was very fleeting, freaky, and disconcerting.

She could shield and protect herself, but there was no way to track it yet.

Once the psyonic-blocking spolymers were applied to 36, the disabling effects were greatly lessened, and the sortie could proceed with its investigation.

Naero and Om attempted to zero in on the strange psyonic energies at work, but they seemed very unstable and hard to pin down. And at first they seemed to emanate from one direction, and then another.

Finally she decided to call in several Marine starfighter strafing and bombing runs on the areas in question. She specifically warned HQ and the Navy that the pilots should be given the same Thellurian spolymer protections against mass psyonics.

The strafing runs came down quickly, crisscrossing the enemy side of that section of the front lines.

After they passed over, a cloaked enemy starship, of a type and designation never encountered before, disrupted and crashed to the ground deeper behind enemy lines.

Shetanna and 36 immediately pursued that strange ship, trying to reach the crash site, feeding Intel and HQ all the data that they could along the way.

Not only had the strange vessel given off wild psyonic signatures, but both Naero and Om thought that they had seen some kind of psyonic projector arrays deployed on the underside.

When they reached where the ship had gone down, it was not on fire and had not exploded. But smoke or steam did escape through several vents and tears in the hull, and burst hatches from the crash. Shetanna led her team closer.

The vessel itself was round and squat like a thick pill, armored with several odd-looking hatches.

They quickly attempted a full scan from the outside before trying to go in. Other enemy forces could converge on the scene at any second.

Om notified her about the fixer scans. *N, as we suspected, that ship is loaded with high quantities of Thellurian alloy in any number of concentrations, and configured with many different types of arrays and psyonic projectors.*

Basically, the entire ship was a psyonic generator that could focus psyonic force. It was a weapon.

And a very powerful weapon at that, N. You and the others must be very careful. But the design of this weapon requires a natural source of psyonic energy. Machines, robots, and tek cannot be psyonic on their own. This generator steps up psyonic force many times over–

I got it, Om. There must be powerful enemy psyonic users on board somewhere to fuel this weapon, whether they are Ejjai or some other alien race.

The ship has been disabled and cannot fly, but the psyonic projector arrays are still active.

Copy that.

They approached the strange starship to enter within. Scanners and fixers picked up the signatures of small arms fire on board.

Some kind of firefight was taking place inside.

Between who? No other Alliance unit was even near that ship.

Who were the invaders fighting? Each other?

Without warning, a furious psyonic blast rocked the ship and everything around it within five klicks, on a magnitude never recorded before. The psyonic waves passed through everything.

Several Marines cried out, despite their protections, and collapsed. Blood streamed from their eyes, mouths, ears, and noses. They had to be floated back to the lines on their gravwings.

Naero and the rest of 36 who could go on, proceeded to close in and gain access to the ship.

Inside, sporadic fire could still be detected up ahead and on several levels.

Shetanna and the Marines performed a direct assault, taking down the Ejjai with direct fire and grenades.

The strange thing was that many of the Ejjai they encountered seemed to have been fleeing, fighting to get away from something, and had terrified looks on their faces when they stumbled into the Marines.

Finally Naero and her team were inside the ship and made their way through about half of it.

Another massive wave of psyonic power, this time telekinetic, ripped through the damaged craft, tearing the hull and supports apart. Fleeing Ejjai troops shrieked and cried out further within.

More Marines dropped and had to be floated out.

Yet another mindblast struck. This time, they suffered a direct casualty. Maurice James, a young Marine with budding telepathic abilities, collapsed without a word. When the medics reached him, his helmet was full of bloody mush.

James had taken a direct psyonic spike, and his skull had exploded. Death had most likely been instantaneous.

Naero could sense the powerful source of the psyonic attacks, dead ahead of them now. It lurked within the core of the ship that the rest of the Ejjai were trying to flee from.

She didn't want to lose anyone else, so she transported right to the source to face it down and destroy it, on her own.

She was in a central psyonic collection chamber, lined with Thellurian step-up rods to gather and intensify psyonic powers.

The first thing she did was race around the chamber, destroying as many of the rods as she could with her Chaos swords. Ejjai dead lay piled up in heaps and scattered in ones and twos. Half of them had been trying to fight their way out of the chamber and escape.

Most had not made it, and like James, their heads had burst open, or their bodies had been telekinetically ripped open and twisted in extremely creepy ways.

Naero heard strange gurgling, chortling sounds as she continued to race around the room, taking down the psyonic collectors.

As she came around a large shielded pod, she beheld two male Ejjai being contained in Thellurian alloy cages.

Hideous psyonic mutants, perhaps grown or developed in some lab.

One was clearly dead, shot up full of holes.

Unfortunately, the other creature was still very much alive, and enraged.

The Ejjai had been trying to kill the mutants and cut off their knots of multiple heads sprouting from their broad, warped necks. So many heads that the mutants could hardly hold them up, they were so top heavy.

The remaining psyonic mutant was wounded and furious, but it hadn't spotted her or become aware of her yet. The damn thing had so many heads that its shriveled, atrophied body could hardly move around.

Each ravening head itself, no matter what various size, was swollen with a distended, blue-violet glowing brain that pulsed with its throbbing black veins and blood flow. The glowing brains were so large that some of the heads did not have eyes.

A psyonic freak–a monster–created by equally sick and twisted minds. These were their enemies. Once more, the Ejjai could not have created such an abomination on their own.

Who was helping them do these things?

Shetanna ignited her katanas and swept in at the thing to take it out.

At last it became aware of her, and her intent.

Psyonic force waves drilled Shetanna back into the shattered hull.

Three times she tried to fight her way back in against those waves of force.

Three times the mutant flung her back.

Glowing tentacles of naked psyonic power lashed out like lightning, wrapped around her, and dragged her toward the mutant's working, gibbering jaws.

Shetanna fought back, chopping and hacking at her bonds, but her swords simply passed through them like ghosts.

If she was going to survive and defeat this thing, she had to engage it on a psyonic level.

Marines broke in and opened fire on the mutant, but it shielded itself against their attacks and sought to entangle them all in hundreds of glowing psyonic tendrils.

Shetanna allowed the creature to draw her closer, putting up a show of struggling in vain.

She impaled it on scores of jagged spears of psyonic Chaos energy, once she was close enough. Then, once the mutant dropped her and the others and stopped attacking, for good measure, she severed all of the still glowing heads off at the thick neck.

After the Marines saw to the body of Maurice James, Company 36 sure had a tale to tell that night.

Word filtered down that overall, the war as a whole was going well. Bravo Command was still the tip of the spear, but even they could only fight on about ten percent of the invaded worlds.

They couldn't be everywhere at once. All of the other Spacer Marine Battle Groups had their hands full on many other worlds, more or less doing the same thing–gutting the invaders. But the Alliance forces and even more and more Corps world forces continued to back them up.

Bravo had plenty to keep them busy, and like most frontline fighting units, they focused on that. Occasionally stories would filter down through the ranks about units facing down similar challenges and threats, or even something new to look out for.

Then there was new gear. All Marines loved their tek.

The 3rd Command Death Eyes were the first to integrate the new phaze rifles throughout their units. The Razor Princes, and princesses, of 6th Command tested new powered suits of combat armor with built in energy blades. The 8th Command Star Walkers implemented the latest gravwings, and advanced microdrone droppods.

They were all kept fighting at the front as it continued to advance, but behind the scenes, there was always good camaraderie and healthy competition between all of the different Spacer Marine battle groups.

A few days later, after the wake, the next Seventhday brought the special dance night beatdown between many Marine units and groups based at the company level, including 36.

They made use of a huge WebBall arena ship.

Company after company sent in their best stompers to do their thing and wow the crowds with their skills and athletic prowess. Some groups were as small as twenty. Others had as many as fifty or sixty dancer.

Then the entire arena shook and shuddered. A full two hundred Marines from Bravo Company 36 marched in dressed in full white parade uniforms. Their MCL Shetanna flashed in, appearing to lead them.

As they danced, their nanosuits melted around their taut bodies from uniforms into tight, flashing and shining dance costumes.

Naero's costume was so skimpy she didn't quite understand why she simply wasn't doing her routines naked. Her gungirls had helped design the lurid thing, and she took their word that it throcked.

They defied gravity, and in zero-G, the entire arena began to spin.

Shetanna summoned intricate glowing platforms, levels, and steps of glowing, transparent red Chaos energy out of nowhere for 36 to perform on and within. She and her Marines danced and flipped through the air. Holograms and light show beams highlighted and featured the hottest acts and dance routines.

For the finale, Shettana shot into the air and seemed to explode like a tremendous living skyrocket, and vanished within an explosion of light and a deafening boom as all the lights went out.

When the lights came back on, all of the units gathered there were left dumbstruck and speechless. Shetanna and Bravo had completely disappeared. Then the crowd exploded in thunderous cheering, went wild, and nearly tore the arena down.

Once things settled back down, other acts came on and made feeble attempts to compare. But everyone present already knew who had won the competition.

28

At Eldratha-2, humanity finally had the invaders on the run. But the Ejjai grew increasingly more desperate and destructive, doing everything they could to cause maximum damage, no matter what happened to their own forces.

The Spacer Navy and Intel neutralization fixer clouds had their hands full–speaking figuratively, since fixers did not have actual hands. Alliance dampening fields kept the invaders from simply blanketing the remaining worlds in atomics and cosmicide devices.

By now, the Corps fleets that had been crippled by the enemy were finally coming back online to assist in a major way, refitted and ready to fight once again. They became a major factor in the High Crusade, near the very end. Their numbers alone made a big difference against a final push on the part of the enemy to flood the Corps worlds with invading hordes.

For once, Spacers and landers–all of humanity–hunted the invading forces down with a vengeance and crushed them, wherever they could be found.

Besides that, working with the lander worlds became much easier with local lander fleets working side by side with the Spacers. As the Spacer forces penetrated deeper into the worlds of Corps space, old hatreds and prejudices, long egged on by the Corps, died hard. Spacer forces still came under fire at times from populations they were fighting to rescue from the Ejjai invaders.

Yet once everyone fully cooperated and coordinated their efforts together to defeat and destroy the invaders, everyone could agree on that much. There were far fewer incidents of prejudice and outright aggression against Spacers.

The local populations quickly learned the value of having the Spacers as their allies.

The Spacer military put the Ejjai down hard and fast, better than anyone else. And that saved lives and shortened the terrible war.

Spacers grudgingly began to be seen as avenging heroes, even on Corps worlds where the Ejjai did not invade.

And the various vid incarnations of Shetanna became a galactic phenomena. Nearly every sentient race had their own version of the legend in every form of media available.

There was even a hilarious Silesian variant of the Dark Angel of Death who grunted and cursed a lot, told rude jokes, and liked to fart at key times during all of the excitement. The frogs loved it.

Naero saw one of the vids and couldn't get past Shetanna having a pulsing throatbag and coming up with creative ways to tell the Ejjai how to dine on her bodily waste products.

In many instances, however, on Corps worlds that had remained cut off by the invasion, it became better to send in some of the lander forces first, especially the heavily populated megacities where the focus was on trying to evacuate people in advance of enemy pushes and attacks.

Some of those lander populations still weren't used to large numbers of heavily armed Spacers suddenly showing up in their cities.

But the new evacuation strategy also saved countless lives. By the time the enemy did strike, they often found entrenched, well-organized Spacer Alliance forces ready to blanket them in waves of destroying fire.

This amounted to a huge surprise for the invaders, when they were expecting to butcher helpless civilians in yet another frenzied orgy of bloodletting.

On a few occasions, the massed lander forces were so enraged that they actually requested that the Spacers hold back in supporting roles, and let them cut the enemy down.

They wanted payback for what the Ejjai had done to their various peoples, and were determined to get it.

The Spacers didn't mind taking a breather here or there, and were always at hand if the enemy got tricky and tried to turn the tables.

Shetanna and Company 36, like the rest of Bravo, enjoyed having the extra forces to implement the various evac strategies. Then the defender attack units, such as Bravo, were free and clear to unleash all-out fury on the invader without being worried about fighting among a packed mass of helpless civies. That cut the hassles with fleeing refugees way down as well, not to mention a major reduction in civy casualties.

Of course, this wasn't always possible. And it took many large additional military groups in massive efforts to effect such large scale evac-strategies. But it was worth it, and now they had the numbers to pull it off, where possible.

Coordinated, large scale evacuations ahead of invader attacks became the standing order and strategy of the day, whenever and wherever they could be implemented.

And it also meant that the horrible war was finally beginning to wind down. Everyone was very grateful for that.

Such was the situation Bravo faced on Eldratha-2. The Gigacorp worlds used huge mining transports to swoop in and evacuate the next gigacity about to come under attack.

They quickly leapfrogged and dumped the population off at another gigacity or between gigacities, in an area with a mild climate, somewhere else on the world that wasn't a war zone. Of course it was a humanitarian and logistics nightmare, but another entire naval group of old ships and swarms of fixers tackled the task at hand. Relocation was better than slaughter, and in most cases, it was only for a matter of days, long enough for the military to wipe out the invaders. Like a big, messy camping trip.

On this world, Bravo and 36 held off the massed invaders and then brought in ground assault ships to eradicate the foe.

The Ejjai could never get the knack of not simply charging all of their forces forward to attack and destroy. Time and time again, this flaw in their strategy allowed them to be jammed up and simply rolled over, exterminating them in large numbers like a plague or swarm of insects.

This seemed to be a major flaw in their mental and strategic mindset and basic make-up.

Things continued to go well for the defenders, until the last few evacuation craft started to lift off, and then suddenly crashed back down into the starport.

One ship even caught fire, causing great loss of life. But the strange thing was, that initial reports from rescue teams said that the people inside were not trying to escape the flames.

The word came down. Everyone on those crashed ships had been stunned or immobilized somehow.

But how?

Scans hadn't picked up any mass stunners at work. They were usually the size of huge vessels, and no such enemy ships were present, cloaked or uncloaked. Fixers detected no nerve gas agents present. How had so many people been incapacitated, and all at once?

Then more landers on the front lines began to drop, including units of the military. Even when they were in sealed EV suits, combat armor, and buttoned-up vehicles.

Whatever was causing the massive sweeps of stunning seemed to be spreading directly toward Shetanna and 36.

Then it began to take down the Marine units around them.

Om, what the hell is happening? Can the fixers detect anything?

As a precaution, she sealed herself with a gel-like suit of defensive Chaos energy.

I've done a nanoparticle scan through several fixer clouds, N. This is a nanolevel attack, far too sophisticated for the Ejjai to develop.

Another gift from the invader masters, then.

Apparently. We can't see them with our eyes, but clouds of insidious tiny drones, or enemy stunbugs, if you will, are infiltrating everything. They are programmed to stun all of us, and leave us helpless before the Ejjai.

How do we stop it, Om?

This is far too big for you and me, N. I've discovered their weaknesses, however. Order the fleets in orbit to bathe this entire area in a low-level disrupting neutrino and electron pulse wave at these concentrated energy levels and frequencies.

At those levels, Om? They won't harm anything. We won't even feel a tingle.

Trust me, N. We won't feel a thing, but the stunbugs' delicate nanocircuitry will be completely fried, and fuse into useless dust. Then the microfixers can start scrubbing, cleaning them up, and recycling them. The entire task will still take days.

Naero called it in.

Haisha, Om. If only we could do something to make the stunbugs show up better on the scans.

I've got it. Tell Intel to flux the wave pulse to these frequencies and intervals. That should activate the stunbugs and cause them to show up toward the bottom of the infrared scans as low-level, ambient glowing light.

Brilliant, Om. That will cause the stunbugs to basically heat up and shimmer slightly, so that our scans can see if we've missed any.

I thought I just said that? I'm setting your helmet screen detectors and scan filters so that you can see them, N.

Naero's face shield flickered before her.

Haisha, Om! We're already swimming in them, like a sea of plankton in an ocean.

36 was about to be overcome by waves of these stunbugs.

Some of her Marines had already gone down. Somehow the little drones were even able to work their way into stealth combat armor and meks.

Then Naero's protective gel suit began to light up, as the stunbugs attacked her protective Chaos field and tried to work their way through.

The enemy stunbugs sacrificed themselves by countless millions in an effort to wear down her defenses and literally chew their way through her active barrier of Chaos energy gel.

She flared her field several times, burning away great swaths of them around her. But as soon as she finished incinerating them with Chaos energy, more of them closed in around her.

Urgently, Naero called in the request for the blanket pulse waves over their positions on all channels.

The stunbugs were persistent and apparently adaptive. They swarmed on her with greater and greater intensity in an effort to overwhelm her defenses.

Om, hurry. Most of 36 is already down. They'll stun me in less that a minute. Naero focused all of her Mystical powers just to hold them off.

On the scans, waves of seemingly harmless disruptor energy swept over the battlefield, bathing the the area from orbit in overlapping sweeps.

Om was correct. Keyed properly to the stunbugs, the energy feedback caused the tiny drones to seize up and became completely inert, falling to the ground or floating in the air as fading dust. Naero walked through them, kicking them up in clouds of extremely fine dust.

But the damage had been done, she saw as she looked around at all of her stunned Marines. Scores of units had been taken down and now lay helpless on the battlefield, at the mercy of any enemy forces who wished to rush in and murder them.

Om, we need antidotes to this stunning effect.

The biofixers and I are working as fast as we can. It's not like they've been poisoned. Stunning is different, and knocks out consciousness in different ways—not at the chemical and neurochemical levels, but the deeper, actual energy levels of the brain synapses and body relays.

You mean, we have to find a way to trigger the stunned people so that they wake up again?

Exactly. Stunning puts a sentient mind and body to sleep basically, and usually for an hour or two. We're working on reversing that process.

Then hop to it, Om. I've got a bad feeling that we don't have too much time.

It is not possible to work on a solution faster. And yes, you are correct. Trouble is heading our way in the form of enemy skirmishers and enemy ground assault craft. They fully intend to pummel and pound this sector and everyone stunned in this area to death, and then suck up the bodies in the mini-meatships that will follow on. They obviously planned it all this way.

First Naero and Om called in all reinforcement units to defend the Marines who were stricken and helpless. The stunbugs were down, so there was no further need to hold back or take precautions.

"All reserves to the front. All available Spacer Navy orbital batteries. Put fire on these enemy ground assault craft that I have painted on the grid. Take them down. Protect our people who have been stunned. The enemy can't be allowed to reach them. Halt and throw back the enemy advance."

At first Naero assailed the enemy on her own. Shetanna smashed into the advancing lines of the enemy skirmishers, cutting, kicking, blasting, and using every lethal trick she could conjure up,

She looked like a flashing wheel of scarlet fire, or a spinning red saw blade of Chaos energy, scything through the enemy forward lines and positions.

Then a thin line of Spacer Marine reinforcements joined her, while the Navy pounded and blasted the attacking enemy ships.

Still, they were too few.

Alone, the Marines could not hold. And Naero and the other MCLs present on the battlefield were quickly exhausting themselves and their abilities.

They would be forced back, or swept away, and their stricken comrades left to the enemy to be slaughtered.

Another tide suddenly swept in.

Lander forces who had originally been part of the evac units soldiered up and flooded in. It wasn't pretty, but it was enough to first hold the enemy, and then begin to throw them back.

The invaders went for broke, and sent in all of their available reserves, in a last-ditch attempt to press their fleeting advantage and overwhelm the defender lines.

There in that firestorm, Spacer and lander fought side by side against the common foe. And no matter who went down, others stepped in to face that wall of fire, and strike back.

All of humanity stood their ground and marched into battle, shoulder to shoulder, to save their fallen comrades who could not fight back. Shields flared and disrupted on both sides. Humans took the fight straight down the enemy's gullet with valor and grit, punched the slasher's tickets, and shot the invaders full of glowing holes.

That night, everyone celebrated Food Night on Thirdday, gorging themselves on an array of delicacies. Naero made fried Guroni cheese and sweet barbecue sandwiches for 36, with help from some of her mates.

She later came upon a somber Jonny Fox, talking with some of their friends while the later still picked at their plates.

Chime and Pete weren't present. Completely besotted with each other now, the couple had taken a well-earned leave together to one of the playworlds in the rear areas.

By all reports they were having a marvelous time. Naero and the the rest of the gungirls could get all of the juicy details after the lovers returned.

Naero studied her friend. "Why so glum, Jonny?"

He shook his head. "I'm still worried about my cousin, N."

Naero rested an arm around her friend's shoulder. "She's fine. Chime's never been happier. She and Pete have it good. Be happy for them."

Jonny made a face and nodded. "You don't get it, Naero. Sure she's happy. Both of them are giddy and delirious. That's the problem. There's still a war going on. Don't you know how this works during wartime? It's like they're tempting the fates or something. This is exactly when something bad always happens."

Naero rested her other arm on the table and nodded. "Oh, I get it. Just when things seem at their best, that's when something really stupid or tragic happens to mess everything up. Yeah, I've seen that happen. Too many times. But you can't think that way. It doesn't always go wrong. I've seen that as well."

Jonny threw up both of his hands in frustration. "You gotta help me, N. We gotta get everyone else in on this. We need to protect Chime and Pete during these last few weeks, to help make sure that nothing happens to them."

Naero shook her head sadly. "Jonny, we always look out for each other. That's all we can do. We can try to do more, but you know as well as I do that there aren't any guarantees for any of us. What, you're gonna start acting crazy like Whip?"

"No. I just have this bad feeling about things that I can't shake."

"We all take our chances in combat, Jonny. That's just the way it is."

"Don't you think I know all of that by now? Look. Just promise me you'll help me in this, N."

"You have my word. I will."

29

Naero relived the same strange nightmare. She was trapped inside some kind of metal pod, cylinder, or missile-like craft. She wore strange, bulky clothes that were also hard and weird. Parts of the nightmare she could not remember exactly right.

Lights flashed; she recalled hearing strange voices in her head and all around. There was fire and an explosion right as she penetrated some kind of unusual energy barrier. The equally strange vessel began to plummet and then proceeded to crash, despite her best efforts to avoid doing so. She struggled to control its descent and protect herself.

Another, even more violent blast tore her free of the stricken craft. She hurtled to the ground, slowed by some kind of odd wings on her back.

Was that it? Was she from the stars, from heaven itself? Was she some kind of angel? If so, what kind was she?

There were supposedly both good and bad angels as she recalled.

Again she wondered. What kind was she?

But her wings hadn't worked right, or she and they had been damaged somehow. Despite her odd protective suit, her head hurt terribly and then, at the very last, her wings stopped working altogether. She still fell toward the rapidly rising ground and her doom.

At the last instant, she had heard a voice inside her head, and together, with the power of that voice, they had somehow slowed hers down enough so that she did not perish.

Then, somehow, she made herself go from one place to another, from several hundred meters up in the sky to just a handful of meters, without gaining speed. In fact, he had even slowed her rate of descent.

What were these strange powers and abilities that she possessed?

Still above the ground, she spotted farm fields as far as the eye could see, in every direction. The pain in her head remained terrible.

A spinning, simple machine like a big fan set up on top of a simple wooden stand broke her fall when she smashed into it. She broke off the thin metal fan blades and crashed through the flimsy, wooden structure.

The structure broke her fall, but Naero struck her head again in the process. Perhaps more than once.

After the farmer and his family dug her out of the wreckage and the ground, she couldn't think straight for a very long while or remember anything about herself.

Who was she? What was her name, even? Where had she come from and why? Why did she come here? Why had she hurtled down from the sky? Why had her wings stopped working?

So many bewildering questions. Even when she recalled that her name was Naero, that still did not tell her very much at all.

Mama Kincaid on the farm plainly said that Naero was clearly a star girl from the star people. And that some of the star people were good, and some of them were very wicked.

Naero smiled. It was just like the angels.

The farm people hoped very much that she was one of the good ones. Naero did not think of herself as evil.

If she was of the good sort, that would make everything much easier, for all concerned.

After Naero healed up, she was more than welcome to stay with the Kincaids and the farm people in that region. But some day soon, the council of elders among the farm people said that Naero would be taken to the great trade station on the capital of the farm world. From there, she would need to return to the other star people, and hopefully go back to her star family.

Naero healed up enough in that one day—at least physically—that the farm people were very amazed. Mama Kincaid said that that was the way of some of the star people, and that they had special blood, it was said, which made them fast healers. Yet Naero's head still hurt, and she could not remember much yet. Mama Kincaid told her that the head took its own time to heal, just like the heart, and that it wasn't good to try to rush either of them.

That second day, Naero was up and out of her sick bed and started walking around the big farmhouse and outside, filled with curiosity and questions about everything around her. It all seemed so strange.

And deep inside herself, she felt that there was something very important that she was either forgetting or had forgotten, like misplacing an object or an article of clothing, and not being able to find it. She had something terribly important to tell the farm people who were helping her and being so nice to her.

Something…if only she could remember what.

Some kind of danger or threat that was coming soon, but Naero could not recall what it was.

Knowing practically nothing made Naero even more full of questions. Where was she? On a special farm world, of course. But why had she come here or been sent here? Sent here by whom? What was a farm world? Why was this one special? Who were these people and why did they live here as they did? Why didn't they seem to know anything that might help her?

Mama Kincaid finally sat Naero down with some of the girls and the womenfolk from the neighboring farms who had gathered together to talk about the star girl who fell from the sky, and what should be done with her in the time they would have together. They all brought things with them to give her. Things that she might need, like clothing, hats, shoes, soap, and brushes. They were very generous. She couldn't go around in a nightgown all the time she was among them.

They tried to answer her many questions, calmly and patiently, but they didn't seem to know very much beyond their world.

Like most of the adult women, Mama Kincaid wore her long brown hair, shot with lines of bright silver, in a long, plain braid down her broad back, with the front parted simply in the middle. She was in her mid to late forties, and held to be very wise and even shrewd, in her own ways, about farm life and people in general. Many of the other older women in the women's circle politely deferred to her as a respected leader.

She was a small woman–still much taller than Naero–which bothered Naero for some reason she could not remember. But Mama Kincaid was both strong and gentle at the same time. She was neither slender like the young girls, nor fat. She had womanly curves without being plump. Her small hands and arms looked powerful and more that able thanks to a daily life of hard work.

The farm people rode horses–even the women, apparently, because most of them wore a long, divided dark skirt of some solid color: brown, green, blue, or gray. The split skirt was belted at the waist with a plain, unadorned leather belt with a plain buckle.

The farm people dressed plainly for work, and did not seem to adorn or decorate themselves very much. On top, their plain white blouses with full, cuffed sleeves and high collars were also without any decoration. Once they came indoors, the women took off the broad-brimmed straw hats that men and women both wore outside to keep off the hot sun. Even children wore them, but never inside.

Men wore their hair straight and clipped short around the back and ears. Men wore similar white shirts and dark pants, but some wore dark leather vests, either buttoned or left open. All of the farm people wore simple, comfortable leather shoes on their feet that laced above the ankle like low boots.

Some men and women carried a basic chronometer–pocket watches of ancient style and design, sometimes on plain leather cords or chains. Ancient mechanical clocks ticked on the farmhouse walls and kept time.

Many small children, younger than ten, went barefoot. Little boys wore a shirt and dark pants. Little girls wore a simple long dress or frock, and usually pantaloons or knickers underneath.

"You ask us where you are, star girl Naero," Mama Kincaid told her. "Our world here is called Yoder-3, and we are called Yoderians by outsiders and offworlders. Some among the star people brought us to these rich farming lands on this world over five centuries ago and gave it to us to work the rich lands here as is our way. One of the great leaders of the star people was somehow descended from a race of farm people much like us and our traditions. They brought us here, and they still give us medicines to keep us healthy and strong.

"This great leader whom I mentioned saw the basic wisdom of preserving us and our ways of life somewhere among the stars, even though he himself no longer followed them. Legends say that he and the star people were wealthy and very powerful. They even changed our weather, in order to make our world here more stable, and suitable for farming and raising livestock, if such a thing can be imagined.

"And the only people who are allowed to live on Yoder-3 are we Yoderians, who uphold and adhere to our simple and sustainable ways. We work hard, and live out our lives in peace. For many generations, we have had extremely little crime. And no wars."

Naero's head suddenly gave her a sharp pain, as if something was trying to break out of it like cracking a hen's brown egg open. The mention of wars had sparked something in her mind that gravely troubled her once again.

"Are you all right, star girl Naero?" Mama Kincaid asked her, resting a firm hand on her arm to steady her.

"I'm fine. It will pass. I'm still very curious. So, the star people leave you alone?"

"Yes. They allow us to live here according to our ways, and they stay apart from us. What's more, they keep others apart from us. Others who would bring their crime and war among us."

"When do you have contact with the star people?"

"Twice each year, at the capital of each hemisphere, the star people come in their great starships. The planetary barrier the star people placed around Yoder-3 has entry points that can be opened only by our grand elders. The ships come down to the established meeting places to barter allowed goods, products, equipment, and medicines for our doctors. We have no use for credits or other forms of money. We barely electrify our homes for lighting and food refrigeration, and heating in the winters. Most of us avoid contact with the star people and all kinds of potential conflict. We keep and have no weapons. We have no armies; not even constables."

Naero thought a moment, her head hurting once more, but she hid it from the farm people. "There must be disagreements occasionally. Even among the farm people. How are such matters resolved?"

Mama Kincaid smiled. "The elders, both men and women of each area, negotiate and resolve all conflicts and disagreements at the local levels, through the circles of men, and the circles of women, and discussion and negotiation between the two. We are a non-violent, peaceful people."

Naero suddenly gasped, as if a hot spike pierced her head.

Invasion.

The word just popped into Naero's mind as if she couldn't control it. Why was that one word suddenly so important?

"So, you and your ways survive here, because of a planetary shield that keeps others out?" Naero stated.

"In their wisdom," Mama Kincaid said calmly, "the star people put up the powerful, protective barrier all around Yoder-3, and taught a small group of our people how to help operate and maintain it. This barrier keeps out the wars and crime and greed and other negative influences that would destroy our world and our way of life, if we allowed them to take root here. Our elders have powerful radios that can communicate with our friends among the star people, and organize the trading times."

Naero considered her nightmare once again. If she was a star girl, perhaps her vessel hit the protective barrier of the planet somehow, a barrier she hadn't known was even there. Perhaps that was why she had crashed on Yoder-3.

Because she had injured her head somewhat; her thoughts were still mixed up.

But strange images and flashes of memory continued to build and buffet her mind like an impending flood. Was she starting to remember more as she continued to heal?

"I think I need to get to one of those radios the elders have in order to speak with my people," Naero said flatly. "I need to contact the star people and find the ones who know me."

"And then what?" Mama Kincaid asked her. "Even if we could do such a thing, which we cannot from where we are. What would you say? You can't remember anything yet. Who would you ask for?"

Naero stammered for a moment, her mind still a confused jumble. "I…I can't remember."

"Just as I thought, Naero. Even though you are a star girl, you will be just fine with us for a few months while we are awaiting the harvest and the next trade time. You can wait a little while also, and live among us during that short time. There is no hurry, and you seem kind, and well-behaved. The time will pass swiftly. Then, when the next barter time comes, you can arrange to go to the meeting place to contact and rejoin your people. That will require a long journey that must be approved by the elders. Perhaps by then your memory will have returned as well. For now, there is no reason to trouble the Elders about the use of their radios."

Naero still struggled and strained.

No, this wasn't right. There was still something important that she was missing. "There was," she began, "a serious reason why I came her. I know there was, but I just can't remember it right now."

"Calm yourself, child. You're getting yourself upset."

"No, it is vital that I recall it. I was sent here for a reason, ahead of many others, I believe. I think…I think that I might have been sent here… to warn you–"

"Warn us?" Mama Kincaid exclaimed. "Warn us about what?"

Naero sighed and shook her head once more in defeat. "Something. I just can't remember what."

Mam Kincaid held her close, patted her on the back, and gently stroked her hair. "It's all right. We're safe here. Nothing can harm us through the barrier."

"I got through," Naero noted.

"Yes, and you were very nearly destroyed. Listen to me, Naero. It's all right. You're safe. All of us are safe. You shall live among us as our honored guest. Now, I must ask you: Will you be able to try to adhere to and accept our ways and respect them, while you live here with us?"

Naero smiled and nodded. "I will try. I'll do my best."

"Good. I must say, you are a pretty little thing, star girl. Somewhere in the stars, there must be others of your kind, your family and friends, who care for you and are concerned that you are now missing from them."

Naero grinned and looked away slightly. "I hope so." Yet deep within, she still felt very worried, for reasons that she still could not bring back to her mind.

The Yoderian women and young girls nearer to Naero's own age helped her dress in her new clothes. She now had two sets of clothing for daily wear and work, and a newer, very clean set of the same clothing to wear to church on their rest day, where they practiced their religion and read from their holy book.

The simple undergarments and stockings were rather funny to Naero. Mama Kincaid's daughters seemed to take great pleasure in brushing and combing Naero's long, black hair and plaiting its shiny tresses into a luxuriant, glistening braid down her back.

Naero quickly learned that women and men washed up each morning and night as needed. Hygiene and cleanliness, as well as modesty, seemed very important to the farm people.

When Naero changed her clothes, many of the women left the room in a hurry, while others turned away while she was briefly naked. Even Mama Kincaid.

Naero did not have any such restrictions in her mind, especially when she was only among other women.

She learned that each of the large dwellings had at least four private washrooms with basins, tubs, pitchers, towels, and washcloths. They used simple, natural soaps and shampoos on their bodies and hair that were barely scented. Everyone in the household was trained and disciplined to keep themselves neat and clean, and to clean up after themselves.

The Kincaids were kind about telling her what to do and how to do things, but they clearly expected her to comply.

In their quest for modesty, humility, and simplicity, as they called it, the Yoderians had very few mirrors in their homes. In fact, they only had small ones in their washrooms for the women to fix their hair in, and the men to shave in, if they chose to do so.

Many of the men who could do so elected to grow full beards, or some kind of beard. No one among them used any kind of perfume or cologne, and the women did not wear any cosmetics. There was no visible jewelry, except for the watches.

The only exception to this rule were the married couples, who wore bands of matching gold or silver on their left wrists.

Naero found the Yoderians modest, humble, plainspoken, unadorned, quiet, and kind.

They were also stubborn, astonishingly hard working–much like ants–and very funny in their own ways. Their sense of humor could be very dry, and so light that if you weren't paying attention, you just might miss it.

They did not ask people to work.

They expected it, and told others what to do right up front.

Within the home and within the boundaries of the fenced-in yard, the mother or woman of the farmhouse was the boss, and controlled nearly every aspect of Yoderian life.

The father, or the head man of the family stepped in only to make his preferences known, as was his right, and to back up his wife if need be.

If a husband and wife had any serious disagreements that they couldn't resolve between each other, the couple could take them to the elders of both the men's circle and the women's circle to help decide them. If they did so, the solutions made by the elders were considered the final ruling on the matter.

Yet few couples did so any longer, because doing that was seen as a serious loss of face and status among the farm people. People were expected to manage their own homes and relationships, and take responsibility for themselves. On occasion, however, some couples would still quietly seek the assistance of the elders in some private matter.

If the mother was the boss of the home, the father was the master of the barns, and the fields, and the livestock of each farm. And at peak times of need, he could even call-out the women and children of the farmhouse to help in the fields.

He could even, in his turn, call upon assistance from family, friends, and neighbors, especially during the planting and harvesting times, when everyone had to work together for the good of all.

It was expected that neighbors would help neighbors during good times and bad. But times were mostly good.

Barns or farmhouses occasionally collapsed during storms or burned down. Young people got married, and if there weren't any homes available in the extended family, a new farm would need to be constructed.

Each month there were periods of time organized for some kind of construction somewhere, and the neighbors and families donated their time, labor, and food until the project was completed. Many able hands made some farms appear like magic in the span of several days.

Most people were farmers, and almost everyone farmed or raised livestock to some extent. For their own needs, if nothing else.

But the Yoderians also had need for smiths, carpenters, millers, coopers, hunters, farriers, tanners, weavers, and shoemakers. Any kind of craft that was needed had crafters who made a living doing such work.

There were also doctors, nurses, and trained midwives who made house calls. Each collection of so many farms, even if they did not call themselves a town, had a staffed medical center to deal with accidents and emergencies.

Each county had a hospital, and a county seat where the elders met together.

There were no large cites, except for the capital trade areas near the two planetary starports, which were only used twice each year.

Most trade was local, and went as far as people wished to take it. There was virtually no crime to speak of. The farm people had no prisons.

In the evening or sometimes in the early morning, the farm people would take their favorite horses or ponies out for a ride. It seemed to be one of their only forms or recreation outside.

Courting and courtship among the farm people was a big point of conversation and a part of their lives, as long as it was all kept respectful.

Courtship could begin at any time after the age of nineteen and was required to last for three years. The farm people lived long lives. Life expectancy was way into the nineties, barring accidents. Illness among them was also rare.

Couples who wished to court had to decide at the end of the three years to either marry or separate. Divorce was frowned upon and extremely rare, but not completely impossible.

Married couples were still expected to be reserved and modest in public, but could be as affectionate as they wished in and around their homes. Sex before marriage was rare with so many people constantly watching, but some courting couples often snuck away to spoon or pet, as it was called.

That night, Naero helped Mama Kincaid and her family prepare for the evening meal. It was the sixth day of their week, and they had to finish supper before nightfall.

The next day–the seventh day–was the holy day of rest for the farm people. Other than simple daily tasks and meals, no work was performed on the day of rest. On that day, Yoderians relaxed, rested, went to their churches to worship, and then visited family or friends, or played simple games, rode their mounts, and amused themselves.

They did not dance, even at weddings, and they enjoyed simple music and gatherings where music was played. They liked gentle singing with or without accompaniment. Only about half of their songs were religious in nature.

Mothers and fathers routinely sang to their children in the evenings. Sons and daughters also sang for their families at night for family entertainment.

Mama and Papa Kincaid had been blessed with five healthy children, as they said.

Lukas was the oldest at twenty and was courting a pretty, young neighbor girl of nineteen from across the way. The girl had golden hair like wheat and big brown eyes. Like his stout father, Lukas was of medium height, with the dark hair of his father as well. But the oldest son also had his mother's green eyes and sharp nose, but his beard was only stubble, compared to his father's full, black beard, almost thirty millimeters in length.

Next came the oldest daughter, Yisel, eighteen and simply dying to reach courting age in another year. She was curvy and pretty, quick-minded and blue-eyed like her father, but with her mother's luxuriant brown hair.

Yisel apparently had eyes only for a tall, handsome rancher boy near her same age, who helped his father raise horses and cattle about two miles from the Kincaid farm. They apparently made eyes at each other at church, every rest day.

That was as far as it had gone. They barely spoke to each other once each week.

The middle daughter was Bekah, dark blond with freckles and green eyes. Bekah was skinny at fifteen and very industrious. She never stopped moving. She seemed cheerful and never complained.

Shiah was the younger son at twelve, gangly and polite. But he stared at Naero with his big blue eyes, his mouth hanging open to the point of distraction and embarrassment.

249

Naero clearly recognized puppy love when she saw it. And Shiah had it bad for her. He was always following her around, trying to help her with something. His sisters giggled and laughed at him slightly, but he didn't care.

The baby of the Kincaid family was nine-year-old Riith, small and dark-haired with brown eyes and ivory skin, like a china doll. Her long, black hair was still naturally curly like her papa's and seemed to burst out of her braid at will like some creature trying to escape. She was funny and loud among her relatively quiet family.

Their meal that night was fried chicken, potatoes with chicken gravy, greens of some kind, and biscuits with butter, gravy, or honey. Dessert was some kind of dark berry pie of a local variety.

Naero struggled to learn and remember all of their names. Papa Kincaid was named Francis, and Mama Kincaid's name was Nelena.

That evening, when the table was set, they all held hands around their table as was their custom, and said thanks to their deity. Naero just smiled and watched. These were good people.

The food was excellent, and everyone had a big appetite, including Naero. They ate happily and quietly together.

Once dinner was finished, the table cleared, the food put away, and the dishes done, the sitting room was too hot from the day, so they all went out on the big porch, watching the beautiful sun set red in the sky. Darkness finally came, and there was a little time yet before they had to wash up for the night and go to sleep.

Even on their rest days, morning would come early in the summer.

The parents took turns reading from their holy book from their religion. Usually they were stories that taught a lesson. They were pleasant enough, but the words and strange names meant little to Naero.

Then Mama Kincaid sang a nice song, and all of her daughters joined in. It wasn't a sad song, but it still nearly made Naero cry. Something was still troubling her deeply.

The family spoke of their plans for the next day, and then Mama Kincaid sent them all in to wash up and get to bed.

At first, Naero was going to sleep alone in one of the guest rooms in the big farmhouse, the one she had been taken to when she was first brought in, in order to tend her wounds.

"Mama," Yisel asked. "It's Naero's first night in a strange place. Can the star girl sleep in my room tonight?"

"If she doesn't mind sharing a bed, and you snoring."

"Oh, Mama. I do not snore."

"You do snore, sister," Bekah noted.

"Like a big fat sow," Riith added.

Some slight laughter followed that.

"I wanted to sleep with the star girl," Riith complained.

Mama Kincaid smiled at her daughters.

It wasn't every day that they had one of the star people literally crash in among them.

"Naero is free to choose," Mama Kincaid said. "She can sleep in Yisel's room, if she wishes, and both of you, Bekah and Riith, can join them on the floor, if you bring some bedding and quilts in with you."

All of the girls looked eagerly at Naero, happy and waiting for her to say yes. Riith couldn't suppress a squeal of delight.

Naero hesitated, and smiled, still somewhat confused and befuddled by all that had happened. "Sure; why not?" she said.

After they all washed up for bed, the four of them sat around on Yisel's bed, brushing each other's long hair.

Naero found doing so very relaxing, and it soon made her sleepy.

Bekah brushed Naero's black hair. "Your tresses are like corn silk in my hands," she said. "It is so black and shiny–just like Riith's."

"Ouch," Riith exclaimed. "Not so hard, Yisel. At least the star girl doesn't have my curls and knots."

Her older sister laughed. "Little bug, if you brush them out more, you won't have so many pulls. That's how you keep the snarls and tangles out."

"I can't help it."

When they were finished, the sisters kissed each other on the cheeks.

They all made a point of kissing Naero on her cheeks as well.

Riith ran out briefly to go kiss her brothers good night.

Yisel's bed was large and comfortable enough. Naero did not mind sharing it.

Out their upper floor window, with the lights down, Naero saw Papa Kincaid walk out to the barn.

Yisel smiled. "Papa's going out to check the barn again," she said. "Same as he does every night."

Bekah giggled slightly. Naero was somehow missing their little private joke.

Riith ran back in and tried jump up on the bed with Yisel and Naero.

Yisel shooed her away. Then the Kincaid girls all knelt and said their nightly prayers.

After that, Riith tried to jump up on the bed again.

"No, no, Riith," Yisel insisted, "down on the floor with you!"

"Come on, little bug," Bekah said, wrestling the child down. "I'll hold you, little sister."

"I'm not a little bug, Bekah. And I'm not even little anymore. I'm nine."

"Of course you are. You're very big. Come here, now." Bekah patted the spot in the thick quilts right beside her. "I'll stroke your hair and sing to you, just like Mama does."

The two sisters settled in.

Naero spotted movement and light outside once more.

"And there goes Mama, Bekah," Yisel said, grinning wide.

Bekah laughed. "Papa sure does need a lot of help checking the animals each night," she added.

Naero finally figured out what was going on.

Yisel grinned even wider at Naero. "Out there in the hayloft, there's a cozy little room and a big bed set up. Up there, Mama and Papa can be as loud as they want. During the winter months, Mama often has to stifle herself. She doesn't like that."

Bekah laughed again. "Yes, sometimes Mama even puts a pillow over her head when she cries out."

"Bekah!" Yisel chided her.

"It's the truth, sister. May our husbands need as much help from us to check the critters at night!"

"You shouldn't talk that way, Bekah. Not at least until you're married yourself. And even then, it's not very nice."

Bekah stuck her tongue out at her older sister.

As they all drifted off to sleep, Naero kept watching the dark sky.

Something about the sky bothered her greatly.

As with most planetary shields, she could not see through it to make out the stars.

It occurred to her at that moment that she was starting to recall certain things.

Then bright, ominous flashes seemed to impact and pound on the energy barrier from without.

Someone–or some thing–was trying to force its way through.

She had an awful feeling that she should know what this was. Why couldn't she bring it to mind?

What was this thing or these things trying to break in?

What would take place if they did?

The flashes continued as Naero and the Kincaids went to sleep. But Naero woke up several times during the night as the flashes continued.

What was going to happen?

Naero expressed her vague fears to Mama and Papa Kincaid the next day.

"Those bright flashes in the sky last night. They are a sign that I need to use one of the elders' radios to try to contact my people. I know it in my heart."

"Naero, we've already spoken about this," Mama Kincaid told her. "There's plenty of time. You'll just have to be patient and wait."

"You saw the flashes as well as I," Naero told them. "Something's wrong."

"We have indeed seen such flashes at times before," Francis said.

"Yet never so many, and all night long," Nelena admitted. "The star girl may be right, my husband."

Papa Kincaid thought a moment, and then nodded. "Very well. I will petition the elders after church. The star people would warn us if there was danger. And either way, the barrier will protect us. It always has."

The family went to church at their local parish. Their local minister gave a very moving speech about the accepted ways of peace and goodness, peppered with readings from their holy book. Lukas sat with his betrothed, taking his turn with her family. Yisel made eyes at her rancher boy beau.

After the service, Mama Kincaid brought Naero forward before the elders in the church meeting room.

Papa Kincaid was already there. "Something more is wrong," he told Naero. "I have learned that the radios we normally use to contact the star people are no longer working at this time. We are cut off from them for some reason. The elders are greatly concerned."

"And the great barrier is under some kind of sustained attack," another elder said.

Naero could swear that someone or some thing was trying to say something to her–in her own mind.

"The radios and their signals are being jammed," she told the elders. She wondered how she knew that.

"Is there any place that your people can hide, if the barrier should collapse?"

The elders just stared at her.

Some of them even blinked, like fish.

"Basements," someone mentioned.

"Storm and root cellars," another said.

"An ice house."

"Perhaps some caves here and there," one elder suggested.

Naero frowned. Somehow, she had an extremely bad feeling that those options weren't going to work very well against anyone or anything that could get past a planetary defensive shield.

The elders were already at a loss, and did not want to alarm anyone.

Someone else noted, once again, that the barrier had protected them for centuries. To their mind, it always would.

Naero could readily see that they had no plan in place if the barrier ever did fail.

Even while Naero rode home in one of the two Kincaid family buggies with her Yoderian family–a flaming star fell burning from the sky.

That was definitely not good.

The elders rang a certain signal with the church bells that ordered everyone to their homes, while a group of several single men still at the church with the men's circle were sent to investigate the crash site.

Naero was adamant about going with them. She and Papa Kincaid joined the men on the investigation team. She told them that it could be other star people.

It wasn't.

Clearly, this was a section of a starship that had crashed down and was completely destroyed. And from the mangled guns and weaponry, it was obviously a warship made of some kind of strange, red alloy with weird markings.

Next came the shocking and mind-numbing sight of the charred alien bodies. These creatures looked tough, vicious, and animalistic, all in armor and bristling with weapons, explosives, and blades All of the aliens were apparently female, if that mattered.

The elders quickly ordered any weapons collected to be disposed of, and the bodies buried. For now, the wreckage was left smoking where it was, in a crater.

But when they were burying the bodies one of them suddenly exploded. The concussion knocked everyone off their feet.

Naero flew back and smacked her head into a tree.

When she regained her senses, she at last heard the actual voice speaking to her clearly in her mind, and quickly began to recall her memories, who she and what she was and why she had been sent to Yoder-3.

She gasped as everything rushed back into her head.

Haisha! The Ejjai invaders were coming, still ahead of the main forces of the Spacer Navy and Marines.

If even a small number of the enemy broke through the planetary defense barrier, the peaceful Yoderians would be completely helpless against the invader onslaught.

Even worse yet, the Ejjai could capture the planetary defenses, put the barrier back up, and then take their time sucking the farm world dry and processing the entire population to bloat the meatships.

There wasn't any time to explain all of that to the Elders.

It wouldn't do any good in any case, N. Glad to be back with you.

You too, Om. Just let me think a moment, while I'm still recovering my memories and my wits.

What could she accomplish?

Naero returned to the wreckage and teknomanced a couple of fixers. From there, she put the fixers to work, cannibalizing the wreckage, and forming armor, weapons, and ordnance for her to use.

"Get to your homes," Naero told the farm people. "If the star people can protect your world, they will. But if they cannot, you will see death and destruction beyond anything you can possibly imagine. These invaders are destroyers. You cannot reason with them. You cannot negotiate with them. They only know how to kill, torment, and destroy all that lives."

All of the Yoderians fled the crash site to reach their homes.

Another, even larger star fell out of the sky.

Naero recognized it as an entire invader battleship, all shot up, descending toward the rich crop fields, still barely under its own power. The bright, blood-red warship was on fire in several places along its massive length.

Then it rolled over in midair and exploded, continuing to go up in flames above the fields as it crashed. Papa Kincaid raced himself and Naero up to the farmhouse. They leaped out of the buggy.

Papa rushed inside to warn his family.

Naero led the horses and the buggy into the barn and left them there. She met with her small fixer cloud and her awaiting armory and gear.

She teknomanced into it all. Then she flew out of the barn upon a new set of gravwings. The Kincaids rushed out of the farmhouse to take shelter in the storm cellar along the one side.

That would not protect them much, but it was all that they knew.

Naero dropped down to warn them.

They stared up at her in all her armor and weapons in almost complete fear.

"I'm going to do my best to protect you all and this area. I don't know if I can or not."

Down in the cellar, she spotted pieces of an old, rusty iron stove for heating and a wood burning kitchen stove. She used teknomancy to quickly fashion the pieces into a makeshift barrier with a hatch. Then she had the fixers whip up a hasty shield generator.

"Stay behind those barriers. They won't protect you for very long, but it's better than nothing. I'm going out to fight."

"You don't have to do that for us," Papa Kincaid told her, holding the hatch open. "Fighting is not our way."

Naero smiled sadly. "No. It is not. But it is mine. For I am a warrior, and I will give my life for you all, if I must." With that she had the fixers activate the shield, and seal them in.

Naero flew out into the sky to assess the evolving battlefield before her.

"What are we up against, Om?"

Dozens of gravtanks and gunships, hundred of invader shock troops pouring out of the crashed battleship.

Copy that. How far away is help?

At least an hour or more, N. The Navy and Corps ships are doing their best holding off the invader fleets. The one invader battleship broke through on a fluke and was nearly destroyed.

We can't wait, Om. We know the invaders can do a lot of damage in an hour's time. Let's go take them out. We'll go in cloaked and try to take them all down. We have to destroy the rest of that ship, first, and any forces still on it. Then we clean up the stragglers."

That's a lot of stragglers, N. You know very well that you're going to exhaust yourself before all of this is done. We might not be able to stop them all.

I know, Om. Put up a fixer net. Keep us informed on every enemy location and their actions.

We know exactly what they'll do.

Naero went directly on the attack.

She knew she had to conserve her strength if she was going to fight this many of the enemy alone. She could not afford to pass out.

Chaos bursts exploded the power cores and obliterated the remains of the crashed battleship, while more Ejjai were still trying to pour out.

Then she cloaked and went after the gunships. After that, the gravtanks.

The Ejjai shocktroops continued to scatter and spread out to scout the surrounding area. They cut down animals, livestock, anything living that they came across.

Shetanna found herself low on strength and still outmatched, with more that a hundred enemy troops scattering in all directions.

She hunted, attacked, slew, and eradicated the foe as the desperate minutes wore on.

The fixers alerted her. Thirty Ejjai moved to attack the first farmhouse they came across.

Naero barely transported there to battle them to the death, hand-to-hand.

She was torn between the need to take them all out quickly, and yet conserve her energies.

She engaged the attackers one-on-one and in small groups. Blades, punches, whirling, spinning kicks sent the invaders flying with their chests and heads crushed and their bodies sliced open or in pieces.

Speed and strength. She unleashed the fury of the whirlwind upon them, transforming into a flashing cyclone of death.

She vanquished them all, yet the farmhouse still burned to the ground as she left. The Yoderians living there had fled away as the battle began, hopefully to one their neighbors.

At least Naero had given them the chance to get away from the enemy.

Fixers warned that yet another platoon from the invaders now moved upon the Kincaid farm to attack there.

Naero gasped and stumbled. She could no longer transport.

She raced at top speed to intercept the band.

The rest of the enemy spread out, gleefully killing cattle, horses, sheep, and other livestock exposed in the open fields or the thin forests.

Naero continued to fight to the last ounce of her strength and ability, hunting down the invaders as efficiently as possible.

She engaged them along their own arc of attack.

She remained cloaked as much as possible, so that they could not see where she struck from. Or that she stumbled and staggered toward them, sometimes gasping for breath.

She fought the final dozen as they charged the Kincaid farmhouse. Om did all that he could to sustain her and keep her up and fighting. He took out three of the enemy on his own.

The last Ejjai Alpha blasted the storm shelter doors open and poured fire down into it, trying to punch through the shield. The alpha was about to toss a shield disruption grenade within.

As Naero rushed up, she saw Papa and Mama Kincaid desperately shoving the heavy iron hatch up the stairs before them, trying to shield their children.

The chortling alpha cut loose with her mini-gun and activated the grenade.

Naero split open the alpha's head with her energy cutlass and swept the body away with a kick into some trees. The grenade flared harmlessly off the side.

The last several Ejjai in the area must have detected the fighting, and now converged upon her position from a distance.

Shetanna staggered around to face them, going down to one knee. Her legs would not respond. She couldn't stand.

Om.

Bravo Marines from 36 uncloaked around the invaders, gutting them and punching big glowing holes through their jerking bodies with precise, interlocking automatic fire.

The invaders convulsed in the twitching dance of death and then dropped.

Naero groaned and nearly pitched over onto her gasping face.

Then she heard cries from the Kincaid children down in the storm cellar.

She dropped her cutlass and crawled down into the storm cellar to help. Mama and Papa Kincaid had shielded their children with the shot-up hatch—and their own bodies.

Bot parents lay bleeding from multiple wounds.

Naero passed out trying to use her biomancy to sustain them both and keep them alive.

Spacer Marines must have pulled them all out afterwards.

Naero awoke briefly, next to Mama Kincaid, while the medics worked on all the wounded. Nelena reached over and took Naero's hand.

"Thank you, Naero," Mama Kincaid told her with a trembling smile. "Thank you for saving us…our star girl."

Again, Naero gave her all of the lifeforce energy that she could spare, before blacking out once more.

Yet when Naero came to later, Om informed her that only Papa had survived his serious wounds. Mama was gone.

Naero remained on Yoder-3 for Mama Kincaid's funeral the next day. The farm people did not return to the stars the way the star people did. As landers, and as farm people, they returned to the earth they loved so well.

Overall, the barrier had held up. The invaders had only managed to penetrate the planetary defense shield by accident and attack the locals in that one location. The Alliance even did what it could to further bolster the shield protecting Yoder -3.

Yet without Naero being there onworld, it still could have proven disastrous.

As things stood, only one Yoderian had perished, and that in itself was considered by many to be a fortunate miracle. Perhaps they were right. So many other worlds had suffered so much greater death and destruction, that by the numbers, one death sounded almost trivial by comparison.

Yet that one single loss deeply touched the lives of so many on a world that only knew peace. Although few might understand that.

While the Alliance Navy spent a few days securing the nearby systems, Naero obtained permission to spend her recovery time with her shattered farm world family, helping them to begin to recover.

Thereafter, when the star girl returned to her star people, in honor of Mama Kincaid and all who had been lost during that terrible war thus far, Naero sent for her friend Shalaen of the Yattai–a true angel of light if there ever was one. And the greatest and most powerful healer that Naero had ever witnessed.

The Alliance had great need of Shalaen's unique gifts.

They met on one of the hospital ships in a small, well-lit, but sterile-smelling conference room.

The two friends embraced and caught up for a few minutes, then Naero took Shalaen by the hands. "I'm sorry, my friend. I don't have much time. I have to get back to my Marines. I have spoken with Intel, General Walker, and even your father. I have summoned you here to perform a great task."

Shalaen smiled, glowing with the same serene blue light which she always did. "For you, N? Anything. Tell me what it is that I must do?"

"Follow me, my sister."

Naero led Shalaen down corridors and into a huge recovery room that took up an entire deck of the hospital ship, filled with medbeds and with the lighting subdued. The large chamber had a few medtek attendants posted at desks.

"Who are all of these wounded?" Shalaen asked.

"Casualties of the war," Naero said. "All head wounds. Their bodies have been healed; those we can regenerate. But the brain and the mind is beyond even the limits of our science at this time. Can you try to help them, Shalaen? We have their neural net mindscans and all of their bioscans and medical records. You can access each one through our systems very easily."

Shalaen looked at them all. Then she walked over to the nearest medbed, with a young female Marine with short brown hair. Shalaen linked with the medical systems.

Naero checked the Marine's name: Gemma Lewis, from a sept of Clan Wilde.

Shalaen continued her analysis. "Shrapnel damaged and tore out most of the left side of her brain, causing extensive injury and loss of function."

"Do you think you can do anything for her?"

"Let me try. Like this?" Shalaen placed her hands on both sides of the near-brain dead young Marine.

Blinding white light flared through Gemma Lewis's skull as if it were lit from within by a great force.

As the light faded, a few instants later, Gemma blinked and looked up at them, gasping and confused.

"Where am I? How did I get here? The last thing I remembered… I was fighting beside my mates on Alparona-3. We got stomped on by an enemy arty barrage."

The medteks came running to take over.

Naero threw her arms around her amazing sister and friend.

"It won't work on every case," Shalaen cautioned. "The neural-net scans are all just snapshots, really. There will probably still be significant loss of memory in many cases, even if I can regenerate and re-awaken the living brain tissues."

Naero pulled away grinning. "It's still better than what we have. At least we'll be able to send some part of them back to their families and Clans. Thank you again, Shalaen."

"How many such cases are out there, Naero?"

"Several thousand, unfortunately. It might take you quite a while to work you way through them all, on all of the various wards they're on."

Shalaen sighed. "Well then, I'd better get busy. Nice seeing you again, Naero. I know you have to get back to your unit as you said. When the war is over, we need to see each other more often."

Naero grinned her characteristic half-smile. "I can arrange that."

Shalaen went right to the next head wound case and began studying all of the data and records. One of the medteks came up to Naero, completely flabbergasted.

"Sir? What if I may ask, is that glowing young woman doing with our patients? Orders came down telling us to grant you and her full access, but we never expected anything like this. That patient over there has a complete working brain again. How is that possible? Haisha! What the hell is going on here?"

Naero took the rattled young medtek by the arm. "Relax. But I would alert your superiors and get lots of help down here, if I were you. I think you're about to become extremely busy.

30

The final battle of the High Crusade for Company 36 took place on Viden-4, in the heart of the largest gigacity on the planet.

Naero had had enough.

Before they dropped down, she went to Whip Konrad that day and jerked him to his feet. "For once, you muttering bastard, will you just shut the fuck up! I'm so sick of your crazy shit. Haisha! You won't have to worry about the enemy killing your dumb ass. I will do it myself!"

No one said another word after that, including Whip.

They all finished prepping for what was going to be their final drop.

Shetanna and her Marines had the unenviable task of assaulting more than a thousand Ejjai shock troops, holding out near one of the last meatships to be located and blown up. It burned nearby, almost utterly destroyed, just as it should be.

The last, putrid nest of the invaders barricaded themselves inside a fortified school adjacent to the area, which had at that time been used by the civies as a refugee camp and aid station for non-combatants, most of them young children.

As usual, the invaders now had the whole place rigged with explosives and shielded against mass stunners. They even strapped explosives and mines to themselves, some with kill switches. If they died, the bombs still went off.

Apparently, the way the enemy saw it, they had plenty of food and could die fat and happy, whenever the time came. They had nothing to lose. They knew they were going to go down eventually.

In true Ejjai fashion, the invaders wanted to go out with a bang and take as many people as they could with them when they did.

Shetanna and Bravo Command had a very different endgame in mind. And by that time, everyone was so sick of the war that they all wanted to end things and wrap them up tight, ASAP.

That same night, Shetanna slipped in and out, fully cloaked, with a cloud of Intel microfixers. Together, they swept the school and neutralized as many of the explosives as they could, over ninety-seven percent of them.

The microfixers were so good at what they did, in fact, that the slashers thought all of their ordnance was still live and working properly.

They wouldn't learn the truth until they tried to set the devices off.

Then, back on the outside, Naero and Om helped pweak their unit tactical CPA to first neutralize as many of the Ejjai as possible, who still had active explosives, and defeat the deadman kill switches at the same time. The timing of the coordinated attacks was key to the overall success of the attack plan.

Otherwise, the attempt was still going to result in lots of dead kids.

36 led nine other companies, poised to attack the invaders almost one on one. Some with microexplosives, some with direct fire, and some with blades, right up close.

The combat grid plotted it all out. Shetanna and each Marine all had three priority targets, just to make sure that all of the Ejjai went down hard and lightning fast.

Then the fixers they left behind emitted several warnings. The enemy was moving around and doing something. Shetanna slipped back in like a wraith, flying along the ceiling with her fixers, sometimes upside down.

In the lower levels of the high rise megaschool, thousands more Ejjai were pouring in from hidden tunnels.

Wherever those new forces were coming from, they would need to be hunted down, surrounded, and eliminated at the same time. Bravo scrambled to shoot in other units to compensate.

The basic attack plan was delayed while the adjustments were made.

But they couldn't wait too long, or the enemy reinforcements would filter up into the higher levels where the kids were.

Finally. Green to go in five. Mark.

Bravo ghosted their way in through the darkness, getting into position, many of them hovering silently up in the air above their targets. It would be necessary for many of the Marines to shield the hostages with their own armored bodies.

Bloody piles of bones and shattered skulls in the corners already testified to the grisly hunger of the enemy.

The bitches had had their last meal. Their horror ended. Tonight.

At three bells, Shetanna signaled the attack.

The *whumpf!* of Marine explosives and pulses of direct fire shook and rattled the mega structure from below. Glass and plasteel shattered or burst.

The bulk of the final battle lasted only seconds as the Marines cut down the invaders. The Ejjai perished not like warriors, but like animals. Little fire was returned, their deaths were so swift.

One small pocket of enemy resistance held out on one of the upper floors of the school overlooking the grounds. A last band of Ejjai had a bunch of stunned kids stacked up there like pallets.

Both Chime Fox and Peter Cooper were up there as part of the assault. Chime called for help.

"N, Jonny, get some teams up here! Our unit shields are holding but we've got two dozen slashers using a bunch of knocked out kids for cover and shields, and there are even a couple of those big mutant bitches!"

36 got the call and raced up there, surrounding the area, but only Naero and perhaps a few squads could go in.

First they went in cloaked.

Chime and Pete and the other two squads present were behind their unit shield, holding their fire.

Some of the enemy were firing back at them to no avail, while most of the Ejjai were busy hastily rigging something behind cover and out of sight. The stacked up piles of kids made it hard to do anything or get in close.

N, they're rigging a bunch of fusion bombs back there.

Om, send the fixers in to neutralize those charges.

Then the Ejjai flung grenades at the Marine shield.

As the unit shield disrupted, all bets were off. Chaos quickly took over.

Naero took on one of the three Ejjai sterodan mutants, carving off its heads.

But the thing was also covered in bandoliers of activated fusion bombs set to go off.

There was no way to neutralize all of those devices at once.

The entire upper level was about to be vaporized, and everyone near it. Such a blast could take out the entire upper section.

And there were two more mutants just as stacked up with bombs as this one.

Naero drove into the first one she faced, kicking and smashing into the creature, until she finally drove it through the wall and sent it plummeting down into a deep crater already next to the school.

Om warned the other Marines away. The rest of 36 scattered.

Naero transported the second mutant high up into the sky. Transporting others, especially a creature that size and mass was very tough.

She dropped to her knees, gasping and nearly spent from the effort.

No time or juice left to take out the third one.

By then the other Marines with her had slain the other Ejjai and fought with the last remaining mutant.

Not one of them turned and ran.

The mutant batted some of them away with its great strength.

But the Marines ignored it and tried to duck and dodge around it up close. They did their best using energy blades and knives to slice through the various fusion bombs strapped to the monster.

They disabled most of them.

But they simply didn't have time to neutralize them all.

The first two mutants exploded down below and above, rocking the entire block.

One Marine charged in without hesitation and smashed into the last mutant, activating another unit shield pod around them both as they toppled out of the shattered wall, still thrashing and fighting each other.

Even as they fell, the Marine unloaded a grenade pistol into the mutant's face and tried to kick off.

But just as they went out of sight the next instant, several of the remaining fusion bombs the monster carried went off.

The last Marines present had set their personal shields in anticipation of those coming blasts, and did their best to fling themselves and their armored bodies over the piles of helpless children.

Even a unit shield pod could not hold back the destructive power of so many multiple detonations.

With the last of her strength, Naero attempted to help shield them all from the explosions that rocked the upper level from the outside.

The blasts blew out most of the walls and peeled back the roof of the upper levels, until only the metal frame of the building's upper portion and most of the floor remained intact.

Things could have gone far worse.

But Naero knew for a fact that they had at least one KIA. The other Marines were battered and beat up, but alive. They checked the kids as help poured in. Only three of the kids had perished. Another miracle considering all that had happened.

Clearly, that one Marine had had saved them all. If those fusion bombs had all gone off any closer, everyone up there would have perished.

Naero sighed and looked around in sudden panic. Where was Chime? Where was Pete? She didn't spot them right away with everyone packed in all around her.

"All right. Who is it?" she called out over their link in the aftermath, dust settled down. "Who did we lose? Who's our hero that took that big mutant out and saved the rest of us up here?"

Sarah Maeris, Naero's very distant cousin, sobbed openly. "It's…it's Jonny, N."

Naero sucked in a painful breath.

Someone had just cut her legs out from under her.

She screamed, her voice shaking as she completely lost it.

"No! No… not Jonny. Haisha! Why him? Fuck the enemy, and fuck this bloody, goddam war!" Naero shrieked like a tortured animal.

Sarah continued to mourn, confirming what they already knew. "They've killed Jonny Fox, everyone. Cut him in half and blasted him to pieces. He's gone from us."

Naero broke down and sobbed, rocking back and forth with her face buried in her hands.

Jonny, her good friend. Little brother Fox, the quiet able Marine who didn't like to kill things, who just wanted his own ship like any good Spacer did. All Jonny wanted was to go home to his nutty greatgran, and find some cute gal–someone to love him, and maybe have two or four kids, some day, an even number, to continue the family name.

A day that would never come, now.

Jonny Fox was the last of them.

The last Spacer Marine to die during combat ops of the High Crusade to save all of humanity.

He went out a hero, fighting to the very end. But he was still gone, and he was never coming back.

Naero would see her brother decorated for all his bravery and gallantry and sent forth on the next journey like all good Spacers.

But that would never make up for any of their losses, now or in the past. Nothing ever could.

Once the hostages were secure and the landers took over, the Marines ignored the many thanks being issued and only wished to leave and get away.

They packed up and saw to their own dead, as they always did. They scooped up and collected as much of valiant Jonny Fox as they could find. They even washed away his blood. The Spacer Marines put his remains and his weapons across his shattered armor and body within a standard casualty bag. Trevor Lakota came by and placed one of his precious knives inside with Jonny. Then the Marines put the broken, defeated weapons of their vanquished foes at Jonny's feet, including the main Ejjai general's sword, which Naero obtained and snapped in half herself, with her own bare hands.

They opened his battered face shield and washed Jonny's face. At least they could still see his poor face.

The growing crowd parted. Chime was carried to his side, inconsolable. She closed his staring green eyes with her shaking fingertips, and then kissed each of them once they were closed. In the end, she had to be pulled off the body of her cousin so that they could prepare to take him away.

Pete held her in his strong arms while she convulsed and shook. He kept her from collapsing to the ground in a heap; Chime was like a ragdoll.

Many of Jonny Fox's comrades and mates knelt and kissed that handsome, boyish face, and many held Jonny's one remaining cold hand and said their goodbyes to their battle brother.

Chime, Naero, and Pete rode up with him in the cargo hold and they all held each other during the ride without speaking. All of the heroes of Bravo Command Marine Company 36 went with them when they arrived.

They marched slowly, and followed Jonny into the enormous hold where personnel prepared the honored Marine dead for their burials, after a wake upon the third day.

They carried Jonny Fox forward and within and Naero walked slowly before them, drawing her energy cutlass and saluting as she called out with *the voice*.

LET THE TRUMPETS SOUND INTO THE BEYOND AND LET IT IT BE KNOWN FOR ALL TO HEAR. A GREAT AND GOOD WARRIOR PRINCE–JONNY FOX–GOES FORTH, UPON THE NEXT JOURNEY. LET HIS FEARLESS EYES BE CLEAR

AND GIVE STRENGTH TO HIS SWORD ARM. LET HIM STAND TALL AND VALIANT AND WALK WITH PRIDE AND HIGHEST HONOR. LET HIM BE WELCOMED BY THE BLOOD OF ALL HIS MIGHTY KIN WHO HAVE GONE BEFORE HIM, TAKEN INTO THEIR ARMS, AND KISSED AND EMBRACED BY HIS SPACER, MARINE, AND LANDER SISTERS AND BROTHERS. OOH-RAH!

"Ooh-rah!" hundreds of Marines shouted.

Shetanna and Company 36 knelt for a deep moment of silence. Then 36 took their leave and then returned to their dropship quarters, even as the celebration at the terrible war's end began to spread on the last liberated world below them.

Naero and Pete helped Chime gather her cousin's things.

Chime wept the entire time, tears simply raining down from her eyes.

Naero and Pete both held her, and tried to comfort her as best they could.

"I guess it's just me and greatgran, now," Chime said. She sighed deeply. Then she broke down sobbing again. "How am I going to tell her? I know she just put up with me; Jonny was always her favorite."

Pete took both of Chime's hands and covered them with kisses. "The war is over, Chime. We're done with all of this. Wherever you go, I'm going with you. You'd better get used to that."

Naero smiled sadly. "You know, at the end, all Jonny could think about was protecting you two. He was so worried that something was going to happen to one of you. He never even thought about himself. In the end, he saved all of us. We could have never survived those fusion blasts up close. Jonny saved me, you two, our Marine brothers and sisters, and all of those scores of kids who are still alive because of what he did. He did it for all of us. And he never hesitated one bit. He just did it."

Chime bent her face into her hands. "Oh, Jonny!" she wailed.

Naero hugged her. "Jonny didn't want to die, Chime. I saw him at the last. He was trying to break free and get away. He wanted to live. There just wasn't enough time for him to do so. That's all. He loved all of us. He loved us so much."

Chime wiped her eyes and sniffed, looking up at Pete. "We're getting married. And we are going to have a son. And I don't give a damn about tradition. We're naming him Jonny–Jonny Fox. And he's going to carry my family name, damn it!"

Pete smiled and pulled her close, stroking her hair as she leaned against him and broke down again. "Our son can take any name you give him, honey. And he will bear such a name as that with pride and honor for all of his days."

Naero still couldn't believe it was truly all over, and the final terrible price they had paid. She hugged her own knees and buried her face down in them.

36 remained somber. They rested and kept to themselves, as if they were all in some kind of shock. But while many around them rejoiced, they did not celebrate anything until Jonny Fox's wake came around on the third day.

With her own funds, Naero purchased a small merchant ship, and registered it in Jonny Fox's name. She even had it named and christened *The Green Fox* with a big bottle of Jett, just the way Jonny had wanted his own ship to be named.

When Jonny Fox went into the sun and returned to the stars, he would take his own ship with him, on into the next journey.

They partied and got drunk that night at the wake in Jonny's honor.

The following morning, *The Green Fox* awaited her captain on board.

General Big Jim Walker, that giant of a man, stood beside Major Ivana Luna, and MCL Captain Naero Amashin Maeris on his left. Naero was in her role as Shetanna, the Dark Angel of Death of Bravo Command, as all turned out that third day.

Chime Fox stood in the place of honor on the General's immediate right, his mighty hand upon her shoulder, holding her close to him. She cried but stood tall and ramrod straight and still.

Shetanna also wept openly, as was her want, as Jonny Fox's gleaming Marine casket, decorated with all of his high honors, was loaded into his own starship. Om had programmed it to lead the last sortie of the last batch of victorious Marine dead from the High Crusade into the nearest star, and on toward the next journey.

For a few nights thereafter, Naero and her Marine brothers and sisters knew rest, and ease, enjoying the accolades of all the grateful worlds and countless innocent peoples and sentients that they had rescued and protected.

Everyone on those worlds knew very well whom they owed their lives to. The very next day, Naero and many Spacer forces raced off to save the Spacer Mystic Homeworlds and what came thereafter.

Yet the worlds that Shetanna and the fearless Marines of Bravo Command rescued from the Ejjai invaders would never forget them, or their great sacrifice and valor.

The legends of the courageous and undefeated ghost warriors of Bravo Command continued to grow and spread and would be told again and again among Spacers, and upon many a lander world. And now those expanding legends were forever joined and entwined with tales of the Amazing Shetanna, Bravo Command's very own mysterious, and fearsome: Dark Angel of Death. She often went before them into battle, striking fear in every enemy heart, helping lead all of humanity to total victory, throughout the course of The High Crusade.

THE END

Please Post A Book Review Right Now

Please post a review of this book if you enjoyed it. Twenty little words are all that is required. Twenty words that say what you liked about this book while it is still fresh in your heart, mind, and soul. Please do so now before something else makes you forget.

Here is the smartlink for *The High Crusade* if you purchased it on Amazon:

smarturl.it/TheHighCrusade

Please click on the link and post your review now.
Done? The author would personally like to thank you very much.

In this busy world, everyone is pressed for time. Our time is so important, no doubt. It has reached the point now where authors of nearly every stripe compete not only for sales, but to garner reviews from their readers. Some authors even stoop to "purchasing" reviews in social media that some services now offer in bulk.

In the publish or perish work of competitive fiction, book reviews from readers are golden, they have now become a commodity even.

Many in the business even consider book reviews as important, or even more important than book sales in some ways. As crazy as that sounds.

So therefore, trust us in this. If you have authors whom you adore, and you want to read more of their books in the future, please post as many reviews for them as you can in all of the forms of social media that you use.

Doing so will help your favorite authors in numerous ways that you cannot even possibly imagine. Never forget that fact. Book reviews matter a great deal.

And if by chance, if you find that there is something about this book that you don't like, and you really do want to help authors, before you slam them with bad reviews, try briefly contacting them instead with your concerns through their contact info that is always readily provided, or through their publisher. Most authors, especially new ones, are usually happy to get constructive criticism that will make their books better. Only hating, online trolls slam authors with bad reviews without giving them a chance. Real pros and fen contact authors directly with any valid concerns. That is the current, accepted etiquette. Please don't be a troll.

Amazon Kindle Review Link for The High Crusade, The Citation Series, Book 2:
smarturl.it/TheHighCrusade

Barnes & Noble Review Link

TBA

Good Reads Review Link

Please post one or more reviews for Mason and each of his books, everywhere that you can.

Thank you once again.

Cheers,

Mason Elliott

Please enjoy this teaser for The Citation Series, Book 3:

Naero's Trial Amazon Link : http://amzn.to/1oaMNE3

NAERO'S WAR:

NAERO'S TRIAL

Naero's Trial Amazon Link: smarturl.it/NaerosTrial

by Mason Elliott

On the third day of Naero's trial, the Prosecution and the Defense made their final, closing statements.

Master Jo spoke first, for the Defense.

"In the final analysis, I would both conclude and insist that Naero Amashin Maeris has proven herself time and time again to be an honorable Spacer, and that her word is without question. She is also vital to the survival of her people in many important ways. Naero Amashin Maeris is a noble, invaluable warrior and a proven leader who has served the Clans and the Alliance well, in both peacetime and war. A Mystic Champion who is now part of the great and mysterious Cosmic Prophecy, long foretold. There is still so little that we do not know about those prophecies; who can say what her role will be in the end?"

Master Jo paced a bit. "And on a very basic level, she is a Spacer. As such, she has the right of all Spacers and all sentients to defend herself, to the death, against anyone who attempts to kill her. Reluctantly, she only resorted to lethal force when High Master Vane attacked her with the intent to destroy her, and take her life. Even after she had tried to get away from him, and begged him repeatedly not to attack her.

"She cannot not be convicted of murder for defending her own life against someone trying to kill her. Those are all many good reasons why you must see fit to exonerate her of these erroneous charges. We cannot take the life of this hero."

The Defense finally rested.

Master Tree was given the final word in the trial for the prosecution.

"Hero? First, let me also revisit the reckless side of this renegade, outlaw Spacer, who fled from justice and had to be brought back by force to face her crimes in shackles, in order to keep her from getting away once again. On several occasions, Naero Amashin Maeris has proven herself to be dangerous, unpredictable, and out of control. By her own words, she has more than once declared that if she ever lost control and became a threat to any of her people, that she herself agreed that she should be put down–and destroyed.

"The cold blooded murder of a High Mystic Master has not demonstrated this fact readily enough? Beyond all doubt? If she can slay a High Master of the Mystics so easily, how much more is she a danger to all? And she even admits that she cannot control her abilities. Her very existence has become such a clear and present threat that it cannot be ignored and must be dealt with. I repeat, she has admitted on several occasions that her powers can go out of control and be very dangerous.

"Next, she also clearly admits that she killed Master Vane. Now, of her own accord, she claims that she killed him in self defense. But she has thus far presented no single shred of proof of that. She claims that Master Vane attacked her, attempted to kill her, and that she killed him, as she now conveniently claims–in so-called self defense. And I remind everyone in this court, once again. It does not matter who she is, what she is, or whatever else she has done. No one is above Spacer Law.

"Not even the infamous, Naero Amashin Maeris."

Tree took in a breath and clasped his hands behind his back. "What are the facts, therefore? A High Mystic Master lies dead, murdered by his own student, who openly stated that she could not stand him. Who openly admitted that she killed him. Nothing else can be proven, beyond those facts. Nothing else exists as fact. And this case must only be decided, based solely upon the facts. Nothing else.

"A Spacer on trial for her life could readily claim and say anything. Merely stating something does not make it true. That does not prove it to be fact. According to the facts of what is known, Naero Amashin Maeris is clearly guilty of murder, and will undoubtedly say and do anything possible in order to get away with her crime. As anyone logically would, in order to escape punishment, justice, and execution."

Naero fumed. Haisha! What the hell did they expect her to say? Yes, I offed the asshole, I loved it, and I'm a fricking monster. Go ahead and kill me?

I wish that weren't so painfully funny, Naero.

Me too, Om.

Master Tree went on to demand that the jury uphold one of the key tenets of Spacer Law and Spacer society:

"Spacers do not murder other Spacers and take their lives! Naero Amashin Maeris is not above that law. Naero Amashin Maeris broke that solemn law. And like it or not, the law demands justice. There is no way around that law and no way to escape it. That law demands that she face the ultimate punishment for her being guilty of committing the ultimate crime!"

Tree emphasized his final point with a single, upraised index finger. "That punishment is immediate Death, by execution. To be carried out by beheading, at the hands and the blade of the Mystic Enforcer!"

The Prosecution rested its case.

Admiral Klyne looked slightly pale as he instructed the jury of Mystic Elders to decide the case and announce their decision after their period of deliberation.

Naero went back to her cell in silence feeling sick, unable to meet Khai's utterly heartbroken glance. She felt stunned and numb. She didn't know what to think. All that she could do was await the jury's decision, along with everyone else.

Yet it was her fate alone that was being decided.

But when she thought about it further it wasn't just her fate.

Everyone waited for eight long hours.

Naero could neither rest nor sleep.

Then everyone was summoned back to the court room.

A decision had been made. The jury had arrived at a verdict in her case.

Admiral Klyne announced, "All rise for the verdict to be read."

They did so.

The jury leader stood up and read their decision.

"According to Spacer Law, and based upon all of the facts and evidence presented, we the jury find the defendant, Naero Amashin Maeris, of Clan Maeris…guilty of murder in the death of another Spacer."

Naero gasped, nailed to the bedrock of the planet itself in almost complete shock.

Guilty meant…

Master Tree rose up. "This Mystic trial has ended; it is over. A verdict has been reached. Without question, this grim crime is punishable among our people by death. Under the circumstances, the sentence is to be carried out immediately and without delay."

Naero, I can–

Shut up, Om.

Naero gasped and covered her mouth with both hands as she sobbed and went down on one knee.

Then she dropped her hands to her abdomen and her eyes met Khai's in explosive waves of desperate horror and regret.

Their child from their love within that distant star barely grew within her. Now, no time remained to tell Khai all that she needed to before he performed his duty as the Mystic Enforcer.

Before he took her head…ended her life, and the lives of his own family.

Naero Amashin Maeris clenched her fists, and rose up with her head held high to meet her fate with her eyes clear and wide open, if that was what must be.

Amazon Link for *Naero's Trial*: smarturl.it/NaerosTrial

SF Author Mason Elliott's Contact Information

Please Join Mason Elliott's Readers List

Use either of these links:

http://bit.ly/1L2QpUL

Backup link:
http://eepurl.com/FgQzv

Be among the first to learn about my writing projects and new releases. I promise that I will not share your info or spam you. I will use the list only to inform you about matters directly connected to my writing projects.

About the Author

Mason Elliott grew up loving Science Fiction and Fantasy in all of their myriad forms. That love has transferred into his dedicated writing. Like most writers, he lives a Spartan lifestyle and yearns to devote his life even more to his writing, and someday retire on the Pacific Coast. So be a fan, buy his stuff, and enjoy!

Like and follow Mason on Facebook, where he does most of his blogging at
https://www.facebook.com/masonelliott731

And on Twitter at
http://bit.ly/1nsqOSs

Visit Mason Elliott's website at
www.masonelliott.authorcontacts.com

And for even more information on Mason Elliott and his works, visit High Mark Publishing online at

www.HighMarkPublishing.com

Mason's Acknowledgements

I love writing the Naero books. She is a wonderful and fascinating character. I am so pleased to be able to continue writing this series, and let me assure you, I have many more Naero books planned. First, let me always praise my friends and helpmates at High Mark Publishing SF.

Next, I would be nowhere without my family, my wonderful beta readers, and my invaluable online writers group. And a special shout out and great thanks to my good and wonderful friend and writer, Tracey.

If you have not read Book One of *Mergeworld*, however unlikely that might be, please enjoy this teaser by Mason Elliott and Garan R. R. Faraday. Available now! Here is the Amazon purchase link:

smarturl.it/Mergeworld

1

David Pritchard woke up gasping from one nightmare and went straight into another. A terrible agony tore through him as if the universe twisted him inside out.

Then he snapped back again.

What in damnation had just happened? Something…was very wrong.

Startled, groggy, it only took an instant for his bleary mind to figure out.

Flames engulfed the front of his college apartment building. The stench of smoke, screams, and breaking glass outside only confirmed it.

He was dazed and blinked his scratchy eyes. The first thing he instinctively reached out for was the framed picture of his dead parents.

That was the last picture he had of them from a few years back, right after he started college in South Bend.

They hugged and smiled at each other in medieval garb at the Bristol Renaissance Fair up in Wisconsin. The picture froze both of them happily in time, retired in their forties. Unlike many parents that age, they weren't divorced and they still loved one another. One of their ren-fair pals took that picture for them on their digital camera.

The same camera retrieved from the car accident on the Illinois highways on their way back home from Bristol. A tractor-trailer jackknifed in the heavy rain and took them away.

The same weekend David begged off going with them.

He blew that picture up in Photoshop, printed out an 8 x 10, and bought a nice oak frame for it. He kept it with him wherever he went. He'd die before he'd part with it, fire or no.

All that history and pain flashed through David as he clutched their picture close to him in the dark. He didn't even have to see it, just cling to it in his hands. That picture always sat prominently behind his small alarm clock on his night stand with his smart phone and wallet while he slept. That was how he found it, even in the semi-dark. He also grabbed his phone and wallet.

His clock normally flashed bright green. Power outage, probably from the fire. And the back-up battery must have gone dead. Light switches? Nothing, of course, do to the fire.

The growing reek of smoke triggered his desire for self-preservation. Once he got out, he could call his friend Mason Tyler, who lived in a duplex over on Allen Street. His buddy Mace would help him.

Somewhat more awake now, David struggled not to panic. He staggered out of his room like a robot. His lanky, five-eleven frame stumbled down the hall toward his front door. He stubbed his little toe hard in the darkness. A second later he grunted and cursed the sudden blinding spread of pain, but kept moving.

Oh, hell. No way out the front.

Dangerous ribbons of smoke curled violently through the metal front door frame and snaked up across the ceiling like an upside down waterfall. The paint of the metal fire door already bubbled and blistered. David choked and swallowed hard.

If that door had been wood, his entire apartment might have already been completely engulfed. He might not have even come to. He saw no sense in touching the steaming door knob.

The apartment building stairs acted like a natural chimney, funneling the fire and heat straight up.

A window—climb out a window. He was only on the second floor.

His three richer roomies were already off on spring break for the next week, to the Bahamas or some such. Their parents could afford such junkets. David could not.

He suddenly realized two very important things. The fire hadn't spread to the back part of the apartment building yet.

Next, he was only wearing navy boxers and a gray T-shirt over his shaking frame.

Early April in South Bend, Indiana could be any weather from sun and sixties to a flippin' blizzard.

Clothes. Only seconds to throw some on. Even in the dim, flickering orange light spilling out of the thick curtains, he spotted his laundry basket on the couch.

The smoke in the living room grew thicker. He put his precious picture, smartphone, and wallet down for only a few moments.

Jeans. On. Socks. On. He snatched up his thick blue, gold, and green hoody from the back of the old couch where he usually left it, and pulled into its soft, warm, comfort. Stocking cap. Popped on his head. Wool scarf. Around the neck. He sat down and jammed on his old gray Nike running shoes, feeling a pair of thin gloves and keys in his hoody pockets still, when he bent over.

Ready to ride, or, at least climb out the back window to escape burning to death.

He stuffed his folks' picture, wallet, and smartphone into his dark green Jansport backpack with his pad, gel pens, and a few books. He zipped it all up.

To the back window. He pulled the curtains aside and yanked the big panel open.

He jumped slightly, at some guy who already climbed down the back of the building from the third floor. Their eyes locked, only a window screen between them in the dim, pre-dawn light and the cold morning air.

The guy looked utterly terrified.

"Watch out!" he warned, trying to keep his voice low. "Those things are killing people. They're everywhere!"

"What things?" What was this guy freaking out about?

The guy jolted wide-eyed and then choked.

A bloody iron arrowhead jutted out the front of his throat. In the time it took them both to blink, another arrow punched through the front of his chest, out of his T-shirt. The poor guy's mouth gaped and worked. Then his eyes rolled up white. He fell backwards, head down.

David grabbed for him, but missed, his hands blocked by the barrier of the screen. He tore it away and stuck his head out the window.

He spotted strange movement down in the darkness.

Two dark, twisted, hunched-over figures loped in on bandy legs and clawed feet wrapped in fur and rags. They were smaller than humans, about four to five feet tall and very skinny and wiry.

Whatever they were, they were definitely not human.

One of them slit the dead guy's throat from ear to ear with a long, wicked-looking rusty knife.

Blood spurted bright black in the night.

The other creature sniffed the air and snarled up at David with a greenish-black, twisted, inhuman face. Long pointed ears stuck out of holes in its ragged hood. It had a big warty nose, and gleaming green eyes. It gave full draw to the same kind of short, black bow of jagged horn that the other one carried.

The creature took dead aim at David.

And fired.

Please enjoy this teaser for Mergeworld, Book 2:
Amazon Link: smarturl.it/Mergeworld2

Mergeworld

Book Two

Amazon Link: smarturl.it/Mergeworld2

by Mason Elliott and Garan R. R Faraday

"Several of the enemy mage prisoners have escaped," a runner came to warn them. The young trooper looked terrified.

Mason drew his Spillers. They would have to be enough. After the bath, he didn't have all of his other guns. And there wasn't time to go after them.

It also worried him that he still felt—off his game, somehow. Something was still very wrong with him, but he couldn't figure out what. Perhaps that was merely what sorrow and depression felt like.

Blondie shook the terrified runner. "Calm down. Tell me what you know. Which prisoners? How many of them?"

"S-six, six, I think. They tried to free the rest, but the guards on the scene shot two down. Then the enemy mages fled this way, and started killing everyone they could find with magic."

Troops screamed, and close by to the west, magic blasts went off, and the sounds of battle and further bursts of magical rapidly sped their way.

The runner continued to stammer, "The tall n-n-necromancer is leading them. Five others. I don't know their names. As soon as they broke out, the duty officer sent me after you two and the Thul woman."

Blondie let the runner go. "Try to find the Thul. Go. Keep spreading the alarm."

"Yes, s-sir!" The young runner looked only too happy to keep running.

"They're coming for us, aren't they, Blondie?" Mason asked, hefting his Spillers.

Blondie clenched both fists, and violet magefire flared up to his elbows. "Yep. Just like I said they would. How do you want to do this, Mace?"

"Hmmm…too many to hit them head on. Let's go at them from the flanks. I'll hit them on the left."

His blond friend nodded. "Then I'll take them on the right. The necromancer's going to be the toughest of the lot. Let's peel off the other five, if we can, and then take him on together."

"Sounds good, Blondie. Let's ride."

They skirted around to either side, trying to stick to cover and stay out of sight. Mason quickly lost sight of his friend.

It did briefly occur to him that this would be an excellent time for Blondie to turn on them all, and help the mages make good their escape. But at this point, Mason had no choice but to keep trusting his good friend.

Blondie said that his abilities were returning.

He could tell them anything he wanted. How would they know if it was the truth or not?

From the sounds of things, the militia troops were putting up a pretty good fight and delaying the enemy at least somewhat. Each precious second they could hold them back, more troops would pour in.

Yet even as Mason got into position to attack, the enemy mages continued to push through, causing death and destruction all around them, and leaving many casualties in their wake.

Startled troops could slow the enemy down, but they would be hard pressed to stop six enemy mages bent on a rampage of devastation.

They were lucky that it wasn't all thirteen of the mage captives on the loose.

At Blondie's urging, Major Bill had spread several of the captive mages out to other nearby, secret locations–beyond the limited range of their prisoners' telepathy.

Mason spotted the enemy. The necromancer strode out in front with another sorcerer. A pair of enemy wizards marched slightly behind them on either side, guarding their flanks and watching the rear.

Blondie stepped up and raked the enemy left and the middle with violet lightning that knocked four of the six off their feet, and stunned the two flankers.

The first flanker on the other side turned to attack Blondie. The second one raised his hands and his eyes got big when he saw the Pistolero step out and aim both of his pistols.

Click! Click!

Nothing. Mason's guns wouldn't fire. He cocked and pulled the triggers again.

Nothing.

By then the one mage was charging Blondie, exploding anything that was made of wood around him. He sent the shards and splinters and whirling debris at Blondie, while the necromancer and the other sorcerer still looked dazed and tried to regain their feet. And the mage facing Mason shot greenish-yellow flames out of his hands at all before him.

Mason dove out of the way, tucked and rolled out of sight, and then crouched and ran. The enemy wizard would be on him in seconds.

Finally he came to a building and ducked inside. He scrambled out of sight into an adjoining back storage room and ducked down. He tried his guns again. Still nothing. Why was this happening,? Now of all times?

Blondie needed him out there.

Maybe if he reloaded. Yeah, that would do it.

Slowing his breathing, doing his best to stay calm, he broke out his spare cylinders for his guns and swapped them out. He was fast at it, but every second counted.

He went back out into the fight. As he expected, the fighting quickly turned Blondie's way, and blasts of magic nearby showed where the foes were pursuing Blondie hard and blasting everything around him. Blondie fought back as best he could, but from what Mason could tell, his friend was outnumbered four to one.

He raced that way, not even trying to stay under cover this time. He had to catch up quickly, and take them from behind, if possible.

Mason sped around a building and almost slammed into the same enemy mage as before. This one seemed to be holding back and protecting the rear of the other three while they stalked Blondie.

Mason had intended to shoot them on sight, but he clobbered the mage from behind now that he was right on top of him. The mage grunted and dropped, unconscious.

Pistol-whipping worked better in this instance. Mason dragged the mage back out of sight and quickly gagged him, and bound his hands and ankles behind him.

At this distance, Mason would not have any trouble taking out the other three with one or two shots, once he spotted them again. And their spells gave them away when they fired. Hopefully, Blondie was staying ahead of them.

Mason rushed forward once more, spotted several troops closing in with bows and crossbows, and motioned for them to go around and close in from one side or the other.

Finally he spotted the necromancer and the one wizard, crouched down and making plans of some kind.

Mason took aim at them with both barrels.

Click. Click.

Crap, not again. What the hell was going on?

Even worse, the necromancer turned and locked eyes with him.

"There's the other one. Let's get him!" All of their hands glowed with magefire.

Mason turned and ran for it. Dark lightning and exploding ice covered the area he had just been in.

His foes were right after him. Archers tried to fire upon the mages, but they swept the troops away from their positions with blasts of power.

A stone or outcropping of brick caught the toe of Mason's boot. He hurtled down upon his face, and tried to roll back up to his feet.

The third enemy mage stepped out right in front of Mason.

Now, the three of them had him fairly trapped.

"Kill him!" the necromancer roared.

The wizard still hesitated an instant. Then he prepared a spell, his hands beginning to glow brighter and brighter.

They were only a dozen or so feet away. Mason hurled his useless pistols at the wizard.

One missed as the fellow dodged to one side.

The other smacked him squarely in the face and dazed and bloodied him.

Mason expected to be cut down from behind by the other two enemies any second.

He glanced back just as the two stood ready to unleash their spells.

Amazon Link to *Mergeworld, Book Two*: smarturl.it/Mergeworld2

If you have not read the original Naero Books by Mason Elliott, Please enjoy the following teaser from the first Spacer Clans Adventure, Book 1:

NAERO'S
RUN

NAERO'S RUN

Amazon Link to Naero's Run: smarturl.it/NaerosRun

by Mason Elliott

"We've got more than enough to consider here," Aunt Sleak said. "We'll post our final decisions on the Spacer ClanNet. All crew, take a breather. We're out of jump in less that two standard hours. Everyone on duty needs to be at their ready stations. Dismissed."

Naero went back to her quarters to do some laundry and a little more reading before they emerged. With regular effort, her quarters were less of a disaster than usual. She'd kept her bunk and her floor more or less cleared off, and slept in her bunk regularly now, instead of on the floor or in zero-G or a float bag.

And definitely not in her flex chair, as she had for years because she either couldn't get her bunk panel out or it was too piled up with crap.

Being small had its advantages. She could curl up like a cat and get comfortable almost anywhere for a snooze.

But keeping her quarters in better shape was a promise she made and kept–to herself–and her parents.

They emerged from jump with the customary shuddering of the ship. The fleet spread out into is standard formation, emerging back into real Space-Time.

Naero punched up their positions on one of her screens, even though she didn't have bridge duty for several hours.

The Shinai flanked *The Dromon* on the port side, with *The Slipper* posted starboard. Their two smaller ships, *The Nevada* and *The Ardala*, brought up the rear this time.

A red hot scarlet particle beam, 60mm in diameter, lanced through Naero's walls like they were paper, disrupting her wallscreens.

A direct hit from a big gun.

At the very least, from a heavy destroyer.

Warning lights flashed immediately.

The rupture in the hull led to an immediate explosive decompression.

Naero held on tight to her bunk and went flat on the floor as the hull sealed itself.

All ships were vulnerable coming out of jump. They couldn't activate their shields until right after they emerged.

Someone had been waiting for them.

The Dromon continued getting rocked by multiple hits from what felt like several spinal guns and secondary batteries.

But the big planetoid could take it and give back plenty, her quad main guns humming and whining to life, coming online.

Naero hit her wristcom. All her screens down.

"Bridge. Status?"

"We stepped into it. They were waiting for us. We're under heavy fire. Multiple bogeys."

The general alert sounded.

"Battle Stations. Battle Stations."

Aunt Sleak cut over the com. "All hands. All hands, to your stations. Prepare for battle. All ships, all batteries, return fire. Launch all fighters."

Naero suited up and raced to the drop bay of her fighter. She met Jan along the way.

More intense fire. *Dromon* reeled and fired back.

She and Jan almost got rocked off their feet again.

A security team intercepted them at the launching bays.

Their fighters had already dropped with their backup pilots.

"The fleet captain wants you two at your secondary defense stations, not out in the mix."

Jan started to protest.

"Orders are orders. Get to your stations."

They ran to their remote gunnery stations, small secured cubicles with a chair and a console, operating triple pulse turrets on the hardpoints above them.

Naero brought up her autotargeting displays, weapons already powered up and humming.

The secondary battery gunnery stations operated independently and were well-protected. They were also fully automated, but they still functioned more effectively with a human interface.

Coordinated targeting profiles came online as she watched.

Jan operated a torp turret nearby.

Directly ahead of the fleet. Twelve elite Matayan destroyers, each with a dozen escort fighters.

Half of their number pursued and attacked a convoy of two dozen independent mining freighters.

Aunt Sleak's fleet scrambled, launched, and deployed a total of threescore fighters in a standard Alpha-Charlie-1 defensive screen.

They were outnumbered two to one.

"All batteries make ready. Incoming torps," the bridge com sounded.

Countermeasures took out half of the blips heading their way.

Spacer fighters and the forward defensive batteries blasted the rest.

"That attack's a diversion," Naero muttered.

Shinai's fire control and com computers fixed on and monitored all channels–including those between the hapless freighters and the corsairs.

"Mayday, mayday, we are under intense corsair attack. All ships. Assistance, assistance. Heavy damage and casualties."

"What do you want?" another panic-stricken voice cried out. "We'll surrender. You can board us. We have no goods and few supplies. Please, stop firing. Our ships are full of workers–full of people. You're killing civilians. We're on fire!"

Scanners displayed an awful, one-sided battle among the transports.

Most of the old bulk freighters didn't even have weapons.

Each of the heavily armed Matayan destroyers was more than a match for them or most of the ships in Aunt Sleak's fleet.

Except for the 6m quad spinal guns of *The Dromon*.

One crippled freighter broke apart and exploded under concentrated fire from three destroyers. It didn't have any shields, and only minimal armor. Its two turrets either didn't work or had been taken out already.

Static and Matayan battle language rang out in triumph.

Dromon's four primary guns cut loose, lighting up the entire sector. Its blue-white blasts ripped into the lead corsair flagship and its wingships, disrupting their shields.

The starboard wingship took two hits and listed to one side. Its aft section exploded.

"This is Captain Sleak Maeris of Clan Maeris. Enemy vessels, be advised: Cease hostilities and vacate this system or be destroyed."

Matayan curses and laughter her only reply.

"Clan Maeris," one of the freighter captains cut in. "This is Captain Philsen of *The Botaru*. Help us! Our situation is desperate. The corsairs are trying to destroy us. We don't know why."

"Acknowledged. We're coming in. Disperse if you can. You're still too bunched up. Scatter and concentrate on defensive actions. Jump if you're able. We'll try to draw them off. We're boosting your distress call."

Three more corsairs turned on the fleet, with all twelve dozen fighters full front on intercept.

The other trio of Matayan attackers kept after the freighters.

Naero heard the pleading and the screams on the open channel, just before another freighter got blasted to oblivion.

Naero realized she had tears on her face.

Was that how her parents went? Blasted to death by Matayan guns?

The rage she felt nearly overwhelmed her reason.

She checked her systems, gripped the controls of her gunnery station, and forced her emotions to go cold.

Against superior numbers, Naero and her Clan Fleet closed for battle.

Amazon Link to Naero's Run: <u>smarturl.it/NaerosRun</u>

Please enjoy the following teaser from **a** spinoff series that we call: The Citation Series, Book 1,
Naero's War:

The Annexation War

NAERO'S WAR:
THE ANNEXATION WAR

Annexation War Amazon Link: smarturl.it/TheAnnexationWar

by Mason Elliott

Naero's flagship, *The Hippolyta,* was one of the latest, Dromon Class dreadnaughts. These warships were fashioned out of dense, iron-nickel planetoids, not less than half a kilometer in diameter. Incredibly tough and rugged on their own.

It took the most powerful mining plasma-borers–working in precise conjunction with construction fixers and an army of teks–months to hollow out armored crew quarters, lift and transport tubes, launching and loading bays. Next came space for power cores, sublight engines, jump drives, backups, gravitics, life support, sensor arrays, communications, navigation, weapons, main bridge and backup bridge.

Set in the exact heart of *The Hippolyta* were its signature big guns. A quad of the largest production guns ever constructed on any ship of war: Four, *16 meter*, rapid-fire, particle beam cannons.

Cannons any larger than that exploded, melted, or otherwise were not feasible within the limits of current tek and materials. Thirty-six secondary batteries, assorted specialized weapons and gun emplacements, and forty-five advanced fighters.

Seven hundred and forty able crew, including a full Rifle Company of two hundred and forty Spacer Marines, and all of their equipment, vehicles, and gear for ship's security and rapid response deployment. Strike Fleet Six's Marines came from the 3rd Spacer Marine Division– known as *The Death Eyes*–because of their superb snipers and their overall, excellent marksmanship ratings. Marines made up a third of the warship's complement.

Their motto: *If We Can See It...We Can Kill It!*

The main bridge was a massive armored dome constructed on top of the dreadnaught's big metal, rough-hewn orb, protected by heavy blast doors, and the latest, most advanced shielding in the fleet. Within, the circular bridge was laid out in four levels under the huge dome, a dome sixty meters high.

Each bridge tier was separated by the height of a few steps from one to the next. The inner three levels could rotate in any direction, independent of the others.

The fleet captain's command nanochair and station occupied the highest tier. Each bridge station had its own secondary shielding, in case enemy fire penetrated the shields, the blast screens, and the hull.

In combat, bridges were routinely targeted, for obvious reasons.

From that primary vantage point, the strike fleet captain could direct battles in three hundred and sixty degrees, through an advanced, battleholo display surrounding her, full zoom data-feeds, constantly updated by battle AIs. Naero could manipulate the displays by nanosensors programmed into the fingertips of her nanosuit gloves.

The battle display system also recognized her voice pattern, and would respond to voice commands, or commands punched in manually through pads on her command chair, or via other backups.

The next bridge level down from hers held the secondary bridge stations: Helm, Weapons, Communications, Navigation, and Scanning, spaced out equally along their ring.

The third ring held all of the twelve tertiary bridge stations, that monitored, controlled, and coordinated all of the ship's other important functions:

Engineering
Gravitics
Life Support
Power Supply
Security
Shields
Medical
Jump and Sub-light Drives
Damage Control
Alliance Fleet and Intel Communications
Main Computer
Launching Bays

The fourth ring went to the two powerlifts, leading from the bridge to the other movers, decks, and levels of the ship. All lift and access points throughout the ship were constantly guarded by two battle-ready Marines, stationed on either side.

If a warship was boarded by enemy assault craft during a battle, invaders could be cut off and eliminated between decks, before they could reach a vital area.

Today, Strike Fleet Six had a mission–a simple one.

Captain Naero Maeris and her fifty warships proceeded to probe the next system on the outer, port arcwall of the Alliance advance at Beleron-4.

A routine run. Current intel assured them to expect little or no Triaxian presence or resistance.

By any stretch of the imagination, Beleron-4 was a nothing world, in the middle of nowhere, with zero, nacha–absolutely no strategic or tactical value whatsoever.

Checking it off the list on the pacified worlds of the Alliance system-hopping schedule was more-or-less just a formality.

But it still had to be done. And Naero and her lot drew the duty at random.

So why did Naero's sense of warning go bonkers?

After they jumped in, simple three-stack, Delta-India-3 formation, the reasons for alarm grew perfectly clear.

They came in right on top of twenty Triaxian fleets of the enemy's latest warships.

And a gigantic new flagship–as huge as *The Hippolyta*–the advanced design of which did not even register as existing.

It had never been seen before.

Naero shot to her feet, kicked her command nanochair back out the way and sent it down into the nanofloor of her top-tier bridge control station.

She instantly called her battle display holos up in spinning, horizontal glowing ribbons and rings all around her.

Data relays went wild. Her fingers flashed among the highlighted screen arcs, taking control of them and their parameters.

Multiple warnings sounded, and with excellent reason.

Nothing about this was good in any way.

Haisha! Twenty enemy fleets could chop them into confetti–well before any other Alliance forces could even jump in to help.

No strategy, no formation could possibly save them against superior numbers such as these.

"All ships, full withdraw. Emergency retreat on this vector, in Charlie-Romeo-7, cone-ring formation. Shields and all weapons full front and hot. Maximize all targeting profiles on the lead attacking enemy elements–they'll be on us in seconds. Whatever happens–we fight until our carriers and some of our ships can break free and jump out behind us. Get the carriers out first!"

For a split second, everyone braced for the sheets of flame that would quickly overtake and overwhelm them.

Annexation War Amazon Link: smarturl.it/TheAnnexationWar

Please enjoy the following teaser ... an excerpt, from the next Spacer Clans Adventure, Book 2:

NAERO'S GAMBIT

NAERO'S GAMBIT

Naero's Gambit Amazon Link: smarturl.it/NaerosGambit

by Mason Elliott

Klyne set the huge Mystic testing room on board *The Kathmandu* to muted gray. Smartwalls, floor, and ceiling, Naero saw no equipment, no padding.

The lights were set low.

From experience, Naero knew that in a training room, just about anything could pop up out of anywhere.

She wore nothing but her black Nytex flight togs.

To her surprise, Klyne and his two adepts wore dark gray Nytex togs also, but with hoods and masks pulled up over their heads. Only their keen eyes showed.

All three of the Mystics appeared to be in top physical condition, including Klyne.

One of the adepts was female, with huge green eyes and light freckles across her nose. The other was male, with the black slanted eyes of the Lii-Kim Clans.

If black was the color of Spacers, the Mystics traditionally wore gray.

They all sat with their legs crossed in lotus fashion, focusing their abilities through meditation, and mental discipline. They formed a triangle, each side about three meters apart, with them at the points.

"Follow our instructions," Klyne said. "Take your place among us. Sit in the center; sit as we do. Face the instructor."

A circle of white light appeared at the center of the triangle. Naero walked over and sat down in it, facing Klyne. Her skin barely began to tingle.

A wider ring of similar light appeared, including the instructor and his two adepts.

Every hair on Naero's body went stiff with electric force.

"You have chosen to come before the circle of Spacer Mystics to be tested for Mystic training. Speak your name."

"Naero Amashin Maeris."

"You agree to be tested?"

"I do."

"I am Klyne, the instructor. My assistants are Adept Iselle, and Adept Makita. We shall refer to you as Adept Candidate Naero. Follow our instructions. Respond only if asked to respond. If you require any medical attention, it will be administered at the end of the testing. Until then, you are expected to endure and continue to do your best. If you understand, say yes."

"Yes."

"The training will begin. Defend yourself."

Without warning, Makita's attack smashed into her.

She blocked one or two out every four or five blows.

A snapwheel kick sent her flying twenty meters, nearly winding her.

The only things that saved her at all, once again, were the experience and knowledge she gained from her training sessions with Baeven.

Makita proved stronger and faster than her, but he still paled in comparison to the outcast's terrifying prowess.

Makita charged her.

Naero met him part way.

She took several punishing strikes, but flipped him hard to the ground.

He swept her legs.

They tangled on the ground, wrestling, slipping out of holds, twisting like snakes. They pummeled each other all the while.

They broke, crouched low, and launched themselves at each other again, like Thellurian fighting blue cranes.

Naero landed a whipkick on the side of Makita's head.

He clipped her under the chin, grabbed her leg and ankle and swung her hard into the floor, stunning her.

She struggled to get up.

For a few dizzy moments, she couldn't.

She rose up and staggered back into her fighting stance.

She half-smiled.

"Come on."

Makita bowed his head, just slightly, and drew back.

"Defend yourself, "Klyne said again.

Naero whirled to face Iselle.

Too late.

An invisible force slammed into her arms and torso, flinging her back.

She rolled with the strike and came back up into her stance.

Iselle fought her from a distance, punching and striking with her hands in rapid combinations.

Naero struggled to advance, to close the distance between them, while heavy, unseen blows rained down on her from every direction, knocking her one way, and then the other.

"Telekinetic combat," Klyne called out. "Try to sense and block the blows. You cannot see them. Reach out with your battle senses, with your mind. Feel them coming. Counter and deflect them. True masters can fight thus, without even moving, simply by concentrating."

At least Iselle still had to physically move in order to project her attacks. That was some help.

Closer. Get closer.

Iselle thrust both hands forward violently.

A wall of force drove Naero slowly back. She pushed against it, slowing it even more.

"Resist. Focus on the energy before you," Klyne told her, "before it smashes you into the far wall. Fight back. Defeat it."

She rolled to one side and then the other. The barrier felt solid.

Naero leaped up four meters, felt the top, and flipped herself over it.

Iselle withdrew a step, cupping both hands loosely on the sides of her face.

Spinning orbs of pure telekinetic force shot out, rapid-fire.

Naero barely perceived them where they warped through the air; they made explosive popping sounds.

She tried to dodge them. One whirred past her head like an invisible ball at high speed.

The next clipped her left shoulder, spinning her aside.

Another knocked one leg out from under her.

She kept her feet and ducked, weaving to either side in turns.

Iselle directed her attack at Naero's feet.

Naero lost her footing, slipping and sliding on what felt like a bunch of invisible ball bearings cast beneath her.

She tried to roll back to her feet, but panes of force battered her from all sides, keeping her off balance.

It felt like being a rubber ball, bouncing around in a box that someone shook.

The sides of the box rapidly closed in.

They tightened all around her, threatening to crush her.

She couldn't breathe.

Iselle released her without warning.

Naero sprawled, gasping, face down on the floor.

"I'm somewhat surprised," Klyne noted. "Preliminary tests demonstrate no psyonic aptitude or innate talent to my trained senses whatsoever. That in itself is very rare. After your battle with the former Danner entity, we simply assumed that you would exhibit some kind of psyonic ability."

"I burned myself out dealing with the entity. I burned both of us out. I'm a nud once more." She admitted it openly. "None of my former abilities have returned."

So she wasn't psyonic anymore. Not even a teknomancer. Disappointing, but not the end of the universe.

"Yet I sense something incredibly strange within you," Klyne said. "What could it be?"

Was it Om? He was still inside her somewhere. He had not emerged again either.

"Take your place at the center of us once more. Face me again."

Naero did so, resisting an urge to massage several bruises.

Klyne positioned himself directly in front of her, sitting lotus fashion just like her and the others.

"I'm going to attempt to merge directly with your mind telepathically, one of my gifts. I'm also an Auralcognitor. Once I link with your mind, I can sense any type of psyonic energy field you might have, active, passive, or latent. I might even be able to trigger or bring them out to the surface. There might be some discomfort. Shall we proceed?"

"Sure."

"Do as I do. I will show you how to place your hands to effect the mind merge."

Klyne cupped his left hand firmly behind the base of her skull.

Naero followed his lead.

He placed the fingers of his right hand on precise spots on her face.

Thumb on her forehead, directly between her eyes.

Index finger on her left temple.

The next two fingers curled slightly in front of her left ear. His smallest finger hooked at the point of her ear and jaw.

As soon as Naero placed her right hand the same way, she gasped slightly.

Thin hairs of what felt like burning hot energy threaded their way slowly through the layers of her awareness.

She could feel Klyne connecting with her thoughts, joining their two minds.

The dull ache continued to grow.

"You should be feeling the initial discomfort. Hold still. Keep focusing. Almost there. Almost…"

A spike of pure agony exploded within her skull.

Naero screamed, transfixed as if by lightning.

Through the torment, a voice awoke in her mind full-force.

Protocols unlocked and engaged. We...are.
Interface...partial.
Om awoke, reacting instinctively with fear and vast power.
Threat detected...Protect all access.
Neural net...INTRUSION. UNWARRANTED.
LEVEL 1.359 DEFENSIVE RESPONSE.

An intense blast wave of white-hot psyonic energy fanned out rapidly from the epicenter of her immolated mind.

Naero continued to scream.

As if far away in the distance, Klyne and his two adepts also shrieked.

*

Naero blinked, her eyes and mouth frozen open.

She lay with her head to one side, in a puddle of her own mixed blood and spittle.

More pain struck her when she attempted to move.

Blood continued to stream from her eyes, ears, nose, and mouth–a bloody mess.

It felt as if a fusion grenade had blown her head open.

She reached up with her hands, to make sure her skull was still intact.

Some kind of noise.

Warning alarms sounded.

A ship. Yes, they were on a ship. The Spacer Intel Ship *The Kathmandu*. She was...being tested, for the Mystics.

Something had gone terribly wrong.

Naero focused, getting to her hands and knees.

She heard other voices, groaning and whimpering.

Makita lay sprawled in a broken tangle, blasted across the room. His gray clothing had been shredded and scorched into tatters. He choked and coughed.

To the other side, Iselle fared little better. She lay convulsing, blasted, scorched, a yellow-white bone of her forearm sticking out of her wrenched flesh. One side of her face was blistered, her red hair burned, some of it still smoking. She trembled and shuddered in pain and terror.

Naero looked around for Klyne, and found the instructor in a burned, bloody heap, lying beneath a dark red smear on the far wall. His hands were charred black, and he was missing fingers.

Naero could not walk. She couldn't even stand. She crawled to Klyne as quickly as she could.

He still lived, just barely.

Then she noticed the intense effects of the blast, all around the room, less than a meter up.

A massive expanding ring of Cosmic force had sliced into the duranadium hull of the smartwalls, punching a deep crease right through them where they buckled, all along its full diameter.

The force of the strike disrupted all systems. The entire training room was compacted, crushed, and heavily damaged.

Rescuers struggled to force their way through the various ruined doors and access panels.

Naero's Gambit Amazon Link: smarturl.it/NaerosGambit

Please enjoy the following teaser from the next Spacer Clans Adventure, Book 3:

NAERO'S
FURY

NAERO'S FURY

by Mason Elliott

Naero still hadn't done it much, but going into a direct trance to enter the Astral Plane shouldn't be all that difficult. Master Vane had shown her how once. And she had gone there lots of times in her sleep, in her mind, to speak with Khai, using their astral crystals.

Before her friend Khai had vanished without a trace.

Yet she had never been completely trained in astral travel, and didn't know that much about exploring or moving around. Master Vane had taken her there once, just to teach her the basics and give her his marker. Many other times later to spar with her.

If nothing else, she could probably focus on his marker and locate him.

Zhen had roused Naero and reminded her it was time. And that she and Shalaen would monitor her while she was in the astral trance.

Naero focused her mind and abilities, controlling her breathing. Remembering the little she had recently learned.

Within several minutes of focused meditation, she open her eyes and found herself floating in the Astral Miasma, the nebulae of energy. She hugged her knees to her chest in her astral form.

Om spoke to her, even more easily here than in her own mind before.

I have accessed some of the Kexxian Matrix's data files on The Astral Plane. Like everything else, they explored it quite extensively.

Om, I'm naked here. I'm not complaining–but just tell me–how do I put astral clothing on again?

You control everything here by imagination, and force of will. Concentrate on your favorite clothing and they'll appear.

That's easy.

She looked down and saw her favorite Nytex flight togs, programmed just the way she liked them.

Naero blinked, spinning and twirling in one spot, turning upside down.

Why can't I move more than a meter at a time in front of us?

You're not used to this reality. So it's not clear to you.

The air around her looked opaque. Not mist. Not smoke or vapor. And it glowed slightly with its own bluish-gray light.

In the twilight she glowed softly blue-white with her own light. From within.

"I once heard rumors that the Mystics could travel and send messages this way, but I thought it was all just a myth."

Since the other planes are entire universes within themselves, it is said, they are all nearly infinite. Thus, it is difficult to pin point any kind of location or person unless you already know them.

Naero instinctively tried to stand up, but there was nothing to stand on.

Then she recalled Master Vane's Marker, and it appeared right before her. Where she found him, she would find the other High Masters.

At least she deserved a chance to be heard by them all. To try to explain herself and her actions. What happened with the obelisk was clearly not her fault.

But they would still blame her for it–especially Mater Vane, who seemed to blame her for everything since Hashiko's death.

Naero could not simply stand by and let the High Masters decide her fate without herself being present at her trial, in some way at least.

She focused on the crimson and black star more and swept forward, seemingly at great speed.

She came to an abrupt halt, like a starship coming out of jump at its destination.

The opacity around her partially melted away. She proceeded forward, opening her visual field far wider. She made out the area around her as the miasma peeled back.

Slightly below her, she saw spheres within glowing spheres, all spinning within greater spheres.

Her own sphere, glowing white-blue, suddenly surrounded her like a glittering soap bubble.

Yet it did not pop when she poked at it.

One sphere in particular, the largest, glowed and pulsed blood red, containing a withered old man with a long beard, pacing impatiently.

Burning eyes vanished and re-appeared at random all over his bald head. The red sphere absorbed Master Vane's marker.

Was this his true form? What he really looked like?

His scarlet sphere was also flanked by two smaller spheres with figures inside them.

Om made a calculated guess.

His current guardian adepts, no doubt. The ones you rescued from the enemy Darkforce generators on Janosha.

I think so, Om.

At most times, every High Master had at least two champion adepts protecting him or her, each of them very close to mastery themselves. Just as Hashiko had been.

Naero studied Vane's new guardians for the very first time, and tried to see into their spheres.

Something about each of them did seem strangely familiar.

One of Vane's adepts, the male, appeared to be so deep dark black, he could be a singularity. This adept's sphere was flat black on the surface and barely transparent.

If Naero had been able to breathe, she would have gasped.

Instead she simply raised her hand to her mouth.

She recalled that she had seen many of these adepts long before.

In her dreams, nightmares, and crazed visions. Perhaps even on the Astral Plane somehow.

Vane's other adept was the white female, the exact opposite of the other. So brilliant and blindingly radiant, she could be a pulsar. Her orb was like a high intensity bulb, blinding and almost completely crystal clear.

It occurred to Naero that during her initial testing, Klyne had male and female assistants as well.

She couldn't guess what the significance of that pattern was all about. Perhaps just some weird Mystic, egalitarian tradition.

Then why weren't any of the High Masters female?

Everyone seemed to ignore her where she floated.

The next larger sphere, farther away, glowed silver-blue.

If she focused intently on it, she discovered she could zoom in with her third eye–her mind's eye.

Within that silver-blue sphere, a silver man sat serenely, neither young nor old. Master Tree, in his purest form of order.

Two smaller guardian spheres flanked him.

Master Tree's female adept glowed with intense blue energy in a deep blue sphere.

The male likewise glowed with vibrant green force within a green sphere, a shining sword sheathed down his broad, athletic back. He seemed very familiar somehow.

Naero did a double-take. Long blond hair. Green skin. Big glowing sword.

Yep. In the flesh–or–astral form at least.

It was Khai! She was sure of it. He was alive.

Had he actually succeeded in his great task of forging his mystic sword in the heart of a gigantic pulsar? Was that it on his back?

Naero gasped again. Now that she knew what he looked like, Khai was also the dreamy green hunk from many past, pent up nightmares. The one who kept sticking his astral sword through her head.

What did it all mean? She wasn't nuts enough yet?

Now she knew for certain she needed serious help.

And to do some serious dating at some point, once-and-for-all.

If the Mystics continued to let her live.

Khai must have sensed her inner turmoil, or thoughts, or maybe just her concentration on him.

Mr. Green-god even glanced her way for a second, looking just as confused and puzzled by her sudden appearance.

Neither of them had ever met the other in person.

Naero covered her face with one hand and looked aside, withdrawing her sphere suddenly further away.

How fricking embarrassing.

She crept forward again. Slowly.

The third and final sphere glowed golden, and contained an equally golden child within, energetic and bristling with lightning. He bounced back and forth inside like a gigantic electron.

Master Jo of course.

Two flanking spheres.

One of his adepts had no clear form, eyes gleaming within a shifting, flickering miasma like the Astral Plane itself. His female counterpart shifted shape from one fantastic creature to another.

When she suddenly made out their voices, she could sense that an intense debate had been doing on. One that still continued.

"We cannot be certain in this matter," the golden child insisted. "We do not dare act in any rash way."

"Agreed, High Master Jo," the serene silver man added. "She might yet be another Trickster from what I can tell."

"Yes. Quite possible, High Master Tree."

The old man in the blood red sphere blustered impatiently. "Fools! Always conspiring against me. Taking positions opposite of mine for no reason but to anger me. I've been telling you all along, this child is clearly the Great Destroyer–long foretold. Our duty is clear. She is a threat to all existence. To multiple dimensions. She must be eliminated, at once, before she can grow even more powerful."

"High Master Vane," Tree said. "None of us can be sure of that fact. Including you."

"I am."

"You are always certain when it comes to destroying someone," Jo added. "Your pure Chaos answer to everything. Destruction or Creation."

"It works."

"No. It doesn't. It only delays and worsens the inevitable," Tree said. "The Universe shall have its way. We all know this. You were mistaken with the last savant when he appeared, and now he remains at large–a renegade beyond even our control."

Baeven? We're they referring to her uncle?

Vane rolled his eyes. "Idiots! The Renegade is the Trickster, I say. This child must in fact be the Great Destroyer. Just look at the powers roiling within her. They will surely corrupt and overwhelm her entirely and drive her mad in the end. She will go berserk on a scale that makes her recent outbursts feeble and puny by comparison. She must perish now, while we have a chance to put an end to her. While the only crimes she has committed include destroying an entire planet, and another of the vital obelisks!"

"We still don't understand the purpose of the ancient obelisks. And we've studied the mysterious disappearance of Janosha, and we still cannot be certain in any conclusive way, that she had anything to do with it."

"Really? Who else could it be then? Planets like Janosha aren't in the habit of just obliterating themselves suddenly for no reason at all. Everywhere she goes, destruction follows!"

I cannot allow this.

Quiet, Om. Don't do anything. I'm trying to listen.

Naero...they're discussing our destruction. The Chaos Master means to destroy us.

Master Jo continued to protest. "You can't just kill off every entity that manifests Cosmic Abilities such as these. Our universe is peppered with them. We must continue to locate and guide them–not find excuses to execute them. Like the Others have told us, Tricksters often appear to oppose Great Destroyers. Without the former, final victory is never possible. "

"High Masters," Tree said. "This young woman also possesses the Kexxian Data Matrix. We cannot destroy her without destroying it. Intel and The Spacer Council of Elders value our wisdom, but even they would not agree to such action."

"Regrettable," Vane said. "Yet I cannot take the risk. I have decided this matter on my own."

"You have no such authority on your own," Tree insisted.

"Idiots! I cannot stand by and allow our galaxy–perhaps our entire universe to be destroyed–just to satisfy your foolish, philosophical, and theoretical whims."

Master Vane turned to his adepts. "My finest students, obey me. Delay these fools. Keep them occupied whilst I act for the good of all existence."

More rapid than thought, the male dark ensnared the blue sphere and its satellites in coils and tendrils of darkness. While the bright female enveloped the golden sphere and its companions in waves of of pure light.

Naero tried to pull away, but in her panic she did not know where to go.

High Master Vane sped straight at her with impossible speed.

I must act, Naero.

No, Om. Please, this is already bad enough. Don't do anything.

I cannot comply. I must defend us!

Naero went down on her hands and knees before Master Vane. She called out, using *the voice* to project her words.

"Please, Master Vane. Do not attack me. I only wish to be trained to control my abilities. I have struggled hard to do so. I still don't understand what happened with the obelisk."

Vane bore down on her, arcs of pure scarlet energy bristling around him.

"Far too late for that, monster. Nothing is ever your fault, is it? Now, you must perish for the good of all. I told you this hour would come."

Instinctively, Naero drew back again, trying to evade his attack. She rose within her receding sphere.

Vane closed in once more, gathering his powers.

"Don't do this," Naero begged. "Please. Help me. I know I can't fully control all of my abilities yet. I'm trying as hard as I can. I can't be responsible for what will happen if you attack me. I can't control myself."

"Yes, and look at the results? Countless lives crushed and eradicated. Janosha vaporized–an entire planet. You must never be allowed to reach your full potential. Now–monster–hold still and embrace your fate."

Naero put her hands out before her, holding her palms out defensively. Pleading.

"No. Don't. I can't–"

"I know, Maeris. You can't help yourself. That is why you are *an abomination!*"

Vane smashed into her, piercing all of her defenses as if they were shattering glass.

In the distance, she sensed that Master Jo and Master Tree finally broke free.

Too late.

Master Vane attacked, trying to overwhelm her with raw power.

He pummeled her with impossible blows.

In the end, he beat her up badly, but only succeeded in knocking her around once more.

Om roared in their mind.

Kexxian defense protocols unlocked and on line.

An energized, glowing armor of some advanced origin formed around Naero like a hi-tek battle suit.

Naero saw out of her third eye as it awoke and burst into radiance like a blue-white star.

Master Vane came at her once more, all of his powers focused through his primary scarlet, burning eye, centered in his forehead.

All of his other flaming eyes closed as he concentrated, his skull wreathed in weird cosmic flames like a mane of cosmic fire.

"See how powerful you have already become? No adept could have withstood those lethal attacks. We must finish this now, before the others can interfere."

"Please, Master Vane. Please—I'm begging you—please, don't do this."

"Maeris, just as I foretold—you shall fall before the greatest of all Cosmic attack techniques. And I am one of the few who have ever learned to master it: The Eye of Annihilation!"

The same Chaos technique that had destroyed Hashiko—even she couldn't control it properly.

A massive blood red beam of destroying Cosmic force shot straight at her.

It all happened so fast. Naero heard Om screaming.

Reflection defense. Analyze incoming cosmic assault. Duplicate and reflect attack tenfold!

Just before the incoming blast vaporized her, a blue-white beam shot out of her own third eye to war against Master Vane's powers.

The Cosmic flows flared intensely.

Naero screamed as if her body and soul were being sucked through the eye of a black hole's needle.

The wide blue beam quickly drove the red beam back to its source.

At the last instant, High Master Vane cried out in terror.

"Impossible! There can be no such—"

The destroying energy ignited on contact.

A massive detonation on the Astral Plane blinded the area within a few light years.

High Masters Jo and Tree barely managed to withdraw and shield the others. All of their spheres shattered.

Pure cosmic energy punched into High Master Vane right before Naero's eyes.

It drove him back like a white-hot comet.

He struggled against it with all his might.

To no avail.

The reflected attack obliterated High Master Vane to glowing ash and dust, screaming in the wake of his own annihilation.

Vane's dying force of will echoed off into the universe.

Naero would have caught her breath if she had any.

The outcome left her completely stunned for a shuddering instant.

Om…what did we just do?

We had no choice, Naero. My sole purpose is to defend our current form.

Naero stared down at her hands in terror. Tendrils of Cosmic energy rippled and still curled off of her body and her sphere like smoke.

Om…*Haisha!* We just killed a High Master of the Spacer Mystics!

Amazon Link to Naero's Fury: smarturl.it/NaerosFury

Edition Notes
If you do not see this edition note here in this spot on the copyright page and on the very last page of your eBook or print version of this title, then you are not getting the final, polished version of this novel that the publisher, editors, and author intended for you to receive. Please contact either the publisher or the author via their emails or websites if you do not see the following update code:

High Mark Publishing Update Code J0214G
Become a fan of my books.
Please join my Readers List:

http://bit.ly/1L2QpUL

Thanks, from Mason Elliott